Starlight Saint

Jayden Gilmore

For my mother and all my cousins

PROLOGUE

The patient breathed several shallow breaths. Clinging onto life as though hanging on the edge of a cliff by a pinkie. The patient lifted his eyes. An endless line of LED lights passed by from above and the murmur of muffled conversations echoed throughout the hallway, as the wheels of the bed raced with dire urgency through the corridor.

Hours before, the patient was rehearsing for his final performance. The final showdown before bidding farewell to his music career. As he was leaving for his water break, disaster had struck. A collapse to the ground, and the star was found unresponsive backstage.

Thousands of fans were thrilled with anticipation to witness the grand finale of their beloved idol. Hundreds had been waiting outside the stadium since morning. Don Leonard Jackson would grace the stage with his magical dances and irresistible vocals one last time. The ability to put anyone in a trance regardless of whether one liked him or not. It was all about the magical touch of music to the soul.

This was how Don had envisioned his departure. After having a career spanning over forty years, why not conclude it with one final concert? It would be his greatest gift to fans of the old and new generations…but then this happened. His time was coming to an end but wasn't expecting it so soon. The grand finale was seven hours away. The show would begin at 7PM.

All the preparation, promotion, and devotion would be for nothing if Don didn't recover in time. Tickets had sold out in less than 24 hours from the moment they were advertised. The world was waiting. Waiting for Don to make his final appearance on stage. A set of doors busted wide open.

Doctors rushed into the ICU carrying Don over to another bed. Gently placing a ventilating mask over his face and inserting an IV drip into his arm, the doctors moved with careful imperativeness.

The awareness of a life hanging on a single loose thread.

Don had briefly drifted into slumber and woken up again, his weak pulse still intact. The ceiling displayed an endless shade of white, and the room's stillness was an unwelcoming reality. The distasteful scent of fresh bleach lurked around, putting Don's nostrils in agony. As he settled into the room, Don grew used to the smell, and it disappeared.

As his vision began to clear, he could feel his breathing grow steadier and more rhythmic. With each breath, a sense of calm washed over him, and he could sense his heartbeat becoming more regular. It was as if his body was recovering from a great exertion, finding its way back to a state of equilibrium. The panic that had gripped him was slowly ebbing away, leaving behind a quiet strength and a renewed sense of hope.

BEEP...BEEP...BEEP, the heart rate monitor echoed.

He was going to make it. He wasn't going to die, and the show was still happening. Unordered chants and screams of fans reverberated from outside all the way to the fifth-floor room that held Don captive. It wasn't rocket science for Don to realize that his sudden accident had reached the news, and concerned fans had followed him to St Mary's Hospital.

Prayers were chanted for the pop icon to recover and walk out of the hospital victorious. Don could not let the people down. Only five hours away, the show would happen. Footsteps sounded, but Don lacked the energy to tilt his head and see who it was. As the source of these footsteps came into view, a smile crept up onto Don's face.

It was Angelo Jackson, Don's second-born son. Eleven years old and light-skinned, tears streaking down his cheeks uncontrollably. Behind him a nurse who had escorted him up to see his father.

"Dad, what happened? Please tell me you gonna be, okay?" said Angelo under his breath.

Don gently touched his right cheek. "Don't worry 'bout me, Ange. It's just a seizure. That's all. We must only dare to hope," said Don, uttering his first sentences since he arrived at the hospital.

"I'll be fine. When I get outta here, you and I can watch Home Alone together after tonight's show. I promise," Don smiled again when he mentioned Angelo's favourite movie. "Remember where to put your faith, never be afraid. There's nothing God or your dad can't handle."

Angelo held his father's hand in a firm but not crushing grip and nodded. Watching movies together was a bonding ritual they'd shared for many years. The young boy clinging tight to the prospect of his father's recovery.

"Where's Casey?" asked Don out of the blue.

Angelo shrugged. "Erica says he's on his way here with the others."

By others, he meant the rest of the Jackson family. As soon as they all heard the news, they had made plans to rush to Don's aid. Everything seemed fine the night before, but life could take unexpected turns.

The nurse placed a hand on Angelo's shoulder. "It's time to go. Doctors are coming to do treatment," said the nurse.

Angelo was reluctant to leave, clutching onto the rail of the hospital bed. He wanted to stay close to Don and endure this hardship with him until the end. The nurse had no choice but to drag away the eleven-year-old by force. Angelo squirmed and struggled with all his might, but it was all vanity. All this child could do was try to have faith that his father would make it out and hold onto the promise of recovery like a vice grip.

After Angelo had left, three doctors marched in, each with a facemask and a surgical hat. One looked like a female doctor pushing a table of medical supplies, one looked elderly, and the other looked the youngest, wearing a dark pair of glasses. Good, the doctors were finally here to do their job and save the day. It was these doctors that thousands of fans outside the building would be counting on for their idol's survival. To save the show.

"How are you feeling, sir?" asked the elderly doctor while tapping his finger against a syringe.

"Better," said Don with an optimistic chuckle. "It'll take more than a seizure to stop me from performing tonight."

Moments after responding, Don felt an inflaming prick on his right arm just below his fist. He tried not to groan too much, no matter how unpleasant the needle felt while piercing his vein. Don's heart raced.

"All done," said the elder. A wave of relief washed over Don. He would be out of the hospital soon. The time was eating away.

"So, when do I get discharged?" asked Don. "I have to do this show otherwise I'll disappoint my fans."

"When you give me back what's mine," said the elder.

The elder's response turned Don's world upside down into a state of confusion. He wasn't sure if he heard the doctor correctly. *When you give me back what's mine? What do I have that's his?* Don thought. *This is the strangest thing I've experienced today. What kind of doctor would say such a thing to a patient? Not just any patient but a star icon.*

"Doc, if you want my autograph, just say so. I'll even let you attend my concert for free since you've saved my life," Don offered.

"I don't need your autograph or a free ticket. You owe me something else and after I take what's mine, you're free to go by all means, but I doubt you'll be able to go anywhere," said the elder with a disturbingly familiar laugh that Don struggled to make out.

Don's breathing became heavy again like the weight of metal pressing down on his chest. His arms and legs went numb. The sense of touch and feeling sucked right out of them.

"I can't…move…what's happening?" asked Don.

The upper half of the hospital bed jittered into motion elevating Don into an upright position. There was no energy to make a noise under his series of heavy breaths. None of Don's cries for help would be amplified enough for anyone else to realize something was wrong.

The elderly doctor stared at his helpless patient, cold and menacing. He peeled off his facemask.

Only then did Don realize that his worst nightmare had come true.

"Your time has come Donny. What's rightfully mine is your life," the doctor began, "after that I take your children. It is simply a Jackson's fate. You hold way too much power and influence, which makes you a threat. I won't let you put my company out of business or have me lose my place in our society. Leaving was your worst mistake."

"No, please. You can have my entire music catalogue and publishing rights! Just leave me and my children alone." The last thing Don wanted was to be faced with his archenemy, whom he'd vowed to never surrender his catalogue to. The one he'd fought to escape from for many years, but now he stood before him in the flesh. There was no telling what would happen to Don's children if the doctor had his way. No matter how hard Don tried to bargain, the doctor rejected his final plea with a shake of his head.

"I was recruited at a young age. I didn't know what I was getting myself into until I discovered your evil intentions! I knew I had to leave. My message is about spreading love and peace to people, not what your cause promotes," said Don, fighting for his life defiantly, but the doctor simply shook his head.

"I pity you, Donny, I really do. All these people treat you like their god and yet you misuse your power. It's time we give it to someone else who will use it better than you and actually serve our purposes. I won't be the one to finish you off though. Your successor will," said the elder with a wicked smile.

He snapped his finger, and dark glasses stepped forward, syringe in hand, ready to strike the final blow. Dark glasses kept his face mask on, making it difficult to see his facial expression, but from what Don could guess, he was probably smiling under that mask.

While his nemesis held out a 200mg bottle of medication.

"Drugs are bad for you, Donny. It's sad to lose another icon to overdosing," said the elder, shaking the bottle.

The doctor with dark glasses impaled Don with the needle. He was too helpless. Too weak to scream at the top of his lungs. He sank into the pit of death and descended further and further into the abyss.

"As for tonight, I'll tell them the show's cancelled," said the elderly doctor, checking Don's pulse for any life that might still be left inside him.

The heart rate monitor was nothing but linear and horizontal. He turned towards his two helpers, who assisted him in committing the deed.

"You've done well, my apprentices; now you know what comes next."

The other two doctors nodded as the elderly one left the room.

***

A storm came over the whole world. Headlines of the news were polluted with one shattering report: *Don Leonard Jackson Dead At 51*. Millions worldwide would be talking about this for weeks, months, and maybe even years. May 18th was officially marked as one of the worst days in human history. The day an iconic musician departed Earth. The day, a huge void was left. What would the world and music industry do without him?

At just eleven years old, Angelo witnessed the death of the one closest to him. The sky seemed to get dark. Hope turned into hopelessness. Joy to pain, and life became meaningless. From this moment onward, there was no light to guide Angelo. *Absolutely no light.* The only light he had left was gone and would never come back. The memories flooded back, his father's sermons about giving others love and hope by using your gifts rang in his head. Angelo had yet to learn if he could live up to those sermons.

When Angelo and Erica stepped outside the hospital, they were met with a swarm of fans, police, and paparazzi. Security guards cleared the way for the two. News reporters were persistent in getting their attention.

"Mrs. Erica Jackson, would you like to say anything about this tragic incident?" asked one reporter with a microphone in her hand. Erica brushed her off.

"How 'bout you kid? Do you have anything to say?" The reporter clearly had her eyes on Angelo.

"Leave my nephew out of this! He's had enough already!" said Erica, irritated by the reporter's insensitivity.

How could they try to interview a child who'd just lost their parent? Insensitive and careless the media was.

As they walked further, a familiar figure came running towards them.

"Is he okay?! I need to know if he's okay." Casey, sixteen and dark-skinned with dreadlocks, finally showed up on the scene.

Erica shook her head with sorrow, but Casey dismissed it. He tried running to the entrance, but security guards blocked his path.

"Let me in!!! I wanna go see my dad!" he screamed, but they wouldn't budge.

"Casey, they won't allow us. Let's go." said Erica with finality.

After futile attempts to reach the entrance, Casey finally gave up and followed Erica and Angelo to their limo. The limo glistened with white. A symbol of the abundance of wealth Angelo was accustomed to.

"Tell me what happened," Casey demanded with tears flowing from his eyes.

Erica's response was dead silence. Casey was rambling, but Angelo was too sucked into his own thoughts to pay attention to the conversation happening.

"When I get outta here, you and I can watch Home Alone together after tonight's show. I promise."

Dad never got out.

The promise went void, and life lost its purpose.

Angelo should've been there. They should've let him stay. Angelo wanted to blame himself for not fighting hard enough, but what more could he have done? It was all over.

Newspapers echoed the same headlines: **Don Jackson – Death by overdose.**

CHAPTER 1

APPLE JACK

5 years later

Angelo's Diary

I choose to be set apart.

I come from one of the richest families in America. From a family of successful musicians! My father was in showbiz from the age of five, and my brother's rap career took off a couple years ago. My aunt became one of the most successful R&B singers of her time but now works as a part time radio presenter at Rockingston Studios. Pretty much everyone in my family is famous for something. I could go on, but I'm not like the rest of them. As for me, I never wanted a music career for myself. I got a few mixtapes I recorded when I was younger, but those will never see the light of day. I could've been an actor but that wasn't my cup of tea either. I remember when Disney wanted me to audition for a sitcom, but I declined. I want nothing to do with showbiz. I just want to live a separate life from my family's showbiz. Something different. Going to school, making friends, doing normal things without the stress of paparazzi, and making headlines 24/7. The celebrity life just isn't for me. Being in

Hollyweird which is what I call it would be a nightmare. I've heard strange things about Hollyweird, which I'd rather not think about. I'm fine with my life just the way it is.

***

A fist caught Angelo Jackson by surprise. A rocketing right hook jarred his jaw. Stars burst before his eyes, and he stumbled backwards. Only instinct saved him from getting hit by the cross that followed. Blocking the punch with his forearm, Angelo countered with a kick to the ribs, but he was too stunned to deliver any real power. His attacker, a sixteen-year-old boy with black hair and a shredded body, deflected the strike and charged at him with a thunderous rage. Angelo shielded his head as a barrage of blows rained down on him.

"Come on Bode! Knock that albino out!"

The crowd's shouts were a monstrous roar in Angelo's ears as Bode pounded him. Angelo ducked and weaved to escape the brutal onslaught but Bode had trapped him. The ding of the bell put the fight to a stop, and the referee stepped between the two competitors. Bode glared at Angelo menacingly.

If Angelo was intimidated, he wasn't going to show it. The sports centre was packed. An enormous crowd of spectators filled the room, cheering and screaming in anticipation for the next round.

Angelo returned to his corner. Sixteen years old, he displayed a black hair fade, brown eyes, a slim physique, and pale white skin. He was diagnosed with universal vitiligo at the age of seven, which gradually transformed his original brown skin into snowy white, making him lose his melanin shade over the years. His skin condition made him stand out from the other students at Sun Valley High School like a sore thumb.

Transferring from Los Angeles to a new school in Rockingston was no easy journey for Angelo. Being the child of a celebrity brought isolation as others were not very welcoming to him. Some might have been envious of his status.

"Let's go, Apple Jack! Don't fold now!"

Angelo turned to his far right to see his friends Rex LeClezio and Shawn Kamuta cheering him on in the crowd. This kind of encouragement was what he needed. He spat out his gumshield and thankfully accepted the water bottle his kickboxing instructor Sid handed to him.

"You must always keep your guard up," Sid warned.

"Bode's so quick with his hands," said Angelo between gulps of water.

"But you're quicker and remember it's not about strength. It's about strategy," said Sid. "You can win this thing…unless you want to quit and run away."

Angelo shook his head, refusing to admit defeat. Summoning his last ounces of energy. Shaking his arms and breathing deeply. He tried shifting the stiffness from his burning muscles. After competing in three matches, he was exhausted.

But he hadn't come this far just to back down now.

He wouldn't let his rival Bode get the best of him.

Sid wiped the sweat from Angelo's face with a towel. "See that guy in the first row?"

There sat a man who appeared to be in his early fifties with silver-grey trimmed hair. Blending in among the cheering spectators; his eyes focused on Angelo.

"He's a manager for the National Olympics team, and I think he sees potential in you," said Sid.

A sudden additional pressure to succeed forced Angelo to breathe faster, his chest tightening with each breath. *If he could just win the tournament's quarterfinals and display his tenacity, he could get a chance to compete in the National Kickboxing Olympics.* His family may have been musically talented, but this was something he could strive for.

His opponent on the other side of the ring, Bode appeared to be conversing with the referee.

11

What were they talking about? Angelo stomach lurched as Bode slipped something out of his pocket and handed it to the referee. Angelo couldn't make out what it was, though. He felt the urge to alert someone, but as he wasted time contemplating, the bell rang for the third and final round.

"Now go win this fight!" Sid urged, giving Angelo an encouraging slap to the back.

Putting the gumshield back into his mouth, Angelo stood to face Bode – determined to win more than ever.

His opponent bobbed lightly on his toes and sported a devious smile that read he was up to no good.

Angelo hadn't seen him smile so much in a match like this. *What was happening? Was Bode that confident in winning?* It didn't matter because Angelo prepared to use all his strength to succeed.

The crowd hollered as the two fighters squared up beneath the white-hot glare of the ring's spotlights. They stared at one another, neither willing to show the slightest sign of weakness. Right as their gloves touched, Bode launched. Straight into his attack – a blistering combination of jab, cross, jab, hook.

Angelo evaded the punches and countered with a front kick, responding with a series of blows, forcing Bode back peddling toward a corner. He was gaining the upper hand and Bode was now on the receiving end.

"Ref! Angelo's cheating!"

Angelo turned away from Bode to see where such a claim was coming from. The referee's attention diverted toward a spectator in the crowd. One of Bode's friends, Troy, seemed to be arguing with the referee.

Angelo suddenly felt a knee hit him in his private area. The searing pain sent him stumbling backwards and finally plummeting to the ground.

Bode got up and glared mercilessly at his opponent.

Only then did Angelo realise his mistake. He'd turned away and fallen for Bode's dirty trick. While Troy had distracted the referee, Bode took advantage and struck Angelo with a blow to the private area since the referee had turned his back towards them.

Sneaky cheating bastard! He Thought. Angelo placed his hands between his thighs.

The referee brought his focus back to the match. The bell rang and Bode was declared the winner. The crowd went ballistic, and their cheers reverberated throughout the entire hall. Angelo looked up at Bode who was relishing his opponent's defeat.

"You don't have what it takes to be champion, yeti. Sun Valley ain't for wimps like you," laughed Bode. "Looks like I'll be going to the semi-finals."

The audacity!

Bode's mockery angered Angelo deeply since he'd been the one who cheated, snatching victory from Angelo's grasp like a thief.

"You knew I was gonna beat you. You just didn't want me to embarrass your egotistic ass in front of the whole school," countered Angelo in his defence.

Bode simply walked away, not willing to entertain his cheap shot victory with his opponent.

"Angelo, what happened?" asked Sid, coming to help Angelo to his feet.

"He cheated, coach, but the referee didn't see it," said Angelo under his breath.

Sid became furious, but the winner had already been declared, and they could do nothing if no one noticed.

Angelo told Rex and Shawn the same story.

"What an idiot. I could teach him a few lessons and put him in his place," said Rex. "You literally had this match in the bag, but he decided to be a coward."

"You're technically the true winner. Had the referee been watching, that would've been a straight disqualification." Shawn added.

Angelo was still upset by the unfair play his rival could come up with, but there was no point in complaining about it because no one else besides Rex, Shawn, and Sid was on his side. He picked up his bag and prepared to leave.

Troy grabbed his arm before he could leave the venue.

"Nobody in this school likes you, albino, not even the referee. In fact, Bode bribed the referee to act distracted so you wouldn't win. You're just a spoiled brat who doesn't belong here," said Troy.

He shoved Angelo out of his way and went ahead.

Rex and Shawn caught up from behind.

Angelo emerged from the sports centre in downtown Rockingston and headed for the bus stop on Fulwood Road.

Rays of sunlight splashed the top parts of every building as the sun was getting ready to set. A late afternoon breeze whispered, and the sun took longer to retire as summer was on the horizon. The calmness and friendliness of the weather helped to soothe Angelo's spirit after a humiliating loss. *He wasn't going to let this loss deter him. Next time he fought Bode, he would not let his guard down again.*

"Should we take you home?" Shawn asked as he and Rex walked behind Angelo. "You look like you could use some help."

"Nah, I'll be alright. Don't worry about it," said Angelo, limping through his muscles stiffening. Having gone out of their way to watch and support his match they'd done more than enough. The trio gathered.

"Summer vacation's in a couple weeks. We should figure out what we're gonna do." Rex began, "Any ideas?"

"I got nothing right now, but we'll figure something out. I gotta catch the bus, so I'll...see you guys tomorrow," said Angelo.

"Alright. My uncle isn't well anyway, so I should go help him out," said Rex.

Shawn seemed concerned, and so was Angelo. His heart skipped a beat as Rex's words hung in the air. He furrowed his brows and leaned forward, Angelo's eyes narrowing in genuine concern. "What's going on with him?"

"He's got a bad lung disease, and we haven't raised enough money for a transplant yet," Rex explained. "I'll catch you tomorrow, Apple Jack."

Angelo gave Rex and Shawn a clasp and finger snap handshake as they parted ways.

Apple Jack was often the nickname Rex referred to him as. Instead of calling him by his full name, Rex had decided to name Angelo after a sweet beverage that was more fitting for his persona. Angelo raced to the bus to catch his ride home. *He couldn't wait to see what Aunt Erica had made for dinner.*

CHAPTER 2

FALSE REALITY

Angelo lived in a neighbourhood of sprawling estates, each one framed by towering iron gates, lined with perfectly pruned hedges and expensive cars gleaming in the driveways. His house boasted extensive spacious gardens, well-crafted architecture, and a well-maintained pool. Not too noisy, not too busy, and not too secluded. Ever since the death of his beloved father, it was decided that Angelo would reside in Rockingston under the care of his aunt, Erica, a retired soul singer in her early fifties.

Angelo walked through the front gate of his home his head down in defeat.

As he stepped inside the house, the scent of roast chicken and stew penetrated his nostrils. Angelo's mouth watered, and his stomach growled, anticipating the meal of that evening. The food was already set on the dining table, his plate consisting of roast chicken and rice, with stew sitting at the top.

After showering and cleansing himself from today's intense activities, Angelo finally settled down to eat. Erica hadn't touched her food yet since she'd been waiting to dine with Angelo, who'd made it just in time.

"How was school and kickboxing today, dear?" asked Erica, her tone soft-spoken. Despite her age, many would still mistake her for being in her thirties, thanks to the youthful glow she'd maintained throughout her career.

Angelo's gaze flickered down to his plate as he took a mouthful of the delicious rice, his shoulders slumping slightly. "It was good," he sighed, the words heavy with unspoken disappointment.

Erica's spoon hovered in mid-air; her brow knit with concern as she studied Angelo's downcast appearance. "Well, that doesn't sound convincing. You sure you're alright?"

"I'm fine." Angelo was far from fine because of his humiliating loss, but he didn't have the enthusiasm to narrate the whole situation, so he just left it.

"Honey, it's okay if you lost. You can't win every match."

"Fine I lost," Angelo admitted. "But I'm okay now. Can we talk about something else?"

Aunt Erica's heavenly cooking helped calm his nerves. She chewed on her food, allowing a moment of silence to pass until she'd gulped it down. After swallowing, she broached a different topic. "Okay. So have you figured out what you wanna do for this summer yet?"

Angelo shrugged his shoulders; it hadn't crossed his mind yet. The previous year, they went to Brazil with his friends, and the year before, they visited Tokyo landmarks in Japan. There was something satisfying about being a normal kid and still inheriting your family's wealth. His mind, however, was still blank on options for the upcoming summer vacation.

"I'll figure something out," he said. He was already halfway through finishing his plate. Erica nodded as she took another spoonful of her meal.

"The electrician stopped by today and said there was an issue with the house's electric circuit. No wonder the main switch trips every now and then," said Erica. "Oh, and your Uncle Jace hasn't been feeling too well. He's got one of those sinuses, so be sure to give him a call and check how he's doing."

17

"Sure," said Angelo, patting his lips with a napkin and taking a gulp of cold, refreshing water.

"Don't forget you have bible studies with Mr. Wilson later tonight," Erica reminded him.

Angelo was in no mood for a bible lesson, but Erica always emphasized the spiritual importance of it. He couldn't object. As he was washing his plate in the sink he paused to grab himself a can of *Gummy Bear* soda from the fridge. He headed upstairs to do homework and listen to music. Before he could escape to his room, Erica brought him to a halt.

"Oh! There's one more thing I forgot to tell you. Something came for you in the mail today. I've left it in your room on top of your bed for you to look at," said Erica.

The mention of a parcel piqued Angelo's interest and curiosity. *No one usually sent him anything by post. Not Casey, Uncle Jace, or anyone else he knew.* Everything delivered to this household was always for Erica but not for him. Angelo couldn't remember ordering anything, either. The thought of homework and listening to music left his mind. His focus shifted to the parcel.

Angelo raced upstairs, and as he entered his room, he found a small box residing on his bed. The stamp read:

Angelo Jackson
86 Braxton Street
90002
Rockingston

Return Address:
Starlight Academy Admissions Office
58 Starlight Avenue
70707
Starfire District

After chugging his soda and tossing it into the trash, Angelo moved his collection of Akira and Mary J. Blige CDs off his desk and placed the box there instead. He got a pair of scissors from his drawer and started to cut the box open. Excitement gripped him, and he was eager to know what was inside the box. *A present? Was a family member generous enough to send him a gift? Maybe a friend? Whatever it was, he hoped it would make his unpleasant day better.*

When he opened the box, there was a tape, a cassette player and a note. Not what he'd expected.

"A cassette?" he whispered to himself. Looking at the note it read:

This note is confidential, but you may share it with others if you choose at your own risk. Just be ready for the potential danger you'll put yourself and others in. The fewer people that know about this, the better.

Everything you've ever been told is a lie. You are trapped in a false reality. This world is not what it seems. Listen to this recording of Don Jackson's last phone call. If you want to uncover the truth, then join us. If you're going to save yourself and potentially your family, then join us. Everything around you is a façade from the enemy that holds you captive, but we can help you escape. It's all a lie to mask something deeper. We shed light where darkness has covered. We can free you from deception. If you've received this note, it means you have been called out of the darkness. Choose wisely and open yourself up to a new reality. The true reality.

There are all kinds of possibilities, for if the doors of perception are cleansed, everything will appear to you as it is—infinite.

Find us at this address: Friday 7PM

6 Woodhead Way
94005
Rockingston

Starlight Saints

Angelo paused, confused and stunned by what he'd just read. *It had to be a prank or a big gag. None of this felt real or genuine.* He still had yet to listen to the recording.

He put on his headphones and played the tape. A lot of static was in the background, but Angelo could hear voices.

"What's the matter, Don?..."

"I don't know if I should tell you this. I don't know who may be listening. There may be a group of people. They want to get rid of me and take my children...they don't want me here anymore." It was Angelo's Dad speaking.

Dad's voice sent a chill through Angelo's spine, almost like a ghost whispering in his ear. The tone of his dad's voice was even more chilling. He spoke in a voice that revealed fear. Like he was afraid of something.

"I don't understand. What are you talking about? Tell me what's going on."

A touch on the shoulder sent chills through Angelo's body, and he flinched out of fright. When he turned, Erica was standing there, her presence breaking the eerie spell cast by the mysterious tape.

With his listening interrupted, he instinctively pressed the stop button on the cassette player and removed his headphones.

"You look like you've seen a ghost. I've been calling you several times. Come downstairs, Mr. Wilson's here," said Erica.

She seemed to have no interest in Angelo's parcel and asked nothing about it. He would have to come back later and listen to the full tape. Angelo descended the stairs, his footsteps felt heavy, each one echoing the weight of the cassette's unfinished revelation. Pulse quickening, and his mind racing with fragments of his father's anxious voice, the ominous hints of danger, and the unanswered questions.

In the living room, Angelo and Reverend Terry Wilson had been studying the great apostles of the Bible and each one's significance. Apostle Paul who was beheaded for his faith. Peter, who was crucified upside down, etc. Others were stoned, boiled, killed, and tortured for carrying out the works of Jesus Christ and building the early church during the first century.

These brave disciples travelled across harsh lands, endured brutal persecution, and lived in terrible conditions, all for the sake of spreading the gospel.

"What do all these apostles have in common?" asked Wilson, putting Angelo's knowledge to the test.

The reverend was pushing into his early sixties and had the appearance of a wise, gleaming professor.

"They were all chosen for a very special assignment," said Angelo.

"True, but not the answer I'm looking for."

"They were all Jesus's twelve disciples?" asked Angelo, trying to figure out what answer to give. Wilson shook his head.

"They all died for a good cause. They all suffered for their faith because they believed in the works of Jesus Christ. They never gave up on their mission, and now they're enjoying their eternal rewards in Heaven," Wilson finally explained. "They preached the gospel message to many nations and cities. Some cities outlawed Christianity but that did not stop the disciples. They're part of the reason why our church still stands today and why the word of God is readily available to us."

Angelo finally understood the point his pastor was trying to make.

"Young man, one day you might have to die for the greater good. Are you prepared to die for Christ? Are you prepared to die for what you believe in?"

Wilson's words caught Angelo off guard. *Am I prepared to die?* He thought.

"I… don't know," was simply Angelo's response.

Being sixteen, Angelo still had his whole life ahead of him, and death never crossed his mind. Surely, he would never have to be stoned or crucified to death like Christians in biblical times.

This was modern-age America, where religious freedom could be practised, and no one was punished the way people were punished in the Old Testament days. What would Angelo possibly have to die for?

"You'll know when the time comes," said Wilson, rising up from his seat.

He said it so confidently as if he was prophesying. He put his hand on Angelo's shoulder, and they uttered a quick prayer. Wilson then headed towards the dining room, where Erica had been taking care of important business.

"Thank you for having me, Mrs. Jackson. May God bless you and your nephew." Wilson gave a final salute and headed out the front door.

When Wilson had left, Angelo could feel the cassette's magnetic pull, its secrets whispering to him from upstairs. He would have to put homework aside. Angelo had to finish listening to the tape. He slipped back into his room and shut the door behind him. Angelo slid his headphones back on, his fingers trembling. He pressed the play button, and the tape whirred to life. His dad's voice once again filled his ears.

"What's the matter, Don?..."

"I don't know if I should tell you this. I don't know who may be listening. There may be a group of people. They want to get rid of me and take my children...they don't want me here anymore."

"I don't understand. What are you talking about? Tell me what's going on."

"I can't talk about it here. Something bad is going to happen. I feel it...in my soul, but I don't know what it is. Only God knows. They might shoot me, poison me. They could frame me and say I overdosed on drugs. They can do a lot of things."

Who was they? Who was trying to shoot or poison Dad? Angelo thought. His anxiety levels were rising as he listened to his father speak. Whoever these people were, they must have been very dangerous. The way Angelo's dad described them was disturbing in itself.

"Who are they? You can tell me, it's just two of us on the line and I promise there's no one else around me. Are they a mafia gang or a terrorist group?"

"It's not a terrorist group, no, it's worse than that. But I don't know, James. I honestly don't care what happens to me anymore. They can take me. I just want my children to be safe."

"Don...Bzzz...wait..."

"I have to go."

After Angelo's dad said his final words, static sounded again.

Silence filled the room.

The recording had ended, and Angelo's heart was ready to jump up to his throat. He played the recording again and again, paying attention to every word and making sure he got everything.

It had been five years since his father's death, and to stumble across a message like this was a shocking revelation. *Where did this even come from? Who were the Starlight Saints?* Angelo tried to convince himself that this was just a prank or gag, but his father's voice was too recognizable. It was 100% him. *Why was he only receiving these five years later and not sooner?* It's not like he could bring his father back. Angelo's head started to feel heavy. He needed time to digest all of this.

Should I tell my aunt about this? Angelo contemplated.

Erica was probably the right person to speak to first, but *how would she react?* The note had warned him about disclosing at his own risk, and he didn't want to risk putting his aunt in danger. It wasn't the time to show her yet since she'd also probably dismiss it as a prank. Angelo had to confirm the tape's validity first, but it would happen eventually.

Who are the Starlight Saints? he wondered. It looked like they were some kind of school academy judging by the return address, but he had no way of knowing for sure. Angelo couldn't keep this to himself despite the note's warning. He had to tell someone about it, and the people who came to mind were his friends. His friends could be trusted to keep a secret and the package sender wouldn't know. He would show Rex and Shawn this mysterious tape to see what they thought about it.

"There may be a group of people."

"They want to get rid of me and take my children."

Those were the words that echoed in Angelo's head throughout the night as the painful memory of losing his father resurfaced. His pillow became drenched in tears as he wept. *Who was this group of people, and why did they want to get rid of Dad?* he wondered. *Why were they after Angelo and Casey? Was it revenge for something he did, or did they want something from the Jacksons?*

Only God knew the answer.

CHAPTER 3

ONE DEADLY PRANK

Angelo stood before a grand Victorian entrance and made his way into the library. The tape and cassette, which kept him unsettled all night, were deeply secured inside his backpack where no other hand would access. The heavy oak doors creaked slightly as he pushed them open revealing the library's magnified interior. High, arched ceilings stretched above him, adorned with ornate mouldings and glass chandeliers. The building flooded with all kinds of books, from encyclopedias to philosophy, history, and countless others. He took a glance at the time. The clock read 1:53PM. *Perfect timing.*

2PM was when Angelo and his friends had agreed to meet in a quiet space after school. Angelo climbed up a mountain of stairs and entered into Meeting Room 07.

"Great, you're all here," Angelo said.

The room was occupied by Rex and Shawn. It pleased Angelo that they had kept their promise to meet with him, especially since they'd arrived before him. This was important, and Angelo knew he could count on these two. The matter sounded urgent and dire from what Angelo had described to them beforehand.

"I skipped basketball practice so I could be here. Spill the tea," said Rex with his arms crossed.

Angelo placed the cassette player on the table. He then pulled the note out of his pocket, carefully unfolding it. Angelo then put it next to the cassette player.

"I know. Thanks for coming through. You guys won't believe what I'm about to show you," said Angelo. "You're the only ones who I know I can trust, so what happens in this room stays in this room."

"What's said in here stays here," Rex agreed as he traced an imaginary zip across his lips.

Shawn signalled his pledge with a nod.

When Angelo first moved to Rockingston years ago, he was alienated. The new city seemed to give him a cold shoulder, but his encounter with Rex and Shawn had eased his journey.

Angelo's finger hovered over the play button on the cassette player, anticipation radiating from his tense posture. He pressed it, and the room was instantly filled with the haunting echoes of his father's voice.

Rex and Shawn leaned in closer, their brows furrowing as the words seeped into their consciousness, each subtle shift in their expressions betraying their growing intrigue.

"They want to get rid of me and take my children..."

"They can take me..."

The tape clicked to a halt, leaving the room enveloped in a heavy silence. Rex and Shawn exchanged glances, their eyes widened with puzzlement.

Angelo explained that he had received the parcel from a mysterious group by the name of the Starlight Saints. Their claim that his dad's death was a homicide cast a shadow of doubt and fear.

"You're saying you received this yesterday from the mail?" asked Shawn.

Angelo nodded.

"Have you told anyone else?" asked Shawn again.

Angelo shook his head. "The fewer people that know about this the better."

"They gave me an address, and they want me to come to 6 Woodhead Way next Friday at 7PM," said Angelo, presenting the note.

Rex and Shawn still seemed confused.

"I'm sorry, but THIS sounds like some kind of sick prank," said Shawn confidently, crossing his arms into an 'X' shape. "It's probably Bode and his boys trying to mess with you."

A seed of doubt was planted in Angelo's mind. *Bode, the irritating school bully, was always known for pulling foolish antics and gimmicks, but why would he send the tape by post when he could've just snuck it into Angelo's bag?* It didn't make sense for that imbecile to go through all the trouble despite his detestation for Angelo.

"Bode isn't smart enough to pull off something like this. He's as foolish as they come," said Angelo, dismissing Shawn's theory.

"I mean, it's been five years since your dad passed so even if he was killed, why would these Starlight guys only send this now?" asked Rex. "It seems irrational if you ask me."

Angelo's gaze remained resolute as he responded, "I know, but this isn't just about my dad. Anyone else in my family could be in danger. Someone could be after me and my brother." His voice carried a hidden defiance, underscoring his unwavering intent. "That's definitely my dad's voice on that tape, and even if it is a prank, I'm not taking any chances!"

Rex and Shawn exchanged glances once more, their initial confusion replaced by a dawning realization. Angelo's determination and boldness in the face of uncertainty seemed to leave them with no doubt about the gravity of the situation.

"You sure you wanna do this, Apple Jack? If you gonna go out there you'll need backup," said Rex with his hands behind his head. He leaned comfortably against the wall and glanced at Shawn. "What do you think, four-eyes?"

Rex's point hit home.

Angelo understood that venturing alone into unknown territory would be a reckless endeavour. He needed an extra hand.

"NO! There's no way I'm going. Did you guys forget about the 203 Dragons?" Shawn's tone grew serious, and his facial expression shifted noticeably at the mention of the name. "No one and I mean no one ever goes to that side of town. It's too dangerous for the three of us to be roaming there by ourselves."

Angelo recalled the warnings and stories he had heard about the 203 Dragons. *They were a notorious gang infamous for their ruthless crimes—robberies, killings, and the horrifying abduction of women and children.* Aunt Erica had always urged Angelo to never be out too late because of disappearances occurring.

Angelo was not always current with the news. Still, he had to recognize the dangers of venturing through the Woodhead suburbs where crime was most prevalent. The 203 Dragons were a terrifying force in the city, and the mere mention of them sent a shiver down his spine. He remembered a chilling story of a teenage girl, her life brutally cut short, her body bearing the gruesome mark of the 203 gang.

"As a former gang member, I can assure you these guys aren't messing around," Rex commented. He fixed his eyes on Angelo.

Angelo became tense, recounting a chilling chapter from his past. When he first arrived in Rockingston, the 203 Dragons had used Rex as bait to lead Angelo to them. When Angelo first met Rex at the basketball courts, he would play him regularly while unknowingly under the gang leader's watchful eye.

"I remember when they assigned me to lure you back to the 203 hideout but never told me why. I assumed they were gonna kill you."

Angelo looked back on the harrowing moment, his heart pounding in his chest at the vivid memory.

"But then I showed you there's a better way to live. That you didn't have to be a thug to be accepted, and you let me escape before the other members could find me," Angelo added.

"They won't be merciful like I was is what I'm getting at," Rex warned. "They could try kill us both this time if we go."

The room fell awfully silent as Angelo's mind raced through these bitter memories and risky decisions.

Rex had been deeply entrenched in gang activity from a young age. Being disowned by both parents and sent to live with his uncle, Rex had no friends or role models to look up to. Joining a gang was his last resort, a desperate cry for belonging.

However, Angelo had seen something in Rex that others had missed. Angelo was the only one who could change Rex's heart by showing him they were more alike than they thought. Parentless and both outsiders in their own worlds.

When Rex turned his back on the 203, it came with the downfall of his associates, and most of the chief members were now behind bars. Fortunately, Rex was only sentenced to two months in juvenile after ratting them out, a blessing that allowed him a second chance. However, like a roaring fire, the activities of the dragons were never fully quenched. New gang members meant ongoing challenges for the Rockingston police force.

Angelo could either journey through the treacherous Woodhead suburbs to find an answer to this mysterious parcel or heed Rex and Shawn's initial warnings and simply jump to the conclusion that the tape was indeed just a prank. However, the magnetic pull of Dad's voice on the tape felt too strong to just ignore.

"Most of these criminals are in jail now. We won't stick around for too long, I promise. We investigate, then we go back. If anything happens, it's on me," Angelo reassured his friends.

"What happens if we get attacked?" asked Shawn.

"We make a run for it. Rex is a street gangster veteran, and I can throw some punches, too."

Shawn tapped his fingers repeatedly on the table. "And…what if I'm right and it is a prank?"

"Then I'll have to buy you one 24-pack of *Gummy Bear* soda off my allowance," Angelo challenged.

"Okay, make that two, then we have a deal," said Shawn reluctantly, his scepticism still evident. "But I can promise you're wasting your time with this investigation."

Angelo was finally relieved to have both of his friends on the same page. As farfetched as this whole plan was, his inquisitive hunt for the truth would not be suppressed. He needed to know if something truly happened to his dad.

"Thank you guys so much. I appreciate you for hearing me out." Angelo replied.

***

On Friday at 6:52PM, the late afternoon sun was getting ready to set, and the sky displayed orange and purplish colours painted by the creator of the heavens. The trio headed down Woodhead Way street, making their way across the cracked pavement, prepared to confront whatever they faced. Some worn-out buildings stood desolate, their broken windows gaping like empty eye sockets and graffiti adorned the walls like scars, creating a sense of evergrowing unease within Angelo's gut. Rex had a pocket knife in case anything went wrong. Although Shawn had agreed to come, he had sourness written on his face. Shawn kept trying to convince everyone that this was all just a prank.

They arrived at the specified location. Angelo took the initiative of knocking on the door.

Knock…knock, the door sounded.

There was no answer.

Angelo knocked again, and after some persistence, someone finally answered.

A tough-looking man with an afro emerged wearing sweatpants and a shirt like he'd just stepped out of a gym session. He gazed at Angelo and then peeped at his friends in the back. "How can I help you?" the man grunted.

Angelo held out the note and the cassette player, his hopes rising slightly as he spoke. "I received a note and a tape from this address the other day. I was told to be here Friday 7PM. Do these ring a bell?"

The man glared at him. Confusion was apparent on his face.

"What in God's name is this?" he muttered as he read the note word for word. "I didn't send no letter or cassette. You've the wrong address." He slammed the door shut, cutting off any chance for further inquiry.

Disappointment flooded Angelo's mind. *Dammit, I wasted my time coming all the way here,* he thought. As Angelo turned to face Rex and Shawn, looks of 'I told you so' displayed on their faces.

"What did I tell you, AJ? I was right all along," said Shawn, taking pride in his accuracy. "I want my sodas."

Angelo had never felt so embarrassed. He cursed himself for his stupidity and for believing any of this was real. With a sigh of disappointment, he made his way back. His feet dragged with defeat.

Throughout their journey back, Shawn continuously nagged Angelo about how much of his time he'd wasted. It was several minutes past seven, and the sun was preparing to take its final dip. Shawn was right, but Angelo couldn't shake off the feeling that something was off. He knew the tape had his father's real voice.

What kind of prankster would do a wicked gag like this? It just couldn't be so.

31

The trio walked the pedestrian route underneath Merrion Bridge, and up ahead was a junction where they agreed to disband and walk back to their homes.

"This is where we part ways. I'm sorry for dragging you guys out here," said Angelo.

The Woodhead suburbs were relatively quiet, and no activity was detected, which was expected since dusk had fallen. People had either locked themselves in their homes or gone to other parts of town for Friday night excursions.

Before long, a van blocked one of the exits. Frustration was evident from Shawn. How convenient. Another engine roared from behind. When they turned around, figures began emerging from the shadows. The streetlights illuminated, and nighttime had fallen. In every direction the three looked, strangers surrounded them. Angelo's skin began to crawl. These strangers appeared like they were ready to commit a robbery. Most of them seemed to be adolescents accompanied by one adult woman and two adult men.

"It's the Dragons," Shawn whispered, his voice trembling with fear. "Oh my god, it's the Dragons. This is all your fault, Angelo!"

The assailants enclosed the trio like lions about to eat their prey, leaving no room to escape.

"I've never seen these guys before plus we always wore masks going out. A lot must have changed since I left," said Rex.

Without warning, Shawn made a break for it, sprinting as fast as he could to break out of the circle. The attempt was extinguished in an instant when one of the assailants quickly knocked him to the ground.

Angelo's heart sank as he came to a horrible realization. "We're outnumbered."

They'd fallen straight into the lion's den. They could either surrender or go against the odds.

"They know me as Leclez 17, the best street fighter in town. I can take these guys on," said Rex. No hesitation tinged his voice, only resolute confidence he had in himself.

Angelo tugged at his friend, doubting if it was a good idea to engage in this unfair scuffle despite Rex's faith in his abilities.

Rex, however, remained unmoved by Angelo's persuasive attempts. His statement was met with cackles from the assailants. A boy dressed in baggy jeans and a Compton shirt stepped forward, matching Rex's height.

"You got a big mouth for someone as lowly as you. Talk is cheap but…"

The boy's taunts were abruptly silenced as Rex unleashed a lightning-quick spinning sidekick that struck the boy's abdomen. Without pause, Rex followed up with a devastating knee to the head. The boy crumpled to the ground. All sense was knocked out of him.

"Who's next?" Rex challenged, his defiance echoing through the tense standoff.

Two other youths intervened, igniting a full-on brawl. Angelo, with no other choice, joined in, summoning all his kickboxing training for this moment. Meanwhile, Shawn was already ensnared, tied up by one of the adversaries, and immobilized with nowhere to escape. That left two against seven.

"Don't let them escape! Tie them up and load them into the van!" the woman ordered.

She must have been one of the gang leaders, Angelo guessed. This wasn't a prank anymore. This was an ambush orchestrated by a group of ruthless kidnappers.

Angelo stood toe to toe with a blue-haired girl. Her bright blue eyes glistened in the harsh lights. She wasted no time launching a flurry of strikes, her speed catching Angelo off guard. Luckily, Angelo could block and dodge a few, but she was quicker than he anticipated.

The girl made a false move to the lower body and finally landed a roundhouse kick that nearly knocked Angelo off balance.

When Angelo attempted to land a hit, she cartwheeled back, demonstrating a level of agility he had never encountered before.

The girl launched a series of relentless fists, and Angelo had no choice but to shield himself under the barrage.

"How many people have you guys killed?" asked Angelo, struggling against his opponent.

"Not enough," the girl replied.

"No rest for the wicked I guess."

The two continued to take shots back and forth, but Angelo's energy soon became depleted. On the other hand, the girl still had adrenaline.

Suddenly, a rope came over Angelo, yanking him by his feet. He plummeted straight to the ground. It was one of the adult gang members behind the rope. Angelo lay there helpless while the girl tied him up.

"Get comfortable in these," the girl mocked as the tight ropes bound Angelo, offering no chance for escape.

Angelo's eyes moved towards Rex, the only one left standing. He'd displayed resilience throughout, but that resilience would soon wear out. Bringing another attacker to their knees; the rest were now focused on him. The odds were not in his favour. This was it. Outnumbered and worn out, victory was out of reach. As a last resort, Rex pulled out his pocketknife and held it to the throat of the boy on his knees.

"I'm only gonna ask this once. Let go of my friends and go back to where you came from, or I slit his throat," said Rex, now gaining the upper hand. The defenceless boy had desperation written on his face.

The gang members didn't move an inch closer. The tables were now turned. Angelo became desperate as he observed the standoff. *Come on, Rex,* he thought.

Rex was their last hope. The female gang leader chuckled, her arms folded as if she didn't care about the boy's fate. Something suddenly flew and hit Rex on the neck.

Angelo couldn't make out what it was since it flew too quickly. Rex loosened his grip on the boy and collapsed to the ground. Only then did Angelo realize what it was—a tranquillizer.

What kind of gang has tranquillizers? he wondered.

"Load them into the van." The woman ordered.

Fear gripped Angelo's heart. He was about to say goodbye to freedom. What these kidnappers would do with them was anyone's guess. The horrors and possibilities were endless. Angelo would disappear for good, and Erica would never know where he went. No one would come to his rescue.

The gang loaded their three victims into the van, arms tightly bound and mouths heavily taped. No one would hear their cries for help. The engine rumbled, and the van set into gear. No one would ever hear from these three again, and they would just become part of another statistic of disappearances.

Chapter 4

An Obscure Case

Darkness swallowed Angelo, each dreadful second passing as the van rumbled forward. His heart hammered against his ribcage, and the walls of the vehicle seemed to be closing in on him, squeezing the air out of his lungs and igniting a primal panic within his chest. Handcuffed and tied up, he tried to make out where the others were, but the blackness made it impossible. Making futile attempts to uncuff and untie himself, it was to no avail as the claustrophobic grip of the van held him captive. Angelo could hear shuffling and murmuring from Shawn, but Rex was still unconscious from the tranquillizer.

Wishing he could communicate with his friends, the duct tape sealed his mouth shut, not allowing any words to pass his lips. He tried to nudge Shawn, but seeing in the dark was hard. The kidnappers had taken their phones and most likely disposed of them to prevent anyone from possibly tracking them down. Hope was nowhere to be found. Their predicament would spell doom for them all.

There were no other options left for Angelo and his friends. Yet, he would not give up so easily and couldn't just accept this kind of fate. It looked like God, or the universe had determined this was how things would end, *but no, it couldn't be.* Angelo hoped it wasn't time to meet the creator yet and prayed a prayer of repentance in his heart, asking his God for some divine escape.

If the gang had their way, he knew he'd be all over the news by the following day. Deep down, Angelo had a gut feeling it was him that the Dragons wanted. He cursed himself for getting Rex and Shawn involved in this cluster.

The van suddenly came to an abrupt stop. Doors slammed as the vehicle halted. Footsteps, heavy with purpose, resonated from outside. Without warning, harsh light flooded into the van as the door swung open.

Angelo squinted against the blinding glare, his eyes struggling to adjust.

The kidnappers roughly ushered each of their three captives to their feet. He winced in the unforgiving light and allowed his vision to gradually return. They were in an underground parking area according to the surroundings. It wasn't just them; various other vehicles surrounded them, suggesting they were not the only ones brought here.

The kidnappers escorted them through a set of automatic sliding doors and down a dimly lit hallway. A sense of uneasiness hung in the air as they were eventually ushered into what looked like an interrogation room.

"Go get the seraph," ordered one of the kidnappers.

Angelo and his friends sat in the frigid room, the cold seeping into their bones, a chilling reminder of their captivity. The blue-haired girl, who had clashed with Angelo earlier, fixed him with a cold glare that was ready to pierce his soul. They waited anxiously at a table, each passing minute amplifying the sense of hopelessness. One of the kidnappers had gone to fetch their 'seraph,' further diminishing any chances of escape. Distant voices suggested the presence of others nearby, painting a bleak picture of their situation—outnumbered and with little knowledge of the surroundings, their prospects for escape grew even bleaker.

Two individuals entered the room, instantly recognizable to Angelo. One was the stranger with the distinctive afro, the same man they had encountered during their investigation when they followed the address written in the mysterious note. The other was the formidable female gang leader they had encountered earlier.

"No need to panic. We're not gonna hurt you," said the man, putting his hand up, "no we're here to recruit. My name's Titus and this is Kate," he said, introducing his female companion.

Angelo was taken by surprise. *Recruit? Why would a notorious gang want to recruit them?* His curiosity grew as Titus placed a cassette player and a note on the table, items Angelo recognized. *Could they know something about Dad's death and that note?*

With a wave of his hand, Titus ordered one of the adolescents to untie Angelo and remove the duct tape from his mouth.

Angelo inhaled a deep breath of air and let it out as if he was breathing for the first time in a thousand years. The others were still cuffed and tied up.

"I believe this belongs to you," said Titus with a crooked smile. "Mr. Angelo Jackson, we finally meet."

Angelo was puzzled as he tried to figure out what this was all about. They'd been ambushed, kidnapped, and driven all the way to this unknown location. He had never even seen this man in his life.

"What do you mean finally? Let my friends go and tell me what you want from me," Angelo demanded.

"I'll let them go trust me. All this was to lead you to us. The note, the tape, and the ambush. This was all a test to see what you're capable of in the face of danger and uncertainty. You did just fine," said Titus.

Titus made eye contact with Rex. "You guys put up a good fight back there. Especially you with the tattoo. We could use someone like you to serve our cause."

"This fool almost cut my throat, Seraph! We can't recruit someone like him," one of the boys protested.

"Silence, Tiger! You don't get to pick and choose who we recruit. That is my job as the seraph," said Titus, shutting the boy down.

He put his finger on the note. "Congratulations! You found us. We're the Starlight Saints."

A knot tightened in Angelo's stomach. *So, these people were not the 203 Dragons after all. This whole ordeal wasn't a prank. It was planned from the start and well executed.* His intuition had been right all along. Throughout their journey in the van.

"Who exactly are you people and what do you know about my father's death?" asked Angelo.

"Let me take you on a tour," Titus offered. He glanced at Rex and Shawn, "Your friends can come along too."

The other two were soon uncuffed and untied. As soon as Rex was free, he went into fighting mode and slammed one of the youths who helped untie him to the ground. The other Starlight Saints got into fighting stances, ready to take him out. Angelo had to act quickly to avoid another altercation.

"Rex, stop! These guys might actually be able to help me with my father's case and give me the answers I'm looking for. I promise we can go home after this," said Angelo, grabbing his arm.

Rex reluctantly let his guard down and agreed to Angelo's request.

Titus and Kate led the trio while the other youths were dismissed. They entered an elevator that ascended to basement floor 1.

Angelo couldn't help but notice that most of this place seemed to be situated underground, adding to the mystery of their surroundings.

"You can't be so sure if we can trust these people," Shawn whispered.

"Well, my gut feeling was right about this not being a prank and you were wrong. So, I trust my instincts better than you, Shawn," Angelo shot back.

When the doors opened, they were escorted into a bright and sprawling lobby, where a vast diamond-shaped eye with several wings greeted them. The diamond appeared to be some kind of logo. It featured a singular eye with crosses, inset into a glossy floor. A staircase led down to the lobby on their left and a curving ramp to their right. The environment was swarming with heavy patterns of activity. Security guards walked up and down carrying files and moving to different areas of the building. Angelo had never seen a facility so active before.

Making their way down the stairs, the vast lobby seemed to transform. No longer flanked by security guards, there were seating areas with lustrous couches and coffee tables littered with newspapers and magazines. A small café appeared in the distance, surrounded by little round tables where people were hooked onto their tablets as they sipped from paper cups.

Angelo's attention turned to the television screens dispersed around the room. Some were tuned to news stations, and others to entertainment channels, both local and international.

Rapper CJ Maverick Announces Upcoming Tour with Quinn Parkerson Who Just Came Out of Rehab, reported on one of the news channels.

Angelo recognized CJ Maverick as his older brother's stage name. He and Casey had stopped speaking regularly, but that's what was expected when you had a full-time music career. Family time was scarce these days.

They went through a glass passage, and the three adolescents were led into a vacant meeting room. Kate and Titus ordered them to sit down while they remained standing.

"You three have officially stepped into Starlight Saint headquarters, in fact you're one of the very few outsiders who've seen this place. Welcome," said Titus. "We're a syndicate of agents and a secret society who specialize in fighting against the Illuminati and stopping their agenda. We have bases across the globe including America, Europe, Asia, Africa, and Australasia."

Kate clicked the projector on. As the board illuminated, it displayed an owl, and the Starlight Saint symbol Angelo had seen earlier. It was her turn to speak.

"We're not here to give history lessons but our societies have been at war for over a century. The Illuminati are a powerful agency focused on dominating America and the rest of the world by brainwashing, controlling and perverting civilians into destruction and immorality," Kate explained.

The screen flipped over to what looked like a picture of Lucifer playing a violin to a man in bed.

"Their strongest asset is the music industry. They use many musicians and entertainers as pawns to carry out their agenda. Ever since they came into power their goal has been to usher in a new world system and pave the way for their antichrist to rule over but the only reason why they still haven't succeeded is because of the Starlight Saints. Our agency has sabotaged their plans for decades making us their number one enemy," said Kate.

Angelo took a moment to digest all this information. *This has to be a dream.* He wished to wake up so badly, but he was right in the midst of reality. Deep down, he wished Shawn was right about this whole thing being a prank. He wasn't going to like whatever he was getting into. Growing up as a young child, Angelo entertained himself with conspiracy theories and played songs in reverse. Sometimes, he would play a game with himself called 'Spot the Illuminati,' where he'd watch and pause music videos if he saw occultic symbols.

Angelo always marvelled at conspiracy theories the way kids marvelled at magic tricks, but as he got older, he eventually grew numb to the idea of a secret society running the world. Casey always told him it was fiction. Over time, Angelo adopted that mentality from his brother. However, the possibility of these conspiracies being true never truly left him. They were buried somewhere deep at the back of his mind, waiting to be released.

Everybody had heard of the Illuminati. It wasn't hard to miss with tons of conspiracy videos flying around the internet every day, but no one had ever heard of the Starlight Saints. Angelo, Rex and Shawn exchanged sceptical glances.

"We have spies and secret agents stationed across Hollywood because that's where some of the Illuminati's activities are heavy. They have other bases in France, Germany and England, but our agents there handle those ones," Titus explained.

A series of questions erupted in Angelo's mind. *Where did all these facilities come from? How has the world not discovered you yet?*

"No offense, but this whole thing seems like a hoax. Nice scam you got going here," said Shawn mockingly. He finally had the courage to speak his mind for the first time.

"Shawn is right. This is stuff we believed as kids. It's like Santa and the tooth fairy," laughed Rex.

"And we're looking to recruit more kids like yourselves because you're the future. You all have a greater calling, which is why you're here," Titus explained. "Most of our agents are orphans, but we give them something to live for. We know how risky this profession is, so we compensate our agents with good money. I can assure you you'll be paid well for your work here. We're disguised as a charity group and academy that gives out internships and scholarships."

Angelo wasn't moved by the mention of money. He still battled to comprehend the Illuminati part. *If all of this was true and an evil mastermind was running the entire game of showbiz, then his family was sure to be right in the middle of the enemy's plan.* "I don't care about your money. What does my father have to do with any of this?" asked Angelo.

"There's a lot you don't know about your father. We have every right to suspect that Illuminati agents killed him before his final concert and staged his death as an overdose. When you leave the cult, they come back for you," said Titus.

Angelo couldn't digest this revelation. There was no way any of the words tumbling out of Titus's mouth were true, but he uttered them with solid confidence and certainty. Angelo's heart began to tremor at an idea so ludicrous.

"Where did you find the recording and why did you wait five years to tell me about this?! This is bullshit. My dad was a man of God, and he built many charities. There's no way he was part of this Illuminati business!" Angelo exclaimed, banging his fists on the table.

"I understand this is overwhelming, but I promise it will all become clear," Kate reassured him. She brought up a news article on the screen, "A recent crime has taken place. Your dad's former dietitian, James Kulkarni, bravely leaked their last phone call together, and he paid for it with his life, shot dead in his car just days ago after leaking. This new evidence suggests your dad's death wasn't the result of an overdose. You and your father's case hold a key that can help us destroy our greatest enemy. He possessed knowledge that the Illuminati desperately wanted to keep hidden from the world."

Angelo simply wouldn't listen to any more of Titus and Kate's explanations. *My dad, a man of unwavering faith and charitable deeds, linked to the sinister Illuminati?* Angelo couldn't accept it, not now, not ever. For his dad would be going against the very virtues he'd imparted to him. They were wrong. This wasn't the answer Angelo was looking for.

Angelo surged to his feet; his voice charged with resolve. "Take me home now! This… this is madness. A twisted game!" He wanted to escape from what felt like an ever-tightening web of conspiracies.

"We can assure you this is no game. Records show that the call was made months before Don's final concert was supposed to take place. Your dad knew something was coming for him," Titus explained.

As Angelo stood there, the echoes of doubt crept into his mind. The magnetic pull of Titus and Kate's words. Even though he desperately wanted to believe this was all a lie, a nagging suspicion told him there was a seed of truth.

Reflecting on the day his father passed away, he recalled that he was never actually by his father's side in his last moments. Sure, he had glimpsed him briefly, but the nurse took him away by force so they could carry out medical procedures. None of the family was there in those final moments when Don took his last breath. They only heard a report of cardiac arrest, but when Angelo was in the room, his father looked like he was recovering. The hope of leaving the hospital had shimmered tantalizingly close, only to be shattered. Still, he wouldn't accept the claims of Titus and Kate.

"I'm happy with the life I have right now. I don't need a secret society lying to me about my father and convincing me that I have some kind of prophetic calling. You're delusional!" Angelo exclaimed. "I'll just forget about that note and tape you sent me."

"Very well, but if you do change your mind, you can always give us a ring," Titus offered, extending a business card to Angelo. "I promise we're not toying with you. This is as real as it gets."

The card had an eleven-digit phone number printed on it. Angelo was tempted to chuck the card away, but he hesitated for a moment and placed it in his pocket instead.

"Let's get out of here," said Angelo to Rex and Shawn.

Before they could go any further, three agents blocked their path. Without warning, one of the agents seized hold of Angelo, forcefully pressing a handkerchief to his nose. Panic surged through Angelo as he struggled against the iron grip. He soon became weak and sleepy.

The gas he inhaled carried an intense spirit-like aroma that sapped his strength. Desperation gripped him as he glimpsed Shawn, also being suffocated by an agent, gasping for breath.

Angelo sank into deep slumber before he could react.

***

Angelo woke up. Light-headed and dizzy, it took his brain a minute to reconnect with reality. *Where was he, and what year was it?* He looked over to a collection of Akira and Mary J. Blige CDs, and he was back in his room.

The birds chirped, and the sun was sneaking up behind the horizon. It had to be morning by now. Again his brain was rebooting like a computer, trying to recall last night's events. He and his friends were kidnapped, but here he was in his room. *Was it all a dream?* He glanced over at his bedside table and immediately recognized the tape, and the card Titus had given him. *It wasn't a dream after all.*

"If you change your mind, you can always give us a ring." The words echoed in his head. *What could possibly make him change his mind?*

The dizziness faded away and his head stabilized. He sat staring at the card, analyzing the displayed phone number.

A knock came on the door, and Aunt Erica stepped in.

"Breakfast is ready. It's waffles," said Erica with a gentle smile.

"I'll be down in a few minutes," said Angelo as he got out of bed.

Angelo placed the card and the tape in one of the drawers and dashed to the shower. Turning the tap on, he allowed the shower's hot water to wash away the memories of the kidnapping. *Was the news worth sharing with Aunt Erica?*

CHAPTER 5

FUSION

6 years ago…

10-year-old Angelo had been homeschooled with Casey in Los Angeles. Their dad's estate was expansive and extraordinary, consisting of an amusement park, petting stables, and exotic gardens. A child's utopia, one would say. Children from other parts of the city would visit the estate and play with Angelo, racing one another across the 2,700-acre landscape, petting llamas, and going on rides. Angelo was blessed to have company until the children stopped coming one day.

What happened to them? He wondered.

There were no more visitors and no more friends to play with. Instead, Angelo would witness mean-looking officers in blue trekking across the estate and searching around as if they were doing an investigation.

On a quiet evening, Angelo sat in his room browsing the internet leaning over his computer, eyes glued to the screen. Scrolling through a bunch of videos a light tap on his shoulder brought him about from the trance. He turned around frightened.

It was Casey "Hey, I need my headphones back.".

Angelo reluctantly took the headphones off and handed them to Casey.

Casey was about to leave, but something caught his eye. "What are you up to?"

"Just watching some conspiracy videos," said Angelo, shoving another Dorito into his mouth.

15-year-old Casey rolled his eyes like he'd heard the same story a thousand times.

"I've been doing some research on the Illuminati. These videos are so cool. Did you know the government has a secret lair of shapeshifting reptilians? And did you know celebrities are Illuminati if they cover one eye?" Angelo put his hand over his right eye, attempting to mimic those celebrities who allegedly showed allegiance to the Illuminati.

Casey had no interest in entertaining Angelo's bizarre ideas, heaving a heavy sigh.

"Turn the computer off. Didn't I tell you to stop searching up this stuff? For Christ's sake, go watch cartoons or read some comic books," said Casey, his tone carrying annoyance.

Even with being brothers they were not so alike. Their differences clear as day and night and far outweighing what they did have in common. Angelo had the open and inquisitive mind of an explorer, while Casey had the rational and more logical. Such came with age.

Casey set his sights on becoming the next musical sensation like Dad and the ones before him, but his dad dismissed him and told him he would never amount to such stardom. Dad never gave Casey a chance to prove himself.

Nevertheless, Casey remained persistent.

Angelo slowly started reading aloud from his computer screen.

"For any person to reach a high level of success, they must make a huh?…covenant with the devil, and once they are inducted, they must go through stages of sacrificial rituals… Examples are the sacrifice of a human body and public humiliation," said Angelo, struggling to absorb the words written on the screen.

"There's always a trade-off in every area of life, including this field. To gain something you have to lose something first. When artists join the occult, they are required to promote satanic symbolism in their music videos."

Angelo's brain didn't fully comprehend all that he'd just read, but he was still fascinated.

Casey couldn't hide his disgust as he stared at the computer screen. "Stop, you're making me sick."

"I'm 10 years old and I'm smarter than you. You just can't handle the power of my knowledge!" Angelo teased, putting two fingers on each of his temples.

"Oh, shut up. You're so full of yourself and this is why you have no friends," Casey shot back. "I'm older than you so I know better."

"Do you think every celebrity and politician is involved in the Illuminati?" asked Angelo.

"Not everybody's involved. Some people worked hard for their own success without the help of some secret cult," said Casey.

"But it says here that you can't be successful without selling your soul first and…"

"That can't apply to everyone though. You're saying everyone cheated their way to the top, which is unfair. You know our dad started his career from an early age and I'm on my way to becoming a star myself." Casey was about to walk out of the room after he'd had enough of Angelo's ranting, but a cheeky smile crept up on his face as he headed for the door. "Maybe when you're done with your stupid conspiracies you and I can play a round of Mortal Kombat?"

Angelo's eyes lit up with excitement as he turned away from the computer screen.

"You're on!" Angelo exclaimed, his enthusiasm bubbling over. "Prepare to meet your doom, CJ!"

Casey snickered and shut the door. Over time, Casey's beliefs about conspiracy theories would sink into Angelo's consciousness.

Angelo started to lose interest in conspiracies and had needed to find a new hobby. He could try being a musician like his older brother or try skating.

Angelo needed to put the conspiracy talk to rest.

Present day...

It's time to confront Erica.

Angelo couldn't hide this secret anymore. She needed to know everything about the past few days. Though having told Erica he and his friends had gone for a night out, and they lost track of time, she somehow suspected there was more to what he was letting on.

"So, you didn't tell me much about your parcel hmmm. Care to share with me?" Erica questioned Angelo one morning.

It was time to give up the charade.

Why was he keeping the tape secrets from Aunt Erica, who had loved and taken care of him since his father's passing?

She had stepped up and showed Angelo the affection he desperately needed. *Couldn't he trust her the way he'd trusted his friends?* Even though Erica was biologically his aunt, she was the closest thing Angelo ever had to a mother. Two of Dad's unsuccessful marriages had left Angelo motherless for most of his life. Erica had been the maternal figure he had always cherished.

Angelo's dad kept many secrets from him. There had to be things the rest of the family knew that he didn't. His quest for truth would not be quenched.

"Come honey, let's sit," Erica said to Angelo as they made their way to the living room.

That morning, just before school, he presented Erica with the mysterious tape and note he had received from the Starlight Saints.

"There's a warning on there so don't tell anyone about this yet, please," Angelo cautioned.. As he pressed play, Erica listened carefully with intrigue. She seemed to recognize Don's voice but was beginning to show unease and discomfort.

"They want to get rid of me and take my children..."

"They can take me..."

Angelo pressed the stop button, his eyes fixed on Erica as he patiently awaited her response. The last words casting an uneasy atmosphere across the living room as if Dad's apparition was sitting right there with them.

"So, this is what came with the parcel, and you didn't even bother to tell me?" Erica questioned, her voice trembling and her eyebrows raised in surprise. "What else is there that I should know?"

Angelo shifted uncomfortably, guilt flooding in his heart. "I didn't wanna put you in danger and I thought maybe, 'what if it was a prank'?" he admitted. "I didn't think you'd believe me but now that you know I hope we can figure this out together. I know it's my father on the tape. He says a group of people wanted to get rid of him. Do you have any idea who he's talking about? Who's trying to take me and Casey, and why?"

Tension in the room intensified in the wake of Angelo's question. With a lingering moment of awkward silence. The elephant in the room had taken charge.

Erica's gaze faltered for a brief moment before she responded with a heavy sigh. She shook her head hesitantly.

"Sweetie, your father had a lot of people on his case. The media attacked him, scrutinized him, and made him out to be a bad person when he wasn't," Erica began, her tone carefully measured. "I remember when he faced those allegations, we were all under the bus. Everybody was out to get us, including you and me. They said I was guilty by association."

These were the child trafficking allegations that Angelo's dad faced throughout his career, but he was found innocent on all three trials. Angelo was angered by how the media and the public continued persecuting his father for crimes he never committed, even to the point of defamation after his passing.

"I need you to take me back into our family history, how did we become so successful in the music business?" asked Angelo.

Erica, the retired soul singer, took a contemplative pause, journeying through her memories before speaking. "It all started with your grandfather Ted Jackson. He's the pioneer of our family. He was a well-known pianist and guitarist back in the 1950s in Chicago. He performed many shows for street audiences out in public, but never made a dime from it. He had no manager or agent. No one was willing to recognize him for his talent," Erica explained. "So, he eventually lost hope and became an electrician instead. He married your grandma Ruby, who gave birth to the seven of us."

Erica had Angelo's full attention now.

Angelo leaned closer with intrigue, hanging onto every word. There was a lot about his family history he didn't know, and he was barely scratching the surface. He prompted his aunt to go on.

"Me, Don, and the others discovered that we each had musical gifts, and that's when our father regained hope," Erica recounted, her voice carrying a hint of excitement and melancholy mixed together. "He had this grand vision of making us top-of-the-world musicians and taking us to stardom. Don, Loraine, and I were vocally talented, while Uncle Jace, Bobby, Melvin, and Prodigy could play various instruments. We never had any free time to ourselves. Soon as school was done, our dad would make us rehearse whether we liked it or not, making us create a full song from scratch. If we made mistakes..." Erica trailed off, her mood turning sombre, "he'd whack us with a stick and keep beating us until we got it right."

Angelo winced at Erica's last sentence.

With how Erica described Grandpa Ted, Angelo couldn't imagine living in a household like that. Ted gave the impression of a harsh slave master whacking his servants for every minor error. He had only seen his grandfather twice as a toddler, but his current whereabouts remained a mystery.

"Your grandpa thought if he could meld us into world-class musicians, we'd be able to generate income for the whole family. Soon, we started entering talent shows, and we won almost all of them. Our band became known as *Jackson & Soul Fusion*, *Jacksoul Fusion*, or just *Fusion* for short. We made a name for ourselves back in Chicago."

A brief pause followed as Erica delved deeper into the family's history.

"Then came that fateful night when we performed in front of the Motown CEO, who was scoutin' for fresh talent. After our show, he approached our dad and proposed a record deal that would change our lives. Soon, we were signed to our very first record company at very young ages, with our dad as our manager. Throughout the '70s, we did countless shows, gainin' more recognition and fame with each one. We became a sensation, one of the most successful black musicians of our time, right up there with The Supremes and The Temptations. *Fusion's* popularity spread like wildfire across the entire nation and soon the rest of the world. We finally moved out of our little shack, and our father bought this big mansion in LA thanks to all the money we'd made," Erica narrated gesturing with her hands.

Angelo was left utterly astonished by the story, his jaw on the floor. It was one of those 'rags to riches never give up' stories that could inspire anyone. The Jacksons were hard-working individuals, for sure. However, this wasn't what Angelo was searching for. The information he sought went beyond this impressive journey.

"Wow, that's awesome, but...has our family ever been connected to a secret society or cult business? Is there some kind of deal I don't know about?" Angelo inquired.

Erica seemed flustered, a glint of discomfort passing through her eyes before she quickly regained her composure.

She shook her head, her gaze fixed on Angelo with a touch of worry. "What? What are you talking about? Of course not. Why would you ask something like that?" her voice tinged with a bit of defensiveness.

Angelo explained what happened on the night he went out with his friends. He chose to leave out the ambush and kidnapping part. Angelo explained what the Starlight Saints had said about his father being involved in the Illuminati. Although he denied it himself, he still needed to question it.

"No. I don't know who these Star Trek Saints are or whatever, but you need to get rid of that tape NOW," Erica raised her voice slightly, rising from her seat as she extended her hand, "Let me throw it in the trash. It's for your own good sweetheart."

"No!" said Angelo, holding the tape firmly in his hand. "You know something, don't you? You're hiding things from me, and I won't let go of this tape until you tell me what's going on."

Angelo became hesitant. If he surrendered the tape, his critical piece of evidence would be lost. If he let Erica dispose of it, what was left of Dad would also be gone, and he would never be able to uncover the truth. But keeping the tape in his possession would also create a barrier of distrust between Angelo and his loving aunt, a bitter disconnection.

Erica tried to calm Angelo down. "Sweetie, there's nothing going on. Some crazy lunatic is just trying to pull your leg. I don't know what this is about."

"Stop lying to me!" Angelo picked up the nearest vase and smashed it onto the ground. He didn't even think about what he was doing, his rage acting on its own, this tantrum getting the best of him.

"Angelo, what has gotten into you? Lionel Richie gave me that vase for my birthday! Don't ever raise your voice at me like that," said Erica, infuriated.

Angelo struck back with silence. He placed his backpack on his shoulders and began to walk out of the living room. The lightest smell of smoke came from somewhere, like a dish was burning in the kitchen.

"I'm off to school now. Whatever you're cooking is gonna burn."

"Angelo, come back here and clean up this mess you've made! I've raised you like my own son, and this is how you treat me? Okay, wait, I might know a little something."

Angelo kept walking with his back turned to Erica until he reached the front door. He wouldn't listen to her anymore, so he slipped the tape into his bag. His head spun with the chance that there was something else she was hiding from him, and *like everyone was messing with him.*

Throughout the entire school day, Angelo made no effort to engage or converse with anyone. Even when it had come to Rex and Shawn. Everybody had assignments to hand in before the summer break, but Angelo couldn't be bothered about what grades he got for the semester. Nothing really mattered. After a gruelling semester, he couldn't wait to get away from everyone at Sun Valley, especially people like Bode.

Listening to his favourite Hip-Hop and R&B tunes on the bus back home, Angelo thought hard about his actions earlier in the morning. *Did I overreact? The guilt took over.* He may have gone overboard by smashing Erica's vase onto the ground. His anger got the best of him, but that didn't excuse how he acted towards her. The only way to make this right was to apologize to his aunt when he returned and try to make it up to her by buying a new vase. The bus finally reached Braxton stop.

When Angelo stepped out of the bus, the scent of smoke greeted him. *Was someone having a BBQ?* He walked down the street until he reached his house. The ringing of sirens started beating against his eardrums, and that's when it hit him. A fire truck and a small crowd of officers surrounded his home, or at least what was left of it. Almost three-quarters of the house was burnt down. Panic and distress took hold of Angelo.

"What's going on? What happened?" Angelo approached one of the firefighters, begging for an answer.

"The house caught fire a couple of hours ago. There was a lady by the name of Erica Jackson inside," explained the firefighter.

Angelo's heart dropped at the mention of Aunt Erica.

A shadow of despair had suddenly been cast over.

Only the debris of the burnt house remained. Ashes scattered in charred heaps across the ground .The pungent stench of smoke and ash hit him like a wave. His home was now unrecognisable, a skeleton of blackened walls barely standing.

"Where is she? Please tell me you got her out!" Angelo was on the verge of tears, desperation gripping his heart.

"We managed to rescue her, but she's suffered some serious injuries. She's been taken to the hospital. It seems the fire was caused by some faulty appliances in the house. Electrical fires like this are quite rare," the firefighter explained.

A comforting hand touched Angelo's shoulder.

"Come, I'll take you to her," one of the neighbours offered, pointing to his car.

CHAPTER 6

MANY ARE CALLED
FEW ARE CHOSEN

When Angelo arrived at Chatsworth Hospital, he informed the receptionist about his aunt, and she immediately recognized who he was.

Another staff member on duty swiftly guided Angelo to the emergency unit, Ward 3. There lay Erica, vulnerable and helpless. Burns were visible on her right arm and neck. Angelo's heart started aching at the sight of his poor aunt as he approached her, taking hold of her left hand with a gentle touch.

Erica opened her eyes and turned to face Angelo.

"Please tell me you're gonna make it, I can't lose you like this," Angelo whispered through heavy sobs.

The weight of his father's loss, suffered five years ago, still bore heavily on Angelo's heart. Dreading the thought of losing another loved one. He had regret buried inside him after the tantrum he threw in the morning.

"I'm so sorry for the way I acted this morning. I didn't mean any of it. Please don't leave me," Angelo begged.

"I'll be fine. They say I got second-degree burns, but these anaesthetics should do the trick. I'll be here for two weeks," Erica said with a reassuring smile despite the pain she was enduring. "Forget about what happened this morning. I can always buy a new vase. As long as I got my nephew, that's all that matters."

Erica pulled him towards her and planted a gentle kiss on his forehead.

The gesture filled Angelo with a new sense of hope. He believed only the power of some divine intervention could've brought his aunt through this. *With Erica's recovery on the horizon, things would be just fine, but if she was in the hospital for two weeks and their house had been reduced to ashes, where would he stay?*

Angelo couldn't help but wonder if this was the beginning of his family's destruction. *Maybe even a curse had befallen them. Something like The Kennedy curse.*

***

Summer had descended upon the city of Rockingston, and the school grounds lay deserted, devoid of the usual bustle of adolescents and children who were now enjoying their long-awaited summer vacation. People flooded the parks, playgrounds, and skateparks, seeking solace in the embrace of the blazing sun.

Shawn's parents had kindly offered Angelo a place to stay while his home was being rebuilt.

Angelo couldn't help but feel a pang of sorrow, his mind dwelling onthe precious items he had lost during the fire. *His beloved Akira posters and cherished CDs, which had been his companions since his early years.* Akira had been Angelo's favourite singer since infancy, but ever since she'd died in a tragic plane crash, Angelo would never get to meet his beloved idol. All his most prized possessions were now buried within the house rubble.

The call of the Starlight Saints to become a secret agent seemed to whisper into Angelo's ear more frequently. He remembered his bible study sessions with Reverend Wilson about how everybody was called to do the goodwill of God, but not everyone answered their calling.

After almost losing Erica, he studied his scriptures more religiously, seeking revelation and guidance on whether he was choosing the right path or not. He'd lived a life separate from the *Hollyweird* business and still had luxury, but becoming an agent would most likely force him to leave that lifestyle behind.

He made his choice after several days of pondering. He was going to join the Starlight Saints.

Angelo and Shawn sat across from each other in their shared bedroom one night, lit by the soft glow of a lamp. The mellow rain came pelting on the roof.

"So, you actually wanna do this? You really wanna join this secret agency?" asked Shawn, leaning forward.

Gazing out of the rain-streaked window, Angelo's feelings were a blend of determination and inner turmoil. "You won't understand, I have to uncover the truth. I feel like something worse will happen if I don't go. If what they say is true, then I have to join them. I can't keep losing the people I love."

Shawn nodded, and his eyes softened with sympathy as he absorbed Angelo's words.

Could there have been a greater force working beyond the culprits who killed Angelo's dad? An evil society might have actually plotted to take over the world using the music industry to do their bidding. Such things seemed absurd before, but after everything that had occurred, he was ready to entertain this further.

Uncertainty hung in the air, and who knew what could happen next? The concept of a secret society oppressing the world and paving the way for their antichrist ruler correlated perfectly with some of what Angelo had read in the bible.

"They said I should call them with this number if I change my mind. I've decided to go back," Angelo felt a stroke of sadness with making such a decision. "This means you and Rex will have to enjoy summer without me this year, so…"

"Hold on just a sec," Shawn cut him off. "I'm coming with you. If this agency pays good money like they said, then I might as well join. Rex's coming along, too."

Angelo's eyes narrowed with concern, and he shook his head. "No, Shawn. Remember what happened at Merrion Bridge? We're lucky it wasn't the dragons who caught us that time. I can't put you guys in danger like that again. They said this profession is risky. Uncovering my father's case is my battle to fight, not yours."

Having dialled the number on the business card a few hours ago, Titus advised that the best time to meet him was at night.

"Same place as last time", Titus had said.

He had already devised a plan to leave the house later that night and make his way to Woodhead Way, where Titus would be waiting. With his raincoat and sneakers on, ready for the night excursion. He opened the window with the gentleness of a trained assassin where he was to sneak out of.

As he was about to leave, Shawn blocked his path.

"Angelo, are you seriously gonna do this without us?" Shawn questioned, his tone becoming more solemn. "I thought we were a clique. What happened to sticking together?"

"Like I said before, this is my fight. You're not risking your lives again because of me, plus you were the first to get your ass kicked at Merrion. If your parents ask about me just tell them I signed up for summer school," said Angelo.

He jumped out the window and landed on his feet. A heavy gust slapped him across the face, and rain splattered across the garden. He left through the garden gate and dashed across the street, where the road was populated with several cars.

6 Woodhead Way was the address. He and his friends were led to this place weeks before, believing it was a prank. Only to go back and be ambushed. However, this second visit would be different. He would come with the desire to join the Starlight

Saints. The rain became heavier, leaving Angelo dripping in its cold wetness. He walked up to the house, his feet dragging his weight. Jaw clenching, his hand greeted the door with a knock, footsteps resonated, and keys rattled from the other side.

"It's good to see ya again. Come inside," said Titus with his booming voice. Angelo stepped in, shutting the door behind him. Titus offered to hang Angelo's raincoat on a rack. Observing the house, the living room was furnished with state-of-the-art couches and a flatscreen television. Titus insisted that his guest take a seat. A series of files and papers lined up together in an office drawer.

"Welcome aboard, Angelo Jackson."

Titus placed some papers in front of Angelo, one front page containing all of Angelo's details, including his birth certificate:

> **Full name:** *Angelo Ezra Jackson*
> **DOB:** *10 April XXXX*
>
> **Eye Color:** *Brown*
> *xxxxxxxxxxx*

Angelo became uneasy. Titus recording all these details was uncomfortable, but it wasn't the biggest of surprises either.

Angelo flipped through the pages, each filled with paragraphs containing information about which school he attended, where he lived, his skin condition, his father, and his family.

"Where did you get all of this?" he asked.

"I'm sure you can guess the answer to that."

But he didn't have the need to ask again. Part of a secret agency's job was to acquire details of people, whether for recruitment or elimination.

"There are terms and conditions to understand...number 1, you do not disclose any information about our operations to anyone outside of this agency," Titus urged.

He began to make all kinds of movements with his hands. He did it so fast that Angelo couldn't comprehend what was happening.

"Just like Freemasons, we have our own secret hand signs. One way to test if somebody is a saint is if they can do the sign of the phoenix just like I've demonstrated. You'll learn all these in training."

Titus went on, "You're not the only one we've got our sights on. We've been recruiting a lot of other teenagers, as no one usually suspects them of working for an agency, and that's the advantage."

Angelo was still struggling to believe this. Only partially convinced.

"Where do you get the funds to build all your facilities and operate?" Angelo inquired. Titus's smile disappeared.

"Many philanthropists have supported and funded our cause for years. We also take some money from our enemies. These corporate devils have billions of dollars under their names, so sometimes, when we assassinate them, we use the money they've left behind for ourselves," Titus explained.

Angelo's trust started to waver. "So, you assassinate and steal from others? I thought you guys were supposed to be saints."

"It's not stealing if it's for a good cause. When you see the atrocities the Illuminati have committed, you'll understand."

Taking Titus's words into consideration he decided not to press any further questions about the matter. The only way forward would be for him to commence his journey.

Titus presented two pieces of paper and a pen. "I need you to sign this non-disclosure agreement."

Angelo did as he was told and wrote his signature across the contract.

"Induction begins this Thursday. Get ready, Mr. Jackson, because your whole perception of reality is about to change," said Titus, handing him a piece of paper. "Keep this other document with you. It has all the details of where you need to be and what time."

Angelo took the sheet, folded it, and placed it in his pocket. The meeting had come to an end. Angelo stepped back out into the persistent rain. The adolescent slipped his hoodie on and journeyed back to Shawn's place. His heart staggered, and he still had no way of knowing whether he was making the right decision. *What would his older brother think?*.

***

Casey, Angelo's older brother AKA CJ Maverick, was hosting a charity drive in Rockingston a few days later. He had secured himself a massive record deal with their father's former record label, Sonic Scope Records, months after Dad died. Casey was residing at a luxurious mansion in Beverly Hills. His ever-growing fandom and status as a rapper made him Rockingston's hometown hero. Even though he wasn't born there, the city still saw him as their icon. The charity drive mainly consisted of children. Toys, gadgets, and other accessories were given away freely under the management of Casey's charitable organization.

Angelo planned to use this as an opportunity to tell Casey about the tape and his decision to join a secret agency. His brother was the only family member Angelo would trust since they were both mentioned in the tape. If any secret could be kept, it would be between siblings.

The park stretched out before him, filled with a vast number of children and parents that day. Groups of families spread blankets across the grass while children ran in wild circles around playgrounds and food stands. The park was packed, leaving barely any room to breathe. Angelo dreaded having to push through this sea of people just to get to Casey. The heat of the scorching sun's rays also didn't make things easier. As Angelo moved through the crowd, he drew some unwanted attention to himself.

"Ayo, check it out. It's that white albino kid! CJ Maverick's little bro!" A boy yelled, obviously referring to Angelo.

Angelo was fed up with how people always took a jab at his skin condition.

"It's called vitiligo, dummy!" Angelo yelled back.

Angelo carried on, squeezing between clusters of families, his shoulders brushing against strangers and the press of bodies making it hard to move. He finally arrived at the front of the crowd where Casey and his management staff were giving away free items at stands. Casey sported the most glamorous designer outfit anyone could dream of. The jewellery he wore glowed in the sun and complemented his outfit. Everyone desired the lavish lifestyle of a rapper, but not everyone could get it.

"Angelo?" Casey exclaimed, genuine surprise and pleasure lighting on his face as Angelo approached him. "Wow, it's been ages since I've seen you. I was hoping you'd show up."

Angelo gave a warm smile as he closed the gap between them. Their hands clasped, and Angelo pulled Casey into a gentle, heartfelt hug. "I know. Long overdue."

"I heard about the fire and what happened to Aunt Erica. Hope she's okay," Casey mentioned, his eyes clouding with sorrow.

"She'll be fine. Should be outta hospital in the next few weeks while they're rebuilding the house," Angelo reassured him. "I've been staying at a friend's place for now."

As the two siblings caught up with each other, Casey enlightened Angelo on how hard and complex the celebrity life could be, including how challenging things were for him when he'd visit Quinn Pakerson in rehab, his new apparent girlfriend. This was part of the reason why Angelo wanted nothing to do with stardom. After a brief update on Casey's busy life, it was time for Angelo to reveal what had occurred in the last several days.

"I gotta show you something, but you cannot tell anyone else. Promise?" Angelo felt driven by urgency and confidentiality.

"Promise," Casey responded. His eyes locked onto Angelo's, indicating a sign of unwavering trust.

They snuck away from the stands and crowds of people to a more secluded space with only the two of them. Angelo checked their surroundings and ensured no one else was following or listening. Before retrieving the cassette from his bag he handed Casey his headphones. Angelo pressed play, and a sense of apprehension crept onto Casey's face as the tape began to roll.

Casey's brows shifted in alarm as he listened. The weight of the tape's revelation seemed to be sinking in. When the tape finally ceased, he removed the headphones and held them in his hand, too stunned to utter a word.

Angelo couldn't bear the heavy silence any longer and decided to break it. "Casey, there are people after us. I'm joining a secret agency called the Starlight Saints. They might be able to help me uncover the truth about Dad's death and help protect us both."

Casey remained silent, but he seemed to be absorbing Angelo's words.

Angelo reached into his pocket and retrieved the folded note that came with the parcel he had received from the Starlight Saints.

Casey proceeded to examine it and became more alarmed by what he had read.

Angelo was sure Casey would laugh his socks off and call this a prank, but his reaction came as a surprise.

"So, this secret agency can help you uncover the truth? You don't think Dad overdosed?" asked Casey with intrigue.

"Nah, I'm convinced there's more to it," Angelo replied firmly. "I think the rest of our family and the media are trying to hide something from us."

Casey nodded, his brow furrowing as he appeared to be in deep contemplation. "I've felt it too, AJ. Ever since I got that record deal, I've sensed hidden enemies lurking within the industry, waiting for a chance to strike. That's why I always got security around me. If what's on the tape is true, then I could be next on the list. There could be darker forces at work, coming after our souls. I can feel it."

Angelo placed a reassuring hand on Casey's shoulder, silently acknowledging the shared burden they now faced.

"I feel it, too. This agency is my best chance of finding out what we're up against," Angelo admitted. "I'll be leaving town soon, but I need you to promise me you'll be careful."

Angelo was having second thoughts about leaving Rockingston and its familiarity. His heart was torn. The city had cradled him in its arms for so long, but recent events, like the raging fire, felt like ominous omens, urging him to venture into the wilderness of the unknown.

"Of course. But before you go, I should give you this." Casey handed Angelo an old, outdated-looking cell phone.

"It's my old phone. I'm still on tour, but we'll need a way to communicate when you get to this agency. Keep me updated on what you discover about Dad, and I'll do my best to help out from my end. There's enemies out there who probably want us dead. If we're gonna stop them, we must work together," Casey explained.

Angelo smiled and accepted the phone and slipped it into his pocket. He had to trust Casey on this. If Angelo was going to stop both himself and his older brother from suffering the same fate as their dad, he would need all the help he could get.

Chapter 7

The New Apprentice

Angelo tossed his bags into the luggage compartment of a bus. The bus's exterior gleamed in the light, a logo plastered on its side. Around him a sea of people bustled about, some pacing with bags slung over their shoulders. Distant conversations filled the air with the roar of engines as more buses pulled into the station. He clambered up the stairs, and the bus was packed with other recruits as soon as he entered. He scanned the area for a vacant seat and found a window one. *Perfect.*

The bus filled to the brim with teenagers squeezing in until every seat was occupied. Angelo glanced around and observed a diverse group of fellow passengers, their faces mixed with excitement and uncertainty. The air became thick with nervous chatter. As Angelo gazed out the window things became gloomy. The city of Rockingston, the home he knew for the last five years would soon become distant.

A short, muscular supervisor stood at the front of the bus and blew the whistle, the sound cutting through the commotion for everyone's attention. The man wore a shirt with 'Starlight Academy' printed on it, obviously a disguise for a secret agency masquerading as a summer school. Angelo knew this was necessary for the Starlight Saints to avoid raising suspicion from the public.

"Enjoy your last few hours of freedom 'cause once we get to the academy, you're all prisoners," the supervisor joked.

Angelo's lips curved into a polite smile, but the humour didn't ring. His stomach tightened with nerves and once again, the thought of leaving Rockingston and entering new territory made him uneasy. It was the fear of what awaited him, the fear of not knowing what he was getting himself into.

Angelo glanced out the window again, his thoughts drifting to Aunt Erica, whom he'd embraced before leaving. He was relieved about her safety but leaving Rex and Shawn to enjoy summer vacation without him felt like a betrayal, though in his heart, he knew he was doing them a favour. They wouldn't have to suffer at the induction and risk their lives working for an agency.

This was too much for Angelo. *Was there still time to change his mind? What if he decided to get off the bus and forget about leaving Rockingston? No, it was a little too late for that now.*

The engine rumbled, and the bus set off. Angelo plugged in his earphones and prepared to listen to some J Cole, Lauryn Hill, and Wu-Tang during the three-hour journey. Glancing out the window, the landscape started transitioning from a bustling city to a beautiful countryside.

Angelo was amazed by the incredible view. Green fields stretched endlessly dotted with patches of wildflowers that swayed in the gentle breeze and cows grazed from afar as small farmhouses peeked out from behind the fields. t His eyes soon became heavy. Before he knew it, he dozed off.

***

The sharp blast of a whistle tore through Angelo's drowsiness, jolting him awake. Rubbing his eyes, he peered outside. It was late afternoon, and sheets of clouds painted the sky, casting shadows over the sprawling landscape. Lush green hills covered in a vibrant carpet of greenery stretched as far as the eyes could see. Towering trees formed a secluded forest in the distance. The passengers soon passed through a pair of imposing iron gates.

Angelo's heart quickened at the sight of a high brick wall with coils of barbed wire at the top. His palms began to sweat, and he couldn't help but feel like he was entering a concentration camp. The bus rolled along a gravel driveway that wound its way deeper into the heart of the secluded academy. His gaze darted from window to window as he spotted several elegant buildings, which he guessed were all part of the Starlight Saint's academy. The campus was larger than he'd expected, that was for sure.

The bus came to a stop at a huge building that looked like the main reception. Angelo stepped out and retrieved his bags. At the entrance of the building was a registration table where all the recruits lined up in a single file.

"Name?"

"Angelo Jackson."

Angelo presented his registration form to the receptionist. The man read through the paper, ensuring it had all the details and signatures of approval. He then looked at Angelo with interest.

"You must be that Don Leornard singer's son," he said. "You're a new apprentice, I see."

Angelo nodded and tried to put on a friendly smile. The man nodded back and stamped the registration form.

"I need you to place your thumb and index finger here starting with your right hand and then your left," he indicated a small biometric machine.

Angelo did as he was told.

After scanning his fingerprints, the man handed Angelo a name tag, a wristband, a map, and a room key.

Titus stood with the other recruits, waiting for everybody to register. The apprentices were escorted to a building further down, which would be their accommodation.

As Angelo walked through unfamiliar surroundings, he felt a gentle tap on his shoulder that startled him. He turned and met the warm smile of a boy of Asian descent.

"Hey, I'm Sanji," the boy introduced himself, his enthusiasm evident. "I can't wait to see our rooms."

Angelo nodded with a nervous smile, a flicker of uncertainty in his mind. "Angelo."

If he was going to survive in this place, starting new friendships would be his best chance.

The accommodation looked brand new or had recently been refurbished. Old beautiful paintings from the Renaissance era hung on the walls of the passage, and the sun's rays filtered through a roof window.

Angelo checked the number on his key and located room number twelve. As he swiped the card, the doorknob light turned green.

The bedroom was small and basic, consisting of a desk, chair, lamp, single bed, a bathroom, and an old wooden wardrobe. Angelo dumped his bags on the bed with a sigh of disappointment, hoping it would be bigger and fancier, but a basic room was better than nothing. He looked out the window, and it instantly felt like a boarding school campus prison in the middle of nowhere. Having high barbed walls in the countryside made Angelo wonder if the Starlight Saints were being a bit too overprotective. *What if he wanted to leave the premises and explore more of the country? Was he even allowed to do that, or would he be confined in this space 24/7?*

"Dinner is at six. Start unpacking and settle in," A loud announcement echoed from Titus on the other side of the hallway.

Angelo began unpacking his luggage and was glad to have brought his bible with him. They may have been miles away from Aunt Erica, but reading scripture would give him comfort and hope throughout his time here. Angelo also pulled out the phone that Casey entrusted him and placed it safely in a drawer. He retrieved the tape cassette, which he'd held onto like a forbidden treasure and slipped it underneath his bed, where it would be hidden from plain sight.

The apprentices were led to a large dining hall when they made their way downstairs. The hall was expansive. A vast number of boys and girls were scattered around, sitting at circular tables while chatting and eating. It had been hours since Angelo last ate. To the left was an open serving area, steaming with freshly cooked food. His mouth watered as he glanced at tonight's menu: chicken chow Mein special for dinner and ice cream for dessert.

"Maybe this isn't a prison after all," Angelo mumbled to himself, shovelling a batch of chow Mein onto his plate. He helped himself with some raspberry juice at the drink dispenser, too.

As Angelo followed an apprentice group to a free table, he wasted no time digging into the food. Swirling his fork and devoured his noodles like he hadn't eaten in days. The flavours caressed his tongue, and the sensation melted his tastebuds with each mouthful. When he looked down at his plate, nothing remained but a spotless surface. Angelo had chowed everything, leaving no trace of leftover chow Mein.

Heading to the drink dispenser next to get more raspberry juice, as he pushed the lever, a teenage girl with beautiful curls approached him.

"Hey, you must be one of the apprentices…Angelo, is that right?" she said, smiling as she examined his name tag. "I'm Vanya. It's pretty cool to have you in our society. I know all about your dad and how much of a star he was. My mom even has an autograph from a concert she attended in the 80s. Sorry that you lost him. It must have been hard." Her smile faded, and her eyes glowed with compassion.

"It's okay, and yeah, that's me. An autograph? That's pretty cool…your mom must be a really big super fan," said Angelo, smiling at her with a friendly chuckle. He tried his best to conceal the inner pain Dad's death had caused him over the years.

This was the first time somebody besides a recruit approached him, and he instantly felt welcomed amongst the pool of complete strangers. However, his attention shifted as he spotted the blue-haired girl from the earlier ambush. Angelo decided to reach out to her, hoping to make a proper introduction.

"Hey, remember me?" asked Angelo with a friendly wave.

The blue-haired girl responded with a glare that could freeze fire. Her words cut through the air like an icy wind laced with hostility.

"I don't know why Seraph Titus decided to recruit you. We don't trust you one bit," she declared, her tone unwelcoming and unwavering.

Taken aback by her statement, a sharp stab to his heart. Angelo was already facing hostility on the first night and didn't know what to make of it. The blue-haired girl grabbed her drink and walked back to her table.

"That's Luna. She can be uptight sometimes, but she's quite a veteran, second-degree phoenix. All the phoenix saints respect her," Vanya explained.

"Second-degree phoenix?"

Vanya chuckled softly, leaning in to share a bit of insider knowledge. "Oh, there's different levels of saints here. You'll learn all about that in your training."

Different levels? Starting at the apprentice level meant there was a long way to go. Angelo would climb up the ranks and prove himself. If he was going to take revenge on his father's killer, then he needed to reach the highest status.

After taking a scoop of ice cream, Vanya led him to her table.

Just like any new kid at a high school, Angelo's shyness got the best of him as he tried to converse with the other boys and girls. Two feet suddenly landed on the table, causing the dishes to clatter.

"Criminal! Trespasser!"

Startled by the abrupt disruption, Angelo's gaze rose from his bowl and found a finger pointing directly at him. Standing above him was a boy of Hispanic ethnicity, sporting a taper haircut.

He shouted so loud he got the entire hall's attention, and all eyes turned toward them.

Angelo immediately stopped eating his ice cream, and his heart raced in his chest.

Did he do something wrong already? Had he unknowingly broken a rule?

"This is the son of a criminal trafficker. He's a Jackson and as we all know the Jacksons are involved in human trafficking and occultic stuff. People like him are not welcome in our society," the Hispanic boy declared.

Angelo's ice cream remained untouched; his spoon suspended in mid-air. His discomfort grew as he felt the penetrating gazes of other saints around him. They all were like vultures ready to seize him.

"Dwayne, stop it! That's not how a saint is supposed to act," said Vanya, coming to Angelo's defence.

Dwayne, the accuser, remained unyielding. "A saint doesn't tolerate criminals in their society. You should know better, Vanya. He could be working for our enemy. Those Don Leornard Jackson allegations tell us everything we need to know about their family."

The cafeteria buzzed with mixed reactions, and Angelo found himself in the uncomfortable spotlight. Angelo couldn't allow this. *Letting someone else defend him would make him look weak, and he hated being weak. Allowing this arrogant bastard to insult his family would be dishonourable to them.* "The allegations are not even true! You'd know that if you did your research. My dad was proven innocent three times, but hey, maybe math isn't quite your thing," said Angelo, rising from his seat.

The rest of the hall erupted with gasps and snickers. The apprentices and other saints seemed amused by Angelo's audacity to talk back.

Dwayne swiftly jumped off the table and landed on the floor with a thud to face Angelo. "Watch yourself apprentice or you're not gonna last very long around here," warned Dwayne, pointing his index finger for emphasis.

Determination filled Angelo as he stood his ground. "Oh, I'll watch myself alright. Watch myself kick your ass all over this building," he shot back, his words laced with bravado.

The hall erupted with cheers and chants, almost as if they were eager for a fight to break out. From the corner of Angelo's eye, Luna noticeably observed the confrontation with interest while sipping her drink.

A glint of surprise in her icy, glaring eyes hinted either an admiration or detestation which Angelo couldn't discern.

Angelo stood toe to toe with Dwayne, neither of them making the first move. Soon enough, Vanya intervened and separated the two of them.

"Both of you stop. Grandmaster Rin will not tolerate this!" she admonished.

Angelo was determined not to show any sign of weakness. Coach Sid had always told him to never let his guard down, no matter what. He continued to stand his ground.

That was when Dwayne decided to turn away. "I warned you, albino. You're in for it now," said Dwayne with a devious sneer, taking a cruel dig at Angelo's vitiligo condition.

Chatter continued to buzz throughout the hall, and Angelo sat back down only to find that the remainder of his ice cream had melted. *Great.* He stood up and put his bowl away in the disposal area. Dinner had come to an unexpected and somewhat unsatisfying end.

Angelo lay on his bed that evening. His thoughts turned to the incident in the dining hall. *The reality of what he signed up for hit home. He was probably going to make a lot of enemies in this agency. It was only the first night, and he already had a target on his back.*

***

The next day, the apprentices were required to wake up early at six in the morning for physical fitness training. According to the campus map, a gym, swimming pool, and basketball court were readily available, which were facilities Angelo hadn't anticipated. Among these facilities was also a gaming lounge and a TV room for leisure, which left him pleasantly surprised. It was hard to believe that a secret agency had such facilities, but Angelo was determined to make the most of them, but also needed to be in training and orientation classes by nine.

"Your training will be led by Cherub Skye and Cherub Hugh," declared Titus, introducing the two agents.

The cherubs wore matching spectacles. Hugh was visibly elderly, while Skye embodied features of a young adult in her late twenties.

Angelo was seated close to the front, fighting to stay focused and running on five hours of sleep. He sat next to Sanji in the lecture hall. The lecture hall was unlike any classroom Angelo had ever seen. It boasted HD flatscreen projectors, state-of-the-art computers, and ergonomic high-backed seats that comfortably embraced their occupants.

Sanji leaned in close, his voice barely above a whisper. "What you did at dinner yesterday was really impressive. Most of us are too afraid to stand up to the higher-ranking saints. We're just apprentices, after all, but you made quite a statement."

Angelo's gaze remained fixed on the front of the room, but he nodded in acknowledgement. "I couldn't let that fool disrespect my family," he replied in a hushed tone.

Just as the cherubs were about to delve into the lesson, there was a sudden knock on the door, and everybody's attention diverted away from them. The door swung open, revealing the figure of an agent.

"Sorry to interrupt the lesson, but we've got two other apprentices joining us," the agent announced, stepping aside.

Angelo's jaw dropped as the two apprentices entered the room. His eyes widened in disbelief as they were the last people he expected to see.

"Rex and Shawn will be joining your class," the agent announced.

CHAPTER 8

STARLIGHT ORIGINS

Angelo's Diary

They Killed the Mockingbird,

I hate the media, and it's that simple. I hate the way they portrayed my father as a pedophile and human trafficker. The media will only sell lies and half-truths to the public to fill their pockets. What did my father's demise profit you? I'm still young. I never want anything to do with Hollyweird, but if I ever become president of the United States, I want all censorship removed. People deserve to know everything about their government. They deserve to know the truth. No more bias, no more deception, and no more manipulation. If life ever allows me to step into the White House, then I can right society's wrongs. The media will be the first to go down. I'll do away with all their evil tactics and prove that my dad was indeed innocent. I will avenge all other celebrities and individuals who fell victim to the media's injustice. I know I've always wanted a life away from stardom, but what if I could change the world? What if I'm a prophet assigned to deliver an important message to humanity? Ok let me not get ahead of myself. I'm only sixteen. I get carried away sometimes when I write.

My name is Angelo Jackson, and I am the future.

***

The training class was in session but Angelo struggled to suppress his shock. Wanting desperately to yell something out but kept it in to save himself from embarrassment.

"You know those guys?" asked Sanji with curiosity.

He seemed to notice Angelo's perplexity.

"They're my friends. I left them back at my hometown before I came, and now they're here," said Angelo, confused.

What an unexpected surprise. Rex and Shawn had somehow managed to find their way to the Starlight Saints. Several questions ran through his mind. *How did they get here?* But the cherubs called back for everyone's attention. On the screen was the symbol of the archangels, its significance known to all as the Starlight Saint logo. Cherub Skye stepped forward, her voice firm as she began to speak.

"The Starlight Saints were founded by Malcolm Stern in 1848 as a rebellion group against the rising Illuminati," Cherub Skye declared, clicking up an ancient black and white photograph of the founder. The image seemed to carry the weight of history itself. "Now, it's important that we teach you about our enemy first so you can understand how our secret society emerged. I'll let Hugh to speak now."

She handed the remote to Cherub Hugh, and the screen transitioned to an image of the triangle of providence. Angelo was well familiar with that symbol. It was on every one-dollar bill, making it common knowledge for everyone in the room. No surprises there. The image, however, soon shifted to an owl.

"Many of you may not know this, but the Illuminati's original symbol was the Owl of Athena. The group was founded by Johann Adam Weishaupt in 1776 from the lands of Bavaria, Germany," Cherub Hugh began. He cleared his throat and continued, "The Illuminati claimed to promote self-enlightenment, liberation, rational thought, and self-rule. They believed eradicating government rulers, religion and completely removing God from society would help mankind to better itself and live happily in peace and equality."

As the lecture continued, Angelo couldn't help but steal a glance at the back seats where Rex and Shawn were seated. He tried to get their attention by using subtle hand gestures. After a moment, Shawn's eyes eventually met Angelo's. Angelo began to communicate silently with the movement of his lips, hoping Shawn could read his words.

The cherub's stern voice cut through the room, and their brief communication was brought to a halt. "Angelo, is there a problem? No talking when I'm talking, please," said Cherub Hugh, evidently irritated that his lecture was being interrupted. He did as he was told, quickly apologized and turned his attention back to the front.

"As I was saying, more citizens and revolutionaries began to support Adam's ideas, and the secret society's members grew in numbers. Eventually, the ruler of Bavaria officially banned the Illuminati in 1785 when he discovered some of their activities. He suspected that the secret society was planning to overthrow the government and defy authority. The Illuminati had failed to take over the world at this point," explained Hugh.

As Hugh delved deeper into the Illuminati's history, Angelo found himself torn. *Enlightenment and freedom from authoritative rule sounded like ideas he could get behind, but the notion of removing God from society stirred discomfort within him. What would the purpose of life be without the existence of a god? He couldn't imagine humanity purely existing on its own. Humanity had to be created for a purpose by a purposeful being.*

A girl at the back raised her hand. "Sir, what's so bad 'bout wantin' to enlighten the world and giving folks the freedom to think for themselves? Ain't that what our world needs?"

Hugh acknowledged the question with a nod. "Good question Maddie, we're getting there. Skye, please continue,"

"As we were saying," Cherub Skye resumed, "although the Illuminati was banned in 1785, the society was later revived in the 1800s across other parts of Europe. They continued to carry out Weishaupt's philosophies and principles of enlightenment. Our founder, Malcolm Stern, was born a member of the Illuminati and ordained from birth. However, as Malcolm grew older, he started to disagree with the Illuminati's doctrines, especially the idea of removing Christianity from society and replacing it with secularism," Skye explained. "He believed removing God would lead to humanity's destruction because there would be no morality to guide the human race."

Angelo's intuition was correct. He knew that without the guidance of a god or higher power, humanity was lost. History had shown the dark consequences of humans governing themselves without a moral compass. Slavery, World War II, the Holocaust, and apartheid were all proof that humans were incapable of ruling themselves. They needed a divine being to govern their ways.

"Because of his opposing views, Malcolm started his own secret society and named it the Starlight Saints. He would secretly recruit people and encourage members to rebel against the Illuminati. He started leaking the Illuminati's top secrets and operations to members of the public, but once they found out, they executed him and his whole family. However, those who supported Malcolm's ideas continued the work of his agency to this present day," Skye concluded.

"As Starlight Saints, we promote the ideas of order, collectiveness, righteousness, and truth. These principles are what hold society together and keep everything balanced," Hugh explained. "There are five major rankings. Apprentice which you all are, phoenix, cherub, seraph, and grandmaster. There are sublevels that vary between these rankings. Apprentices must complete three different rituals in order to progress. We'll explain more in the next lesson."

Skye clicked up ancient writing text on the board for everyone to view. "Lastly, there are also five mottos every Starlight Saint must live by."

The five Starlight mottos were the following:

1. *Nothing is real, and every truth must be questioned*
2. *Reality is a gift to the awakened eye and a curse to the deluded blind*
3. *What is unseen, and intangible is often what holds the most significance*
4. *Order shall prevail, and perversion must cease*
5. *If there's no god or archangels guiding our purpose then let our existence be a lie*

Angelo and the other apprentices were taking notes as the cherubs were explaining. The class was soon dismissed, and he was thankful he had that early morning fitness training. His brain was active enough to take in all the information.

Each apprentice was given a personal laptop to read over their learning material and do assignments. Angelo couldn't hide his disappointment anymore. This was supposed to be a so-called agency, but he felt like he was in school again. From what Angelo had seen, the agency provided saints with private education courses like math, accounting, physics, etc. Starlight Saints needed to blend in with everyday society, whether that meant adopting the roles of doctors, accountants, or athletes. Fitting into the world's standards and customs of everyday life was essential for the secret society to keep surviving and operating discreetly.

"*We're very good at what we do. You could meet a teacher, or a janitor and you wouldn't be able to tell that they're a secret agent. We have saints in all occupations. Whether in low or high-income positions, it doesn't matter because they ultimately work for us,*" Hugh had said during the lesson.

Being sixteen and still in high school, Angelo found himself at a crossroads. Unlike many of his peers who were thinking about their future careers, Angelo still wasn't sure which path he wanted to pursue. He had already ruled out any involvement in

Hollyweird and enjoyed kickboxing as a hobby, but there wasn't any professional job he could see himself doing in the future. He'd overheard Rex asking the Starlight Saints if they could get him drafted into the NBA, which was bizarre, but considering the agency's vast resources, it was totally doable.

Angelo's favourite subjects were geography, economics, and social studies, which seemed to offer some direction. He decided to study these courses during his time with the Starlight Saints.

***

Angelo stepped out of the lecture hall, the murmur of students trailing behind him as they scattered to their next destinations. He took a quick glance at the clock. *Lunchtime.* He still needed to confront Rex and Shawn about their unexpected arrival and headed toward the cafeteria. The lunch menu featured chicken burgers and fries, quite the appetizing spread. Angelo scanned the bustling dining hall until he spotted Rex and Shawn at the left corner, mingling with other apprentices.

He approached them with a mixture of frustration and concern. "How'd you guys get here? You should've stayed back in Rockingston."

Shawn leaned back, a mischievous grin on his face. "And let you get all the reward money? Ha, as if. Rex and I finessed our way in. The seraph got us a ride."

Angelo couldn't help but shake his head. "Money? Is that really all you care about? You have no idea what you've signed up for."

Shawn simply smirked and took a bite of his burger, unfazed by Angelo's warning.

Angelo placed a chunk of fries into his mouth, shaking his head at the foolish decision his friends had made. *All he wanted was to keep them out of harm's way.*

As lunch came to an end, Angelo finished the remainder of his meal, and the trio walked outside onto the grassy grounds.

Angelo couldn't help but catch a glance of Dwayne, the foe he clashed with on the first night, sitting on a nearby balcony.

Dwayne gave him a disgusted glare of suspicion, but Angelo did his best to ignore it.

"You guys are idiots. Y'all should've stayed back home like I told you," Angelo chastised, facing Rex and Shawn.

"Nobody tells Leclez what to do. I'm tryna raise money for my uncle's lung transplant, and this agency might be my only shot. Talk smack to me again, and I won't hesitate to cut your throat," Rex warned.

Angelo was no stranger to Rex's violent tendencies and was practically used to them. Rex still had some traits from his street fighting and years of gang activity. He finally understood Rex's motivations and nodded with sympathy. He made no further comment, unwilling to entertain Rex's threat any further.

"Plus, we're a clique and we stick together," Shawn added.

"Okay, fine. I understand. Just promise me we're all gonna look out for each other. I've got people here gunning for me already, and there's a target on my back," Angelo implored.

"When have we not looked out for each other, Apple Jack?" Rex grinned. "I've saved you from trouble multiple times."

Angelo couldn't dispute Rex's statement. With their camaraderie reaffirmed, he took back what he had said earlier and was glad his friends had decided to join the Starlight Saints. Having familiar faces in unfamiliar territory alleviated some of the stress he had been going through.

As they prepared for afternoon training, Rex and Shawn strolled toward one of the training halls. Angelo would soon follow behind. Before he left, he took one last look at the balcony where his rival, Dwayne, had been seated, only to find out that Dwayne had vanished.

***

"This afternoon's training exercise is about protection and defense," Skye announced.

The intense heat of summer was taking its toll on everybody. Each apprentice carried their own water bottle to stay hydrated in the sweltering weather. Angelo was relieved that the training hall had air conditioning and embraced the cool, refreshing breeze. Rex, Shawn, and Sanji stood by his side, awaiting the cherub's instructions. Skye held up what appeared to be some sort of vest. She scanned the crowd of apprentices, and after a while, her gaze settled on Angelo.

"Angelo, would you please come up?" she commanded.

Why me? He thought. *There were dozens of other apprentices Skye could've chosen. Could he object to the cherub's instruction if he wanted?*

He'd probably get punished if he did, judging by how strictly the Starlight Saints conducted themselves. Angelo's heart raced as he reluctantly made his way onto the stage with the eyes of other apprentices glued onto him. He despised being the centre of attention, especially when surrounded by so many watchful eyes.

"Put this on," Skye instructed, handing Angelo the vest. He obediently slid it over his head, securing it around his shoulders and waist. The vest had a surprisingly smooth touch to it, and it felt comfortable against his skin.

"This is a protective vest that every saint is required to wear when going out on missions," she explained, pointing to Angelo. "It's made up of promethium-lined armour. When attacked, the vest hardens up in specific areas struck to protect you against impacts such as bullets. Angelo, please face me for a moment."

He complied and turned his body ninety degrees to face Skye. Suddenly, out of nowhere, in a surprising twist, she swiftly whipped out a gun and shot Angelo directly in the chest. Everyone gasped, and the suddenness of the shot made Angelo's heart skip a beat. He'd instinctively shut his eyes, bracing for the worst, only to reopen them and find himself miraculously alive.

"Ouch," he complained. He reached for his chest where the bullet had struck, and behold, to his amazement, there was no sign of blood or injury anywhere. While the vest had done its job protecting him and preventing harm, the shot had left a slight lingering sting on his chest. Nevertheless, the vest had performed exactly how the cherub said it would. The entire group of apprentices watched in awe at this impressive demonstration.

"The vest is also powered by kinetic energy so when you move around it keeps your vest completely charged," Skye explained, revealing the added functionality of the gear.

Skye presented shin pads and arm pads crafted from the same advanced material.

"These pads come in handy too. The shin pads can enhance the impact when kicking an opponent because of the kinetic energy. In most situations, you won't have protection over your face so the arm pads can be used as a makeshift shield when positioned in front of your face," Skye elaborated, providing essential insights. "For today's training exercise we'll be focusing on blocking and defence techniques. Everyone, please grab a vest, pads, and a staff."

The apprentices were required to work in pairs and practice defence. Rex chose Angelo as his sparring partner. Together, they practised blocking and evading each other's attacks. Angelo's kickboxing skills gave him the upper hand, and he was quick to learn the movements. For a moment, he felt invincible, as if no one could touch him. However, when Rex got an opening, he skilfully swept Angelo off his feet.

Angelo landed on the floor with a thud, feeling embarrassed. His pride fell along with his body.

Rex couldn't help but chuckle at Angelo's miscalculation. "Caught you slipping," he teased.

Angelo recognized his lapse in focus and nodded. He had gotten carried away and let his guard down as a result. He couldn't be too confident in his abilities.

"Alright, your turn," said Rex, handing the staff to Angelo.

He was now on the offensive side and eager to take his shot at Rex. This would be fun.

CHAPTER 9

THE POWER OF MUSIC

Angelo's body was still drained from the relentless training and learning of the previous day. The apprentice's schedule was an unending whirlwind, offering no time to rest. Angelo was already tempted to call it quits and leave the campus, but the charred remains of his burned-down house served as a painful reminder of why he had no choice but to stay. He had committed to the agency by signing that contract, and there was no backing out of it now.

Cherub Hugh's voice pierced through the exhaustion. "Today's lesson is about the Illuminati's role in the music industry and how vital it is for us to liberate it."

Hugh brought up an image on the screen depicting Lucifer, the fallen angel, gracefully playing the violin. "According to biblical scriptures and scholars, the devil was once the angel of music before his fall from Heaven."

The image transitioned to a vivid artistic depiction of the celestial rebellion, capturing Lucifer and his fellow fallen angels plummeting from the heavenly realm.

"Last lesson, we spoke about the Illuminati's downfall in 1785 and its great revival in the 1800s. We also covered the rise of the Starlight Saints and how we came to be," Hugh continued, his words drawing the apprentices deeper into the historical narrative. "Now, by the early 1900s, the Illuminati had extended its influence on all corners of the world, including our own. The 20th century saw a significant increase in power and tension between the two secret societies."

Angelo's curiosity was piqued, and he leaned forward, eager to understand the connection between the Illuminati and the music industry. He could sense other apprentices were charged with anticipation. When he was younger, he'd heard multiple conspiracy theories about the music industry being run by the Illuminati. Still, he never knew if they were accurate. Now, the cherub was going to shed light on the matter.

"So, what connection do Illuminatists or Illumiknights have to the music industry?" Hugh posed the question. "I'll allow Skye to do a demonstration of one of our greatest inventions before we get into it."

Skye presented a small device for the whole class to see. She turned a knob, and a haunting melody began to reverberate from the device throughout the room. The music sounded like a heavily distorted bass and violin clashing against each other, trying to fight their way out of something. The distorted notes sent shivers down Angelo's spine. A surge of discomfort and confusion washed over him, and his heart raced. It was as though all his pent-up anxiety, anger, and frustrations had suddenly awakened, threatening to engulf him.

Angelo felt a strong urge to smash his laptop to the ground as if some evil entity possessed him, his temples throbbing as his pulse quickened. As Angelo's eyes darted around the room, he noticed that other fellow apprentices, including Rex, Shawn, and Sanji, were also affected by the device's tormenting sound. They all covered their ears, begging for the agonizing music to stop. Skye stood there with a smirk and stopped the music at last. She removed what appeared to be earplugs from her ears.

"This device," Skye explained, "is called the frequency box. One of our weapons that we use against the enemy. What you all just experienced was a dark frequency designed to bring out all negative emotions. This tool can prove invaluable in situations where you're trapped or outnumbered by enemies. Just play the dark frequency, and it'll bring chaos, giving enough time for you to escape or finish off your adversaries while they're ensnared under your spell."

She turned the knob once more, and the music resonated again. This time, a gentle and soothing tune filled the room. Angelo's earlier feelings of aggression and panic were soon replaced with tranquillity and ease, as if the music had cast a soothing spell upon him.

"I've adjusted the frequency to 448Hz, which is lighter than before," Skye continued. "The frequency box also possesses healing properties if tuned to the right frequency. It can help heal some sicknesses by stimulating the body with harmonious sounds. Though you can't see frequencies with your eyes, they have significant impact, which relates to the third Starlight motto. That, my fellow saints, is the power of music frequencies."

Angelo's mind was blown away by the astonishing demonstration of the frequency box. He had never imagined the sheer power of music and frequencies. He couldn't help but feel a growing eagerness to try this remarkable weapon out for himself. All the apprentices gave a round of applause, and the lesson pressed onward.

Skye took hold of the remote and projected an image onto the screen. It depicted soldiers marching, accompanied by the backdrop of an orchestra. Unmistakable swastika flags indicated the picture's origin in Nazi Germany.

"Now, for the next part of this lesson," Skye began as she took a swig from her water bottle. "The Illuminati began infiltrating the music industry as early as the 1920s. Every song you listen to, whether it's hip-hop, rock, pop, or jazz, carries a certain frequency. The Rockefeller Foundation, which was part of the Illuminati, had an agenda to control the population through the manipulation of certain frequencies."

Skye paused for a moment, allowing the class to take notes and digest this information. "Frequencies make people think and act in certain ways whether happy, angry, or sad. The Rockefellers adopted the 440Hz standard from the Nazis and enforced it across America, which led the masses into greater aggression, distress, and disunity. It's almost like mind control. Some of these dark frequencies were so powerful, they could inflict illnesses and were even used as military weapons for war."

Angelo scrambled to take notes of these unsettling revelations. There was something evil and sinister about 440Hz. He was already familiar with the name Rockefeller, one of the wealthiest families in America. Skye passed the remote back to Hugh, and he carried on the presentation.

"The Illuminati knew that music could be their greatest weapon because everyone likes music. We tend to think music is harmless but in reality it is the most powerful delivery system of propaganda because it influences people without their conscious awareness. Which is why we see so much evil, violence, and division in today's world," said Hugh. "I remember when a satanic panic movement emerged in the 80s because of musicians adopting satanic culture. Our enemy has corrupted millions using this weapon, which is why we must stop them."

There was a ring of truth to what the cherubs were saying, even if Angelo didn't believe all of it. He started to question the very music he listened to on a daily basis. The insidious notion of being influenced by hidden frequencies crept into his thoughts. *Was he unknowingly allowing himself to be programmed by certain songs?* The weight of this newfound knowledge left him feeling overwhelmed.

Angelo felt the weight of dozens of eyes fixed on him, their gazes probing and judgmental. He couldn't help but think about his family of talented musicians, including his brother. That was probably why he had everyone's attention. Raising his hand, he caught the attention of both cherubs.

"Surely not every artist in the music industry is part of this evil agenda. It would be unfair to accuse everyone of being involved, wouldn't it?" Angelo questioned with a slight quiver in his voice.

Cherub Hugh and Cherub Skye exchanged a knowing look before Hugh responded. "Of course not, Mr. Jackson. We can't say every entertainer is involved in the Illuminati. Some entertainers could very well be one of us. The purpose of this lesson is only to raise awareness and provide insight into these matters."

Angelo acknowledged the response with a nod, feeling relieved that they weren't implicating his family in these sinister schemes. Not wanting the other apprentices to start asking or making accusations about them.

Another seed of Hugh's words sparked a dawning realization in Angelo. If there was darkness, there also had to be light, so if entertainers were members of the Illuminati, there also had to be entertainers who were Starlight Saints.

Angelo's perception of reality began to shift just like Titus said it would. The class came to an end, and more assignments were handed out.

***

The cherubs took the apprentices for a tour through the sound room for their afternoon training session. The room was vast and highly sophisticated. The walls and the ceiling were adorned with stars and galaxy patterns, creating the illusion of being in a celestial chamber. There were endless rows of chairs, each equipped with tablets and headphones, awaiting the apprentices.

"Today, you were introduced to the frequency box, and now we will introduce you to the sound room. This is where all saints can come to relax and heal by channelling positive frequencies," Hugh explained as they continued walking. "For instance, 174Hz relieves pain and stress, whereas 396Hz helps liberate you from fear and guilt. The benefits are indeed endless. Just put on these headphones, and you'll be transported to another realm."

"Now, this is awesome," Shawn exclaimed.

Angelo was taken by surprise. Were agents actually allowed to relax? From his experiences so far, he had barely had any time to rest. He marvelled at the idea of coming in here and taking a breather. He would make it his priority to visit the sound room regularly.

"Be warned, though," Hugh cautioned. "If you stay in here for too long, you could die or go insane. Too much exposure to this stuff can be detrimental to both the body and the mind."

Angelo's initial excitement suddenly turned to dread, and his trust started to waver. *Were positive frequencies capable of killing people, too?*

The science behind these devices was something Angelo couldn't comprehend. It made him hesitate and question if he should be handling such technology. The cherubs invited apprentices to try out the sound room equipment as part of their training.

Angelo took a seat next to Sanji and cautiously put on the headphones. A digital tablet before him displayed a vast selection of songs, all available in binaural mode. Without further ado, Angelo selected a random song and let the music flow into his ears. The sound was so stimulating it was intoxicating. The sound waves massaged his brain, and he experienced a fascinating type of high that he couldn't explain. An out-of-this-world experience. Angelo closed his eyes and drifted off to another realm in no time, just like the cherub had said.

Eyes shut; Angelo found himself floating in what looked like a celestial realm. Bright, vivid colours and ethereal patterns painted his surroundings. He whispered to himself in silent awe, *"I never wanna leave this place."*

The song eventually came to an end, jolting Angelo from his reverie. That was it. He reluctantly removed his headphones, wishing the moment would last longer. He had no clue how long he'd spent listening to the music but being in there felt like a trance. Angelo's mind and body felt more at ease and healthier after tuning into the frequency player. What a phenomenal piece of technology the Starlight Saints had at their disposal. They probably deserved more credit than Angelo was giving them. The afternoon session came to an end, and the apprentices were escorted out.

"That was amazing!" Rex exclaimed, his eyes wide with wonder. "It's like I took a whole acid trip in there."

"You can say that again. We should totally go in there at least once a week," Shawn chimed with an excited grin.

What the apprentices had just experienced was the extraordinary power of music. More importantly, the power of frequencies.

***

After savouring a hearty lamb curry for dinner, followed by a sweet serving of jelly for dessert, Angelo decided it was time to retreat to his room. Meanwhile, his friends opted to enjoy some leisure time in the gaming lounge. His sleepiness got the best of him, and he decided to get some shut eye. Walking down the corridors toward his quarters, he turned a corner and encountered an unexpected obstacle - someone standing in his path. The last person he wanted to encounter.

With a sinister gesture, Dwayne clicked his fingers and signalled to two figures lurking behind him. One of them, displaying the physical prowess of a club bouncer, ensnared Angelo in an unyielding grip. Angelo attempted to escape, but it was to no avail. The grip was too firm, rendering his attempts useless.

Dwayne, the ringleader of this unwelcome encounter, approached Angelo with a menacing demeanour. "I told you, albino, you're in for it now. Meet my amigos Blake and Neel."

He punctuated his words with a backhanded blow to Angelo's face, the resounding smack of flesh against flesh echoing through the corridor.

"Have you figured out who I am yet? I'm Tom Chandler's son. You remember my father, don't you? The prosecutor who tried your father for trafficking," Dwayne revealed.

Angelo couldn't believe it. He didn't even try hiding his shock at this revelation. This was Dwayne Chandler, the offspring of the man who had relentlessly prosecuted Angelo's father. Tom Chandler had led the investigations against his dad. When Angelo's dad was proven innocent for the third time, Chandler stepped down as district attorney. Angelo couldn't fathom the irony.

How had the sons of two bitter enemies ended up in the same agency?

"Ever since your dad ran scot-free from all charges, my dad lost his job as district attorney. Don was able to settle the case by paying hush money to families of his victims," said Dwayne, connecting a punch to Angelo's gut. "To think the seraphs would allow someone like you into this society is beyond me."

Angelo wheezed as the punches landed, each blow delivering a painful message from his assailant. The wind was almost knocked out of him. However, Angelo's resolve held firm even as pain surged through his body. He couldn't let Dwayne's words break him.

"None of that is true. Go to hell!" Angelo yelled.

"That's where your dad is," Dwayne taunted, landing yet another backhand slap to the face.

"Tom Chandler just hated my dad's guts and wanted to see his downfall. Just accept your dad was an evil scumbag," said Angelo enraged.

"I could accept that. I couldn't care less about that poor excuse for a deadbeat dad anyway. I just have a problem with the Jacksons thinking they can get away with things," said Dwayne.

The onslaught continued, but Angelo refused to back down.

"Dwayne stop it!" Vanya came running from behind.

Angelo felt a wave of relief wash over him as he saw her approaching. She had arrived just in time to intervene.

Dwayne's friend, Blake, released Angelo from his grip, and he lay helpless on the ground.

Vanya came to his aid, her presence a comforting sight. He was beaten, but there was nothing too severe. "Dwayne, shame on you. Imagine what the seraphs will think," said Vanya.

"Don't be like that, Vanya. Are you forgetting that I'm Phoenix Council president? What I say goes," Dwayne retorted. "Angelo is working for the enemy. You guys just don't see it yet."

"You're wrong!" Vanya shot back. "You're just taking advantage of these apprentices, and I won't let that slide."

"If you tell any of the seraphs about this, you're as good as dead. I will make you regret it. I'll show you what I do to people like you." Dwayne turned his attention to Angelo with a devious grin. "This isn't over yet albino. Wait till you see what I have in store for you. Blake, Neel. *Vamos*"

With those ominous words, Dwayne and his friends walked away, leaving Angelo and Vanya alone.

She helped Angelo to his feet and walked him back to his room. Tonight's revelation would haunt Angelo. *He was on the same campus as his enemy. This wasn't a mere rivalry anymore. This had turned into war.*

CHAPTER 10

JOURNEY OF FAITH

Angelo awoke the next morning, his body aching from the assault by Dwayne the previous night. The unsettling truth that Chandler was in the same secret agency as him was not something he could put off. The memory of his helplessness against Dwayne and his friends haunted him. It was only Vanya's timely intervention that had saved him from further harm. He couldn't allow Dwayne to throw him around like this any longer.

Angelo needed to escape the cloud of suspicion that hung over him due to Dwayne's influence. Who was using his position as Phoenix Council president to turn other saints against Angelo, making them believe that Angelo was secretly working for the Illuminati and that all Jacksons were terrible people.

After explaining the incident to his friends, Rex had offered to teach Chandler a lesson or two, easing the journey slightly. Rex, Shawn, Sanji, and Vanya were the only trusted friends Angelo could confide in.

As the afternoon lesson approached, the apprentices were headed to the lab. Angelo could constantly feel a sense of unease and isolation, like a lone wolf amidst a pack of strangers.

"Our scientists are making modifications to another one of our greatest inventions. Today, Doctor Khan will show you the starlight watch," Skye announced.

The apprentices were bundled together in a crowd as Dr. Khan, a well-groomed and charismatic figure, stepped forward, wearing the starlight watch around his wrist. As he pressed the device, a staff materialized in his grasp. It seemed almost ethereal, with a radiant blue glow that captivated Angelo and the others, leaving them in awe. But this wasn't magic; it was something entirely different.

"The starlight watch uses energy projection to project the weapon of your choice. Each weapon has its own time limit before it disappears and has to recharge. The more advanced the weapon, the harder it is to project." Dr. Khan explained, his voice filled with enthusiasm. "Producing these watches consumes a significant amount of energy, but the results are well worth it. Today, you'll have the opportunity to try these watches for yourselves."

With excitement, each apprentice received their very own starlight watch. Angelo secured the accessory around his wrist, his anticipation growing. Deciding to summon a dagger, to his amazement, it materialized perfectly in his hand—a tangible weapon ready for action. His eyes widened in amazement, heart racing with exhilaration. He could feel the cold, solid grip of the dagger, its blade glinting with potential.

Angelo pressed his finger against the tip of the blade to see if the blade had actually been projected but mistakenly cut his poor index finger instead. *"Ouch!"* he yelled in his head to avoid other apprentices laughing at his blunder.

The watch made a formidable asset. He hesitated and contemplated on trying to summon another weapon while staring at his bleeding finger. Angelo carefully projected a katana and was met with the same amazement. A watch that could project anything you desired would make it easier to take enemies down. The cherubs observed the apprentices and helped them get familiar with the watches.

***

"Welcome to the trial of three. There are three rituals an apprentice must complete. I will be overseeing your progression throughout these trials, and your first ritual tonight is the Journey of Faith," declared Seraph Nigel.

Angelo had tried to catch a few hours of sleep prior to the ritual, but he had no success. Fatigue clung to his bones, and he yearned for the sweet comfort of his bed. Skye and Hugh both stood beside Nigel as he took command of the room along with two other cherubs known as Clyde and Faye. An unexpected wave of anxiety washed over Angelo. The looming trial at hand made him contemplate walking out of the hall and calling it quits. *Was he ready for the first ritual?* Doubt gnawed at his core, sapping his confidence despite the training he'd undertaken.

He felt crushed by an overwhelming sense of pressure. *What if he couldn't complete the three rituals?* The prospect of failure haunted him. He wouldn't qualify as an official Starlight Saint if he screwed up. Angelo's thoughts drifted to his dad, whose need for vindication pressed on him. His memory of Dad weighed heavily on his heart like an anchor. He also remembered Casey, who would be counting on him and allowed his family to ignite the motivation he needed.

"The Journey of Faith is done in pairs. You and your partner will be chained to each other by hand. One of you must be blindfolded, and you cannot remove your blindfold at any time during the ritual. Only the one with the blindfold can move objects around and it is up to their partner to guide them," Nigel explained. Angelo's heart pounded as Nigel's words echoed through the hall, casting a shadow of uncertainty over the room. "The purpose of this ritual is to establish trust and loyalty between saints. I'm confident that some of you will succeed, though unfortunately, some of you may fail."

Nigel's piercing gaze seemed to settle on Angelo as if addressing him personally.

Angelo's anxiety intensified with Nigel's intimidating glare.

Surveying the hall, everyone else appeared to share the same fear of failure as him. Other apprentices began pairing up. He spotted Shawn standing across from him, a familiar face amidst the sea of strangers.

Without a second thought, Angelo made his way to Shawn, placing a hand on his shoulder.

"Let's do this," he said, choosing Shawn as his partner.

Angelo wasn't sure if he could trust the other apprentices with the ongoing Jackson hostility.

Rex had already paired up with Sanji.

"Quick game of rock paper scissors. Loser has to go blindfolded," said Angelo, proposing a fair deal.

Shawn agreed to the proposal, and the game ended in a few seconds.

Angelo's fist was clenched like a rock while Shawn chose scissors.

"Damn it," Shawn muttered, a hint of frustration in his voice. "You better know what you're doing. If you try anything funny, I'll make you regret it."

Angelo sighed, trying to ease the tension. "Dude, we're gonna be chained together. I wouldn't wanna jeopardize our chances of passing the challenge," he said, rolling his eyes at the idea of sabotaging their own success.

A nervous boy in the crowd raised his hand. His curiosity evident his face scrunched up in thought. "Eh, Seraph, what happens if ya take off your blindfold?" he inquired.

Nigel's response was unwavering. "You'll be penalized. You fail the ritual and you'll be required to start over. Fail the same ritual three times and you're out. Our blindfolds have trackers that alert us when someone removes theirs, so you can't cheat your way out of this," Nigel explained with a sly grin.

That warning should've been enough for Shawn not to dare try his luck.

Angelo would do everything to make sure that Shawn stayed blindfolded throughout the ritual to avoid costing them the challenge. Shawn had no choice but to trust him.

"You will venture outside these walls into the hilly forests. Each pair will receive a small bag and a book with twenty marked altars scattered throughout the forest. The task is to say a quick prayer and collect a gemstone from each altar, then cross the altar off your map so we know you've been there," Nigel instructed. "You're allowed to stop on the way to sleep or eat, but at your own risk. If you fall behind it's to your disadvantage. Working with other pairs or giving them assistance is not allowed. Only you and your partner will partake in this journey. Lamps will be lit along the way to guide your path, and you must return to the lodge with all your gemstones before the first light of dawn."

Nigel examined each of the apprentices. His gaze weighed on them, penetrating each of their souls.

Angelo had never camped out in the woods before. He'd been surrounded by luxury his whole life. Sure, he connected with nature from time to time, but he never imagined himself hiking for an extended period of time. He may have belonged to one of the wealthiest families, but his status meant nothing here. All apprentices were treated the same and would endure the same challenges. Agents started chaining apprentices to their partners and handing out blindfolds, bags, and notebooks.

Cherub Hugh was the one who chained Angelo and Shawn together. Shawn accepted the blindfold, and as the cuff tightened around their wrists, Hugh began to speak.

"I've been observing your progress during our classes and training. You're a dedicated student, and I see potential in you, Angelo," Hugh remarked, placing a firm hand on Angelo's shoulder and locking eyes with him. "I believe you have what it takes to be a promising Starlight Saint. Throughout this ritual, make sure you guide your partner and trust one another. I have high hopes for both of you."

Hugh's words acted as a calming balm on Angelo's frayed nerves, lightening his load of anxiety. The fact that one of the cherubs was rooting for him added extra motivation to push through this difficult task. The apprentices were escorted toward the rear gate that led to the forest.

They were to leave in intervals. Shawn put on his blindfold and adjusted it to a suitable grip.

"Better get moving. Clock's ticking," announced Nigel, his eye lingering on Angelo, adding a weight of urgency pressed upon him.

"You ready?" asked Angelo.

"Ready." Shawn replied, determination clear despite the blindfold.

Their shared notebook held the prayer: *May the archangels be with us.*

It was their turn to step out. With that, they ventured beyond the campus walls and embarked on their mysterious journey.

Chapter 11

Race Against Time

The pair had long lost track of time, their weary steps taking them only as far as fourteen altars out of the twenty. Shawn shouldered the small bag with the fourteen gemstones they'd collected from each altar. Being, blindfolded, meant he relied on Angelo's whispered directions to navigate, and the chain probably made it easier for Shawn to sense where Angelo was going.

Angelo had reached his limit, a relentless fatigue clouding his vision, making every step a gruelling challenge. The flickering lamps made their path visible, offering guidance through the forest's shadows. Angelo couldn't go on, his exhaustion deepening with each passing moment. His weakened legs began to rebel, and heavy desperation fell upon him as they walked up a steep, hilly area. The cool night breeze brushed against his skin. A distant rumble of thunder sent a shiver down Angelo's spine, and he prayed there wouldn't be a storm. His legs ached even more, and he wondered how Shawn was coping in this laborious trek. His mind briefly drifted to Rex and Sanji, as he was also curious to know how they were progressing in this relentless Journey of Faith.

"The fact that we have to do this totally sucks, man," Shawn muttered, his voice heavy with fatigue. "I can't even feel my legs."

"I feel mine giving in, too. Some *Gummy Bear* pop would do right now," Angelo grimaced. "But we gotta keep going. Can't fail this ritual."

"Why'd I even sign up for this? I swear if I knew it would be this gruelling, I'd have stayed back in Rockingston," Shawn grumbled.

Angelo couldn't deny that he'd entertained that thought, too, but now they were in this together, and there was no going back. He couldn't afford to quit now, no matter how overwhelming this trial was. They had to make it to the last altar at the top of the hill.

"You will experience a lot of pain on this journey, but you must endure this together and have faith in each other," Nigel had said during the briefing.

Angelo found the pain too unbearable to overcome. He was hungry and weak from exhaustion. The energy from his last meal was fully depleted.

"Next altar is across this bridge. There's a lake underneath so be careful," Angelo instructed while giving the chain a slight yank. "Stay behind me and just follow my voice."

Angelo led Shawn toward the bridge with a cautious step. The wooden planks creaked and swayed under their weight. He inched forward, guiding Shawn along with him.

As they ventured further, a sudden jolt and tug on the chain stopped Angelo from moving any further. As he looked down, Shawn was hanging on for dear life. The bag of gemstones hung precariously from Shawn's shoulder, slipping perilously close to the edge.

"Damn it! Hold on," Angelo exclaimed, struggling to pull Shawn to safety. The effort drained his weakened body as he fought to keep the precious gemstones from plummeting into the water below.

"Whatever you do, don't drop them stones!" Angelo shouted to emphasize the importance of their mission.

They weren't taking any chances. If the gemstones landed in the water, they would fail the ritual. Shawn desperately clung onto the bag with a determined grip as Angelo pulled him up. Managing to get a secure hold on one of the bridge's planks.

Angelo grabbed his partner's hand, bringing Shawn up to safety with the bag of gemstones still intact. Relief washed over them as they continued their journey toward the next altar. However, as Angelo looked back, he wondered how other pairs before them had crossed the bridge without one of the planks giving way. Perhaps he should've done a better job at guiding his partner. He couldn't dwell too much on this, though, as time was of the essence.

After their prayer, Shawn handed Angelo the bag, and Angelo guided his hand to securely place the fifteenth gemstone inside.

"Got it. Five more to go now," said Shawn.

Thunder rumbled again, and gentle raindrops pelted softly on his skin. A drizzle had started. He couldn't wait to get this ritual over and done with. The two plodded on, collecting three more gemstones.

The end was in sight. He wanted to push forward, but Shawn insisted that they take a short break underneath a tree. As reluctant as Angelo was, he, too, had to admit he had no stamina left. A short break was all it was. They were almost at the end anyway. The rain became heavier, but the shade of the tree's canopy provided some shelter.

Angelo drifted in and out of sleep, trying to restore his stamina. He caught glimpses of shadows moving about. Yet, did not have the energy to pay close attention. He was starving, his stomach grumbling in protest but they hadn't brought snacks for the journey, and food was nowhere to be found in these woods. He drifted back to sleep once more.

Angelo woke up again, staring into the spooky trees of the forest. The rain had calmed down, falling gently. "Shawn." His voice cracked with urgency as he shook his friend, but Shawn remained in deep slumber.

"Shawn! Come on."

Frustration crept into Angelo's voice, but the rain-drenched forest offered no response. Only the soft pattering of raindrops and the distant, ominous rumble of thunder. They couldn't afford to delay. Angelo yanked the chain connecting them and gave Shawn an insistent nudge. A groan finally escaped from Shawn, and his bleary eyes fluttered open.

Dawn was lurking, waiting to sneak up on them at any moment. As Shawn stood up, he dusted himself off, awaiting Angelo's instructions. However, something seemed out of place.

"Our gemstones. The bag. They're gone," Angelo exclaimed with his voice quivering.

The realization hit him like a sledgehammer, and he couldn't imagine how they could've lost the gemstones.

"What do you mean they're gone?" asked Shawn. "We had the stones right with us. We better find them ASAP."

Angelo searched where they had placed the stones, but they were all gone. A cocktail of anger and frustration welled up within both of them. The vital treasures they needed to complete their ritual were no longer in their possession. Someone or something must have taken them.

"I told you we shouldn't have stopped! We shoulda kept going. Now we're never gonna finish this challenge," Angelo lamented.

They were on the brink of success, so tantalizingly close, yet they failed. Stopping for a snooze was their biggest mistake. He wanted to collapse on the ground and be left soaking in the rain.

Hugh's words echoed in Angelo's mind. *"I see potential in you...I have high hopes for both of you."*

Angelo couldn't cope with the thought of letting down the cherub. He pondered on running away and not returning to the lodge. Maybe he wasn't worthy of being a Starlight Saint. As the two walked in defeat, there was a rustle nearby in the bushes. He raised his guard up, preparing for the worst. Suddenly, a lone raccoon emerged, hissed at the pair with aggression, and scurried away. It was nothing more than a wild animal. Angelo scanned their surroundings, and still, there was no trail of where the gemstones could have gone.

"Looking for these?" a female voice resonated from above.

Confusion filled the air. Shawn, still blindfolded, couldn't see a thing. On the other hand, Angelo looked up to find a masked stranger perched on a tree branch. His eyes widened as he realized their predicament; the stranger had the precious gemstones they sought. The stranger leapt off the tree branch with a blade, coming toward Shawn. Angelo, realizing the threat, quickly tackled Shawn out of the way, making the stranger miss by just an inch. Shawn was undoubtedly confused, but Angelo had just saved his friend from being assassinated.

"Did you just try to kill my friend? Who are you, and why do you have our gemstones?" Angelo demanded with a tinge of anxiety while getting up. "Give them back."

The woman responded with a chilling laugh, echoing through the dark woods. Shawn's lips parted slightly, trembling with no word coming out as if the scream was trapped deep in his throat, unable to escape. Angelo could see him itching to take off his blindfold, but they would fail the challenge if he did.

"I was aiming for you, but your friend was in the way. It's not really your gemstones I want, although they make a nice souvenir," the stranger taunted. "It's your blood I want, Angelo Jackson."

Angelo was taken by surprise. *How did this woman know who he was?* "What did I ever do to you?"

The stranger cackled again. "I've been given a very special assignment to take you out by…let's say an insider. I go by Willow but that doesn't matter 'cause you'll be dead soon. Carving you two up will suffice my hunger for blood."

Angelo felt a chill running down his spine, grappling with the realization that he was face-to-face with a hitman. What did he do to deserve this? *Which 'insider' was Willow referring to?* Angelo's mind buzzed with questions.

This woman openly admitted to murderous intentions and said it so casually, like it was nothing. Who could've possibly assigned her? If she was in this forest reserved for Starlight Saints, then it could only mean one thing. Someone within the secret society had a vendetta and desired to get rid of Angelo. He'd felt that hostility from the day he arrived. Angelo's heart raced as he realized he was in the presence of a psychopath.

"Look, no matter who sent you, I won't go down that easily," said Angelo. "Give back our gemstones."

Shawn seemed to be growing increasingly anxious. Challenging this woman was dangerous, but their lives and the Journey of Faith were at stake here.

"You talk a little too much, kiddo. You have no idea who you're up against," said Willow. "I'll just get this over with so my boss can pay up."

"We won't let you have your way," said Angelo, relying on his training.

Despite his display of bravery, deep down, Angelo was afraid. He had no way of knowing just how brutal Willow was.

"Angelo, are you forgetting that we're chained together and I'm blindfolded?" Shawn reminded him with a panicking voice. "We literally don't stand a chance."

"We either back down, die, and lose the challenge, or we fight for our gemstones. Just follow my lead and trust me," said Angelo.

If Angelo was going to fight, that meant Shawn would have to follow. He seemed to hate this but reluctantly assumed a fighting stance, ready for Angelo to guide him into this perilous confrontation. Shawn had no idea what was happening, and what made matters worse was that he would fight blindly.

CHAPTER 12

TRESPASSER

Angelo's heart raced as he braced for the impending threat. The hitman could strike from any direction or angle. He knew he had to do everything in his power to protect Shawn. Angelo recalled Hugh's words from before the ritual. *"Make sure you guide your partner and trust one another."*

Angelo understood that trust and cooperation were paramount. Shawn might've been blindfolded but still had his senses of hearing, smell, touch, and taste. If Angelo could effectively utilize his voice to lead Shawn, they would have a chance of winning.

"Watch out, she's got a knife," Angelo warned. The two apprentices took a defensive stance, standing back-to-back, prepared to face their adversary.

"I really wish we had those starlight watches. They'd be really useful right now," Shawn murmured with a shaky voice.

Shawn was right.

Angelo was desperate to have a starlight watch around his wrist, but they would have to rely on their own strength.

Willow began walking in circles around the pair like a spider wrapping its prey, an unsettling presence of murderous intent. Without warning, she lunged, stabbing Shawn in the leg.

Shawn let out a howling scream of agony and crumpled to his knees. Of course, she would make Shawn her first target since he was blindfolded. With Shawn groaning in pain, Angelo acted as a human shield, determined to fight back against this heartless assassin.

"You sick lady!" Angelo spat, his fury boiling over.

"Oh, I couldn't help myself. You lot make this dead easy and straightforward," laughed Willow, licking the fresh stained blood off her blade. "Bit of a cheeky move, but still does the job."

Angelo became more furious at Willow's heartlessness, and Shawn continued to suffer.

Willow had gained the upper hand.

Angelo had no weapon and no starlight watch to activate. *How would he win?* They were sure to die in this forest and fail the challenge. Whoever had sent Willow to do the task had been very strategic. They knew He would be vulnerable, and it would be easier for them to cover their tracks with the blood on the assassin's hands. No one else from outside the secret society would have known about the rituals of the Starlight Saints. *It was an inside job, as Willow had revealed before, and Angelo suddenly pictured none other than Dwayne Chandler in his mind.*

Chandler's words from their last encounter buzzed through Angelo's mind. *"This isn't over yet, albino. Wait till you see what I have in store for you."*

Dwayne's detestation was enough to make Angelo believe that he was purposely trying to sabotage his success in the rituals and get him killed. He would not let his rival get away with such.

No help seemed to be near, and Angelo wished the seraphs could come to their aid. An epiphany struck. Angelo assessing the situation, realized he had to use his environment to his advantage. He surveyed the area for any objects he could use as weapons and spotted a sturdy branch near him close to his right. Being chained to Shawn was the only issue, but the chain was long enough, and it would allow him to reach the branch. Angelo gave Willow a serious glare of determination.

"What do you think you're doing, little brat? You're as good as dead," said Willow.

Angelo sprinted towards the branch, dodging Willow's attacks, and grabbed it just in time to block the assassin's dagger strike. With the branch in hand, Angelo hit Willow with a swift kick to the side before knocking the dagger out of her hand with the branch. As he followed up with a knock to her head using the branch, Willow fell to the ground, defeated.

Angelo took a moment to catch his breath and turned his attention back to the injured Shawn.

Shawn's leg was still bleeding, and the wound needed critical attention. Angelo hesitated, torn between helping his injured friend and completing the Journey of Faith.

"We should go back and tell the seraphs about this. You're hurt," Angelo urged.

"No! We have to finish the challenge," Shawn insisted with determination. "We got two gemstones left."

"But…"

"I'll be fine, trust me. Just help me up," Shawn assured him.

Angelo reluctantly picked up the bag, and Shawn placed his arm around Angelo's shoulder while limping. They powered on for the last stretch, leaving Willow unconscious.

"We should tell the seraphs about the assassin when we get back. I have a feeling Dwayne's behind this," said Angelo.

As they collected the last gemstones, the faint sounds of birds chirping signalled the approach of morning. Angelo could sense the urgency of their situation. "We can't fail. Let's hurry."

With Shawn on his back, Angelo mustered his remaining strength and determination to complete the ritual. Step after step, within a few moments, they finally made it back to the main lodge just when dawn arrived.

***

"Congratulations, you've successfully completed your first ritual," said a voice.

Angelo, his body sore and exhausted, felt relieved as Titus welcomed them back. Looking around, other apprentices were similarly worn out and covered in mud. Angelo was drenched in mud and was due for a shower. He was on the verge of collapsing from all the strain the challenge put on him. He was relieved he wasn't amongst the unfortunate who didn't make it. Angelo placed Shawn gently on the floor and removed the blindfold. The wound on Shawn's leg had stopped bleeding out but still needed attention. Rex and Sanji approached them. They were also covered in dirt, and both appeared drained by the challenge.

"What happened?" asked Titus, concerned about Shawn's wound.

Angelo explained how they ran into Willow, the assassin, and how she tried to kill them. Titus grew alarmed and examined Shawn's wound. Rex and Sanji were shocked by the encounter, too. They shouldn't have slept during the challenge and didn't want to inform the seraphs about it either.

What would others think if they admitted to sleeping during the ritual?

"If there's an assassin roaming out there, I'm not leaving these walls again," said Sanji, fearing for his life.

"This whole land, including the forest, is only reserved for our saints. We haven't had anybody trespass our secret location in years. I'm sending a group of saints to scout the forest," Titus explained. "This is so odd. Any member of our society found guilty of an inside job is dealt with severely."

"What if the intruder escapes?" asked Rex.

"We won't let that happen. Trespassers open us up to the risk of our academy being discovered, and we can't have that. We will track this assassin down until we find her."

110

Titus ordered a few agents to take Shawn to the sanatorium for medical treatment. As Shawn was escorted out by Titus and other saints, Angelo saw Nigel approaching, his hands hidden behind his back.

"I commend you on completing your first ritual, Angelo," Nigel began, his tone serious. "But I wouldn't get too comfortable if I were you. Your next ritual will be more intense, and you will taste death. I advise you to brace yourself."

Nigel's words made Angelo shudder, and the prospect of a harder ritual was far from comforting. "Of course, Seraph. I'll do my best."

The apprentices were granted permission to rest during the day as they prepared for the next ritual, which would be held in the evening.

Later in the day, Angelo heard the news that Willow had been captured. He and Shawn were ordered to meet the assassin and confirm this was who they fought. Willow sat there, shackled and surrounded by agents, ensuring she had no opportunity for escape.

Looking down on the assassin, Angelo was still enraged by how she tried to mutilate Shawn. "Who sent you? Answer me."

Willow, however, kept her mouth shut, her resolve unwavering. She seemed determined to keep her employer a secret and not reveal anything. Her eyes were still cold and menacing.

"You know what must be done to trespassers. Someone has clearly disclosed our location. We must investigate further," said one of the seraphs.

Suddenly, Nigel intervened. "Everyone step aside. I'll deal with this repulsive intruder. Since I'm in charge of the rituals, it is my responsibility to take her to the grandmaster for questioning."

With a forceful grip, Nigel seized Willow by her hair and hoisted her to her feet. The other seraphs seemed content with Nigel's insistence and backed away.

Angelo and Shawn could only watch as Nigel escorted the assassin away. Angelo dreaded Willow's fate but was eager to see the culprit who hired her exposed. His sneaking suspicion kept convicting him that it had to be Dwayne.

Her fate rested in the hands of the saints, and the outcome could be either merciful or dire.

***

Angelo and his fellow apprentices were gathered once again in the main lodge, awaiting the seraph's instructions with heavy anticipation. Hugh, the cherub who had been a source of encouragement, approached Angelo in the midst of conversing with his friends.

"You and your partner displayed outstanding bravery in the last ritual. Don't lose that fire in you," said Hugh.

Angelo nodded, grateful for Hugh's unwavering belief in him. "I won't let you down, cherub."

Hugh's words of praise made a comforting anchor amidst the apprehension of the upcoming challenge. Angelo understood that not everyone would share this faith, but Hugh's support was enough to sustain his confidence. Nigel brought the hall to silence and took ownership of the room.

"The next ritual is the Nightmare Room. It's important for every saint to master and control their fears," Nigel announced.

A collective gasp rippled through the hall at the mention of the Nightmare Room. Shawn appeared terrified, and so did Sanji, their faces mirroring the unease that rippled throughout the hall. Rex seemed to be the only one composed, and if there was any inner turmoil, he did well concealing it. As Angelo gulped and felt his heart sinking, he braced himself for the inevitable task ahead.

"A famous occultist named Aleister Crowley used nightmare rooms to reach a higher level of spiritual enlightenment and master fear. In our line of work, we must not let our fears control us. We control them.'" Nigel explained. "A wise renegade once said, *'One cannot be brave who has no fear.'*"

Nigel rubbed his chin, taking pride in the apparent quote. A hulky, muscular boy in the crowd raised his hand, and he allowed him to speak.

"Yo Seraph, I thought we was Starlight Saints, not no *Renegades*," the apprentice challenged.

"True, but that doesn't mean we can't learn from others," Nigel responded. "Wisdom is a precious commodity that can be drawn from different sources."

"What's inside the Nightmare Room?" asked Shawn, his voice quivering.

Angelo didn't want to imagine what could be in there. It could only be the worst thing possible. He dreaded the prospect.

"Ask yourself what's inside of you and how you can use it to conquer the room. It's more about the mind than the environment," Nigel explained. "What's inside you is far greater than what you face around you. You just have to find the key and unlock that inner power."

Angelo absorbed Nigel's profound words, resonating deeply within him. He had a new, inspiring sense of determination that fuelled him.

***

The apprentices gathered outside an eerie, cathedral-like building situated in the far southern corner of the campus. Unlike the previous rainy night, the skies were clear, allowing the full moon to glisten in its glory. The building, resembling an abandoned cathedral, had an air of desolation as though it had stood unoccupied for centuries. Each apprentice was required to take on this challenge alone. They all stood in line, anxiously awaiting their turns. One of the agents unlocked a set of double doors and ventured inside to light a sequence of candles.

"Whoever passes out inside the Nightmare Room fails," Nigel declared.

Once everything was set in place, the first apprentice was beckoned forward. As the girl stepped inside, the massive doors slammed shut behind her, sealing her in with whatever awaited. Blood-curdling screams echoed from within, which made Angelo's heart race. Whatever lurked inside that building had to be demonic. After several minutes of disturbing silence, the doors finally burst open, and the girl was carried out by two agents.

With the help of the moonlight, her face contorted with fear was unmistakable. The agents supported her unconscious body, a clear sign of helplessness.

"Fail. She must learn to control and master her fears," said Nigel, unfazed. "Next!"

A few more saints stepped in to assist the unconscious girl and carefully led her away from the sinister building. The agents guarding the entrance were prepared for the next participant. However, no one seemed eager to step forward. The boy at the front was hesitant.

"I'll go next since the rest of you are too chicken to do it," Rex declared, pushing his way to the front of the line. With his fearless demeanour, he ventured into the Nightmare Room.

Everybody waited and made small nervous chatter. Rex feared nothing. If anyone was to be feared, it was him.

The doors flung open, and Rex emerged, drenched in sweat but notably unbroken. He still appeared to be in shape. Great exhaustion was apparent, but there were no signs of trauma. Agents escorted him away, and the rest of the apprentices were left to wonder about the harrowing experience inside the room. The line continued to move forward, and Angelo's turn would soon be approaching.

"I can't do this," Shawn whispered. "I'm gonna bail and skip out on this ritual. Nobody's looking. They won't know I'm gone."

Angelo shared the same feelings, but would ditching the challenge with Shawn be worth it? Seraph Nigel would surely notice if they escaped, and cowardice would be frowned upon.

They could dash for a hiding spot somewhere behind a building while the seraph was distracted, but the punishment for attempting to bunk a trial was something Angelo didn't want to risk facing. Despite how distressing the Nightmare Room looked, Angelo refused to let Shawn slip away. Before Shawn could run, Angelo grasped his arm firmly and stopped him from moving further.

"Where do you think you're going? This is what we signed up for, remember? I ain't letting you get off easy while the rest of us suffer. It's time to man up for once," Angelo admonished.

Angelo pulled Shawn back and gave him a strong push, propelling him to the front. After Sanji and the other apprentices had gone, it was Shawn's turn. He was evidently shaking like the winter had come. His trembling limbs reflected the mounting terror, and as the heavy doors swung shut, the only sounds that emerged were bone-chilling howls. Angelo had never heard Shawn scream like this in his life. He dreaded at his friend's peril, with his eyes widened.

Shawn finally came out. His traumatized look spoke volumes of the Nightmare Room's horrors. He walked like he was on the brink of collapse, but he still managed to put one foot in front of the other. Two agents helped him out and escorted him away. Angelo looked back, wondering where everybody went after completing the ritual. After two other apprentices, it was finally Angelo's turn to enter the Nightmare Room. As he stepped forward, he found Nigel's penetrating gaze glued onto him. Whatever monster he was about to face would either break him or make him.

CHAPTER 13

THE NIGHTMARE ROOM

The heavy doors swung closed, sealing Angelo within the suffocating embrace of the unknown environment. The nightmare room now held him captive. The soft glow of candles lined the path ahead, casting eerie flickering shadows. He ventured steadily down the pathway. In the dim illumination, another door appeared, and a figure suddenly came into view. Angelo's pulse quickened. Fright clawed at his chest, ready to consume him. However, as he looked closer, an elderly-looking man was holding a cup. It was an agent, by the looks of it. The man slowly approached Angelo.

"Your adversary awaits behind that door," said the agent, pointing to the weathered entrance. "But first, you must drink this."

Angelo accepted the cup with both hands, a storm of questions brewing in his mind. "What's this? Why do I have to drink it?"

"Just drink," the agent ordered, irritation creeping into his voice.

Angelo hesitated for a brief moment, but the agent's firm gaze left no room for negotiation. He lifted the cup, the drink gave off a strong, ugly odour that could make anyone puke the moment they took a whiff. Despite the vile taste that followed, Angelo forced himself to chug the drink down. Each gulp was nauseating as he kept chugging, but no matter how unbearable it was, he would finish the drink. Once he had drained the cup, it began to melt out of his grip. The gooey, liquified remnants dripped on the floor, and a bewildered Angelo blinked multiple times to make sure he was seeing right. With an abrupt gesture, the agent swung the door open, and Angelo, his mind still grappling with the uncanny scene, stepped into the unforgiving den.

Finding himself in a dim room full of paintings. The dampness and coldness of the room enveloped him. A creeping sense of unease settled into his gut. His head began to swirl like a whirlpool, unable to grasp the sudden transition. He questioned if he had drunk some sort of deadly poison.

The size of the room started expanding, appearing to defy the logical laws of physics. The paintings began to move like something had brought them to life, and they morphed into sinister-looking creatures. The grotesque transformations sent chilling waves of fear through Angelo. Ominous hisses echoed throughout the room.

"Wh-what's happening? How did..." Angelo stammered, attempting to make sense of the surreal spectacle. He rubbed his eyes, hoping to snap out of it, but to his disappointment, the creatures were still alive, bearing down on him. His mind had to be playing tricks on him. None of this could be real. Angelo looked upward and fell back in terror.

A black, hairy monster-sized creature clung to the ceiling. The sight of the arachnid creature was gruesome and hideous, it's fangs dripping with saliva.

Angelo was paralyzed with fear, and he thought perhaps he should've agreed with Shawn's idea of ditching the ritual. The hope of escaping this nightmare was nowhere to be found.

"Go away! You're not real," Angelo cried out, trembling with disbelief. He desperately wanted to believe he could erase the illusion with the power of his words.

The giant spider dropped down, one of its legs striking Angelo with the force of a sledgehammer and swatting him like a broken toy. This was no dream at all.

"Oh my god, it's real," Angelo cried, scrambling to his feet.

Desperation gripped him, and he made an apprehensive dash for the door in an attempt to escape, but the monstrous spider was quick. It blocked his path, diminishing his only chance to break free from this hellish ordeal.

The spider, aware that it had him trapped, slowly closed in on him. Its fangs were flicking with anticipation, ready to devour its prey.

Angelo backed away and started mumbling prayers, each word trembling on his lips.

"Though I walk through the valley of the shadow of death, I will fear no evil, for you are with me," Angelo recited this scripture several times, making a desperate plea for some divine aid.

The creature continued advancing.

He tried different prayers, but the spider remained unmoved no matter how many he chanted. In his final moments, Angelo's gaze fell upon an old fireplace adorned with two sets of antique swords. Something clicked in Angelo's head at that moment.

The profound words of Seraph Nigel. *"What's inside you is far greater than what you face around you."*

That was it. This challenge wasn't about overcoming or eradicating fear completely. It was about controlling and mastering one's fears with the courage left inside despite the circumstances.

Angelo still trembling with fear, but with a realized will to survive and succeed had to outweigh his fear. He picked up a sword and got into a fighting stance. With his heart pounding, he recited the sacred verse.

"Though I walk through the valley of the shadow of death, I will fear no evil, for you are with me."

Summoning up all the courage he could muster, he charged toward the spider and with a thrust pierced one of its malevolent eyes, bringing out an agonizing screech from the monster. The creature convulsed, vaporizing into a wisp of black smoke.

A wave of relief washed over him.

The ritual was over now, and he was still standing. He would walk out victorious.

However, his relief was short-lived when a demonic-looking creature manifested and materialized from the spider's smoke.

Angelo jumped back and aimed his sword at the demon. It seemed like the ritual wasn't quite over yet. "Your eyes have been opened to the spirit realm," the demon declared with a wicked grin. "We are your demons, and we will take your soul with us to hell when you die."

So, these were malevolent spirits that Angelo was dealing with. The strange concoction that the agent had made him drink opened his eyes to a spiritual world. An unseen world Angelo wasn't fully aware of until now. Angelo swung his sword with determination, ready for action. For once, Angelo was grateful for the tiring bible lessons he'd had with Reverend Wilson as they now held significance. They helped him understand that physical and spiritual elements were both at work.

"Everybody fights their demons. I won't surrender my soul to you. I'm sending each of you back to hell," Angelo declared with burning resolve.

Four other demons surrounded Angelo and converged upon him, encircling him like a storm of viciousness. But he was in control of his mind and not the demons. They made him see what they wanted him to see.

The demons had the power to manipulate his perceptions, but he would no longer be their puppet.

Angelo chanted prayers as he slashed each demon with a sword, wielding not just his weapon but his mind and soul against the unholy intruders. Since he was dealing with demons, a physical attack wasn't enough.

"I am in control, not you. I am the master of my own fears. My own thoughts," Angelo proclaimed as he slashed through the demonic entities.

One by one, each demon succumbed to his newfound strength. They vanished into black vapour until none were left. Angelo let out a heavy sigh of relief. Having conquered the nightmare room. It had to be over this time.

"Congratulations," said a voice from behind. Angelo's heart raced as the uncanny voice resonated behind him. It was eerily familiar, and he dared not believe it was what he wished for. The concoction was still in effect, but Angelo turned to face an unexpected surprise.

"Dad?" His voice wavered.

"It's me, Angelo," came the response. Angelo's eyes welled up as he grappled with a sense of disbelieving astonishment. His father, healthy and radiant, stood before him. This couldn't be real.

"No, you're not real," Angelo muttered, dropping the sword to the floor. "Stop it. Just go away."

Dad's explanation cut through the fog of Angelo's scepticism. "That substance you drank opened your eyes to the spirit world, remember? What you see now is me in spirit form. I'm physically dead, but my soul is very much alive."

Angelo's dad's explanation made logical sense. More tears flowed freely down Angelo's cheeks, and he fell gracefully to his knees. He was astounded by how this concoction allowed him to see his dad again. *Was he able to touch him or hold him? Probably not, but what mattered was that he could see him.*

Angelo battled with finding the right words to say. His father standing before him was like a long-awaited family reunion. "I've missed you so much. Nothing's been the same since you left. Everything's changed and… life just isn't as colourful as it used to be," he whispered, still doubting if this conversation was real.

"But some things have changed for the better. Look at ya, all grown up," Angelo's dad smiled, but it soon faded into a sombre warning. "But some things have changed for the worse. You made a huge mistake by choosing this path, and I've come to warn you."

Angelo was caught off guard by Dad's unexpected words. Having joined the Starlight Saints to seek vengeance for his father's death what could he have done wrong?

"What do you mean?" asked Angelo, quivering with confusion.

"This secret society you've joined is a big mistake," his dad warned. "The Starlight Saints are not who you think they are. You must leave now."

Silence enveloped the room.

A seed of confusion was sown into Angelo's mind. He couldn't comprehend what was coming from his dad's mouth. *There were saints that had been hostile towards him since the day he'd arrived. Pests like Dwayne, but there were ones who embraced him like family.*

"Dad, what are you talking about? There are people responsible for your death, and this agency can help me avenge you. Tell me who did it. Which one of the Illuminati did it? Or was it the saints?" Angelo inquired, desperate for an answer.

Silence remained as Dad's sole response. Angelo's father appeared to still be thinking about his answer. He breathed out a sigh of grief. From the corner of his eye, Angelo noticed the room starting to condense back to normal size at a slow rate. *Was the concoction wearing off?*

Angelo had no way of telling, but his father still stood there. His burning question remained hung in the air, awaiting an answer.

"I don't remember who killed me, but Ange, you have to trust me when I say the Starlight Saints are bad news. They lured you in. They're only using you to get to our family and push their own agenda. They're not who they say they are, which is why God sent me to deliver this warning," His father explained. "You think I'd ever lie to you? You're my son, and I love you."

Dad's words pierced deep like a needle.

Angelo sobbed again with regret momentarily but composed himself. *His family was prominent in the entertainment industry, and most saints suspected they were involved with the Illuminati, which Angelo knew wasn't true. Even Dwayne had accused him of working for the enemy. What if all the Starlight Saints were doing was using Angelo to get something from his family? Was that the only reason they recruited him?*

Angelo was filled with bitterness and rage, Dad's words seeping through him like venom. He couldn't believe he'd been tricked so easily.

"What should I do? I'm stuck here with these people in the middle of nowhere and all the gates are heavily guarded. How do I escape and what about my friends?" Angelo questioned.

A smile crept up on Dad's face as if he'd been waiting for Angelo to ask that question. Angelo had to put all his trust in his dad if he was going to get out of this predicament. His father could always be trusted when he was alive, and it was more imperative to trust him now when dead and godsent.

"Never mind your friends, it's you the saints want, not them. The only way for you to escape is to escape this world and be with me," said Dad, pointing at the sword Angelo had used to fight off the monsters earlier.

"What?" Angelo stuttered, his mind racing, torn between a profound longing for his father and the weight of the decision before him.

"You said you trust me, so I'm telling you to kill yourself. You can join me in heaven, and you won't have to suffer anymore."

A door of radiant light suddenly illuminated out of nowhere. It appeared to be a portal to somewhere. *Was this the doorway to heaven?* Angelo's love for his dad was unwavering, but the course of action suggested was almost too much to comprehend. He contemplated heavily on this life-and-death decision. This seemed oddly contradictory to the values Angelo was accustomed to. Dad stood at the door, ready to walk through as the afterlife prepared to welcome Angelo.

"Just slit your throat and join me," Dad extended his hand. "Everything will be okay, Apple Jack, I promise."

Angelo realized something was off at that moment. Throughout his lifetime, his dad had never called him 'Apple Jack.' That was the nickname Rex had given him. This raised many red flags.

Something was terribly wrong here, and the dots were not connecting. If Dad was godsent, wouldn't God have shown him who his killer was? More importantly, wasn't it a sin to kill oneself? Joining his dad in heaven by killing himself didn't correlate.

"Hold on a second, you're not my real dad. Dad would never ask me to do something crazy like this, plus only my friend calls me Apple Jack. You're a spirit masquerading as him," Angelo declared, scepticism replacing his initial trust.

He grabbed the sword he wielded earlier and pointed it toward the false spirit of his dad. Dad's facial expression suddenly contorted, and he became enraged. His face transformed into something sinister, and his eyes turned to a wicked shade of red. The deceit was unravelled, revealing the true nature of the entity. Another demon. The demon roared menacingly, but Angelo was ready for action.

"How dare you use my dad to try make me do somethin' I'll regret? I am in control, demon!" Angelo pierced the demon's chest with his sword, and the entity dissipated into vapour.

This marked the third time Angelo had battled formidable monsters within his own mind. This last one almost got him, but thankfully, at the very last second, he saw right through the deception before taking his life. Angelo glanced around, and the room was back to normal. The paintings hung still on the walls, and there was no movement. He released a grateful sigh of relief. The ritual was officially over.

Angelo stepped out of the room, exhausted with sweat, almost collapsing, but he stood his ground and made his way to the exit. Exiting the building, he found a few terrified apprentices still waiting their turn. Whatever monsters they'd be facing was anyone's guess.

Nigel stood there with his eyes widened in astonishment. The seraph must have been impressed by Angelo's conquering of the Nightmare Room.

Two agents escorted Angelo away, and he found himself in a waiting lounge with all the other fatigued apprentices. They all had to wait until every apprentice had attempted the ritual.

"So, how'd it go in there?" asked Shawn, curious.

Angelo thought hard about how to answer his question. "I'd rather not talk about it, the journey was my own."

After such a tormenting trial, Angelo was in no mood to converse with anyone for the rest of the night. There was another lesson the Nightmare Room had taught him, which was to master one's emotions. The last demon that pretended to be Dad had used Angelo's longing for his father to manipulate his actions. Had Angelo allowed his feelings to overpower him, he surely would've failed and enveloped himself in death.

A Starlight Saint didn't only have to master their fears. They also had to avoid succumbing to their deceitful emotions and stick with reality instead.

CHAPTER 14

CIRCLE OF TRANSFORMATION

The sun hung high in the sky, beating down relentlessly on the campus. Heatwaves rippled off the stone paths and the air was thick with the heavy stillness of the afternoon. The time had come for the third and final ritual, known as the Circle of Transformation. All apprentices who had made it this far anxiously awaited their turns outside the main lodge and were called to go in individually, one at a time.

Angelo's heart pumped with nervous energy that no amount of preparation could stop. He had successfully passed the Journey of Faith and conquered the Nightmare Room. However, no matter how far he'd come, doubt still found a way to creep into his thoughts. The prospect of the final ritual left him uneasy. *This would be the hardest of them all. Angelo could feel it in his gut.*

Without warning, Angelo's name was called out as the next apprentice to walk into the lodge. Situated in the centre was a man seated on a gold throne. The man wore midnight blue robes that boasted royalty and high class, glistening with gold imprinted on his upper body and sparks of silver glitter around his sleeves. With a gleaming piece of jewellery around his neck, Angelo noticed the Starlight Saint symbol of the archangels. He was in the presence of the grandmaster.

Cherub Hugh and Skye were standing on each side of the throne. The grandmaster's sheer presence was captivating. This was the highest-ranking member amongst the Starlight Saints he'd been taught about. Grandmaster Rin.

Angelo approached the throne, bowing, overpowered with a strong level of reverence. The thrill of finally meeting the grandmaster excited him but also terrified him at the same time.

"Please stand," the grandmaster ordered.

In front of Angelo was a hardcover book with the symbol of the archangels imprinted on it. He placed his right hand on his heart and raised his left. Cherub Skye placed a noose around his neck, and his heart froze.

"Angelo Jackson, it is time to test your knowledge," Grandmaster Rin announced, his piercing gaze locked on the apprentice. "Are you prepared?"

Angelo nodded, his heart racing like a drumbeat, increasing pace with every breath. This final ritual seemed to be an enigmatic test. All the classes he'd had throughout his training led to this.

"Please state the five mottos every Starlight Saint must live by, starting with motto number one," Grandmaster Rin instructed.

"Nothing is real, and every truth must be questioned," Angelo answered confidently. *The cherubs' lessons were paying off.*

"Number two."

"Reality is a gift to the awakened eye and a curse to the deluded blind."

"Three."

"What is unseen, and intangible is often what holds the most significance."

"Four."

"Order shall prevail, and perversion must cease."

"And the final one."

"If there's no god or archangels guiding our purpose, then let our existence be a lie," Angelo concluded.

"Excellent," the grandmaster declared, a flicker of approval in his eyes.

There was a surge of confidence. *He had passed the test with ease and was quite surprised. That was it.* Angelo was about to become a saint. He couldn't help but think about Aunt Erica and the rest of his family. *What would they think of him now?* His family were supposed to be Hollywood entertainers, but Angelo had chosen the path of a secret agent. Part of him felt like he was betraying his family values, but part of him also knew he wasn't meant for *Hollyweird*. His calling was different from the other Jacksons.

"Place your right hand on the archangel book," the grandmaster commanded.

The book had a hard texture to it, like an ancient bible.

"Repeat after me. I, your name, pledge my allegiance to the archangels and the Starlight Saints, from now until death," Rin instructed.

"I, Angelo Jackson, pledge my allegiance to the archangels and the Starlight Saints from now until death," Angelo repeated.

"My purpose is to enlighten and awaken the world from deception with truth, righteousness, order, and fine wisdom."

"My purpose is to enlighten and awaken the world from deception with truth, righteousness, order, and fine wisdom," Angelo repeated.

The grandmaster instructed Angelo to remove his hand from the book and stand still.

A saint fidgeted with the noose around Angelo's neck, ensuring it was securely in place like a criminal being put on trial for treason. The noose caused great discomfort, and he was itching to know the purpose of it.

Was this also part of the final ritual?

"The noose around your neck symbolizes the death of the old you. You are about to die and be reborn," Rin explained.

The word 'dic' erupted a wave of panic in Angelo's heart. He did not want to taste death when he was so young and wanted to run out and escape the lodge, it would be a vain and worthless attempt.

"You will be reborn with a new perception, a new way of thinking, and a new way of living. Cherub Hugh and Skye will take you through the process," said Rin. "We change our rituals every ten years. Some, we replace with new ones and some we bring back."

The two saints held Angelo tightly by the arms. They had a firm grip, and there was no way he could overpower them. No, this wasn't right. They were going to hang him. He didn't consent to any of this, and surely, this was a violation of human rights. No matter how much he struggled or pleaded, the saints wouldn't let him go. He'd taken the pledge and sealed the deal. Angelo started to have regret. Maybe the spirit in the nightmare room was right. Maybe the Starlight Saints were the evil ones. Rin ordered the saints to take Angelo into a semi-dark chamber. Seraph Nigel stood there visibly eager.

There was a big, rounded pool, and the water displayed a clear crystal glow. From what Angelo observed, the pool was quite deep. In the middle of the pool was a circular floating platform.

The noose was still around his neck and was loosened up slightly. The saints strapped a small device to Angelo and handed him a wooden staff. They ordered him to swim across, climb onto the platform, and stand there. As Angelo planted his feet on it, he felt the surface of the platform wobble, meaning it wasn't so stable. He had to be careful with how he moved and try keep his balance. Nigel's eyes were trained on Angelo, and he felt a wave of panic at the prospect of what this task entailed.

"This final ritual is about rebirth and death to the old you," said Nigel.

Suddenly, the water began to bubble. Angelo was in a sea of confusion as he tried to make out what was happening. Out of nowhere, a slither of snakes emerged from underneath the pool and began to swim around the platform Angelo was standing on in a circular motion. There appeared to be hundreds of them swimming around, and Angelo's stomach tightened as he'd never seen this many snakes before, his heart racing with terror. If he lost his balance, he would die the moment he fell into the water.

Angelo couldn't help but notice something unusual about these reptiles. The snakes began to change colours like neon LED lights in a mesmerizing, otherworldly dance. Each snake transitioned through a kaleidoscope of vibrant colours, shifting from deep emerald greens to sapphire blues, fiery reds, and electric purples. The colours intermingled, creating a breathtaking spectacle that was unlike anything Angelo had ever witnessed.

"You must maintain balance on the platform throughout this ritual. You must release your old self with each lap the snakes make around the platform," Nigel explained. "If you fall into the water with the snakes, you will fail the ritual…and possibly die." Angelo's heart froze at the last sentence.

"How's this even happening?" asked Angelo.

"That device on you is a harmonizer, which is slightly different from the frequency box. It emits a subtle frequency which the snakes perceive as communication and only they can hear it. This frequency influences their behaviour, and as the harmonizer communicates your emotions, it allows you to establish a connection with the snakes. Let go of your old self bit by bit, and the snakes will respond positively as they circle around you, show resistance and they'll attack," Nigel explained. "Right now, there's a chaotic display of colours that mirror your inner turmoil and past burdens. If you can let go of your old life and old self the snakes' colours will synchronize, indicating balance and harmony. This is how you succeed in the Circle of Transformation."

So, frequencies could influence animals, too, and not just humans.

Angelo started to comprehend the task ahead, and he gave a nod. He focused on keeping his balance and observing the glowing pool.

At first, the snakes seemed calm as Angelo took deep, anxious breaths.

"Let go of your old self bit by bit 'til you find your inner peace," Hugh encouraged.

Angelo closed his eyes and tried not to think about the lingering snakes.

His thoughts turned to his family and their Hollywood careers. He thought about his luxurious life in Rockingston when attending Sun Valley High. Angelo had to admit that he missed the comfort of living a simple life as a teenage high schooler ever since he joined the saints.

As he opened his eyes, without warning, a snake jumped at him, hissing with spite. Luckily, Angelo swatted the serpent away using his staff before it could bite him. More snakes leapt out of the water and attacked Angelo. He hit each one with all his effort, panicking, and the platform started to wobble. Soon, Angelo found his balance giving way and was on the verge of plunging into the water. An inch away from failure.

"Look at you. You don't have what it takes to be a Starlight Saint," Nigel commented. "How disappointing. I expected more from you. Looks like you won't be getting ordained."

Seraph Nigel's words struck a nerve in Angelo. *He had made it so far only to lose now. But again, was this really Angelo's calling? Doubts began to circle about whether joining this secret agency was really the best decision.*

He could forfeit the ritual now and forget about becoming a saint and investigating his father's case, which weighed heavily on his shoulders. *But what if he could succeed and prove all the saints who'd doubted him wrong?* Memories of Dwayne's taunts ignited fury within him. The injustice that his dad faced throughout his career only added more fuel to the fire, sparking his determination to power through.

130

"There is still something you're holding onto. Until you let go, you cannot be reborn. Every saint must forsake their old ways. You must let go of everything that holds you back," said Skye.

She was right. Angelo had to accept his new profession. There was no way of changing his path. Angelo regained balance and fought off more snakes with fiery determination. He closed his eyes again and pushed back against the wave of old desires.

"I let go of everything!" Angelo yelled with a shaky voice.

As he opened his eyes, the snakes swam around him calmly like before, and their colours started to synchronize, indicating a transformation. Angelo was finally beginning to forsake his past desires and accept the new calling. His emotional state had transitioned from inner turmoil to tranquillity, and the snakes responded positively as a result.

He breathed and maintained his balance until the ritual was called to a close. Angelo was reborn, a strange sensation washing over him as he observed the snakes radiating in harmony.

Once the ritual was finished, the snakes slithered back underneath the pool, and Nigel beckoned Angelo to swim out of the pool. At the same time, the cherubs handed him a towel to dry off.

Nigel gave a satisfactory nod. "Congratulations, you've completed the final ritual of an apprentice."

Angelo acknowledged the comment with a bow of thanks and turned to the cherubs.

"Welcome to the family, Angelo. You're now one of us," said Hugh, patting Angelo on the shoulder. "Your perseverance is impressive. You remind me of *Starlight Johnny* in some ways."

"Starlight Johnny? Who's that?" Angelo inquired.

"A former student of mine. One of the greatest saints I ever trained," Hugh revealed.

Angelo was flattered by the fact that he resembled one of Hugh's best proteges. He was eager to know more about this

Starlight Johnny figure and hoped Hugh would enlighten him more in due time.

Angelo had completed all three rituals. He was officially a Starlight Saint! His journey had been full of unexpected turns, and he wasn't sure how to take it all in. Shawn's parents had probably relayed the message about a summer school by now, but could he tell his aunt the truth? No communication with outsiders was allowed, and the agency made sure of that by creating a firewall on the network. The saints escorted Angelo to the waiting room, where apprentices had to linger until everyone had attempted The Circle of Transformation.

Chapter 15

One of the Saints

An induction ceremony was held later in the evening to officially welcome the successful apprentices into the agency. The main hall was occupied by several saints. The polished marble floors beneath Angelo's feet were glittering, reflecting the light as the hall burst with chatter. Some saints wore black uniforms with the symbol of archangels embedded in them; others wore more sophisticated marine-blue uniforms with more décor. Angelo observed that saints had different attire depending on their ranking. He'd heard that uniforms were only worn for special ceremonies and gatherings within Starlight Saint territory. The cherubs had informed Angelo that he'd be presented with his own attire at a later stage. He sat with Rex, Shawn, and Sanji as they eagerly awaited the grandmaster's arrival. The scent of incense burning in delicate brass holders by the stage filled his nose- earthly and bitter. All the apprentices who had succeeded sat on one side, and all those who had failed were seated on the other.

"Can you guys believe it? We're officially Starlight Saints now," Sanji exclaimed, struggling to contain his excitement.

"Definitely the most bizarre way to spend a summer vacation together. Like, who knew we'd become secret agents?"

said Shawn. "I almost failed the Circle of Transformation, but here I am. Many forfeited, and I heard one apprentice died like…they got devoured by them weird glowing snakes."

Angelo shuddered at the mention of death and the poor apprentice's fate. All recruits had signed non-disclosure agreements before joining, and the agency, therefore, wouldn't be held liable for deaths within the academy. The apprentice was probably just another orphan, like most apprentices in the agency.

Angelo still couldn't help but feel sorry for the lost soul. The Starlight Saints seemed harsh when it came to these matters, but they were, after all, a secret society which had to protect its secrets.

Shawn was right about this unexpected summer venture. He had never imagined a summer like this, not in his wildest imagination. Angelo had tried to dodge the calling the first time, but it eventually found its way to him.

Grandmaster Rin entered the room, escorted by seraphs. The entire hall rose up and became silent as a sign of respect for the grandmaster. One of the saints opened a box of rings beside Rin. This was it. The failed apprentices were called up first.

"I have observed your eagerness to be part of our secret society but I'm afraid since you couldn't complete all three rituals, you can't be ordained," Grandmaster Rin declared. "You have the option to either try your failed rituals again or leave."

The failed apprentices were dismissed, and Angelo couldn't help but feel sorry for them. Their faces were written with disappointment and gloom but was grateful that he'd made it along with Rex, Shawn, and Sanji.

The successful apprentices were instructed to form a line and receive their rings individually. After fitting their ring, the grandmaster would ordain and appoint them.

It was finally Angelo's turn to be ordained. As he walked out of his seat, he could feel the weight of hundreds of eyes glued onto him because most saints despised him, the remnants of prejudice and disdain still alive since he'd arrived. But despite that he'd proven himself throughout the three rituals. *Surely, he must've earned a certain level of respect.*

Among the sea of onlookers, Angelo spotted Cherub Hugh and Skye. They had an enthusiasm that indicated they were proud of their student, reaffirming his triumph in the three rituals.

Angelo reached for a gleaming gold ring with the symbol of the archangels etched on its surface and gently slid it onto his finger. He then inclined his head in a gesture of profound respect as he approached the grandmaster's throne. In this pivotal moment, as Grandmaster Rin's hand rested upon Angelo's head, the world seemed to hold its breath.

"Angelo Jackson, from this day going forward, I hereby ordain you into the order of the Starlight Saints," Rin declared.

Despite completing the three rituals and being ordained, would the other saints accept him now?. He would likely still be persecuted and doubted if being ordained into a secret society with unwelcoming members was the right step forward.

Nevertheless, the declaration was made, and there was no going back. Angelo made his way back to his seat, feeling like a student graduating from high school. As he kept walking, he caught a glimpse of Dwayne glaring at him with disgust in his eyes. A smirk crept up across Angelo's face. *He'd proven himself. He was officially part of the secret society, and there was nothing Dwayne could do about it.*

There was something thrilling about rubbing his accomplishment in his rival's face. The other saints would have to respect him now.

***

As Angelo walked outside, he bumped into Seraph Kate, the same woman who was part of the Merrion ambush. She appeared to be in a rush somewhere. Kate had a glowing aura of radiance, leaving Angelo momentarily breathless.

"There you are," Kate began, her tone softer and more approachable than their previous encounter. "I gotta say you were pretty impressive durin' the rituals. I know we got off on the wrong foot last time we met, but I'll be your leader for the upcoming investigation. Your seraph."

Angelo couldn't help but be drawn in by Kate's praise. They hadn't had a proper introduction before, but as she spoke, he found himself discovering new aspects of Kate he hadn't seen before. He felt a strange connection he hadn't felt before.

"Oh, that's cool. Uhm, I'm glad I joined this agency," Angelo laughed with nervous excitement. "You kinda remind me of my favorite singer. She passed away a few years back." Angelo commented on Kate's resemblance to the late Akira.

Kate acknowledged the comment with a nod and seemed rather intrigued. "Right…well, come this way. We have our team meeting now."

When it came to missions, the Starlight Saints were divided into groups, and apprentices were allocated to different teams. Angelo, Shawn, and Rex were assigned to the Shadowbreakers team, while Sanji was put into the Astral Hawks team.

Kate led Angelo to computer lab 5, where they would do a briefing on their first mission. As Angelo stepped in, there were other familiar faces.

Luna and Vanya were there. Luna shot Angelo another one of her icy glares, and Angelo, sensing the tension, kept a reasonable distance from the blue-haired phoenix.

"Congratulations to the three of you on getting ordained, but now the real work begins," said Kate. "My name is Kate Ramirez, but you will address me as Seraph, understand?"

Angelo and his friends nodded respectfully. The computer screen flashed 'Operation: Jackson's Soul Quest.' Angelo was intrigued by the name and wondered how significant his role would be.

136

"As y'all know, famous singer Don Leonard Jackson died a couple years back from an overdose, and our goal is to uncover what really happened," Kate explained.

This was it. The saints would finally help Angelo discover the mystery of his father's death. Whatever secret was being kept from him would soon be uncovered.

"It's not uncommon to hear about celebrities dying from overdoses. But we have reason to believe that Don's death was a homicide and that there's a darker power at work here. The man had too much influence over the music industry, which made him a target. We figure he was the key to takin' down the Illuminati," said Kate.

A picture of Angelo's dad flashed up on the screen. Angelo found it hard to look. A sharp feeling of sorrow pierced his heart, and his dad's memory flooded him with waves of grief.

"When James, Don's dietitian, leaked Don's last phone call, he was shot and we found the crime connected to Dr. Cory Marshall," Kate began. "What's strange is Cory was sentenced to prison for involuntary manslaughter for two years after prescribing the medication Don overdosed on. The unnamed culprit responsible for James' death said he was hired by Cory somehow, then poof, he vanished before the cops could arrest him. Cory, however, swears he's innocent. Sounds fishy, right? Unless there's somethin' Cory desperately wants to keep hidden, then it's unlikely he'd pull a stunt like that. There could be more people involved, but for now, he's our first suspect."

The screen flashed to an image of a doctor, and Angelo recognized that face. This was Dad's personal physician during the days leading up to his final concert. Angelo remembered when Cory was blamed for his father's death, and he'd developed a bitter detest towards the doctor since then. Looking at the image brought back unresolved anger and bitterness. Dr. Marshall was part of the homicide, but who else was pulling the strings?

"According to official records, Don's cause of death was propofol intoxication, which isn't so accurate. Don was said to be healthy and not addicted to such drugs. The equation doesn't balance, which is why we must investigate," said Kate as the screen transitioned to dreary images of a fearsome facility. "We're paying a visit to Los Angeles State Prison."

Angelo shivered at the mention of a prison visit.

The menacing images, the prison's interior appeared filthy and suffocating. Angelo felt his heart tighten as his claustrophobic panic arose. The prospect of the visit seemed dreadful to Angelo, a deep seeded fear of prison. The temptation to opt out of this mission bore down on his conscience, but no, that would be frowned upon. Chickening out wasn't an option. Not if he wanted to uncover the truth about his father. He would have to push through it just like they taught him in the nightmare room— control the fear, swallow it down. That's what it was all about wasn't it? .

Angelo's fists clenched. Memories of the accusations, trial, and unanswered questions flooded back.

The screen flashed up some names. Angelo, Rex, and Shawn had to choose their codenames. Kate had explained that anyone could be listening to their communication network, which was why codenames were essential. Rex went with Leclez 17, and Shawn went with Sparrow. Angelo still needed to figure out what codename to choose.

"How about Apple Jack," Rex suggested.

And so, it was settled. Angelo would go by the alias of Apple Jack. Whoever would hack into the communication wouldn't suspect a thing.

"As for the prison visit, Angelo, you're obviously coming since you're the centre of this entire operation," said Kate, her tone firm. "Rex, we could use some of your fighting skills in case things get out of hand. That makes three of us, and the rest of you will communicate from the base here."

"What? How come I don't get to go on the first mission?" Shawn complained.

"If there's too many of us together, it will raise suspicion. You gonna do as I say and stay behind," said Kate.

The seraph silenced Shawn, and he didn't object any further. "How will the guards allow us to visit the doctor in the first place? Doesn't the inmate need to know beforehand?" Angelo questioned.

"Lucky for us, we have a saint who works as a correctional officer at the prison. He'll be able to get us access into the building," said Kate.

The first mission was set in stone—a doctor's appointment. The lab meeting came to an abrupt end. This was the first step to discovering what happened with Dad and who was out to get him.

As Angelo walked out of the lab, he unexpectedly bumped into someone he'd been hoping to talk to.

"Seraph Nigel? I'd like to ask something," Angelo began. Nigel halted abruptly and allowed Angelo to continue. "It's about the assassin from the Journey of Faith. Did you find out who the culprit was? What did the grandmaster do to Willow?"

"Not now," Nigel replied firmly, dismissing Angelo's question. "I have somewhere to be."

Nigel rushed away with haste. As Angelo looked over his shoulder, the seraph mumbled something to himself. "Need to get that firewall under control."

That's when a stark reminder came to Angelo's head. *Casey. He couldn't keep this investigation to himself. He'd promised to keep Casey informed. Dad was important to Casey just as he was essential to Angelo.*

There was a firewall, which created a barrier to outside communication. Angelo had a risky idea, and Sanji was good with tech. He could either hold his promise and risk getting caught or play it safe, probably making Casey worry and feel betrayed for not keeping his promise. Sanji would show him how to access a VPN and communicate with his brother.

"You're gonna get me in trouble for this," warned Sanji. "If I do this, then you owe me something."

"Of course. Don't worry, they won't catch us and if I do get caught I'll take the blame," said Angelo.

Angelo knew better, but he was confident in his own abilities. *It's not like he was intentionally going against the rules. He just needed to communicate.*

Once Angelo had the VPN, he texted Casey about the Starlight Saints, everything that had occurred so far, and the first mission. Casey swore not to tell another soul and assist where he could.

CHAPTER 16

DOCTOR'S APPOINTMENT

The California state prison emerged into view, surrounded by imposing electric fences that crackled with latent danger. The prison's walls, painted with dull grey, loomed like a fortress, and grim puddles of water circled the complex. Heavily armed guards, carrying their menacing rifles, patrolled the perimeter, ready to blow someone's head off.

For the Shadowbreakers, the day began early. They had travelled and parked an SUV outside the prison for their investigation. Angelo barely got enough sleep, while Kate and Rex showed no signs of fatigue.

Angelo shuddered at the thought of ever going to prison. The stories he'd heard of ruthless inmates, brutal assaults, or rampant abuse were enough to instil a lifelong promise to himself. Whatever he did, he would never set foot in a cell for the sake of his sanity. As the team approached the prison entrance, a stern officer was stationed at the booth, his gaze firm and authoritative.

"State your business here," said the officer.

"I'm here to see Dr. Cory Marshall about the recent murder of James Kulkarni. I'm a detective. I made prior arrangements with one of the officers here," said Kate, producing a fake ID and presenting it to the officer. The officer looked for a while as if sceptical, but Kate remained composed, knowing what she was doing. As the officer's gaze bore into Angelo, a glint of recognition finally appeared in his eyes.

"You're that mega star's son," he muttered. His gaze shifted to Rex. "But who's the other kid?"

"A friend," said Angelo. The officer examined them, making a long observation that could pierce one's soul.

"This way." After a moment of contemplation, the officer grunted and motioned for the three to proceed. They entered and walked through the prison grounds, filled with guards and inmates moving about. Several inmates gave Angelo a deathly stare, and he shrank nervously at the intensity of their gazes.

"How'd we get in so easy? I thought this dude would put up a fight," said Rex, whispering to avoid being heard by anyone nearby. He was puzzled by the ease of their entry.

"Like I said, we have saints working in these facilities, and we can count on them," said Kate, who managed to hear what Rex had said.

That was a relief. Getting past the officers would've been a lot harder had arrangements not been made, especially with a detective and two adolescents.

As they entered into a building, the atmosphere shifted dramatically. There were volumes of cells boasting iron bars gleaming coldly. Up ahead, the faint clatter of trays and distant voices signalled what appeared to be a cafeteria.

The air inside carried an icy chill compared to the warm air outside, making Angelo's skin crawl. An officer led the saints into one of the visiting rooms, instructing them to wait while they summoned Dr. Cory Marshall.

The muffled chatter and shouts came from outside as they waited. 'Get those lunatics back in check!' came a stern command.

The chaotic noise served as a grim reminder that prison life and prison guarding was no easy job. Angelo recalled stories of a rebellion where some prisoners managed to kill a few guards some years ago, and they almost lost control of that section of the prison. These inmates were not to be played with. That was for certain and being in such an environment chilled Angelo to the bone.

The door swung open and unleashed an ageing man with a receding hairline. Though most of his hair remained black, only little strands of grey could be seen, suggesting he wasn't as old as he looked. Accompanied by two guards, Cory Marshall, dressed in standard prison attire, seated himself in handcuffs. The saints were given a set amount of time to ask questions. Judging by the look on his face, the man had just been out. Cory observed his visitors carefully, but when his eyes landed across Angelo, they widened in shock, seemingly uninterested in the others present.

"What are you doing here?" Cory directed his question to Angelo, his eyes locked onto the adolescent. "You…I got nothing to say to yuh. If you come here to accuse me and ask me what happened, you're wastin' your time."

It was almost as if Dr. Cory knew exactly what Angelo had come for. Rex and Kate were fazed by the tension between Angelo and the doctor.

"Dr. Marshall, we're here to discuss the events leading to Don Leonard Jackson and the dietitian's recent death. Records say you hired someone to kill the dietitian after he leaked a tape of Don's last phone call in an attempt to stop info about Don's death from getting out," Kate spoke. "Is that true?"

Cory simply shook his head. His gaze held firm. There seemed to be truth in his body language, and his stoic demeanour suggested he had more to reveal.

"As we suspected. Someone else is behind this, desperately tryna keep their identity hidden. Now, let's move on to Don's case. We believe there's more to the story than what was presented in court. Can you shed some light on the issue?" said

Kate. She placed an empty 500mg propofol bottle on the table, its presence an eerie reminder of the past. "Two years ago, you were convicted of involuntary manslaughter and were sentenced to four years in prison," her eyes fixed on Cory. "Reports indicate you prescribed Don this drug, correct?"

Cory hesitated, avoiding direct verbal confirmation, but gave an involuntary nod instead, acknowledging the truth.

"You gave him propofol for insomnia, correct?" Kate pulled out a report file of Don's condition and medication. "We don't think the reports are accurate. Are there any details or people involved that weren't disclosed during the trial?"

Cory shook his head.

"Were you qualified to administer this drug?"

Cory nodded his head.

Angelo's impatience was growing, and he decided to interfere in the conversation, knowing that they only had limited time to interrogate the doctor before he was called back to doing his prison labour. "Doc, it's clear you know more than what you're telling us. Who signed you up to this, and what was their motive?" asked Angelo.

Cory simply kept quiet, pretending to not acknowledge Angelo's presence anymore.

"Who'd you work with?" Angelo demanded.

"Look, kid, I don't know what yuh talkin' about. I've been wrongly accused. That pop star's death was an accident. The media twisted the facts to make me the scapegoat. I was trying to help the guy by givin' him other medicines, but he wouldn't listen. He overdosed, and dat was it," Cory declared.

Despite his words, there was unmistakable hesitance in Cory's tone, as if he was fighting to keep something from escaping his mouth.

The Shawdowbreakers could see it.

The doctor was telling only parts of the narrative, not the whole story. Just what he thought they wanted to hear. The tension in the room escalated.

"We ain't here to judge, doc. We need to uncover the truth. Was his death really an accident? Stop playin' dumb and answer the damn questions," said Rex, impatience evident in his tone.

Cory kept his mouth zipped and maintained his silence.

Rex looked like he was about to do something drastic, but Kate restrained him and tried reasoning with the doctor herself.

"What are you afraid of?" Kate asked. "Were you sworn under an oath to keep a secret and not tell anyone?"

Cory shrugged, not giving a definite yes or no. Body language communicated better than words in this case. His expression was a clear giveaway.

"I can assure you whatever you say in this room stays in this room. Nobody else will know. We can help you," Kate reassured, but Dr. Marshall still wouldn't budge.

What would it take for the doctor to speak and reveal what he knew? There was clearly more to this story than what appeared on the surface. Time was almost up, and in a last-ditch effort to extract the truth from Cory, Angelo's mind raced with ideas, desperate for a solution. He could tell that the doctor detested his presence, which would be an obstacle in getting Cory to warm up to him.

Angelo had been deep in his thoughts and came up with something on the spot. A bargain. *If they were going to get anything out of Cory, they had to offer him something in return for his cooperation.*

"Listen, how 'bout if you talk, we bail you outta jail?" Angelo proposed. "We can pay your bail, get you out, and you can go see your family again." He shifted his glance to Kate for reassurance and turned back to face Cory.

Cory's expression seemed to lighten ever so slightly as if he might take the deal. "No."

The door to cooperation seemed to slam shut, leaving Angelo disheartened. That was the final answer from the doctor's mouth. Just a simple no. At this point, the saints had exhausted their options. With Cory unwilling to speak, they would have to pursue alternative means of investigation. The disappointment was shattering, but at least they'd put in the effort.

"If you bail me out folks are gonna suspect something. However…" the three saints immediately paused to listen to what Cory had to say. "I could make dis one exchange. Yuh see, my family's finances ain't too good, and someone needs to pay my daughter's college tuition fees. We need a $5k check for it. Agree to dis and I'll talk," Cory proposed.

They had no time to ponder the decision, so Kate, as the group leader, agreed.

"Don and I were very close," Cory began, his posture becoming tense and uneasy as if talking about Angelo's dad unsettled him. "He trusted me, and I did my best to help him. I prescribed medication as per his condition. The dosage was within the recommended limits, but something else must have gone wrong. When Don spoke to me, he kept saying people were coming for him, and he warned me, saying they were gonna try frame me when he died."

Cory paused momentarily, his words hung in the air. Sorrow and regret filled his eyes. "I didn't believe him. I just thought that was the paranoia effect of the drugs I gave him. I should've listened, but I didn't. The doses I prescribed were not lethal enough to kill him."

"Who do you think was trying to kill him? Any idea of who the perpetrators could be?" asked Angelo, desperate to unlock the mystery behind the doctor's case.

"There were others who had access to the Don's medical records and could have tampered with them. The truth lies in those records. You might wanna investigate the autopsy report which is hidden in St Marys medical facility. The truth is I'm just the fall guy and the real killer is still out there," Cory confessed.

Dr. Marshall looked like he was about to reveal more. The doctor opened his mouth once again, and before words could escape, the door swung wide open.

"Times up!" an officer declared.

The other guards came and escorted Cory out of the visiting room. Angelo pondered on the word 'autopsy'. *That was how people traced the cause of death, wasn't it? His father's autopsy would be the next matter to look into.*

Cory looked back at the three with sincere hope.

They had a promise to fulfil, which was to help the Marshall family.

The good thing was now the saints had confirmed that the death of Angelo's father was no accidental overdose. There was a bigger picture in the grand scheme of things. The saints had a solid foundation to continue the investigation and find the missing pieces relating to Angelo's dad and the dietitian.

CHAPTER 17

SERVING TIME

As the team was led by guards toward the exit, Angelo and Rex conversed with each other about what had just occurred, with Kate strolling just behind them.

"I can't believe they'd make an innocent man rot in jail. This killer is more cunning than I thought," Angelo began. "We must retrieve that autopsy report as soon as we can. What do you think, Seraph?"

"Seraph?" he called out, but no response came. Angelo scanned the hallway ahead and noticed Kate's absence. His eyes widened in shock as he spotted her farther down the corridor. The guards had handcuffed Kate and brought her to a halt.

As Angelo and Rex rushed to Kate's aid, their running fuelled with alarm, the other guards surrounded them in a circle.

"You're under arrest," one of them declared, fastening a pair of cuffs on Angelo.

Angelo's heart dropped and sank like a rock. *What were they being arrested for? They hadn't done anything wrong.* Angelo pleaded their case and begged the officers to let them go, but nothing worked. His pleas fell on deaf ears. Kate and Rex were also puzzled by the sudden arrest.

"Officer, I don't know what this is about, but I can assure you, we've done nothing wrong. We just visited an inmate," said Kate, maintaining her composure.

"Oh, cut the crap," snapped the officer.

Rex took a verbal jab at the guards, unable to read the situation while they also handcuffed him. "You guys stupid or somethin'? We're not criminals."

Kate remained calm despite how quickly things escalated in the last few seconds. Angelo's heart was beating at light speed, his mind unable to register what was happening.

"You three are working for a terrorist group called the Starlight Saints," the guard declared, his words shrouded in suspicion. "You have every right to remain silent."

A terrorist group? The label hit Angelo like a cold wave. *How could these guards have known they were secret agents? Somebody's mouth had slipped, and no one was supposed to know what they were doing.*

Another officer, chubby and authoritative, walked in and greeted them. "It's nice to have some secret agents on these grounds. Don't want our visitors leaving so soon. Please make yourself at home here. Name's Officer Gerald." His smile cruel and calculating.

These words left the saints bewildered and exposed. Their true identities had been revealed, and the reason remained a baffling mystery. A gun was drawn, and anyone's head could be blown off any second.

Such a precarious position the saints found themselves in.

Angelo's body tensed, leaving him paralyzed in the face of danger. Gerald continued mocking them, leaving no room for resistance.

"Take those watches off them and confiscate all their weapons," Gerald ordered. "We got plenty to discuss. I wouldn't try nothin' funny unless you wanna lose your head."

The saints had no choice but to comply, their powerlessness apparent as their starlight watches were seized. They were outnumbered.

The guards escorted them through the prison halls as looming guns held their lives in a delicate balance.

Angelo's breath came out in heavy, anxious gasps. It didn't seem like they would pull the trigger.

Not yet at least. What did Gerald know about the Starlight Saints, and what were his intentions?

They continued walking until they were led to a series of vacant cells. Angelo was forcibly shoved into a cell, and the door shut behind him.

Kate and Rex were led into their respective cells, leaving them confined.

"You can't do this! I'm too young for jail. This is illegal!" Angelo protested, but all the guards did was snicker.

Locked within the cold, dimly lit cell, Angelo's heart thumped in his chest with a potent cocktail of dread and anxiety. For once, he was tasting the horrors of imprisonment, the suffocating atmosphere, and the haunting realization that his freedom had been stolen from him.

"Shut up, kid. We'll be back in an hour to interrogate the three of you," laughed the guard.

Angelo grabbed the metal bars, struggling against them in anguish. The cell was cramped. Its concrete walls seemed to whisper hopelessness, and Angelo's claustrophobia kicked in. He quickly glanced at Kate from across and Rex in the left cell. *How could these authorities make such accusations against them without evidence or fair trial? This was a setup.*

Angelo gazed at Kate with desperation, hoping the seraph would have a plan. "Seraph, they have no right to arrest us. How we gonna get out?" asked Angelo, his voice trembling with uncontainable fear.

"Just calm down and be quiet. We'll find a way," Kate replied.

Kate was right, but Angelo's fear and paranoia about jail were getting the best of him. He knew his outbursts and panicking would only make things worse. The other option would be to simply trust Kate and follow her lead.

Kate's calming words were the lifeline in this sea of uncertainty.

"I ain't scared of jail. If they sentence us, Leclez 17 will be running the place," said Rex, cracking a sly grin.

Rex often overestimated himself, which was typical of him, but how long would he keep up with this bravado?

An hour passed, and a guard came over to unlock the cells. This guard had a cop hat and a pointy nose. Other guards came and escorted the saints to a big interrogation room. The saints were forced onto their knees with their heads down. One guard let go of Angelo and shoved him beside the other two. Other guards had their guns trained on them, ready to open fire. The three knew it would be a blood bath if they attempted to resist or escape.

No way out and no way to fight.

"I'll let you guys in on something," Gerald began with a devious grin. "I'm part of the Illuminati, and I'm here to rid our world of criminals like you."

"I shoulda known. No other officer would've known about our watches and other weapons," said Kate.

Angelo's heart sank as he realized they'd fallen into the hands of the enemy. The guards' weapons remained poised and ready.

Rex grunted as an unempathetic guard bumped into him and kicked him as if he were nothing more than a domestic animal.

Minutes passed in tense silence until Gerald decided to shatter it.

"Starlight Saints are nothing but poison to this world. We simply can't co-exist. You're gonna tell me everything about your secret hideout and where you train all your pesky saints," said Gerald.

The statement was so cold it froze the atmosphere. Angelo, Rex, and Kate remained silent, bound by their code to protect their agency's secrets.

Gerald observed the saints, and his cold gaze fixated on Angelo. "Ah, maybe the mega star's son can share some details. Talk, and I'll let you go free," Gerald proposed. "I've got a sweet deal I can offer you while these two rot in jail. We'd value someone like you, especially with your family name."

Angelo found himself in a whirlwind. He would do anything not to end up in jail and was desperate to be free.

The horrors of everyday prison life were too much for Angelo's mind to bear, but now, his chance to escape damnation was here. He didn't have to go to prison if he took Gerald's deal. However, guilt weighed on his heart at the thought of abandoning Rex and Kate to suffer a cruel fate in exchange for his freedom. *How could he run free knowing his best friend and seraph were locked away?* With a heavy heart, Angelo shook his head ever so slightly, indicating no for an answer.

"Not taking the deal? Very well. Take them in!" Gerald snapped his fingers, and the guards immediately seized the saints.

There was no escape route left. The saints would be sentenced to prison among the other inmates. As the guards grabbed them, tormenting drone-like music resonated through the prison walls, and no one had a clue where it came from. It perplexed the guards. The intensity and unordered rhythm mimicking a bomb. *Someone must've been using a frequency box. But how? All their weapons were confiscated.*

Amidst the chaos, the guards crumbled under the assault of these unseen sound waves, all except one. It was the pointy-nosed guard who'd unlocked the cells earlier. That was the fellow

Starlight Saint who worked at the prison. His badge read 'Officer Frederick.' Frederick swiftly helped remove the handcuffs from Angelo and his team. He handed back their weapons amidst the ongoing turmoil, signalling their freedom.

"Leave now," Frederick admonished.

Angelo, Rex, and Kate already had their specially designed earpieces shielding them from dark frequencies. Fortunately, these were the pieces of equipment the guards hadn't confiscated.

The guards, including Gerald, were all still scattered in distress, begging for the noise to stop. While they were all too focused on covering their ears and engaged in tracing the source of the sound, the saints seized their chance.

Kate signalled Angelo and Rex, and they sprang into action. A brief scuffle with a few unarmed guards cleared their path, and they raced towards the nearest exit. The other guards were too disoriented by the dark frequencies to even notice their captives escaping. They made it out the back, where there were prisoner transport vehicles. The gate was just up ahead. Two guards were stationed there.

"Hey, you!" one of them shouted.

Rex took the initiative to knock the guards down.

Kate pushed a button on her watch.

They kept running until they left the boundary. The saints reached their vehicle and, with roaring engines, sped away from the prison.

Angelo cautiously glanced over his shoulder. "I think we lost them," he murmured, his breath still ragged from the adrenaline rush.

"Don't be so sure about that," Kate warned.

She was right. They couldn't take chances. They couldn't just assume that their pursuers had given up the chase. They had to move in all directions and turns to test if they were still being followed.

"At least we've got some leads now," said Rex.

"The doctor confirmed it himself. He's not the one responsible. He's just the fall guy for the whole operation," said Angelo.

"I think it's time we head back to the academy," Rex suggested.

Once they returned, they would hold their meeting again and upload the data they'd collected to their mission's database. *Although things hadn't gone precisely as they'd planned, which most of the time never did, who's to say that their first mission wasn't successful?*

CHAPTER 18

BACK FROM THE DEAD

Five Years Before...

The whole world was as dull and empty as a void, as if someone had robbed it of its joy. The atmosphere had its liveliness sucked right out of it, and there wasn't a single sign of happiness anywhere. Dystopia had arrived. Society entered a new era. One they could not turn away from and one that would remain forever. The people most affected were almost the entire globe.

The roads in Los Angeles were flooded with traffic, different vehicles fighting to make their way through. Above were helicopters zooming around and news broadcasters capturing every detail of this historic event. From a slight bird's eye view, a black hearse navigated toward its destination with other smaller black vehicles surrounding it. From a television watcher's perspective, the news broadcast. The cameras were focused on the hearse and its progress along the road.

"As we prepare for the late Don Leonard Jackson's memorial service, we'd like to note this traffic is crazy, don't ya think, Theresa?" said one of the TV news broadcasters.

"Absolutely, Jimmy, and it's no surprise, as this will be a massive event for a big icon. Rest in peace to him."

"Oh yeah, you know the news came as a shock to fans across the world. Don was supposedly meant to be performing what would be his final concert a couple weeks ago, but sadly, it never happened."

"Hundreds of fans and celebrities are gathered here to honour the life of the beloved star. Reports say celebrities like Usher, Chris Brown, Jay-Z, Kobe Bryant and many more are in attendance."

The reporters continued their chatter, going into every detail of the upcoming memorial service. Don Leonard Jackson, the icon who tragically lost his life to an overdose, was now sound asleep in his realm of eternal bliss. His soul had said farewell to his flesh. Now, it was time for the world and the fans to say farewell.

The memorial was held at the O3 arena in Los Angeles. The venue swarmed with thousands of people, most of them dressed in formal black dresses and suits. It looked like the arena was about to burst from all the crowding. The eleven-year-old Angelo was accompanied by Casey, Erica, and the rest of the family. The family all wore black and sat at the front of the stage where the coffin lay as still as a rock in the ocean. The casket glistened with radiant gold like the tomb of an ancient king. On top was a pile of red roses. Roses that were meant to symbolize love and appreciation. As the proceedings went on, a choir stood up and sang a tuneful hymn.

'God be with you till we meet again
Till we meet, till we meet
Till we meet at Jesus, feet
Till we meet, till we meet,
God be with you till we meet again…'

Angelo's eyes watered at the sight of the lone coffin, and the choir's harmonic singing only intensified his grief. He still couldn't believe this was his reality—so much hope lost and so much pain gained. How could he bear all of this? Casey, on the other hand, seemed more composed. It appeared like he was trying to fight back his fears, but one drop managed to escape and trickle down his cheek. Angelo initiated small talk.

"Why did God let this happen to us?" asked Angelo.

"Who knows? I wish I did," said Casey coolly.

"He's an angel now and he's with God in heaven, right?"

"Humans don't become angels when they die, Angelo, that's a false teaching. They gain heavenly bodies," Casey explained. "That's what I remember from one of our Bible classes when we were young."

"So, he's with the Lord as a human?"

"Exactly, he can rest now, and he doesn't have to suffer from the pain this world throws at him."

Casey burst into tears, and so did Angelo. They embraced each other like two peas in a pod and poured out their grief. Soulful music filled the entire venue, and the atmosphere suffered the weight of more gloom. Various people stepped up on stage to deliver their eulogies. The service stretched for millenniums until Angelo and his family were finally called to come up and give their speeches. Just before the first Jackson came, an elderly-looking man with long white hair and a luxury suit that signalled billionaire status walked up to give his speech. Blu J was what they called him. He stood in front of the audience and was silent for several minutes as if trying to find the right way to begin his speech.

"At the age of ten, Don had a dream. A dream to become one of the greatest entertainers in the world. He was willing to do whatever it took to achieve that level of success… I'm struggling to find the words to…" Blu J's words drowned in sorrowful sobs. The audience waited patiently for him to regain his footing.

"I met Don when he was fifteen. He had such a loving heart, and when he left us a part of me left with him…Don, I know in recent years we weren't always on the best terms, but you were the greatest friend I ever had. I saw what you were capable of and as you're looking down on us, I promise that we will continue to honour your legacy. I will always cherish you." Blu J burst into tears, and one could only show sympathy for his hurt. Everyone knew what it was like to lose a great friend in that moment. Officials came to escort the man off stage, and Angelo also cried out of compassion for him.

They had saved the family for last, allowing them to do the honour of closing the memorial. First, it was all of Don's siblings, followed by other relatives, and then the children. Erica had been on the verge of breaking down during her eulogy but had maintained her composure in front of the audience and finished what she'd started. It was Casey's turn and then Angelo's. The microphone stand was a few inches taller than Angelo, and the family had to adjust it to his height. Now, it was the second born of Don Leonard Jackson, whom the whole world was waiting to hear from. What would this child say? What would be his farewell speech?

Angelo began to breathe rapidly, hyperventilating as if he was having an asthma attack. Casey stood on his right. Erica stood on his left and patted him on the shoulder, assuring him everything would be okay. Angelo carefully unfolded a paper in front of him while his hands trembled.

"Ever since...I was little...Dad has been the best father you could ever imagine," said Angelo, stuttering. Tears flooded from Angelo's eyes like never before. His face was all red, and he couldn't stop crying. "And I just wanna say I love you so much, Dad." Angelo couldn't utter any more words. His speech drowned with weeping. Erica embraced him in a comforting hug that should've cushioned the pain, but it made little impact.

The world mourned in unison. Nobody could really imagine the family's turmoil. The whole Jackson family walked off the stage, and the music began to play once again. Two ushers moved onto the stage and started carrying the coffin away as the sombre tune continued to flow through the venue. Different images of Don from his youth until his last days were scattered on the screen, making things more emotional. All the celebrities who had paid their respects and sang a tribute to this legend mirrored the family's grief.

The memorial came to a sad close. People began to exit the venue. Angelo was accompanied by Erica, Casey, and the rest of his family. However, as Angelo continued walking, he glanced over his shoulder and noticed that his family was caught up conversing with some celebrity attendees. Angelo recognized them as prominent figures like Jay-Z and LL Cool J, which he had no interest in. He decided to wait for his family outside. This was a chance for him to weep more and get some alone time.

The sun was blazing, and the brightness didn't let up. It looked like a fine day to be at a festival or something. Although the weather was joyful, it contradicted how Angelo was feeling. If he had the power to alter the weather based on his emotions, it would surely be raining and pouring.

"I can't believe he's gone, papa when will I see you again?" Angelo mumbled to himself.

He sobbed quietly for some time until his sixth sense detected someone standing next to him. When he turned around, he got a fright, and his heart raced. He looked up and saw a mountain of a man with long white hair and dark, weathered eyes. Angelo felt like he was looking up at Godzilla! It was the man from the memorial, Blu J. He seemed even taller now when he was standing beside Angelo.

Angelo felt inconvenienced and put his crying on pause. He wiped his tears away quickly and tried his best to act normal as if nothing was wrong, but that was obviously futile. Blu J looked down at him, his presence imposing. A warm, friendly smile appeared on his face, making Angelo feel safer around this elderly giant.

"Today hasn't been easy for any of us. We're all sad about the loss of Don," said Blu J, putting a hand on Angelo's shoulder and embracing him. Blu J was at least twice as tall. Angelo's head only managed to touch his hips.

"Your father and I were really close. We had our fights, but deep down, I cared for that man. He meant the world to me. I would do anything to have him back," Blu J confessed.

"You were best friends?" asked Angelo, his voice tiny quivering.

"Yes, we were. I promised your father that I'd look after you and your brother if anything ever happened and I must keep that promise."

Angelo was comforted by the man's words. He was one of those friendly seniors you could trust no matter how unfamiliar he was. Blu J had a kind soul at heart.

"I'll be taking Casey under my wing, and I will be helping him with his music career. You're still too young so I'll come back for you when you're old enough. I promise to take good care of you and your brother. You guys are family to me."

"Thank you mister…mister?"

"My name is Jason Radisson, but just call me Blu J, like my favourite bird," said Blu J with a smile. After the sweet, comforting interaction, he strolled away, bidding farewell.

"I'm always here for you and your family. You can count on me," he said with a wave.

'Blu J'—what a beautiful name. This man was the only person who'd given his undivided attention to Angelo that day. The family needed all the help and support they could get. It was time for Dad to make a home from the earth underneath and return to the dust he came from. It was Memorial Service Day.

***

160

Present Day...

Angelo left the dining hall in a hurry. The cool evening breeze greeted him. He needed to speak with the seraph. Angelo had several questions to ask Kate about his dad and why he played such an essential role in the Starlight Saint's mission to take down their enemy. He remained cautious for any sign of Dwayne as he walked through the campus. Their quarrel was far from over, and Angelo remained alert, reminiscing their last encounter. He strolled carefully to the Shadowbreaker's lab, where he would find Kate working on the computer. That's where she usually was at this time. As he stepped in, Kate didn't seem to acknowledge his presence.

"Hey, Seraph? I need to talk to you about something," said Angelo,

"Not now. I'm busy," Kate replied.

"It's important though."

The seraph would not let Angelo speak, no matter how hard he tried to reason. It was better for him not to press further and leave. He couldn't help but feel disappointed.

Angelo turned away and walked back the way he came. Just as he was about to exit, Kate suddenly caught his attention and commanded him to come back.

She turned away from her computer screen and faced Angelo. "What is it?"

Angelo quickly pulled out a chair, straightened his posture, and made himself comfortable. He still had to show a certain level of respect for his seraph by being seated as they conversed. It was common courtesy.

"I remember you said me and my dad's case hold a key to destroying your enemy, but what key do I hold exactly?" asked Angelo. "I obviously wanna find the killer, but why is your agency so keen on helping me?"

Kate paused for a moment and in deep thought. "We believe Don knew about a secret and dangerous operation that the Illuminati is planning. If we can get a hold of that knowledge, we can be one step ahead in this deadly game, which is why it's crucial for both you and our organization. Don knew more than people thought, and finding his killer could help us piece the puzzle together before it's too late. I was once in the same position as your father."

Angelo widened his eyes. The last sentence piqued his curiosity. "Same position? What do you mean?"

Kate hesitated for a moment; her eyes focused on a point beyond their surroundings. "Well, to begin with, my real name isn't even Kate," she began, her voice soft and almost vulnerable. "My real name is Akira, and I used to be a singer before I faked my own death."

The sentence dropped like an explosion of unexpected revelation. Time itself seemed to have paused. A wave of disbelief overtook Angelo, and he found himself questioning reality, unsure if he had heard right. His fatigue must have been playing tricks on him. Angelo asked Kate to repeat herself, thinking he might be dreaming, but got the exact same answer.

"Which Akira?" Angelo inquired. "Didn't know there were two singers named Akira."

"I'm *the* Akira, sweetheart," Kate revealed, the irony of the situation unfolding. "I had a whole army chasing after my music catalogue and publishing rights. My label desperately wanted to take me out and keep my art for their pockets, fearing I'd one day turn against them. So, I had to fake my death."

Angelo's mind reeled, grappling with the astounding revelation.

Akira had been his favourite musician since he was a toddler, and he'd decorated his room with all her posters. The news of Akira's death a few years back had shattered him and his dreams of ever meeting his idol. This had to be another test orchestrated by the agency, just like the ambush.

Angelo refused to get his hopes up. He would not allow himself to give into false hope. He stared into Kate's deep, hazel brown eyes, the resemblance evident, but his heart still trapped in denial. "That's impossible," Angelo argued, still very sceptical. "Akira died in a plane crash. There's no way she could be sitting here now. If you're really Akira then prove it. *Nothing is real, and every truth must be questioned,* right?"

"I see you've started applying the Starlight mottos," Kate observed, somewhat impressed. "Very well."

Kate began to click her fingers in a rhythmic dance, snapping like a metronome. She started humming, and her melodic voice instantly drew Angelo in. As her fingers continued their subtle choreography, Kate sang an acapella.

Angelo sat dazzled by the cadence of her voice. A soothing melody to calm the soul.

"Baby, you don't know what you've done to me. Between you and me I feel this chemistry..." she sang, the words carrying an intimate power.

The enchanting melody flowed, and Angelo slowly started to recognize that singing voice. It was precisely the way his favourite singer sounded, each note hitting the mark perfectly, each word flawlessly on key. There was no mistaking it.

Angelo was so amazed, caught in a moment where he must've entered heaven.

> *"Your love is one in a thousand*
> *It's forever and ever and ever..."*

Tears trickled down from Angelo's right eye, caught in the trance of a beautiful symphony.

It really was Akira. He was breathing in the same room as his longtime celebrity crush. A distant fantasy he had for many years had finally come true. Angelo's gaze settled on Akira. There was a weight in his heart he couldn't deny, building up the longer he stared at the resurrected singer. A strong feeling that he didn't want to admit. The song had hypnotized him. He'd fallen in love with the seraph. The leader of their team.

How would he convey such feelings? Could he tell her how he truly felt? Surely, it was forbidden for an apprentice and their seraph to have romantic relations.

"So, you've been a secret agent all these years?" Angelo marvelled, his voice still quivering from the shock of the revelation. "I collected all your CDs, stuck your posters on my wall, learned all your dance moves. I watched you on TV, then I heard the news, then..." Angelo trailed off, trying to hold himself together, his emotions too complex to put into words. "How did you survive the plane crash?"

Akira's eyes reflected a flicker of truth. "I was never on the plane, to begin with," she confessed. "I made them think I was because I knew somethin' wasn't right. I set up a decoy and managed to fool them into thinking it was me. I was signed to a different label under the same owner as Sonic Scope. I have a feeling Blu J was the one who orchestrated my death but have no solid proof to confirm it. When the plane burned up, and they found no human remains, they declared me dead. That's when they took my entire music catalogue and profited off my work."

Her voice trembled. Her anger was evident, but she also had a stern determination. "My family was left with nothing. Since I'd faked my death and gone into hiding, I had to find a new identity, a new occupation. I will get my revenge on those corporate scumbags one day, though. They can't control artists like puppets forever."

Angelo's heart ached for Akira, and the mention of Blu J, the man who had kindly taken Casey under his wing, became a disturbing shock. The record label had devoured Akira, leaving her with nothing. Seething with anger at the exploitation of artists by these labels he was also relieved to learn that his father wasn't the only victim.

"I started out as a child star just like your dad," Akira went on. "Made my debut when I was thirteen, and all the kids looked up to me. As I grew older, people across the world screamed my name. I remember being up there with Mariah Carey and Missy Elliott till it was all taken from me. But my hope was restored when the Starlight Saints found me. I trained for years to become a seraph and vowed to free the industry from the Illuminati's control. When we recruited you I took it upon myself to become your seraph and guide you on the right path of a Starlight Saint."

Tears welled up in Akira's eyes as she continued.

This was the first time Angelo had seen his seraph so vulnerable. "Blu J isn't the man you think he is. He may have signed your brother to Sonic, but I wouldn't trust him. Casey could become the next victim if he's not careful."

He recalled the tape and knew Casey was right in the heart of danger. *The threat growing every single day. The killer was after both of Don's children. Casey had warned Angelo about enemies lurking waiting to strike.*

Akira stood up, her resolve radiating through her.

Angelo couldn't help but be moved.

"Those motherfu…" Akira restrained her tongue. "They deserve hell. I will make 'em pay. I won't let them win," she declared with unscathed determination. "It's not even just about freeing the industry and getting revenge. Our fight goes beyond that. We're here to dismantle the dark powers that rule society and set this world free."

She paused for a moment. Out of nowhere, as if led by instinct, Angelo suddenly embraced Akira with a firm hug, and she froze, caught off guard by this unusual behaviour of an apprentice toward a seraph.

As Angelo held her, Akira's presence enveloped him. He was met with an irresistible aroma of her perfume. A blend of jasmine and cherry blossom.

Akira had a sweet, comforting scent that was, well, Akira.

How else could he describe it? Angelo kept her in his embrace until she gently pushed him away.

Akira was slightly thrown off and seemingly embarrassed by the act of affection displayed.

"Sorry, I got a bit...anyway, Seraph, I understand. I can't imagine the pain you've been through." Angelo began, hoping he wasn't blushing. "I promise to avenge you. I'll destroy the Illumiknights for what they did to you and my father. You have my word."

Akira nodded and managed to give a warm smile. As she acknowledged Angelo, his heart started racing, his feelings intensifying.

Any acts of intimacy with his seraph would be deemed inappropriate. He had to remember he was still an apprentice until he completed his first operation. Angelo suppressed his emotions and started to back away. "I should probably go now. Sorry I disturbed you." With a sense of reluctance, he walked towards the exit. But before he left the room, he glanced back at Akira, who was in the midst of packing her belongings.

"Don't worry, Angelo. I really enjoyed our convo. We're in this together, and if you ever need to talk, I'm here," Akira assured him. "Outside this secret agency work, you and I can be friends."

Angelo stepped out into the corridor and touched his heart. He could feel its rapid, relentless beating, and he knew what that meant. No matter how hard he tried to suppress these feelings, they would overpower him. Angelo had a new problem to deal with now. His love for Akira held him and chained him.

CHAPTER 19

SERAPH SERENADE

Angelo's Diary

Love can kill,

Yo, it's me again. I can't believe I'm writing this, but I've accepted the fact that I'm in love with my seraph. Akira. She stole my heart from the moment she started singing. I still feel like I'm in a dream. This is Akira. The woman I've admired my whole life. Now I'm in a secret agency with her, trying to take down the Illuminati. Could life get any crazier? I love Akira but there's 2 problems. I'm 16 and she's 29. I'm still an apprentice and she's a seraph. Why should I give myself hope that this will work out? Dad always told me time waits for nobody, so I might as well give it a shot. I'm gonna ask Akira out on a date. Stupid of me, right? I can't help the fact that my heart is tied to her now. Matter of fact I wrote her a poem. Not really a poem but more of a rap song cause I can rap too. I call this one <u>Akira 'Til Infinity</u> mixed with that Biggie Smalls vibe and a touch of Lauryn Hill magic. Imma show it to Leclez and Shawn to see what they think first.

Anyway, the bottom line is I made a promise to avenge my seraph. If I can beat all Illumiknights she'll definitely love me. It's up to me to put an end to all this industry madness. I got the platform. Time for a new movement in Hollyweird. Call me the modern-day Moses 'cause I'll free my people. I do this for you, especially Akira.

***

Akira 'Til Infinity

"Dear Akira, I'm in love with your features
Stole my heart I don't care if you're my leader
I got somethin' to confess you like my red rose
You and I are meant to be, and it really shows
I'm the nigga you deserve for real
I'm the one that you deserve for real
Can't you see?
You my dream
When two stars collide
Nothing can ever divide..."

***

Angelo stood amongst the serenity of the west campus gardens which were usually peaceful with the soft rustle of wind brushing through neatly trimmed hedges and the occasional chirp of hidden birds Anticipation mingled with his nerves as he unveiled his poem to his closest friends, gathered in a small circle, in the fading afternoon light.

Rex and Shawn exchanged amused glances, and before long, they burst out laughing.

Angelo's irritation simmered beneath the surface, but he should've known they'd make a mockery out of this. He expected nothing less from his friends, and the two continued to cackle uncontrollably.

Shawn's words cut through the laughter, direct and matter of fact. "Hate to break it to ya but you'll never get a date with the seraph. She's way out of your league."

168

Out of all people, Angelo at least expected his two friends to support him. *Who was he kidding? No one would truly understand the depth of his feelings for Akira.*

"What's going on here?" said a voice from afar.

Luna entered the garden. Her hair was tied into a ponytail, and her features glistened in the golden rays of the late afternoon sun.

Angelo and Luna never got along very well from the day he arrived, but he couldn't deny that there was something about the girl that seemed to hold his attention.

Luna still had her suspicions about him working for the Illuminati, most likely from Dwayne's brainwashing, and Angelo wouldn't hear the end of it.

Shawn jumped in to answer her question. "Angelo here wants to ask our seraph out on a date. Can you believe this guy?"

"A date? Seriously?!" Luna snapped as she shot Angelo a glare. "You're sixteen, and she's a grown woman. The hell's wrong with you?"

Angelo could sense the intensity of Luna's displeasure, almost as if she were offended by such an idea. "Why do you care so much?" Angelo questioned. "My relationship with the seraph is none of your business."

"Oh, yes, it is," Luna countered. "You're trying to get close to the seraph in hopes that she'll give you top secret information that you can show to our enemy, so they'll find a way to take us down. A typical Illumiknight's strategy."

Angelo folded his poem and tightened his fist around it with frustration. Luna's words pierced deep like a needle. *Why did she and the other saints always have to assume the worst of him? Hadn't he proven himself already that he was on their side?*

"In Apple Jack's defence, he did hold his tongue about the academy's secret location during the first mission when an Illumiknight held us at gunpoint," Rex intervened. "I'd say that's fair game. But this whole poem and dating the seraph thing? Absurd, I tell ya. Have to agree with you there, sweetie."

Rex smacked his leg as he burst out in laughter once again.

Angelo's heart shattered at the dismissal of his fellow teammates. They didn't even take the time to try to understand him and his feelings. They simply shrugged it off like it was nothing. He wanted to yell something but couldn't bring himself to do it. Trying to explain his feelings would be like talking to a brick wall. They would never comprehend.

Luna would no doubt spread the news about this to other saints, making Angelo even more of a target.

"You know what?" Angelo began. "Forget it. If you guys won't help me score my date, I'll just do it myself."

Angelo turned his back toward the three and stormed out of the gardens. He could still hear faint snickers of Rex and Shawn.

They had enraged him. He didn't need them anyway. He was determined to prove that he would be perfectly fine on his own. All he needed was confidence and his 'game.' Charisma ran in the family.

He muttered to himself, "I got this".

As he wandered aimlessly around campus, the radiant sun cast a warm glow, painting the skies with shades of orange. Angelo found himself by a beautiful fountain, its intricate architecture captivating his attention. He took a few deep breaths to calm his racing heart and smoothed out the crumpled poem. Out of the corner of his eye, Angelo spotted Rex and Shawn strolling toward him.

"Go away!" Angelo couldn't help but lash out.

Rex chuckled once again but, this time, offered supportive advice. "Don't be like that, Apple Jack. We were just pulling your leg. Honestly, your poem or rap song isn't even bad. If that's how you really feel about the seraph, then show it to her and ask her out."

Rex's words put Angelo's mind at ease. The bitterness he'd had towards them before was gradually fading. With newfound resolve, he started reading the poem out loud to himself.

"Dear Akira, I'm in love with your features…"

"There you are."

Before Angelo could continue, a sudden voice nearly made his soul jump out of his skin. Akira appeared as if summoned by Rex's words, her presence unexpected and abrupt. Rex and Shawn nodded with encouragement.

"Seraph? I didn't see you there," said Angelo, his heart racing intensely, his breathing shallow. "Do you need me for something?"

"I need to brief you on our next mission. You and Luna are with me on this one," Akira explained. Her gaze noticeably shifted. "What's that in your hand?"

Angelo was still holding his poem. This was his golden opportunity to showcase his heartfelt words, but the pressure and anxiety proved too great. He quickly crumpled up the poem, shoved it in his pocket and darted his eyes around without focus.

"Nothing, I mean…I wrote something for you. I wanted to ask you out on a d-date," Angelo stumbled over his words. He tried to correct himself. He couldn't form his sentences right. "Update. I wanted to ask you for an update on the operation. Yeah, that's it."

Confusion was apparent from the way Akira raised her eyebrows.

Angelo's heart pounded more as if seeking to escape his chest. He might have messed up and said the wrong thing. *Had he given himself away? Someone needed to shoot him in the head at that moment so he wouldn't have to deal with embarrassment.* Akira finally composed herself.

"We're meeting with Dr. Khan tonight. He's got something to show us before our next mission. You and Luna must be there pronto," said Akira.

Angelo nodded and secretly exhaled a sigh of relief. His secret was safe, and Akira hadn't seen through him.

"When do I get to go on a mission?" Shawn protested.

Akira responded firmly. "Soon. You still need some additional training. I hope you've been keeping up your private lessons with Cherub Marc."

Shawn grumbled out of disappointment and nodded obediently to Seraph Kate's orders. The seraph finally walked away, and Angelo was about to beat himself up for not having the courage to ask Akira out.

Rex glanced at Angelo, shaking his head, disappointment etched on his face. "That was your chance, Angie. Shoulda went for it. If you don't tell her sooner, you might end up regretting it. Take it from me."

Angelo hated the fact that Rex was right.

He couldn't keep his feelings buried forever. He would have to confess at some point, but the question was when? It was only a matter of time.

***

Angelo, Luna, and Akira convened in the science lab with Dr. Khan later that evening, an array of high-tech equipment surrounding them. Rows of advanced gadgets were dispersed around the room. They were to test their equipment and ensure everything was set before the upcoming autopsy retrieval mission. Their attention centred on a 3D holographic map, its luminescent display casting beaming glows.

"There's a medical facility in Los Angeles called St. Mary's known for treating some of the biggest celebrities. They have a designated place where they keep autopsy records of deceased celebrities, but access is restricted to the public," Dr. Khan explained.

"Hmmm, I wonder why they'd restrict access. It's obvious they're hiding something," Luna commented. "Hollywood and their weird shenanigans."

St. Mary's was the medical centre where Angelo's dad used to be treated. After his death, an autopsy was reportedly done, and the conclusion was an overdose of drugs. No further information was given. Angelo recalled Dr. Marshall's suggestion to look into the autopsy report.

It was the Shadowbreaker's next lead. They had to carefully plan how to access the building without raising the alarm. Once they retrieved his dad's autopsy report, it would reveal the real cause of death, bringing them one step closer to finding the killer.

"Retrieving the autopsy in broad daylight is just plain dumb. Unlike the other medical facilities, St. Mary's is the only one that's got closing times. Eight o'clock is when the staff leave," said Akira with her arms folded. "We'll infiltrate under the cover of night."

"So, we're breaking in?" asked Angelo.

Akira gave a firm nod and pointed her finger to the roof of the building displayed on the holographic map. There was a trap door hatch. That would be their point of entry into the building. Akira then touched a screen, and a red dot appeared.

"They store their autopsy report files on the sixth floor. That's where our jackpot is," said Akira.

Angelo raised another concern. "What 'bout security and CCTV cameras?"

"Our tech expert, Vanya, will disable the alarms and cameras by hacking into the network. As for security guards, they'll be a walk in the park. We'll take 'em out if necessary," Akira explained.

Angelo admired Akira's confidence in their mission. She appeared to have considered every detail, leaving nothing to chance. *That was the job of a seraph anyway, wasn't it?*

He had come to realize that the Starlight Saints were proficient in their work, and they left no stones unturned. *No wonder they were the Illuminati's greatest enemy.* The chances of anything going wrong on this operation looked slim, and this reassured Angelo. Los Angeles had to be far from where they were, though. They would probably have to drive for hours just to get an autopsy report. The distance was trivial compared to the importance of retrieving the autopsy report, which was a critical piece of the puzzle.

"I will now introduce Angelo to the *Johnny Skyblazer*," said Dr. Khan, holding what looked like a futuristic jetpack gleaming under the lab's bright lights. "This jetpack was named after *Starlight Johnny*, one of the greatest saints to ever live. With this marvel, you can reach speeds of fifty miles per hour, making a journey to LA under forty-five minutes. It's one of our own creations, and it's convenient for missions like this one."

With deliberate care, Dr. Khan placed the jetpack down, and Angelo widened his eyes with anticipation. The prospect of flying in the air excited him. But Dr. Khan hadn't finished yet. He followed up and produced a pair of high-tech sneakers.

"These are called *star strides*. These shoes allow you to run up walls and buildings. They have a special magnetic and gravitational pull to them when the user stands 90 degrees on the wall," Dr. Khan explained.

"Like Spiderman?" asked Angelo.

"Not quite," laughed Dr. Khan. "Spiderman naturally possesses a spider's abilities and setae. Our strides are more mechanical and designed with gravitational pull."

The scientist prompted Angelo to try the *star strides* on first, and the two of them, accompanied by Akira and Luna, stepped outside. They positioned themselves beside a campus building, the moon casting its illuminating glow over the land. The night's symphony of chirping crickets enveloped them as Angelo eagerly fitted the footwear on.

"Let's start with a simple walk against that wall, then progress to a jog when you're ready," Dr. Khan instructed.

Angelo pressed one foot against the wall with caution, followed by the other. At first, he jerked back as if he were about to topple, but he quickly found his balance. An incredible sensation washed over him as he stood sideways on the wall, feeling as if he were firmly rooted to the ground. With every step, Angelo marvelled at the power of the *star strides*, walking up the wall with ease. After a moment, he couldn't resist the urge to pick up the pace, breaking into a run as he ascended until he reached the top. The thrill of running up the wall was mind-blowing. Angelo turned around to look down at everyone on the ground.

"Running up this wall feels so rad!" Angelo praised with a smirk. "Care to race me, Luna?"

"Uh, shut up and come down already," Luna responded, her annoyance evident.

Angelo ran back down and landed on the ground.

Dr. Khan handed him the jetpack, the *Johnny Skyblazer*.

Angelo fastened the support buckle in front of him, securing the jetpack on both his shoulders. An attached controller awaited his command, resembling one of a PlayStation, and Khan instructed him to press the green button. As soon as he pushed it, mechanical wings started emerging. He felt like he was transforming into an angel or mystical being. He had always entertained the idea of being able to fly in the sky, and now he would be given the opportunity.

Dr. Khan gave a summary of the safety measures and how to use the jetpack effectively, emphasizing the importance of wearing goggles to shield his eyes from the brisk wind.

Angelo would be moving at a high velocity.

"This controller is your steering wheel. Think of it like playing a video game. The touchpad on the controller functions as your GPS," Dr. Khan advised.

Angelo had been playing video games for years. He reminisced about his old PlayStation console and yearned for simpler times before joining the agency.

"These high-tech goggles can alert you to any potential dangers while you're airborne, though chances of that happening are minimal," said Dr. Khan.

With everything set, the group moved to an open field under the gleaming moon for Angelo to conduct a series of test flights. As the jetpack's engine rumbled to life, the earth beneath him was slipping away, replaced by a sense of weightlessness.

"Now let's begin with a couple of laps in a circular motion by using the analogue stick. Keep your speed low," Dr. Khan instructed.

Angelo followed the scientist's directions, smoothly gliding through the air like an eagle. He embraced the thrill of the flight. When he looked down, Akira, Luna, and Dr. Khan were mere specks on the ground below.

"This is dope! You guys should make flying a regular thing," yelled Angelo.

"Okay take it easy, kid," said Akira.

Without warning, the jetpack began to shake, and the touchpad on the controller flashed red. Angelo soon found himself ascending rapidly and uncontrollably. His heart raced at the unexpected glitch, and he knew that if he let go of the jetpack, he would fall and splatter on the ground. *If he didn't find a way to regain control, he would risk a fatal accident that could jeopardize the whole mission.* He kept ascending toward the full moon as if going to space, and he quickly recited the Lord's prayer out of despair. The jetpack continued ascending on its own, taking the user with it, and Angelo would soon meet his end. A voice suddenly cracked into his earpiece.

"Press down on the left analogue stick, hold it and tap X repeatedly! This should help resolve the glitch. It's a force land function like force quit on a computer," Dr. Khan urged.

Without wasting time, Angelo followed Dr. Khan's instructions. In an unexpected turn of a hazardous situation, he began to descend gracefully toward the field where the team was.

Angelo finally made a safe landing on the ground, still sweating out of panic and his heart rapidly pounding. He caught Luna grinning and could tell she relished his flawed test run.

176

"You made a good attempt, but you'll need more practice using the control functions," said Dr. Khan.

After a few more careful rounds of testing, everything for the mission was set. Starlight watches, bulletproof jerseys, frequency boxes, star strides, and the Johnny Skyblazer were all in order. Angelo and the team were dismissed, ready to embark on their major hunt for the autopsy report.

CHAPTER 20

CHANDLER'S CAMPAIGN

Under the weight of the day's tensions, Angelo and Luna trudged back to their respective hostels, making no effort to converse. After the exhausting activities throughout the day, he couldn't wait to put his head down and sleep. Amongst the silence, Angelo could sense Luna's irritability of being in his presence.

Arriving at a walkway junction, they locked eyes briefly before parting.

"So, have you asked the seraph out yet?" Luna challenged, her tone harsh and interrogative.

Angelo dug into his pocket, ensuring his poem was still tucked away safely. "Why? So, you can spread rumours to the other saints, hoping I'll be kicked out when I'm a vital key for your society in stopping your enemy?"

Luna went silent momentarily, seemingly unable to give a response until they unexpectedly crossed paths with Dwayne.

"There you are albino. I was surprised you actually completed all three rituals," said Dwayne. He glanced at Luna with scepticism. "Don't tell me you trust this spy. Never trust a Jackson."

Angelo felt the weight of Dwayne's resentment bearing down on him. Having grown weary of Dwayne's constant attempts to discredit him. *Chandler had already turned most of the saints against him, so what more could the Phoenix Council president want?*

"I don't trust him at all," Luna affirmed. "Just waiting to catch him then he's finished."

Even Angelo's teammate had animosity. Luna's words stung him, but he tried not to show it. He'd proven himself during the three rituals and was ordained into the society. Clearly, that wasn't enough. *What was it going to take to show that he could be trusted?* A boiling anger then washed over Angelo as his memories flashed back to the first ritual.

"I know you tried to sabotage me in the Journey of Faith. You hired that assassin. Admit it!" Angelo yelled. "That's some move for a council president. Why don't you explain yourself?"

"Huh? What are you talking about? I did no such thing. I didn't even participate in the rituals as I'm not an apprentice," Dwayne hissed, eyes widened, offended by the accusation. "Trying to make me lose my position as council president so you can cover up your spying act won't work!"

"For the last time I'm not working for the enemy, and I know damn well it was you who sent the assassin," Angelo shot back.

Dwayne took a step closer, his anger intensifying, but before the confrontation could escalate further, a commanding voice intervened.

"Step down, Chandler."

Angelo caught a glance of Rex coming from afar, accompanied by Shawn. He couldn't help but curl his lips into a smile as his friends had come to his aid. This time, Dwayne was alone as he didn't have his other two friends.

"You might be the big shot 'round here, but to me, you're just an insecure maggot looking to scrape his dirty shoes on everybody," said Rex, his gaze stern and unwavering.

"You hired that assassin and almost got us killed. Now thanks to you, I got this," said Shawn, lifting his trouser sleeve to reveal his leg injury. A bandage was wrapped around it.

Dwayne's face contorted, his frustration evident with the nagging truth. He knew he was the culprit, which is why he tried so hard to deny it. Angelo was sure of that.

"So, the two of you have sided with the son of a paedophile? *Depreciable!*" Dwayne spat. He focused his gaze on Rex with a mischievous grin. "Heard your uncle isn't doing too great. He's running out of time as we speak, so I'd focus on finding those funds for the transplant if I was you. Before he drops dead."

Rex began to tremble, not out of fear but out of rage.

Dwayne's jab had undoubtedly infuriated him, and Angelo knew his rival had struck a nerve in Rex.

"You shut up about my uncle! I'll pummel you all over this academy and cut you to pieces," Rex yelled.

Dwayne had made a terrible mistake, and he was about to face the full extent of Rex's wrath.

Angelo couldn't be more eager to see Rex put Chandler in his place.

Rex came charging toward Dwayne like a raging bull, and as he got into close proximity, he launched a rain of aggressive blows. As Rex hammered at Dwayne, Chandler surprisingly dodged his attacks with ease, displaying unexpected agility. Before Rex could land a hit, Dwayne dodged and countered with a powerful strike to Rex's ribs. Rex groaned in agony before collapsing to the ground, much to Angelo's shock. How did Dwayne, of all people, manage to bring the best-proclaimed street fighter of Rockingston to his knees?

The fight was far from over.

Dwayne didn't waste a second. Swiftly capitalizing on Rex's vulnerability, he locked him in a painful arm hold.

Rex groaned in desperation as Dwayne twisted his limbs, and the tables had turned.

"Who's the maggot now?" Dwayne taunted, relishing Rex's agony.

"Let him go!" Shawn intervened, delivering a kick to Dwayne's shin, which forced him to loosen his grip on Rex.

Dwayne winced at the unexpected attack, buckling to his knees. This was Shawn's chance to follow up with another hit.

Angelo couldn't help but marvel at Shawn's bravery. For the first time, he was actually acting instead of running away.

Shawn went for a knee to Dwayne's head, but Chandler's quick reflexes allowed him to dodge in time.

Dwayne then grabbed a hold of Shawn and lifted him in the air. He then slammed Shawn to the ground in a devastating Supplex on the grassy floor.

Angelo's friends were down, and he couldn't fathom what he'd just witnessed. Dwayne's combat skills were too advanced, even for the likes of Rex. He boiled with rage.

Was he just going to let Dwayne scatter his friends like this? He couldn't stand seeing them suffer at the hands of his rival.

"I've had years of training. Did you fools really think you had a chance at beating me?" Dwayne gloated, looking at his defeated opponents, who lay helpless on the ground.

Dwayne turned his attention back to Angelo. "Now, where were we before these degenerates interrupted us?"

"Everyone will know you sabotaged me and Shawn," Angelo declared. "I'm sick of all your lies. I won't let you disgrace my family name any longer."

Angelo would have to rely on his kickboxing and training from the cherubs.

Dwayne cackled and cracked a devious grin. As the two prepared for a tense standoff, a hand grabbed Angelo's arm with an excruciating twist, and in an instant, he was pinned to the ground. Taken off guard by the unexpected attack, Angelo rolled over and found Luna pinning herself onto him. She was the attacker.

Angelo looked into her crystal blue eyes and became bitter. It was clear whose side she had taken.

"Not even your own teammate trusts you," Dwayne snickered, savouring Angelo's defeat. "Go ahead and finish him, Luna. Break his damn…"

"What's goin' on here?"

Dwayne's celebration was cut short when Akira appeared out of thin air.

As Luna released her grip on Angelo, he dusted himself and observed the confrontation. Dwayne, who was triumphant moments ago, was now seemingly intimidated by the seraph's authoritative presence.

"We were just practicing and doing a little friendly sparing, Seraph," Dwayne offered as an explanation. Shawn and Rex groaned in response. Angelo knew that his explanation was far from the truth.

"Shouldn't you be attending to more important duties, Mr. Council President? Leave now," Akira commanded.

"As you wish, Seraph." Dwayne had no choice but to obey Akira. He immediately walked away, and as he glanced at Angelo, his lips curled in a wicked grin, signalling that this rivalry was far from over.

As Akira helped Rex and Shawn get to their feet, Angelo shook his head at Luna for her attack. "Why the hell did you do that? Can't be on the same team for this operation if you're taking his side."

"I had to stop you before you became a punching bag," Luna explained. "Dwayne's vicious and has way more experience than the three of you combined."

Angelo considered Luna's justification for a moment. *Why had she gone out of her way to protect him? She could've easily left him to be pummelled.* He was confused, started having second thoughts about Luna's intentions and wondered if she was just abiding by the code of a Starlight Saint. Still, he wouldn't let his guard down around her. Saints like her- too dangerous to trust If only he'd had the starlight watch with him to fight. But of course, no. It was only allowed on missions and not on campus.

"I won't tolerate higher saints taking advantage of apprentices. They will be dealt with if I catch them," said Akira.

"I was just goin' easy on him. Didn't even use my full strength. Next time, I'll show him the full power of Leclez 17," said Rex, trying to find an excuse for his loss.

His friend never wanted to admit defeat. It was in his blood to win.

With Akira's dismissal, everyone dispersed, and Angelo returned to his hostel. Not a word was spoken. Angelo had one final task: updating Casey about the next mission. In his room, he activated the VPN and began typing a message.

Going to retrieve Dad's autopsy report...

He sent the message, and it was delivered.

CHAPTER 21

THE BIGGER PICTURE

Angelo's newfound love for flying engulfed him. The sensation of soaring through the air with the Johnny Skyblazer was akin to becoming a real-life superhero. As he gazed down, the city's night lights stretched out like an endless decoration of stars.

Akira, leading the way, glided ahead of him, followed by Luna and Vanya.

Vanya was to accompany the team on their mission as an extra safety net for assistance. The GPS on the touchpad indicated they were in close proximity to their destination, the medical facility. Lowering their altitude, the team began to descend onto the rooftop of St Mary's.

"Tempest, are you there?" Akira's voice sliced through the night.

"Right behind you, Seraph," said Vanya.

Akira issued orders to Vanya, instructing her to initiate the disabling of the security systems and alarms. The CCTV cameras would be dysfunctional by the time they got in.

Vanya pulled out her laptop and began analysing the building's defences.

"Damn it, these security systems are more complex than I imagined. This might take me a while," said Vanya.

There were security guards stationed around the building.

"We'll wait. Once you're done, we'll take out these guards. You'll remain up here while we put 'em to sleep," said Akira.

The minutes ticked by each second feeling like an eternity as they waited for Vanya to work her technological magic.

After a fair bit of time she reported, "Got it. Keep in mind security systems can only be disabled for a short amount of time."

With a nod from Akira, Angelo began his descent down the wall using his star strides. Needing to be as discreet as possible and utilizing all his training in stealth not to alarm the guards scattered around the building.

One of the guards stood close to a nearby bush, seemingly frozen in place.

Angelo activated his starlight watch and projected a staff. If they didn't deal with the guards quietly, the entire operation could be jeopardized. *He couldn't let that happen.* Creeping ever closer, he moved like a shadow, conscious of every step, trying to maintain utter silence. When he was within striking distance, he rose and delivered a precise blow to the guard's head, rendering him unconscious.

The guard mumbled like a drunkard and crumbled to the ground and lay there, helpless and no longer a threat, while Angelo unsummoned his staff. *Angelo couldn't just leave the guard exposed. If any other guard discovered an unconscious body, this would undoubtedly raise the alarm.*

The Shadowbreakers had to take all the guards out silently.

Muscles straining and sweat beading on his forehead, Angelo summoned all his strength to drag the unconscious guard to the safety of the nearby bush, praying that no other guards were watching or approaching. It was a Herculean task, dragging the heavy body, but it had to be done. He hated every moment but finally reached the bush and concealed the guard, taking a moment to catch his breath.

"What's this guy been eating? Dude's a freakin' tow truck," Angelo whispered to himself.

Dragging the guard to the bush exhausted him, and he swore he could drop dead. Grunting and hitting came from the other side. It was Akira and Luna taking the other guards down. Nearby footsteps made Angelo's heart race, and he quickly got into a stealth position behind the bush.

He peeked through the bush, and there was another guard approaching. Angelo quickly projected his staff again to incapacitate the guard like he'd done to the previous one. Smacking the guard from behind, he collapsed to the ground.

"Apple Jack, you there?" asked Akira through the earpiece.

"I'm here, Seraph," he whispered.

"That should be all the guards now. I tranquilized them, and they should be down for the next two hours. Let's hope they don't remember much when they wake up."

"Yes ma'am."

Angelo wished he'd used Akira's method. It proved much more effective than his. *Why didn't I think of that?* he thought.

Akira urged Angelo to start making his way to the rooftop, and he scaled up the wall with urgency.

The team worked to prepare for entry into the facility. The night sky above was partly veiled by clouds, with only sporadic glimpses of the moon illuminating. The distant hum of vehicles travelled through the air and was proof of life in the city.

Vanya distributed three headlights.

Akira secured the rope to a sturdy, anchored pole, ensuring it was ready for their descent. Angelo stood there, his eyes locked onto Akira's, waiting for the signal to proceed.

"Here we go into the abyss," Angelo commented, a tinge of anxiety stirring within him.

"Go on then," said Luna, gesturing for Angelo to slide down the rope.

"Ladies first," Angelo replied playfully.

Luna rolled her eyes and went first instead of causing a hassle. She grabbed the rope and ventured into the darkness.

He followed closely behind, and after that, Akira.

Vanya stayed behind on the rooftop to communicate with the rest of the team.

Luna's headlight was the first to illuminate.

Angelo followed suit, and finally, all three headlights illuminated the area they had infiltrated. The place looked like a regular medical facility, but it was clouded by a wicked atmosphere Angelo couldn't understand. He became tense, his shoulders growing stiff and his heartbeat drumming. He held himself as if he might shrink.. He tried to suppress the vivid imaginations of horror movie scenarios that swirled in his mind. The very thought of a grim figure or a sudden, unexpected scare sent shivers down his spine. Whatever happened, Angelo was determined not to show his fear. *He was the man here, so he was supposed to be the least scared.*

As they ventured deeper into the facility, Luna playfully executed a subtle jump scare on Angelo, taking him by surprise with a sudden, mischievous move.

He accidentally bumped into something as a result of panic.

"Try not to wet your pants," Luna laughed, amused by Angelo's fright.

"For crying out loud," said Angelo, growing irritated. "You made me lose focus. This mission's important, and we can't be screwin' around."

Annoyance quickly replaced his fear. *An environment like this was not the kind of place to play tricks on someone.*

Luna reminded Angelo, "Saints aren't supposed to be scared. You're supposed to control your fear no matter what Mr. Jack Apple Einstein."

As the team proceeded, they couldn't risk taking the lift, so they walked down the stairs until they reached the sixth floor.

The team was finally at the autopsy office, where Angelo's dad's report was supposed to be kept. The medical facility kept people's files for over twenty years. The door was locked, and they couldn't see another way in. They could simply break the door down, but an encrypted keypad flashed red.

"Tempest, I thought you disabled all security systems," said Akira, talking into her earpiece.

"Looks like I missed one. Hol' on, seraph," Vanya responded.

They waited anxiously for a couple of minutes. Akira stood patiently and allowed Vanya to do her tech work.

"Shoot, this door has high-level security encryption. I can't seem to unlock it," said Vanya.

The saints found themselves in a crisis. Time was hastily ticking, tightening its grip on their impending mission. The operation would be compromised if they didn't go through the door and retrieve the autopsy in time. The alarms could reactivate at any moment.

"Stay vigilant. Keep an eye out for any signs of danger," Akira admonished.

Luna whispered into her earpiece, urging Vanya. "Come on, girl, think of something."

"I'm tryna find a weak spot in the system. This should help me bypass the encryption algorithms," said Vanya.

They waited for what felt like hours, idle in such a precarious predicament. Vanya was intensely focused on bypassing the security system of the door to the autopsy. It was hard for Angelo to stay calm with the sense of dreadful urgency weighing on him.

The security guards could've woken up by now and been alerted. There was a limited time frame for how long the other security systems could be disabled, and the alarm would set off at any given second. *If the guards caught them, they would suffer prosecution for attempting to trespass into restricted territory. He was not willing to entertain it. What if there was another way to unlock the door?*

Angelo was willing to suggest that they may have to abandon the mission and try again another time when more prepared. He, however, doubted they'd have another chance to retrieve the autopsy. The facility would know that someone tried to break in, and they'd enhance their security measures to make a break-in impossible.

"Got it!" Vanya exclaimed as the keypad turned green.

The door finally opened, granting them access to the room.

The Shadowbreakers stepped inside, and discovered a space filled with a desk and rows of drawers neatly organized by the alphabet. Each section was labelled with letter ranges, such as A-C, D-F, and so on, which indicated the surnames of the individuals whose files were stored there.

The team fanned out and explored the area, moving between the rows of drawers.

"Bingo," Angelo exclaimed, making sure the others heard him. Finding the section labelled with the letter 'J' he pulled the drawer open and began sifting through the folders, searching for the one marked with 'JA.' His eyes quickly located the folder he was looking for: *Don Leonard Jackson*. Angelo took hold of the folder and carefully removed it.

Akira instructed him to place it on the desk so they could all read its contents together.

This was the sacred autopsy report beckoning the three to discover its secrets. First, it was all the personal profile details, followed by weightier content:

Case Report
Case No: 20XX-0975
Name: Don Leonard Jackson
DOD: 18th May 20XX
City: Los Angeles
Synopsis

THE DECEDENT IS A 51-YEAR-OLD MALE WHO SUFFERED RESPIRATORY ARREST WHILE REHEARSING ON STAGE FOR HIS FINAL CONCERT. ON THE DAY OF HIS DEATH, THE DECEDENT COMPLAINED OF DEHYDRATION AND NOT BEING ABLE TO SLEEP. SEVERAL HOURS LATER, THE DECEDENT STOPPED BREATHING AND COULD NOT BE RESUSCITATED. PARAMEDICS TRANSPORTED HIM TO ST MARY'S HOSPITAL, WHERE HE WAS PRONOUNCED DEAD. THE DECEDENT'S CAUSE OF DEATH WAS A LETHAL INJECTION. IT IS UNKNOWN IF HE WAS COMPLIANT WITH HIS MEDICATIONS. THE DECEDENT SUFFERED FROM OTHER EXTERNAL CONDITIONS BUT HAD NO HISTORY OF HEART PROBLEMS.

Angelo scanned through the synopsis again until he spotted a key detail.

... THE DECEDENT'S CAUSE OF DEATH WAS A LETHAL INJECTION

"Lethal injection? One of the doctors gave Dad a lethal injection on the day he died. Dr. Marshall didn't even work for the hospital as he was Dad's private physician, so it definitely wasn't him," said Angelo, recalling the time when the nurse dragged him away from his dad's room for the doctors to carry out medical procedures.

"That's definitely a big lead. Check this out," said Luna.

They continued going through the report and eventually came across some disturbing pictures - Polaroids. These polaroids showcased what appeared to be Dad's lifeless body stained with blood and depicted from various angles. Photographs of his face displayed hauntingly empty eye sockets with the skin around them bruised and discoloured, suggesting the removal of his eyeballs had been neither clean nor gentle. Then came his chest, the skin pulled back to reveal a gaping emptiness where his heart and lungs should've been. Another shot showed that the edges of the incision were lined with fresh, dark stitches.

The last photograph was perhaps the most unsettling.

Angelo's dad's throat had been surgically opened, revealing the raw interior. A small label on the polaroid indicated Don's vocal cords had been removed. It was as though Dad's body had been purposefully dissected. This was far from an overdose. It was homicide in plain sight. Angelo almost wanted to vomit at the horrendous sight of these photographs.

"What the hell?" Angelo questioned with tears of grief and disgust welling up in his eyes. "Who would do such a thing? I think I'm gonna be sick."

This act of brutality was beyond comprehension, leaving Angelo and the others in shock. It indicated a blood sacrifice.

"I heard Illumiknights remove organs for preservation after someone dies," Akira commented. "An absurd ritual beyond our understanding."

Angelo became sicker to his stomach as he allowed Akira's knowledge to digest. When he thought about the removal of the vocal cords, it started to make sense. He thought perhaps Illumiknights would try to somehow replicate his dad's voice and generate posthumous music for their own gain.

"This confirms what the doctor said. Homicide, but why would the media leave out something like this and not tell the public?" Akira questioned, the severity of the situation sinking in.

Angelo's head was spinning as he struggled to process this horrific revelation. The truth was undeniable. His dad had genuine enemies and had lived in fear for years. He had failed to see the signs, and he didn't know if he could forgive himself for his ignorance.

"We'll take this report with us and file it away for safekeeping. This evidence makes our case stronger," said Akira, holding the autopsy report.

"Don was a sacrifice. The Illuminati had everything set up so his death would look believable," said Luna. "Framing Dr. Marshall, being rushed to the hospital. It was all part of the plan."

Luna's words struck a chord in Angelo.

The Illuminati had orchestrated his dad's death so well it didn't raise suspicion. They made Don look like he was descending into madness, which explained why no one took his words seriously.

Angelo's anger welled up, and he had to fight the urge to destroy everything in the room. He was furious with how the Illuminati got away with such a wicked act. *They had gone way too far.* Slamming his fists abruptly on the table as if to deny the evidence presented in front of him and wept. *This couldn't be what the world had been hiding from him for so many years, but it was.*

"There's more to these things than what the natural eye sees. It's hard to take in but remember that *reality is a gift to the awakened eye*," said Akira. "You'd rather be aware of the deadly vipers that live among you than be ignorant and fall victim to their venomous fangs."

Angelo absorbed Akira's profound words of wisdom. *The reality of his father's murder was brutal and difficult to accept. Yet, it granted him a deeper understanding of his enemies.*

The conversation was cut short by a thud of an object and the slam of a door reverberating from afar.

"What was that?" Angelo asked, his mind and instincts immediately on high alert. The whole team shared his sense of alarm. It was evident that someone else was in the building, and the logical assumption was that it must be one of the guards.

"Guys, you've got company. My computer tells me someone just entered the building, coming up from the ground floor," said Vanya into their earpieces.

They had no time to guess how many guards would be approaching.

The Shadowbreakers had to leave fast.

***

The trio quickly switched off their headlights and put on night vision goggles instead. The gadgets only allowed them to see objects in the dark. A distant door slammed shut, and the echoes filled the space around them, but Angelo could only discern vague shapes in the dimness. He knew they had to retrace their steps to the point of entry, but they maintained silence, relying on their movements to guide them.

No matter who was in the building, they would use their starlight watches to take them down.

The plan was to knock enemies' unconscious but not to kill anyone, as Akira instructed. Angelo's attention darted around, catching sight of a figure clutching a flashlight down the corridor. This person posed an obstacle, blocking their escape route.

The team huddled behind the corridor's bend, concealed from the enemy's view.

Angelo shifted slightly to get a better look at the guard's position, but in his haste, his foot nudged a small metal cart. The cart's wheels squeaked loudly, echoing through the corridor and alerting the guard of their presence.

The figure's voice broke the silence, a deep and gruff man's voice. As he drew nearer, the Shadowbreakers were left with no option but to launch an assault.

"Who's there? Show yourself!" the man demanded.

"Stop right there."

Akira and the rest immediately sprang out of their hiding place and went full speed to attack their assailant.

Luna delivered a flying kick to the man's chest, which sent him plummeting to the floor. He didn't even have time to react.

The man was pinned down, and Akira prepared to incapacitate him with a taser. "Wait! Please stop," the intruder, now at their mercy, pleaded. "I don't want any trouble. I wasn't stealing, I promise."

They removed their night vision goggles and shone a light on the man's face. He looked fairly young, probably in his twenties or thirties.

"Stealing? Why would you be stealing, and what exactly are you here for?" asked Akira inquisitively. They allowed the man to get up and explain himself.

"I work here full time, but in all honesty, I don't like my job here very much," the man began. "My name's Xavier. I've worked here six years but recently discovered this place ain't what it seems."

Xavier's testimony piqued the interest of Angelo and his team. *What did he mean by that?*

They urged him to go on.

"They're hiding something. Lots of autopsies are taken here. The place is enforced with demonic activity. I'm surrounded by cultists. I come here at night to uncover secrets in hopes of becoming a journalist," Xavier explained.

Under normal circumstances, people might have dismissed such claims as the ravings of a madman. But the Shadowbreakers had experienced enough strangeness that night to make Xavier's story believable. Angelo recalled the eerie chill he'd felt when they first entered the facility.

"Tell us more," Angelo prompted.

Xavier continued to elaborate on his unsettling discoveries. He shared how rituals took place in the facility and how many of his colleagues were members of a cult. The basement floor was often used for these ceremonies. As Xavier went into the horrific details, Angelo could only assume this to be the work of Illumiknights. The worker believed that some deceased Hollywood celebrities had been sacrificed within these walls. While these colleagues appeared friendly at work, Xavier was certain they concealed a darker side. Xavier feared that revealing his knowledge could put his life in danger.

Angelo was sympathetic for Xavier, understanding the unease of working in such a sinister environment. People often had hidden depths, and one had to be careful not to trust anybody too closely. Secrets like this should've been exposed out there in the media.

"We came to investigate Don Jackson's autopsy report, and we saw photos. We have reason to believe he was a sacrifice," said Akira.

"Oh, you mean that superstar who passed a couple years ago?" Xavier nodded, still cautious but willing to cooperate. "You're probably right. They don't allow me into the sixth-floor office to read the reports. I'm just the assistant but whatever you've found I bet it's disturbing. As part of my own investigation, I found Don's enemy list of his three biggest enemies, who he claimed would come after him. I got it from a biographer, and it might be able to help you." He gave the team a file.

Angelo and the team examined the file. The enemy list contained the following names:

Yato Yukimura
Tom Chandler
Zayn Hopkins

Angelo's eyes widened in shock. "So, one of these three must have killed the dietitian to avoid exposure. One of them probably snuck into the hospital and gave the lethal injection too."

Angelo recognized Yato Yukimura as his dad's former manager, Tom Chandler as Dwayne's father and the former prosecutor, and Zayn Hopkins as a well-known magician. They could've all had a connection to the Illuminati, but the main objective was to find out who delivered the killing blow to the pop star. The team exchanged glances. This would be the next lead.

Xavier dug into his kit bag and pulled out a notebook. "I journal down info, take notes and record every detail. My gut tells me this medical facility is secretly owned by a cult but I don't know who exactly. I hope to report this to a media outlet and get this story on the news once I've got enough evidence about this place."

It was an intriguing yet shocking revelation to hear. Xavier's commitment to collecting evidence about a sinister organization astounded the saints.

"What happens if you get caught?" asked Angelo.

"They'll definitely kill me," Xavier stated with no sign of doubt. "I've seen some of my colleagues disappear without trace. Every case that turned up reported that they died of an accident or disease, but my intuition now says otherwise."

Xavier shivered, evidently dreading the possibility of being found out. This medical facility was far from ordinary, hosting dark secrets and enshrouded in wickedness.

Akira stepped forward. "We're actually an agency ourselves. We'd be willing to recruit you into our society if you left your job."

"We can protect you. Train you to become like us. You could help us in our fight," Akira continued, putting her hand on his shoulder.

Xavier shook his head, declining the offer. "I'm better off staying here. I can uncover more secrets that way and expose this facility for what it is."

Akira's nod signalled his agreement.

The Saints had not only gathered more evidence of the disturbing ongoings in the facility and Don's true cause of death but also received help from an unexpected source.

A loud siren suddenly burst into the air, and a red light flashed repeatedly throughout the building. The team wasted no time. The alarm had reactivated, and it was time to escape.

"Leave now! Before the authorities come," Xavier urged the saints. Pulling out his employee ID card, he swiped it across the door's keypad, granting the team the opportunity to escape.

"Let's move," Akira declared. The saints dashed through the building, with Xavier leading the way. They'd gathered the lead they needed for their next mission as the risk of being discovered threatened to engulf them with every passing second.

CHAPTER 22

A HAPPY ENDING

Angelo spent the night tossing and turning in bed after the unsettling visit to the medical facility to retrieve his dad's autopsy report. The chilling truth of Dad being a sacrifice lingering in his mind throughout the day. The media, perceived as the most trusted source by the public, were selling lies all this time.

Just as he'd thought. He now knew the following three suspects to investigate. Yato Yukimura, Tom Chandler, and Zayn Hopkins would be found out one way or another.

Three of Dad's biggest enemies.

Angelo, consumed by the desire to bring justice, sent a text message to Casey and informed him about the autopsy photos, which also horrified Casey.

Dad was sacrificed. HURRY AND FIND THE CULPRIT BEFORE IT'S TOO LATE, Casey had replied.

After returning from dinner, Angelo sensed something amiss. He couldn't quite put his finger on it at first but a nagging sensation tugged at him. He reached into his pocket, his heart skipping a beat when he found it empty. He inspected his desk, rifling through the stack of papers, and realised his poem for Akira wasn't there. Angelo searching through the drawers and cupboards had sweat beaded on his forehead, but the poem was nowhere to be found.

A growing worry stirred within him. "Dammit, I thought I left it on my desk."

Angelo quickly plunged into his laundry basket, rummaging through the pockets of his worn trousers and shorts. Clothes flew, cluttering the room. *It had to be somewhere.* Yet he still had no success finding his sacred rap song. Worry grew into panic and frustration. He couldn't afford to lose the piece that tied Akira to his heart. *Perhaps he'd misplaced it.*

As he pondered on all the possible locations of the poem, Angelo's mind went to the computer lab where he'd been earlier. Could it have fallen out of his pocket there? Clinging to the slim hope, Angelo hurriedly dashed out, hoping no one had touched or disposed of it.

As he approached the computer lab, the murmur of voices grew louder. Peeking through the window, there was a group of figures standing in a circle together. Among them, he instantly recognised Akira, along with Titus, Nigel and other seraphs. They were gathered for an important meeting that he wouldn't dare to interrupt.

Angelo's frustration grew as he was desperate to find his poem, but the meeting proved to be an obstacle. With a resigned sigh, Angelo decided he could always come back later. Yet just as he was about to turn away, a snippet of the conversation captured his interest.

"...that autopsy report proves why the Illuminati are always two steps ahead of us," said one of the seraphs. "Listen to this."

Intrigued, Angelo hesitated, then crouched down against the wall, his full attention drawn to the discussion about the previous mission.

The tuning of a radio resonated with a news report. "Late pop icon Don Jackson's autopsy report has reportedly gone missing from St Mary's medical facility. Persons reported a break-in, but the culprits are still to be found. A deceased staff member Xavier Philman who was suspected of aiding the theft reportedly jumped from the seventh-floor balcony in an act of suicide before more investigations could be done."

Angelo's heart dropped at the mention of Xavier's fate. Suicide seemed farfetched unless Xavier was desperate to protect his secret. However, now that Angelo knew what Illumiknights were capable of, he could assume that the death had been no coincidence - a homicide staged as a suicide to manipulate the media.

Guilt brewed from within. *Was it his and his team's fault that Xavier got killed?* They had put the man's life at risk on that mission, but then again, Xavier had declined Akira's offer to join the Starlight Saints. *Xavier had chosen his own fate.*

"The Illumiknights were so crafty in covering up Don's death and deceiving the public," said Akira. "If they managed to keep this autopsy info hidden for five years, imagine what else they've got up their sleeve?"

"Remember that eight-year chart plan our saints discovered decades ago? We haven't seen one thing through the news media that did not happen according to that chart," Titus mentioned. "It's like prophecy. They're always on schedule. They own some of the biggest corporations in the world, controlling the masses through music."

"Hate to say it, but the Illuminati's strategies are way beyond us. The only reason why we've probably managed to stop some of their plans is because they want us to play their game, thinking we've won only to drain and catch us by surprise," explained one of the seraphs. "If we don't solve Don's case soon, then society as we know it is damned."

Angelo grew more anxious as he comprehended these terrifying revelations. He didn't realise just how meticulous his enemies were until now. He continued to eavesdrop with intrigue, hungry for more revelation.

"Seraph Owen, with Don's connection to the Illuminati, do you really think we can trust his son Angelo?" said Nigel.

Angelo's heart froze as Nigel made him the conversation's subject. Nigel continued. "Recruiting him was a risk. He might turn on us when he gets the chance. Teaching him our ways so he could use them against us. I say we get rid of the boy now and reevaluate this case."

"Nigel, stop!" Akira interjected. "We're not getting rid of Angelo. That boy has the Starlight Saint spirit, and he's on our side. I believe he wants to destroy our enemy just as much as we do. I have faith in him."

A wave of gladness washed over Angelo as Akira leapt to his defence. Dread coiled in Angelo's stomach as he couldn't bear to imagine the consequences if the Starlight Saints deemed him unworthy of trust. *Facing their judgement? Being labelled a traitor?* This sent shivers down his spine and his hands began to tremble. Part of Angelo still struggled to believe that his father could've had any involvement with the Illuminati, but the mounting evidence threatened to shatter his illusions.

"Here's what I suggest," a seraph began.

Heavy footsteps sounded from behind, jolting Angelo into high alert. Someone was approaching, likely another seraph. Facing a crucial decision: stay hidden and risk getting caught or escape and potentially miss out on more vital pieces of information from the meeting. The footsteps drew closer, amplifying the pressure. If he got caught, he could only imagine the punishment the seraphs would dish out for eavesdropping uninvited.

Angelo quickly abandoned his hiding spot against the wall, darting behind a nearby pillar. With heart pounding, he made a split-second decision and dashed away from the computer lab before risking detection. He didn't spare a second glance as he navigated through the corridor, focusing solely on escaping unseen.

As Angelo pushed through a door, relief flooded him. He found himself in his treasured location - the sound room.

***

The sound room had become a peaceful sanctuary of refuge, and Angelo became somewhat attached to the facility with each visit. Though Hugh's cautionary words about staying in for too long echoed in his mind, he continued, finding himself unable to resist the allure of the facility. When life's tribulations became too much, the simple thing to do was put the headphones on and zone out.

"Who needs drugs when you can get high off music?" Angelo mused to himself.

Angelo eased into the chair and placed a pair of headphones on his ears. He browsed the tablet and adjusted the frequency knob to a level that would resonate with his soul.

Soon, the music began playing, and Angelo surrendered to its embrace, shutting his eyes. Laying back, he began to drift off to another dimension. As the positive healing frequencies pulsed through him, Angelo was convinced that this was the most outstanding work the Starlight Saints had ever done. He couldn't get enough of it.

He found himself floating in outer space, surrounded by beautiful stars and patterns that resembled the Milky Way. The sight was mesmerising enough, but as the tempo and melody of the music changed, the scenery transitioned into something more spectacular. Angelo found himself in a beautiful mystical land flowing with rivers of gold and crystal.

An epiphany hit Angelo at that moment. What he was seeing reflected the mood of the music. So, however the music sounded, his mind would try to replicate that sound visually. *Fascinating! Could this be any more amazing?* The sky glittered with gold that screamed heaven. There were maple and acacia trees of blue scattered around the area, too. An unexpected deer came running by and stopped to stare at Angelo. This was different from any deer Angelo had seen before. The mammal was coated in various colours that resembled a rainbow pattern. Whatever these light-positive frequencies were doing, Angelo loved it. The deer soon ran off and left Angelo in awe. He kept walking across this mysterious land, hoping to discover more extraordinary sights.

Angelo soon came across a waterfall and a lake. The water was nothing but glimmering gold, and he felt the lake beckoning him to jump in. A yellow-furred otter covered with intricate purple spots suddenly emerged from the depths of the water. As soon as its eyes locked with Angelo's, it shook off the wetness with a graceful twist. The peculiar otter sprung a pair of bird wings, began to flutter, and eventually flew away, defying nature's expectations. Angelo glanced up as the flying mammal soared through the sky, which had now transitioned from gold to light pink.

After another surreal encounter, he removed his shirt and trousers, leaving only his trunks. Without a second thought, Angelo did a cannonball dive into the water and swam like there was no tomorrow. It was as if all his troubles were washed away by the cleansing of the gold lake. Wanting to forget about everything back in the outside world and stay here forever.

Why go back to that miserable existence when he could just remain here in paradise?

Angelo kept floating in the golden lake until something suddenly grabbed his leg from underneath. His heart raced. He screamed. He tried to resist, but the grip was too strong. Angelo plunged deep into the water, his lungs starving for air, and emerged back to the surface. A giggle came from his unexpected attacker while he caught his breath.

"Gotcha!"

Akira wore a smooth-looking swimsuit, her hair beautifully soaked in the wetness, dripping gracefully. Her skin was radiant, almost like bronze, leaving Angelo utterly captivated. She had a wonderful glow that complemented her features. Time seemed to slow down as Angelo was stunned by Akira's divine beauty.

"Seraph? What are you doing here?" asked Angelo, almost too stunned to speak.

"I came here to find you, silly," said Akira with a playful grin.

Was he in trouble? Was it possible to access other people's dreams in the sound room? Angelo was learning something new every day.

Akira stepped out of the water, put a sundress over her swimsuit, and signalled for Angelo to follow her. After Angelo got dressed, the two strolled across a field of purple grass. The effects of the music still had hold of him.

They came to a grand fountain flowing with pink water in the middle of the field, which was another sight to marvel at. Angelo knew he was high on music frequencies and was convinced he'd reached peak highness.

"There's something I gotta tell you, Angelo," said Akira.

"What is it?" Angelo's heart began to race, and he could feel a surge of emotions rushing through his veins. *This world couldn't get any weirder.* The sky had noticeably transitioned to rich purple as he looked up, and the sun hung low on the horizon.

"When two stars collide," Akira began, staring into Angelo's eyes, creating an intense connection, "no shadows block the sun."

Angelo found himself momentarily stunned into awkward silence and confusion. He had no idea what Akira had just said.

"What? What do you mean by that? I…"

Akira gently pressed a finger to Angelo's lips, silencing him. Her tone became soft while her words poured out as if coated with sweet honey. "As your seraph, I order you to kiss me."

Angelo's eyes widened, his mind grappling with the unexpected command. "What?" He couldn't wrap his head around it.

There was no way the seraph had just asked him to lock lips. It didn't add up, but his heart compelled him to do it. He hadn't even shown her the poem yet, *so how would she know about his feelings for her? This was what he wanted, though, wasn't it?* A chance with his love, his all-time celebrity crush.

However, he remembered that romantic relations between a seraph and an apprentice were not acceptable by the standards of the Starlight Saints. Luna's words echoed in his mind: *"You're sixteen, and she's a grown woman."*

Angelo felt a strong pull tugging at him as he contemplated such a critical decision. Akira seemed okay with it, so why wouldn't Angelo? There was no reason to hold back, no reason at all. An opportunity like this- he couldn't just let it slip away.. He felt Akira's alluring lips beckoning him the longer he contemplated. *"Time waits for no one,"* as his dad always used to say.

"Okay, let's do it." Angelo couldn't hide his excitement. It was impossible. He knew this was what he desired.

Akira gracefully leaned toward him, and Angelo reciprocated, his heart burning with anticipation. Their lips were inches away from touching, on the brink of an intense bond. *This was it.* The moment Angelo had been waiting for. *His dream of dating and kissing his star idol would finally come true. This was the perfect date anyone could ask for.* Just as their lips were about to meet,

The music finally came to an end.

Angelo found himself back in the sound room and realised his session was over. One inch away from a kiss, and it was cut short...

"No, no, no! I didn't get to kiss her," Angelo cried to himself. "I need to go back."

Disappointment washed over him. The sense of longing for what could've been lingered in his mind. Angelo tapped the tablet uncontrollably, trying to get another listening session and fulfil his wish, but deep down, he knew it was just a fantasy. A projection of his desires.

"Everything okay, dude?"

Angelo looked up and another saint was standing over him. This boy displayed a clean, spiky haircut. About to die from embarrassment, he quickly composed himself as if nothing happened.

How could he let himself be so emotionally vulnerable in front of others? Considering how most saints were against him, the boy would probably spread the word about this to the other saints.

"I'm fine. Just need another session," said Angelo, putting his headphones back on.

The boy grabbed his arm and halted him abruptly.

"Dude, no. They said one session a day. Too much exposure to this will kill you. Don't you listen to instructions?" he emphasised. "We can't have anyone dying in here. Zack signing out."

The boy headed towards the exit, shutting the door behind him. *Zack was right.* The cherubs did say that too much exposure to frequencies could be fatal. Angelo knew better than to attempt another round. He was desperate to finish off his dream and fulfil his kiss with Akira.

Despite his conflicting emotions, Angelo needed to focus on the present and the mission at hand. He couldn't let his feelings for Akira consume him. With determination, he pushed away his disappointment and regained his focus. His bond with Akira was built on friendship, admiration, respect, and shared goals of the Starlight Saints. Nothing more than that. But a small, stubborn part of him still held onto the fantasy of winning Akira's heart.

Angelo decided to retreat to his hostel and call it a night. Maybe the right opportunity would eventually present itself. He still needed to find his missing poem and showcase it to Akira. A part of Angelo sought for something beyond friendship with Akira, *but would that ever be possible?* He would only find out by confessing the truth to her. He was going to do it. *It was just a matter of when.*

CHAPTER 23

FAMILY REUNION

The Shadowbreakers stood at the crossroads of their investigation. *Were they getting closer to the truth or veering off course?* Dr. Cory Marshall had been cast as the fall guy, the autopsy report revealed a homicide, and Xavier, the late aspiring journalist, had disclosed Dad's enemy list. The next target in the conspiracy web was Don's former manager, Yato Yukimura. The one who Angelo's dad had fired a couple of years ago because of alerting suspicions. The saints had every right to suspect that he was the culprit. If anyone had a grudge against Angelo's father, it was him.

The Shadowbreakers assembled in the lab for a briefing.

"Yato Yukimura got fired a couple years back, and now he manages this rapper named Dean Rozay under Capital Records," Akira typed out, reading every piece of information she could find. "He's out in San Francisco. We gotta track him down and grill him."

Angelo, Rex, Shawn, Vanya, and Luna were all grouped together, absorbing the details of the upcoming mission. There was a lingering awkwardness in Akira's presence since Angelo's dream in the sound room. His closeness to kissing the seraph in the dream still haunted his memory. He wouldn't dare mention it to Akira or anyone for that matter. Some things were better left unsaid.

"Dean Rozay's got his last show in San Francisco tomorrow night. His manager goes with him to everyone. Yato's bound to be there," said Akira.

"So, are we all goin' this time?" asked Shawn.

"Absolutely. This mission needs all of us. We'll have other saints posted outside the venue for backup. We're outta here tomorrow," Akira explained.

"Yes! Finally!" Shawn punched the air with excitement, clearly unable to contain it.

Angelo cracked a smile, glad that his friend would finally be part of the investigation and team.

The path to Yato's location was strewn with challenges, and the saints needed to approach the task with caution, recognising the potential risks involved of which death loomed for them all.

"The plan is straightforward. We sneak into the arena while the concert is happening, go backstage then boom. We capture Yato." Akira concluded the group meeting once all the details were ironed out.

***

The lively atmosphere of San Francisco greeted the team with warmth, partly cloudy skies adding to the city's charm as the sun was sinking below the horizon. Angelo's memories of childhood visits to the town resurfaced moments shared with his father and Casey. Recollections of vacations while his dad performed shows intertwined with the city's vibrant energy. The city and its people were more vibrant than the residents of Rockingston.

The team maintained a composed and vigilant demeanour to avoid drawing attention to themselves as they strolled through the city.

"My mom used to take me out a lot when I lived here as a kid," said Vanya, her face lit up with a nostalgic smile.

"My mom's paralysed," Rex revealed. "Can't take me anywhere 'cause of an accident." The weight of Rex's words created a solemn gloom, silencing the team and the lively atmosphere.

Angelo couldn't help but empathise with his friend. "I've never had a mom. It's always been me, my dad and aunt," Angelo shared, with a sense of vulnerability. "I wish I knew who my real mom was."

"You've got us," Shawn reassured, offering some words of comfort to fill the void.

The saints reached a bustling junction. The skyline bristled with high-rise buildings while cable cars clanked in the distance, cutting through the traffic. They were close to the heart of the Financial District. They took a right turn, following the signs to Elite Stadium, the venue for the concert. As they approached, the distant cheers from the crowd inside confirmed that the concert was already in full swing.

"Looks packed in there," Shawn remarked.

Elite Stadium was heavily guarded, with security personnel strategically placed like military sentinels. To navigate their way in, the saints would need to rely on their charisma and persuasive abilities to interact with event organisers, staff, and fans—whatever way would work. Direct confrontation was to be avoided if possible. The Shadowbreakers would go in disguised as VIP guests.

Vanya had prepared fake tickets for everyone and handed them out.

"It's showtime," Akira announced.

Each team member presented their tickets as they approached the entrance, where vigilant guards stood. As they handed the tickets for scanning, one of the security guards raised an eyebrow.

"These tickets don't seem valid. You VIP guests?" the guard inquired; his voice gruff.

Angelo became enveloped with anxiety. *Had the guard found them out?* If he didn't allow them through, the saints would have to force their way in. Judging by the heavy presence of security, attempting to fight all the guards off was too risky.

Luna responded with an innocent smile that was hard to resist. "Yep, we sure are. Got special tickets 'cause we're Dean Rozay's biggest fans."

The security guard hesitated for a moment, evidently charmed by Luna's smile. "Well, I ain't gonna keep you from witnessing musical greatness. Head on through that door," said the security guard, pointing in the given direction.

The saints entered the venue, navigating the path to the backstage area where Yato Yukimura, the manager, was expected to be. The muffled bass of the music vibrated through the walls, signifying the escalating of the lively show. A door labelled 'Yato Yukimura' beckoned them.

With a twist of the door lever handle, they entered. Disarray greeted them - papers scattered and glasses broken. Remnants of a disturbance were evident throughout the space.

"What the hell happened here? Looks like a fight took place," Akira observed.

They investigated the manager's jumbled room further. There was a broken glass and a spilt cocktail. Some spots of fresh blood were stained on a mirror. *Had Yato been killed or kidnapped?* Angelo wondered *who could've done this and why.*

Drawn to a jacket discarded on the floor, Angelo uncovered an unusual emblem. The jacket had the number 203 imprinted, and Angelo's eyes widened when he spotted a disturbing graphic he instantly recognised. The jacket had a picture of his father emblazoned on it, with two dragons surrounding it. The discovery startled him.

"Guys, I found something!" said Angelo, presenting the jacket to the rest of the team. "It says 203. I think that means 203 Dragons but...why does it have a picture of my dad?" He gave Rex, Shawn and the rest disturbed glances.

Confusion rippled through the room.

Rex looked the most disturbed out of everyone. A shadow from his past was resurfacing. "The Dragons are back," his tone becoming icy cold as if the mention of dragons activated a curse. "I don't even know how they could possibly have Don's face on their coats? What if they were somehow involved in your dad's murder?"

The thought of his father's face on the jackets of ruthless gang members was surreal and unsettling. Recalling the time Rex was tasked to lead him to their hideout, Angelo realised the Dragons must have been working with the Illumiknights to take him and his father out.

"Who exactly are these Dragons?" asked Luna, out of the loop with Rex's conflicted history. "I'm a little lost here."

"My old gang from Rockingston. Looks like they've expanded or moved here," said Rex. Rex and Angelo shared the same feeling of disturbance. It was as if the demons who'd tormented Rex had come to strike again.

Worry filled the air as the team grappled with the implications.

Akira, taking charge, directed Vanya to use her tech glasses to trace Yato's potential whereabouts. The group became charged with urgency as Vanya, collecting a DNA sample from an abandoned cocktail and blood, initiated the process.

A trail led them outside toward the rear of the stadium, unravelling a mystery that beckoned them toward an ominous warehouse. Scuffles and distant sounds of conflict echoed, heightening the team's senses to stay alert. As they approached the warehouse, locked entrances barred their way, leaving them no way to enter.

The Shadowbreakers, acting as an entourage, trod carefully, acutely aware that something intense was occurring within the walls of the warehouse.

Vanya suggested the team get through the windows using their star strides.

Angelo pressed himself against the wall, on high alert. Muffled screams and shouts penetrated the stillness from within the building. The clamour hinted at a commotion unfolding.

***

Through the narrow window, the Shadowbreakers navigated their way into the warehouse, crawling over a precarious high scaffolding. Angelo, the last to enter, gasped at the sight before him. A man, bound to a chair, displayed the grim aftermath of a severe beating—bruises painted across his face like a grotesque masterpiece. *It had to be Yato, the captive manager they were here to interrogate.* The muffled sounds of agony emanated from him.

Approaching footsteps diverted their attention. A menacing figure adorned with a gold tooth that glinted in the light swaggered toward Yato.

"You ready for another round, son?" The man, revelling in the manager's torment, ripped the gag from Yato's mouth, exposing the raw vulnerability etched on his face.

"Alright, listen up. When Don's dietitian got shot, the papers revealed something that could be of value to us. So cut the cheese with the excuses, see? You're gonna help us find what we're lookin' for one way or another."

The man went on. "Ever since Don left us, there's been more conspiracies flying around than pigeons on Michigan Ave. Word on the street is you got a hard drive with a thousand unreleased songs stashed away as Don's manager. Those songs can make us millions. Our pop star lord would want us to have them and continue his legacy. So, spill it, where's the drive?"

Angelo was taken aback by how the gang member referred to his father as their pop star lord. *His father would never want a gang of savages to carry his legacy,* he thought. He was disgusted.

Yato, clearly battered and pleading, denied having the hard drive of unreleased songs. The gold-toothed man, unrelenting, laughed sadistically, degrading the helpless manager by spitting on his face like a beast.

"I don't have it anymore. I'm no longer Don's manager." Yato pleaded in desperation.

Gold Tooth scoffed at the plea, not believing a word Yato was saying. He signalled his henchmen to escalate the torture.

One short-haired lady wielded a crowbar, another man threw punches, and Yato's cries for mercy echoed in the cold room.

"See, we were hopin' for some cooperation but since you won't budge, I think it's time we put you out of your misery," Gold Tooth sneered. "We will find that hard drive."

Angelo, witnessing the impending tragedy, had the urge to turn away but couldn't tear his eyes from the gruesome display of violence.

"What do we do?" he whispered. *They could either intervene or leave the manager to his fate.*

"We gotta save him," Akira declared. "Remember, he might know something that will help our case."

With a nod from Akira, Rex silently descended, launching a surprise attack on the lady with the crowbar. The room erupted into chaos as the rest of the team swiftly followed, ready to confront the gang before them.

"What the-? Who the hell are you people?" growled one of the gang members.

The saints maintained a stoic silence, their presence unwavering. Gold Tooth halted his actions, fixing his gaze on Rex.

"No way! Is that really Leclez 17? I never thought I'd see you again," said Gold Tooth with a crooked smile.

"You're supposed to be behind bars, Fox. How are you walking free?" Rex retorted.

"Let's just say we got a lucky bail. You should be kissin' the bricks to see your own fam again," sneered Fox. "We took you in, treated you like blood and you crapped all over it, turning against us. You oughtta be ashamed of yourself."

The anger emanating from the 203 Dragons intensified at the sight of Rex. They were evidently repulsed by his presence. They were the same individuals who tasked him with eliminating Angelo.

Angelo positioned himself beside Rex, alert and ready to activate his starlight watch.

"You guys ain't my family. I'm nothing like you. I've found a better one," Rex asserted.

"Oh yeah? Why don't you spill the beans about that time you almost killed your own ma? You drove a car right into her, and now she can't walk because of you," Fox spat. "Real nice, huh?"

Angelo's disbelief clawed at him, attempting to reject the unsettling claims about Rex.

"It's why your folks ditched you. You're a cold-blooded Dragon just like us. It's in your blood," Fox continued, revelling in the discomfort that settled upon the team.

The collective gaze of the Shadowbreakers turned towards Rex, his head bowed in shame.

"Leclez, is that true?" Shawn's question cut through the silence.

Rex nodded, a silent admission of guilt. "I was just a little kid, eight years old maybe. Snagged my dad's keys and tried to drive, but I ended up hitting my mom by accident. I wasn't tryna to kill her."

Fox, seizing the vulnerability, pointed a finger at Angelo. "Your assignment was to lure Angelo Jackson to us so he could take his father's place among the Dragons, but you failed," Fox declared, his words coated with bitterness.

Angelo became startled by Fox's words. "What?" he breathed, his voice barely above a whisper.

Chapter 24

Unknown Legacy

A wave of shock rippled through the whole team. Angelo caught unable to comprehend what Fox had just said. There was no way Angelo's father could've been a member of the 203 Dragons. Standing before the people who were somehow involved in Dad's death made his blood boil.

"Keep my dad's name out your mouths and get his face off your dumb jackets! What do you mean I was supposed to take his place?" Angelo demanded. "Are you the scumbags responsible for my father's death? You used Leclez as bait so you could kill me next, didn't you?."

"What? Oh, no no. He never told you?" said Fox, his whole tone changing and becoming sincere. "Your dad was a saviour to us. We never intended to kill you but for you to join us as another Jackson."

Angelo remained vigilant, not buying anything Fox had to say. Fox went on to explain further. "Don visited the Dragon suburbs in Chicago and other cities during his prime. He launched a campaign to end gang violence by donating money to help our community. Performed fundraising concerts in the ghettos. Don had even helped my family when we were desperate."

According to Fox's story, Don's campaign successfully brought peace, as the gang stopped terrorising cities for several years, and crime rates dropped significantly.

"We honoured your father with his very own Dragon jacket for all the support he'd given us," Fox mentioned as he grew sombre. "Everyone else saw us as criminals who deserved to suffer but not Don. No one else besides him looked our way when we were in need. Not even our own corrupt government. Don, bless his heart, secretly became our leader. Instead of tearing things down he urged us to build somethin' better for ourselves and the neighbourhood."

Yet, when Don died, the 203 Dragons were heavily devastated by the void he'd left. Because of their grief, they went back to their gang violence and became divided, breaking the peace the pop icon had brought. With their beloved role model gone, who else would they turn to?

"You honestly expect me to believe that?" Angelo questioned, infuriated. "That's the biggest load of BS I've ever heard. If that were true everyone else would've known about it."

Fox, acknowledging Angelo's scepticism, went on to explain that the story of Don's heroic efforts was never covered by the media. All the press ever presented were negative statements about the pop star, like the child trafficking allegations, but never anything that would make Angelo's father look good in the eyes of the public.

Angelo now saw the pattern.

Fox even presented a locket, which contained a group picture of Don and the 203 Dragons, for further proof. *This gang member was telling the truth after all.* Angelo held the locket in his hand. *Don really was their hero.*

"I believe you now," his heart moved and eyes watering. "But going back to committing crimes while trying to find a hard drive isn't the way to honour my father's legacy. He'd be ashamed of you all."

"Then join us. Be the leader your father was and bring peace again," Fox offered. "It don't matter if you're just a kid. These people, they'll follow your every word, simply 'cause you're a Jackson. It's chaos, and only you can put things back in order."

Angelo found himself on the brink of making a critical decision. His father's death had not only affected him and his family but also wider communities.

"Don't do it, Apple Jack," said Akira.

Angelo had a chance to restore the peace his father had worked so hard to establish by becoming a 203 Dragon member, but he was tied by his loyalty to the Starlight Saints and would likely break their trust if he accepted Fox's offer. *Was it possible for him to be both a Starlight Saint and a Dragon? No, two conflicting agendas wouldn't work.*

Yet if Angelo declined the offer to join, he and his team would have to fight the dozens of brutal gang members. Despite the Dragon's misled intentions to carry his father's legacy, Angelo was a Starlight Saint at heart, and he would never associate with a group that went against his beliefs.

"I won't join your gang," Angelo declared. "My dad did everything he could to bring unity and you guys ruined it. If you can't handle yourselves with my father gone then what good will I do? I won't let you ruin his legacy with your crimes. You belong behind bars."

Fox's eyes widened with shock as if he'd been betrayed. "Have it your way."

Rex summoned a katana from his starlight watch, charging toward Fox, attempting to slice him, but he dodged the blade. The clash between the former gang members erupted into a chaotic brawl, weapons drawn and swung with deadly intent.

Angelo, summoning a staff from his own starlight watch, faced an opponent wielding a chain with a blade attached. Struggling to dodge the chain's lethal swings, He found himself disarmed as the chain skilfully disentangled the staff from his grip.

Now defenceless, Angelo summoned a stun gun in a desperate attempt to fend off the relentless attacks. However, his shots proved ineffective against the agile assailant.

Cornered and facing a potential defeat, Angelo's back met a shelf, causing the items to tremble as if on the verge of falling. With the assailant poised to strike, a sudden jolt of shock ran through him, and he collapsed to the ground. Luna, wielding her own stun gun, had intervened just in time, saving Angelo from imminent danger.

"That was close. Thanks," Angelo expressed his gratitude.

"Don't mention it," said Luna as she continued her struggle against the other gang members.

When he looked around, Rex was still brawling with Fox while Akira, Shawn, and Vanya were dealing with the other gang members. Soon, most of them were lying on the floor. These gang members could fight, but it was nothing the saints were not capable of handling. Fox threw Rex to the side, broke off and dashed to the manager. He now had Yato in front of him and a knife by the poor manager's neck.

"I pity you people. How dare y'all tell us we belong in jail? Don loved us," sneered Fox, the knife's edge threatening Yato's flesh.

Tension encircled the room like a coiled dragon.

"Come one more step closer, and I off this guy," Fox taunted, his voice dripping with malice. Angelo felt paralysed, uncertain of the best course of action. His gaze sought guidance from Akira. Yato held vital information crucial to their mission.

"Let him go," Akira commanded, her tone unwavering. Fox scoffed at her demand.

"Or what, doll? How 'bout I take you on a date in exchange for your friend? We can grab some Italian bites, hmm," Fox teased, his smile radiating menacingly. Yato, muffled and pleading, faced imminent danger.

Angelo couldn't bear Fox's audacity, feeling an unexpected surge of defensiveness towards Akira.

"I won't ask again. I'm giving you one chance. How about we make a deal?" Akira proposed, stepping closer to Fox, attempting to navigate the dangerous waters with her charm.

Angelo grew uneasy.

Shawn's absence in the heat of the moment, though he dismissed the concern, prioritising Yato's peril.

"I saw how you decimated my goons. What are you? Some kinda secret agents? How's about you ditch whoever you're working for and join my gang. We could be runnin' the cities together?" Fox suggested.

"I guess we could make that work. You ain't half bad looking, so yeah, I'm in," Akira played along.

Angelo remained conflicted between watching Akira play a dangerous game and stepping in to take Fox out himself. The mission's success hinged on Yato's survival, forcing Angelo to suppress his emotions and let Akira do her thing.

Just as Akira neared Fox, a sudden thud echoed.

Fox released his grip on Yato collapsing to the floor.

Shawn, wielding his staff, stood behind the fallen Dragon. He had put Fox to sleep before Angelo could endure any more torture of watching Akira flirt with the gang member. Distraction was the plan Angelo realised. *Good thinking,* he thought.

The apparent boss wallowed and lay helpless on the floor.

Rex held a blade over Fox's body, ready to finish the job, the blood thirst in his eyes.

"Rex, stop. Killing him will make you just like them. You're different." Angelo placed his hand on Rex's arm and gently lowered it. He finally cooled down and composed himself, no longer blinded by rage.

Yato fell on his knees as if praying. "You saved me! I don't know how to repay you, but I must say thanks. They kidnapped me from my room backstage tonight. I thought I was a goner for…"

"Why'd the 203 kidnap you? They mentioned something about a drive," said Angelo, getting straight to the point.

"They wanted me to give them unreleased material from one of my former clients, Don. No way in hell was I gonna give it up," Yato explained. "That drive is invaluable."

One would most likely be sympathetic towards Yato, but Angelo wasn't willing to show such a man sympathy, especially since he could be one of the co-conspirators.

"You better hand over the drive then. I won't let you profit off my dad's music," Angelo declared.

"We have reason to believe you were involved in Don Jackson's death," said Akira.

The statement caught Yato by surprise. He didn't expect such a topic to be brought up by a bunch of people who'd just rescued him from certain death.

"Don's son? Are you detectives?" He tried to move and get up with all his might, but it was futile.

"We know you have something to do with Don's death. He had you on his enemy list," said Vanya.

"I have no idea what you're talking about. You're not getting nothing out of me. Go back to where you came from, you detective wannabes." Yato gave a look of bitterness and defiance.

"We could tie you up and leave you here with these guys if that's what you want, but trust me when I tell ya, they ain't gonna be very happy when they wake up," said Rex. "Jail's the only place for them."

Yato looked at the unconscious bodies scattered around and shivered out of fear. Things wouldn't end well for him if these criminals still found him here.

"No, please! Don't leave me here with these lunatics! I'll do whatever you want, honest! I swear on my great monk grandpa, I will!" Yato begged.

Now, the saints had Yato at their mercy.

Shawn crept up behind him and pulled him up with the staff positioned against his throat.

"Tell us what happened, tell us who killed Don?" Angelo demanded, bitter.

Yato panicked even more. "Look, I don't know who killed him, but I know people were scheming and conspiring to see him fall. It wasn't exactly a secret."

"Go on..."

"Back when I was Don's manager, Tom Chandler offered me a deal that would pay me good money if I agreed to leak information and, well, kinda helped him take Don down.. Big mistake on my part. I betrayed Don and worked with shady people. I deeply regret it now. I should've stuck by Don when I had the chance," Yato explained.

"So, you backstabbed my father after all he'd done for you, helped your family, showed you kindness? You took that all for granted," said Angelo, infuriated. "You're the biggest scumbag out here."

He was right. The manager, who was with Dad for years, showed his true colours. It proved that one can never fully trust someone, no matter how close they are.

"So, let's get this straight. You were involved in the killing of Don?" asked Shawn.

"Yes, I was in on some of it, but I didn't do much at all, really. Tom Chandler had a bigger role in this. He pulled the strings and was most likely the one who delivered the final blow. He swore to take down the star when he failed to convict Don as prosecutor in trial," Yato explained.

"So, where's Tom Chandler?" Asked Akira.

"Last I heard, he lived in Oakland, but that was years back. It's all I know of his whereabouts. If you go there, you might find him," said Yato. "Might be your best bet."

That was all the information the saints needed. They'd need to find Chandler in Oakland and confront him. He had to be the one responsible. But now, one thing needed to be dealt with. *What were they going to do with Yato? The Starlight Saints had facilities to take people into their own custody, give them food, and interrogate them further. That was the best option.*

Akira called for other agents to take Yato away, and their next stop would be Oakland. Before leaving, Angelo decided to strip all unconscious 203 Dragons of their jackets with Don's picture and burn them so his father would never be associated with savages again.

They were getting closer to the killer. *The answer was almost unlocked.*

CHAPTER 25

INDUSTRY SCAPEGOAT

Trial...

"We, the jury of the above-entitled case, find the defendant, Don Leonard Jackson, not guilty of child trafficking charges."

Don Jackson was put on trial for approximately two months after being accused of child trafficking. The downfall of an admired pop icon. A target had been on his back ever since he started having disputes with his record label, Sonic Scope Records. Don hated how they treated him and decided to use his platform to speak up. He began to drink the cup of Sonic Scope's wrath. Reports circulated, and more rumours of Don grooming children spread. He was forced to pay some alleged victim's family $2.5 million.

As a result, Don's last record performed poorly in sales, his music was boycotted, and he was no longer the respected icon he once was. Don's allegations put the entire family through persecution, and things only worsened.

Erica and her husband sometimes had to watch over Angelo and Casey when Don was absent handling legal matters.

In the days of Angelo's early childhood, the estate was eventually restricted, and no more children were allowed to visit. He would never see any of his childhood friends again. He would try to ask his dad why they stopped coming, but he simply answered, "I wish I knew." These were confusing times for Angelo. His dad looked distraught. Something was bothering him, and Angelo knew that no matter how hard his dad tried to hide it.

On the other hand, Casey was more composed throughout this ordeal and less concerned about the whole situation. The family was hanging on a loose thread.

"What's going on? Why do cops keep coming?" An anxious Angelo would ask Casey.

"Dad's been accused of trafficking kids. That's what this whole mess is about." Casey explained.

"Like stopping kids at a traffic light?"

"No hurting them and doing all these nasty things your mind wouldn't understand."

"But why? Dad would never do such."

"Oh, yeah right. With all of them kids he been hanging with? It's all over the news," Casey said. Something about Casey's tone made it sound like he actually believed the news.

"Dad's just tryna help other kids. That's why he built that creche and an amusement park. So, they can have fun," Angelo said in his dad's defence.

"I don't give a damn. He's making us all look bad. Plus, he never supports my dreams of becoming a musician like him. So why bother helping?" Casey said.

"That's all that matters, huh? Your music? Maybe there's a good reason he don't support you. We're in a crisis. We gotta be there for Dad. You bein' selfish. I'm outta here," Angelo stormed out and slammed the door.

Things were in shambles and would only get worse from here. Angelo feared all the future possibilities. What if his father ended up going to jail? Who would take care of the two boys, then? He dreaded that possibility and prayed it would never come to that.

Tom Chandler was the one orchestrating the trials and the prosecution. The family couldn't let that devil win. They had to beat the case one way or another.

The Jacksons' stood alone against the world turned hostile toward them.

Present Day...

The Shadowbreakers found themselves in the meeting lab once again. They were to set off the next day to find and interrogate Tom Chandler, the former district attorney and prosecutor.

Angelo was itching to bring this adversary to justice. After losing the case and failing to convict Don of any child trafficking charges, Chandler had gone into retirement, and that was the last the public heard of him. He had sworn to take revenge against the one who had ultimately decimated his career.

Two members from the Astral Hawks team were to accompany the Shadowbreakers on their mission. Zack, whom Angelo had bumped into in the sound room, and an older raven-haired girl, perhaps eighteen, named Kiko.

"We got one more saint joining the crew on this mission. He'll be of great help," Akira announced as she looked past Angelo and the others toward the door.

As Angelo glanced over his shoulder, he became overwhelmed with displeasure.

Dwayne entered the room, seemingly unbothered by Angelo's presence. Rex and Shawn mirrored the same animosity as Angelo, diffusing a strong tension within the room.

"No! There's no way we're bringing Dwayne on this mission," Angelo protested. "He'll just sabotage us like he did to me and Shawn during the rituals."

Dwayne stared daggers at Angelo. The standoff was on the verge of escalating until Akira, sensing the imminent conflict, stepped in to mediate.

"Stop! Dwayne was on a mission during the three rituals, so he couldn't have hired the assassin," Akira explained.

Angelo stood dumbfounded; his assumptions having been shattered by the explanation.

"What?" Angelo had a mix of disbelief and embarrassment.

"Seraph Nigel says the assassin got away and the real culprit is still to be found," Akira elaborated.

The revelation struck Angelo like an unexpected blow, a sudden jolt that left him reeling. He had invested so much in his assumptions about Dwayne, convinced he could expose his rival's misdeeds during the rituals. Instead, reality unfolded like a cruel joke, exposing Angelo's misjudgement and making him feel like a fool. The truth, once hidden, now stood glaringly in the open, leaving him with a bitter taste of regret for his misguided suspicions.

"That's right," Dwayne spat. "Check yourself before pointing fingers."

Angelo stood silent having nothing else to fall back on. He grappled with this troubling reality. Cunning, manipulative – how could he trust Dwayne with this mission? .

However, if he kept opposing, it would just delay and hinder his search for the truth. The mission's success hinged on unity, and Angelo would have to make an unsettling compromise. Accepting Dwayne onboard was the only way forward. Still, he would keep his eyes closely on Chandler, wary of any move his rival might make to jeopardize the mission. Shawn held his head down, guilty of the same false accusations.

"We're sorry," Shawn muttered under his breath.

"Leclez 17 wants his rematch," Rex declared, reminding Dwayne of their fight the other night. "Just remember I was goin' soft on you. You've yet to taste my full power."

Dwayne simply brushed off Rex's threat and walked toward Akira, "My father's still in the same city but he's relocated to West Oakland. We'll find him there. Greenville to be exact."

"Excellent. Your loyalty to this agency is profound despite your father being a suspect for Don's murder," Akira commended.

"I stand by the code of the Starlight Saints. No matter if I'm up against my own flesh and blood, order shall prevail and perversion must cease," Dwayne declared.

Angelo had to admit that Dwayne's commitment to the Starlight Saints was admirable. Despite how difficult Dwayne had made his life since he first arrived, the fact that his rival was helping him find his dad's killer spoke volumes. The tension between them seemed to momentarily subside in the face of a shared mission.

The database swiftly processed and assimilated all the pertinent clues and facts regarding Tom Chandler. Akira sifted through the data, carefully narrowing down the information until she pinpointed the exact address of the former district attorney. *Bingo!* With all the essential elements in place, the Starlight Saints were primed and ready. At the conclusion of the meeting, the team stood fully equipped for their upcoming mission.

Angelo stepped out of the lab, weaving through Luna and Vanya to reach Dwayne. As he approached, Dwayne shot him a frustrated glare, squinting his eyes.

"Look, I owe you an apology after accusing you. I was wrong about you, and I gotta admit you've shown me what it means to be a Starlight Saint. Since you're helping us find my father's killer, let's put the bad blood aside and work together, council president," Angelo extended his hand, a friendly smile on his face, hoping they could finally bury the hatchet.

However, Dwayne remained unmoved, making no effort to reciprocate Angelo's sincerity. "Don't get it twisted," Dwayne scoffed. "I'm not going on this mission 'cause I wanna help you. I'm simply under the seraph's orders, and I've got a bone to pick with my old man. I know he's innocent, and he's going to prove Don guilty of his crimes." Dwayne turned his back and strolled away, leaving Angelo hanging.

What seemed like a chance at reconciliation turned out to be a continuation of their feud. Angelo had briefly hoped for a thaw in their relationship, only to be met with Dwayne's confession of ulterior motives.

Once again, Chandler proved to be untrustworthy.

***

The Shadowbreakers soared above a van, utilizing their Johnny Skyblazers at a moderate speed. Dwayne, an unexpected ally, glided behind while Kiko and Zack took charge of the vehicle below. Angelo's resolve deepened with each passing moment, fuelled by his determination to confront another adversary.

They reached the neighbourhood where Tom Chandler was believed to reside, the team grounded themselves, parking the SUV safely in a nearby alley to apprehend the suspect. Dwayne, with his insider knowledge, had provided the exact address, yet as the saints knocked on the door, it remained unanswered. The entrance stood locked, adding an unexpected obstacle.

"If you are looking for Tom Chandler, he went to grab some grub at his favourite spot, Riverside Diner. Ain't too far from here," said one of the neighbours.

Within a few minutes, the Shadowbreakers found themselves waiting outside the diner. A weathered man in his fifties, marked by the subtle birthmark on his face, emerged from the establishment, wearing a contented smile after indulging in his favourite meal.

"We got him," said Shawn.

As the sun edged toward the horizon, the team, having eaten before reaching Oakland, observed Tom Chandler in good physical condition for his age. Following him with nimble movements, utilizing their star strides to run up walls, the Starlight Saints closed in on their target. By the time Tom detected their presence, it was too late—he was surrounded. In a swift move, Kiko handcuffed him, and Zack held a gun to his head, silencing any potential outcry.

"Don't even think of making a sound. You have the right to remain silent," said Zack.

"This way," Akira instructed.

They escorted Tom to the alley where the van awaited its captive. He hadn't even made any effort to resist. His movements were calm and deliberate, displaying neither surprise nor resistance. The evening shadows danced around them as they approached the waiting van.

"What do you people want from me?" asked Tom.

"Shut up and don't speak unless told to," ordered Vanya.

"A kid like you has no business talking to elders like that. Did your folks do not teach you manners?" asked Tom.

Vanya simply discarded the prosecutor's questions as if she didn't hear.

"Just keep walking," Akira ordered.

The saints made it to their meeting place with their captive. Tom realized he was outnumbered.

"Wait. I know who you guys are. Starlight Saints. I…" Tom froze as his eyes landed on two particular saints, "Dwayne? You're one of them?"

"Surprised to see what I've become, Papa? Ever since you vanished, I trained to become a Starlight Saint," Dwayne declared.

Tom fought back the urge to burst into laughter but managed to cover it with a forced smile. "You and Angelo working alongside each other? Very intriguing, I must say," he chuckled.

"Enough! Rumours say you're a member of the Illuminati and that it was you who killed my dad," Angelo shot back. "Is that true?"

Kiko held Tom firmly, ensuring he made no attempt to break free and escape. The soft light of the alley cast shadows on Tom's face, revealing a sly grin. The atmosphere crackled with a load of unanswered questions.

"You tell me. Your father was part of it," Tom taunted.

"My father would never be part of that corrupt society!" Angelo was tempted to use his fists. He almost lost control.

"Apple Jack! Control yourself," Akira admonished.

She was right. He took a deep breath, suppressing the surge of anger that threatened to consume him and couldn't afford to let his emotions win out especially when facing a possible source of information. The goal was to find out whether Tom Chandler was guilty of murder.

Rex, Shawn, Luna, and Vanya remained composed, leaving Angelo and Dwayne to take charge of the confrontation. This was clearly their business.

"You have nowhere to run, so you might as well confess," Angelo demanded. "We got evidence pointing right at you. You're on my father's enemy list. So, I'll ask again. Did you kill my dad?"

"Who knows? Perhaps I did, perhaps I didn't." Tom laughed with mockery.

Angelo raised his fists at Tom, ready to unleash his frustration, but Dwayne intervened, halting Angelo's attempts to intimidate the prosecutor.

"Come on, pops. Tell them how much of a pedo Don was. How you sought justice for all those poor kids," Dwayne encouraged. "I'll forgive you for abandoning me once you testify your innocence in front of them."

Dwayne's words struck Angelo like a blow. *It's evident that Dwayne was taking his father's side and would go to great lengths to prove him innocent of murdering Don.*

The Chandlers, clear as day, couldn't be trusted.

Angelo wished Akira hadn't brought Dwayne along with the Shadowbreakers on this critical investigation.

"Is this supposed to be a court case?" Tom scoffed. "Well, since we have an audience, I might as well expose the truth."

The night's confrontation grew tense as Tom's words hung in the air. A grin crept up on Tom's ageing face. Dwayne's mirrored smile hinted at a shared anticipation for the truth to surface. The truth would finally be exposed. Tom was either going to confess or deny killing the star icon.

"No, I didn't kill Don. I swear I was only the prosecutor. Had nothing to do with that bastard's death," said Tom.

Dwayne's triumphant gaze swept across the team, lingering on Angelo with a hint of great delight. No further evidence to suggest attempted murder. "See? He's telling the truth. I knew my father was innocent."

"But here's the thing. The allegations were all a setup," Tom cut his son's triumph short. "We, the Illuminati, orchestrated it as punishment when Don started disobeying orders."

Everyone froze, and Tom took vindictive pleasure in witnessing their startled reactions. Angelo couldn't believe what he was hearing. The shockwaves rippled through the rest of the Starlight Saints, and even Dwayne seemed taken aback by the revelation.

"A setup? You mean you planned the whole thing?" Angelo inquired, stuttering on his words.

Tom leaned in, his words coated with cruel malice. "What I'm saying, boys and girls, is Don was no pedophile. We framed him, and we did it so perfectly. All those kids who spoke out against him? We paid them to do it. Think of it like chess. I'm one of the pawns in this wild game of ours."

Angelo's eyes widened with a combination of disbelief and horror. He and Dwayne exchanging bewildered glances for a moment, sharing the same shock despite their differences.

The confession settled like a stone in Angelo's stomach, anger simmering beneath the surface. He knew his father had been innocent all along, and now the prosecutor had confirmed it.

How could these people falsely accuse his dad of something so serious?

Dwayne, standing beside Angelo, trembled as if he was on the verge of a breakdown.

A devious smile crept up on Tom's face as he watched his startled son's reaction. "Wait, but there's more," said Tom, adding more weight to the unsettling revelations. "The truth is I'm part of a child trafficking agency disguised as the Gummy Bear Association hiding behind the scenes. It's where we groom and sacrifice kids like yourselves to our own authority. Some of our everyday products and beverages like *Gummy Bear* soda include organ cells from the children we sacrifice."

This couldn't be real. An underground child trafficking cult?

The mere idea was a poison seeping into Angelo's mind, further shattering his understanding of the world he once knew. His favourite soda had been contaminated with the shedding of blood all this time.

Luna looked like she wanted to throw up at the mention of organ cells.

Doubt and disbelief flickered across Rex, Shawn, and everyone else's faces, a collective realization that the revelation was more nauseating than it seemed.

"Poor Donny didn't like what we were doing, so he tried to protect the kids. Bringing them under his umbrella. Such a big heart but a weak mind. So, we just put the blame on him. It never mattered whether we won or lost the case; all we wanted was for the public to think he was guilty. We successfully diverted the media's attention to him," Tom explained.

Angelo's hands trembled his face hot with rage as he lunged forward, grabbing Tom by the collar with a fierce intensity. The air crackled with the fury that surged through him, a storm of emotions unleashed by the cruel tricks and manipulations that had ensnared his father.

Luna, quick and decisive, intervened, pulling Angelo away with a strength that matched his anger.

Dwayne's voice quivered with disbelief as he confronted Tom. "So, you've been part of the Illuminati and a child trafficking network this whole time?" Dwayne stumbled on his words. "I thought you were innocent. All those children? It was you, but I thought the Jacksons were the criminals."

Despite his distrust, Angelo couldn't help but sense the ache in Dwayne's soul. *The shattering truth of knowing his father was behind the malicious occurrences was taking a toll on Dwayne. The whole allegation and child trafficking story had been fabricated, yet the majority of the public believed it to be true.*

Angelo having to remind himself of the first tenant of the Saints that nothing is real, and every truth must be questioned.

"Wait a sec," Luna added. "We're your enemies, but you've just exposed your secrets to us. Why give yourself up like that?"

Tom's chuckle resonated with a sinister buzz that betrayed a lack of concern for the consequences of his actions. His eyes bore into Luna, devoid of any fear or regret.

"Fair question," Tom mused, his tone nonchalant. "I revealed these things because I know that no matter how much you uncover, you'll never be able to stop us. Our agenda is going exactly as planned. In fact, we're very ahead of schedule. I never killed Don, but I was simply an instrument for distraction," he explained, his words suspended like a looming threat.

The whole group exchanged concerned glances. If the Illuminati's agenda was going as planned, the Starlight Saints urgently had to step up and take control of the situation before it was too late.

"We're giving you to the authorities," Akira ordered Kiko and Zack to take Tom away. "The public will know about your whole Gummy Bear shenanigans!"

"Handing me to the police won't do you any good. We're always one step ahead of you. It's honestly pathetic how you claim to be saviours of the world," Tom laughed.

"Shut up and keep walking," Zack ordered, escorting Tom to the waiting van.

Angelo, scanning the scene, caught a glimpse of something amiss.

Tom had managed to slip his hands out of the handcuffs.

In a flash, Tom shoved Zack away with aggressive force. From within the folds of his jacket, he produced a small cylinder containing a mysterious green substance. Before the team could react, Tom injected the substance into his neck. A moment of tense anticipation passed before the truth unfurled.

The green concoction seemed to surge through Tom's veins, and with newfound strength, he seized Zack, toppling him to the ground. Kiko, determined to prevent his escape, charged forward, but Tom, now a formidable adversary, overpowered her, slamming her to the ground with startling ease. *Where was this sudden boost of strength coming from?*

Tom had managed to beat down two saints in a single round, and only the Shadowbreakers were left standing.

Dwayne, seemingly frozen in denial, stood like a statue, oblivious to the chaos that had just unfolded before him.

"You're not gonna arrest me," Tom declared. "You took my son and corrupted him."

As Tom spoke, Angelo couldn't shake off the feeling of unease. There was an unsettling shift in Tom's demeanour after injecting himself with the mysterious substance. His actions were calculated, his gaze devoid of the humanity it once held.

Angelo's bewilderment mingled with dread. He grew alarmed by the impending effects of the substance coursing through Tom's veins.

"Your son's with us. He'll never be like you," Akira asserted. The rest of the team, sensing the imminent danger, readied their starlight watches.

"I'll just have to make you all suffer then. No mercy for Starlight Saints," Tom proclaimed.

Chapter 26

The Prosecutor's Vendetta

Tom sprinted towards the saints with an almost unnatural speed.

Akira projected a sword and began slashing through the air, but Tom deftly sidestepped every strike.

In an instant, he closed the distance, seizing Akira by the neck and effortlessly pinning her to the ground. A chilling smile played on his lips as he applied a chokehold. "Let's make this simple," said Tom, his voice cold and calculating. "Look at me as you die."

Angelo, reacting on instinct, projected a spear, urgency pulsating through his veins. "Get away from her!" Angelo thrust the spear into Tom's back, the impact forcing him to loosen his grip on Akira.

Blood spilt from the wound as Tom groaned, and Angelo pulled out the spear. A gaping hole revealed the brutal force of Angelo's attack.

Tom finally collapsed to the ground, signalling a clear victory. Angelo was shocked by his own strength. He'd killed the prosecutor without hesitation.

The triumph was short-lived when the hole in Tom's back began to close, the flow of blood stanching and disappearing. In an unexpected twist, Tom's back healed, leaving no trace of the injury. It was as if the impaling by the spear never happened.

"What the hell?" Angelo questioned as his spear disappeared.

"I can regenerate after every blow you throw at me. You can't lay a single scratch on me," Tom revealed, his delight evident in the wicked grin that twisted his features. "You also shouldn't have sided with the Starlight Saints, Angelo. They're not who they say they are. Don't be like your father who tried to run away."

With a speed that defied the laws of nature, Tom seized Angelo and hurled him across the space.

Angelo's body tumbled through the air like a discarded rag doll, colliding with a trash can with a sickening thud. The metallic echo of impact reverberated through the surroundings as Angelo lay there, growling in pain. As Angelo struggled to rise, a horrifying realisation crept over him.

If Tom could regenerate, that would render the Starlight Saint's attacks against him useless. "Who'll suffer my wrath next?" Tom challenged.

"Let's see if you can keep up with me, old man," Rex said confidently, and summoned two gleaming dagger blades with a glint of determination in his eyes and lunged towards Tom. His movements were swift and precise, each strike executed with calculated skill.

Yet, Tom, despite his apparent struggle, danced cautiously through the onslaught, evading every attack at a pace that challenged Rex.

"Seems like you're losing your touch," said Rex.

Amidst the continuous dance of dodges, Rex finally managed to land a hit across Tom's face, a thin line of blood appearing on the prosecutor's right cheek.

Tom and Rex, locked in a brief pause, exchanged a charged glance.

Angelo, despite the pain coursing through him, felt a surge of satisfaction at the sight of Rex successfully making a fool of Tom.

"Not so invincible are you?" Rex taunted with laughter.

"You impudent brat. Nobody hits me and gets away with it!" Tom roared, his rage visible. The wound on his face began to repair itself, the tissue knitting together until it vanished completely.

Rex, undeterred, allowed the daggers to dissipate, summoning instead a fiery sword that blazed with bright blue. With a determined swing, he charged at the infuriated Tom.

Angelo couldn't help but admire Rex's strategic thinking. *If Rex could make Tom catch fire, it should be harder for him to regenerate.*

Rex's attacks were swift and purposeful, each swing intended to catch the prosecutor off guard.

Tom exercised all of his efforts to avoid contact with the flaming sword.

"Just one flame, and that's it for you, sicko," said Rex with a devious smile curling on his lips.

Tom, though fast, struggled to evade every strike.

Angelo watched, tense, convinced that Rex would manage to land at least one hit as the fiery sword slashed through the air.

As Rex continued his assault, the sword eventually vanished, the weapon needing to recharge.

"Uh, crap!" said Rex, frustrated. "Forgot this thing had a time limit."

Tom seized the opportunity, unleashing a powerful kick straight to Rex's gut. The blow sent Rex flying several feet above the ground, and he landed atop a van with a resounding crash.

The vehicle's alarm rang off, and Rex was likely unconscious from the impact. Shawn and Vanya quickly made their advances but suffered the same defeat.

Tom's overwhelming power seemed insurmountable.

Luna, however, refused to give up the fight. Quick and strategic, she pulled out her frequency box, activating it with a twist of the knob. The weapon lay discarded on the ground, emitting a haunting melody that travelled through the air as Luna engaged Tom in combat.

The dark music frequencies worked their magic, momentarily disorienting Tom.

Luna seized the opportunity, blades swinging with a grace that belied the chaos. But even in his disoriented state, Tom managed to block her strikes. The invisible soundwaves from the frequency box, instead of subduing him, seemed to only fuel his aggression.

Tom, infuriated by the tormenting melody, rushed for the frequency box and snatched it. With the crushing grip of his bare hands, he silenced the music and destroyed the device.

"I hate that stupid music box of yours!" he spat; his face twisted with fury. The frequency box had inflamed his anger, adding a new layer of intensity to the battle.

Luna, determined and resourceful, summoned a chain in an attempt to restrain Tom's relentless onslaught.

as the links coiled around him, Tom effortlessly broke free and yanked the chain aggressively before it disappeared. Taking advantage of the moment, Tom grabbed Luna's arm, a vicious twist resounding a sickening crack as her joint dislocated.

Luna screamed in agony.

With a malevolent grin, the sadistic Tom held Luna by the head, relishing in her helplessness. "Off with your head," Tom taunted, slowly beginning to twist Luna's head to the side.

Angelo, powered by an urgent rush of adrenaline, couldn't allow Luna to suffer an excruciating death. Ignoring the aches that pulsed through his body, he pushed through the pain and bolted to Luna's aid. "Leave her alone!" summoning a sword, he drove it through Chandler, piercing the prosecutor's gut from a side angle.

Tom released Luna from his grip, and she collapsed to the ground, coughing blood but still breathing. Staggering back from the unexpected blow, yanking the sword from the side of his abdomen, only for it to vanish into thin air.

Tom grabbed Angelo by the neck and squeezed his windpipe. His vice-like grip on Angelo's neck cut off his oxygen supply, and the world blurred as darkness encroached on his vision.

Angelo dangled in the air helplessly. However, Tom eased his grip slightly, allowing his captive some grace to breathe.

"Tell me where your secret location is so we can handle unfinished business with the Starlight Saints," Tom demanded, the threat hanging like a guillotine. "Or I'll murder your family and all those you hold dear."

Angelo, torn between loyalty and the safety of his loved ones, felt the pressure intensify. "I won't..." he managed to rasp out, his voice strained.

"We know where your family lives. How about I take you with me and hand you over to the child trafficking agency, where you'll be cut to pieces and used on the black market?" Tom's sadistic excitement cast a shadow over Angelo's terror-stricken face.

The mere thought of becoming a pawn in the child trafficking cult's exploitative game sent shivers down Angelo's spine.

The prosecutor's wicked eyes bore into him, a glimpse of the hellish fate awaiting him. "You know what, I've made up my mind," he declared with malicious satisfaction. "You'll be worth millions to the network. You're coming with me. You can say goodbye to these Starlight Saints since you won't comply."

Angelo, defeated, made his last plea, the words tumbling out in a desperate whisper. "Hold on, wait. Let's see if we can work out a deal."

With a distant rumble, the sudden whir of a chainsaw sliced through the air, and Angelo dropped to his feet instantly.

Tom's right limb lay severed on the floor, blood spurting out in gruesome pulses.

Angelo, catching his breath, glanced up to witness Dwayne holding the chainsaw, his face streaked with stains of blood. The drastic change in Dwayne's expression took Angelo by surprise; throughout the fight, he seemed immobile, but now, he had intervened to save Angelo.

Tom, on his knees with his arm severed, widened his eyes at Dwayne's unexpected intervention. "Dwayne, how could you?"

The chainsaw soon vanished, replaced by a pair of chain whips with blades. Dwayne clasped their handles around his wrists. With fierce rage, son struck father, the blades of the chain whips slashing through the space. He wrapped the chains around Tom's body, and an electrical shock pulsed through the links, causing him to convulse under the voltage.

The chains disappeared, leaving behind a stunned and weakened Tom.

Angelo realised such a weapon had drained a significant amount of energy from the starlight watch.

Dwayne didn't need to inflict any more attacks, though, as the damage had been done already.

Tom lay on his back as his right arm slowly began to regenerate, growing back into its former glory. He groaned, struggling onto his knees, only to find himself at the mercy of Dwayne's blade.

"I know you can't regenerate if I slice that head off your body," Dwayne declared, his voice trembling along with the blade in his hands. "I can't believe you lied. When you stepped down as district attorney, you left me and my mother to suffer alone."

Dwayne choked on his words as if on the verge of tears.

Angelo could sense an intense emotional standoff between father and son, a battle of unresolved wounds and shattered trust. Tempted to intervene, his instincts tugging at him, warning against interfering in such a pivotal moment.

"We were poor and left with nothing. You just vanished and never bothered to help us. Thankfully, I discovered the Starlight Saints when my mom enrolled me in a program that said they gave out scholarships. You were dead to me, but the only thing that never made me lose hope in you was your pursuit of justice. Your determination to take down child traffickers..." Dwayne trailed off, his voice thick with affliction. "You framed Don! You're an Illumiknight. This whole time, I thought the Jacksons were the ones who separated and destroyed our family, but it was you all along. You lied to me! What kind of father are you?"

The words remained suspended, a damning revelation that signified the shattered bonds of family and trust. Akira, Rex, Shawn, and the others were up by now, making no efforts to intercede, but remained passive as they witnessed the dramatic confrontation unfold.

"I only vanished to protect you. I was gonna come back and recruit you into the order when you were ready, but these pesky Starlight Saints beat me to it. We traffic and sacrifice children for several reasons. The first is to keep the human population size under control," Tom explained, blood running from his lips as he tried to justify his deeds. He rose steadily to his feet, he faced Dwayne, their eyes locking in a moment drowned with sorrow. "I know I haven't always been the best father, and I'm sorry. I haven't always been there for you, but I wanna make up for it now. Join me, Dwayne. Leave the Starlight Saints, and I will show you the path to self-enlightenment."

Tom's proposal was left hanging, freezing the atmosphere momentarily. No one dared to move.

Angelo focused his gaze on Dwayne in anticipation to see what he would choose. *Would he take the deal and betray the Starlight Saints, or would he stay loyal to the secret society that had taken him in when he was in desperate need?*

Dwayne, head bowed, deprojected his blade, a sign of deep contemplation.

Angelo locked eyes with Akira from the other side and shared worried glances.

Rex and Shawn were ready to activate their starlight watches as if expecting Dwayne to turn on them while Vanya stayed by the injured Luna's side.

"Never!" Dwayne summoned two katanas and sliced Tom across the abdomen. With all the saints up except for Luna,

Akira signalled the unified advance, a final standoff against the prosecutor.

Tom, outnumbered and overpowered, suffered each saint's relentless barrage of attacks.

Realising the inevitable, Tom forcefully barged Shawn aside with his shoulder, creating a path for his escape. A collective resolve pulsed through the remaining saints as they made their final push against the prosecutor.

In a sudden twist, Tom began crawling up a building like a four-legged lizard, using his bare hands—a phenomenon unfamiliar to Angelo. Tom wasn't using star strides, either.

"You'll pay for taking my son away from me. Your demise is coming, Starlight Saints," Tom threatened, his voice resonating through the battleground.

Tom reached the top of the building, his escape unfolding with an almost unnatural agility. Jumping from rooftop to rooftop like a ninja in the night, slipping away from the clutches of the saints. The eventful encounter had left everyone weary.

"How did he get so strong?" Angelo's voice cut through post-battle silence.

"Reptilian serum," Akira explained. "It's a weapon the Illumiknights use. Gives them reptilian powers, including strength."

"Injecting it into your body can kill you. Apparently, you gotta go through rituals to develop immunity to the serum," Kiko added.

The use of this serum had left Angelo bewildered.

Tom had almost decimated the group, and Angelo couldn't imagine facing a whole army with reptilian serum. He was chilled to the bone by such powerful mechanisms. Angelo's body still throbbed with pain, although it had eased up. All the saints gathered around Luna.

"Is she gonna be okay?" asked Angelo in alarm.

Vanya helped Luna and started patching her using a first aid kit. "She'll be fine. She just needs time to recover 'fore she's back in the game, but her arm will be fixed in no time."

As the Shadowbreakers huddled to discuss their next plan, Shawn broached the lingering topic: "Tom Chandler got away, but he mentioned an underground circle of child traffickers sacrificing children. Are these the kids your dad was trying to protect?"

Although the question hung in the air, Angelo remained silent, buried in his thoughts. He wasn't in any mood to converse with anyone. *Not only did Angelo still need to find the killer, but he also needed to protect his family after Tom's imposing threat. The thought of Tom hurting Aunt Erica or Casey left him uneasy.*

The burden of the whole operation became more unbearable.

"He was framed. They used him as a cover for their dirty work. I heard they also make child sacrifices to some entity called Moloch for more power and influence," Akira remarked.

"This is personal now. Tom is gonna go after my family," said Angelo.

"We ain't gonna let him. We're sending agents to track him down," Akira reassured.

Despite the comforting words, the saints had another matter on their hands: The child trafficking cult.

"Investigating the trafficking agency will throw us off track from our main investigation. We focus on the main one and leave the other one for later," said Akira.

Akira turned to Dwayne and placed a comforting hand on his shoulder. "You've once again proved your loyalty to the Starlight Saints. The grandmaster will be proud."

Dwayne managed only a nod in response.

Angelo was still bitter about this whole revelation. However, the truth was also liberating. Always having been convinced deep down that his father was innocent and never guilty of any charges he faced brought Angelo a profound sense of peace. *When they said the truth sets you free, they honestly weren't lying.* He would tell Casey to be careful of Tom. He would secretly text his brother about the investigation as soon as he returned to campus.

"We're leaving," Akira ordered.

Everyone prepared to go, and Angelo trailed behind, quickening his pace to catch up with Dwayne. He tapped him on the shoulder, gratitude and remorse washing over him.

"Thanks for savin' me back there. I owe you, and I'm really sorry about your dad. I know what it's like to lose…"

"Shut up," Dwayne's sharp interruption sliced through Angelo's attempt at empathy. "I never intended to save you. I simply had a score to settle with my dad. This changes nothing between us."

Dwayne's words stunned Angelo into silence, and it seemed like the barrier between them would never be broken. Though they shared a common purpose, their differences would always conflict.

As they moved forward, the Starlight Saints, armed with vital information, pressed on into the unknown shadows. That left just Zayn Hopkins to investigate. The final suspect on Dad's enemy list.

The Illuminati's well of secrets only became darker as they went deeper.

CHAPTER 27

DOUBLE TROUBLE

"Mr. Jackson? Excuse me Mr. Jackson."

Angelo jolted awake and found himself in the backseat of a car.

"Wake up. We're here," said a man.

Angelo wondered what 'here' meant. When he looked outside, he saw Erica waiting for him. Behind her was a tall white building that seemed familiar. He felt like he'd seen this place before. Angelo stepped out of the car to meet with his aunt.

"This way," Erica instructed.

Angelo had no clue what was happening, but he followed. As soon as they entered the building, Angelo finally remembered what this place was - St Mary's Hospital.

"Why we here? Did something happen?" Angelo asked.

Erica didn't answer. She simply kept walking as if she couldn't hear him. They kept walking down the white corridor, and as Angelo looked around, a sick-looking patient in a wheelchair passed by.

"Help me!!! I've been in this place of torment for many years. Why didn't I repent?!" The patient screamed.

"Sir we're only trying to help you," said the nurse pushing the wheelchair.

"*I promise I'll do better.*" *The patient was crying in agony.*

Angelo glanced forward and kept following Erica, but the patient's screams of agony persisted from behind until their voices faded. This left Angelo confused. The look in the patient's eyes was one of terror and suffering. Angelo found it strange how the patient described this hospital as a place of torment. Whatever was happening, the poor patient must have been losing his mind and hallucinating. Who could blame him? After being in a place like this for so long, Angelo was sure to start losing his mind, too. He felt sorry for the patient. He kept walking with Erica until they reached an owl-shaped door labelled Dr. Marshall.

Inside was Dr. Cory Marshall, seated at his desk reading some documents. He greeted his two guests with a gentle smile, and they returned the greeting.

"How can I help you today?" asked Dr. Marshall.

"My nephew is here for a blood test," Erica explained. Angelo was perplexed by this.

"Erica, what do I need a blood test for?" asked Angelo. "You didn't tell me anything."

"Just sit there so we can get this over with, alright?" the doctor instructed.

Angelo reluctantly complied, sitting uncomfortably on the bed. The doctor brought out some equipment and pulled out a syringe. "It'll only be a pinch."

Angelo closed his eyes tightly, not wanting to witness the needle pierce his skin. He hoped to get through the process as quickly as possible so he could go home.

"And all done," said the doctor, patting white tissue on the spot where the needle had pierced.

Three containers with samples of his blood suddenly flashed out of nowhere. Erica smiled at Angelo, and he felt relieved, although he still didn't know the purpose of the blood test.

"Toast to all of us," said Dr. Marshall.

Erica grabbed one of Angelo's blood samples, and so did the doctor. They took off the seals and made a toast with each other.

After that, they gulped down the blood like beer. He became very disturbed by this, his heart jumping. It made his stomach turn, and he wanted to throw up. Had Erica and Dr. Marshall just drunk his blood?

Angelo began to question whether he was seeing things right.

"Aren't you gonna drink that?" asked Marshall, pointing at the untouched container, which had now grown owl wings.

"What's going on? Erica, what the hell's this?" Angelo asked.

"Come on, Angelo. Have a drink," said Erica.

Her eyes were turning red, and Angelo knew something was wrong. He got off the bed and ran towards the door. As Angelo burst out, he found himself running down a long, hazy, maze-like corridor. Screams reverberated throughout the hall as he observed countless doors on each side.

"I died, but Lord forgive me!"

"Don't leave me here! Bring me back to life!"

"I'm a sinful man!"

Angelo kept running, wobbly objects in his periphery, and his heart accelerated with horror. With each door he opened, he found patients being tortured by doctors. This wasn't a regular hospital at all. It was a full-on torture chamber. What was even more unnerving was that these patients kept bringing up the topic of death like they were already dead and still being tortured. Did Angelo die somehow and end up in some twisted version of hell? That couldn't be. He kept running and running down the endless corridor. He began sobbing to himself.

"Oh, dear God, please tell me I'm not in hell. I tried my best to live right, I prayed. Somebody help me!" cried Angelo, but his cry was in vain.

He finally reached the end of the eternal corridor, where he met two steel doors. This must've been the way out. He looked back and saw patients scrambling on the floor, crying for a saviour.

"Help me!" they screamed, but Angelo was in no position to help anyone.

If he stayed longer, they would surely get him, too. He bolted through the steel doors and found himself in a quiet, peaceful room. A figure had their back turned towards him, but when they turned around, Angelo felt joyful relief.

"Casey, it's you."

Casey smiled and embraced Angelo.

"You won't believe what I just saw. There's something crazy going on back there." Angelo explained the whole story to Casey about how the patients were screaming for help, how Erica drank his blood, etc.

Casey's response was just laughter.

Angelo should've known that his brother wouldn't believe a single word.

"Come, let me show you something," said Casey.

He beckoned for Angelo to follow. They jumped through a vividly coloured vortex and found themselves in another room. There were two hospital beds, and two patients appeared to be sleeping. Casey gestured for Angelo to examine the patient on the right bed. Angelo was hesitant, but Casey assured him it was safe.

The closer Angelo got, the more he noticed something odd and familiar about this patient. The patient was pale-skinned and bald-headed.

"Is that me?" asked Angelo, perplexed.

"A part of you. We must put death our old selves to death and become a new creation. It seems like part of you's fighting to escape," Casey explained.

"What are you talkin' about? I gave up everything," said Angelo, confused. His memory started returning to him. "I joined the Starlight Saints and left everything behind."

Casey stood next to the patient on the left side of Angelo's patient. Casey grabbed a pillow and slowly began to suffocate the patient. Subtle groans emitted from underneath as the patient fought for breath. The groans finally faded into silence, indicating death. Casey dared Angelo to do the same thing to his patient.

Yet, Angelo hesitated, unsure if he could kill himself or whatever this thing was that resembled his features.

"You know what happens to people who run away from their destiny? If they don't come to their senses and kill their old self, someone will do it eventually," said Casey.

"Destiny?"

"Your destiny is not something you can choose to escape, a different path was meant for you and it's still within you, fighting to emerge," Casey explained.

Angelo suddenly felt a tight grip around his neck. The clone had awakened. It began strangling him as it rose out of the bed. The clone was too powerful, no matter how hard Angelo tried to fight back.

"Casey, help me. I don't know why he's attacking me," yelled Angelo.

"Can't help you if you keep running away from what's meant for you," said Casey.

The clone pushed Angelo through another set of doors, and he found himself standing near an edge leading to a fiery pit below.

"No, you can't do this. Please!" Angelo begged.

The clone showed no signs of mercy, giving Angelo a cold, deadly stare in the eye. The clone forcefully pushed him off the edge, and he began spiralling down the furnace into the fiery abyss.

***

"Angelo, wake up."

Angelo gasped for air with heavy breaths and touched his face and felt the sweat sticking to him. That dream Angelo had felt too real. His heart pounded rapidly, and he tried calming himself.

Luna stood in the doorway wearing an arm cast and sling. A haunting reminder of their encounter with the malicious prosecutor.

"You're late for our meeting. Akira asked me to come get you," she said.

Angelo muttered to himself with frustration and realized he'd overslept and now rushing out of bed and getting himself cleaned up.

"Dammit, just give me five minutes," said Angelo.

In the bathroom mirror his reflection gave him a sudden fright. For a split second, Angelo saw himself but not quite himself. The bald-headed clone from the dream flashed in the mirror for just a moment. When he rubbed his eyes.

The final suspect on the enemy list was Zayn Hopkins. *Once dad's friend and still a proclaimed magician and illusionist.*

The saint's database hinted that the magician was located at the heart of Las Vegas, Nevada. According to the latest updates, Zayn had transitioned from the realm of magic into the high-stakes world of professional gambling. He was known as one of the best gamblers in Nevada, and he even owned his own casino called Zayntopia.

As per his business details, they had scheduled an appointment to meet with the magician-turned-gambler beforehand, a calculated move to unravel the threads of illusion that shrouded their final suspect.

"Zayn's our final target. It's gotta be him," said Akira. "We'll be setting off soon."

The team's collective nod signalled agreement and Angelo felt a surge of newfound resolve. The pursuit of truth now focused on Zayn.

"Sorry, Luna, but you'll have to stay behind. You're too injured and we can't risk jeopardizing the mission. Take this time to rest and heal up," Akira instructed.

Angelo caught a flicker of sadness in Luna's eyes as she nodded in understanding.

Tom Chandler's brutal assault had taken a toll on her, and Angelo silently concurred with Akira's decision. *She needed time to recuperate, to mend both body and spirit.*

The realization, however, left a void in the team, a missing link in their cohesive unit.

"That's a shame. A trip around the Vegas Strip is definitely needed. Leclez can't wait!" Rex exclaimed, his enthusiasm standing in stark contrast to the sombre mood.

The glares from the rest of the team conveyed their seriousness about the impending mission.

"What? I've never been to Vegas," Rex defended himself.

The door swung open, and a commanding figure stepped into the room. Seraph Nigel, a formidable presence, surveyed the team with an act of deliberate observation.

"I'll be joining you guys on this investigation. You could use an extra hand," Seraph Nigel offered, to Angelo's surprise. "This case is becoming a more crucial matter and must be solved soon before the Illuminati can push their agenda forward."

"Of course. We'd be grateful to have you on board, Nigel," said Akira with a formal handshake.

Nigel's glare, always intimidating, seemed to amplify.

Angelo recalled when the seraph had proposed getting rid of him in the meeting and was reluctant to trust Nigel. *Was Nigel looking for an opportunity to catch him out?* he wondered. Despite the intensity, he was glad to have at least another skilled seraph on the team. *They would be an unstoppable force.*

***

The meeting drew to a close, the room clearing as the saints prepared their equipment and finalized the details of the upcoming mission. As Angelo strolled out of the lab, the clunk of his footsteps was joined by another set, and Luna caught up to him.

"You've been acting kinda weird lately. Is everything okay?" Luna's concern was evident as they walked away from the meeting room.

"I'm fine, but it should be me asking you. Since when do you care about me anyway? I thought you and the other saints hated me," Angelo answered defensively , a shield against the unexpected concern.

"Well, I'll admit I had my doubts about you at first. You were a new apprentice, wet behind the ears. But then, back in Oakland, you saved my life, also stuck with us when the Dragons wanted to recruit you in San Francisco. You've earned my trust. You've shown you got what it takes to be a Starlight Saint, that's for sure," Luna's admission caught Angelo off guard.

Despite the guarded nature of their interactions, Luna's sincerity shone through.

No matter how hard Angelo tried to hide his feelings, Luna could see right through him. He wasn't so good at concealing anything as he thought, so he gave in and decided to open up. "I had this dream." Angelo explained everything he saw, including the blood-drinking, the hospital, and his clone.

"I know it's just a dream, but I swear it felt so real. It got me shaking, you know. What if something bad happens to Casey or my family? Especially with Tom Chandler still out there," Angelo's vulnerability surfaced, the fear for his loved ones in imminent danger.

Luna placed a comforting hand on his shoulder.

As their eyes locked, it was like staring into an ocean of shared concerns and unspoken fears.

"Look, the enemy just wants you to be all riled up. Don't give in to what they want. Stand your ground," Luna reassured. "Grandmaster Lady Eszter always said *the one who's persistent should be more feared than the one who's gifted.*"

She was right. Angelo gave his enemies victory by allowing fear to control his mind. He had to stay focused and not let the adversary win.

"Would you mind doing something for me?" Luna removed her arm from the sling and pulled out a permanent marker with a glint of excitement in her eyes. Handing it to Angelo, she said, "I'd appreciate it if you could sign your name here."

Angelo, flattered by the unexpected request, thought, why not. "You want me to write 'Angelo'?"

"Nah, Apple Jack," Luna laughed, a blush tinting her cheeks. "I like that better. I think it's way cooler and cuter."

With a grin, Angelo brushed the marker over the cast, leaving behind his alias along with a heartfelt message: "Get well soon, Moonlight - Apple Jack :)."

Aware of the impending journey to Las Vegas the next day, Angelo retreated to his hostel for some much-needed rest. But before he could leave, Luna grabbed his hand.

"Wait, come with me to the sound room. You need to rejuvenate your soul, and I know it's your happy place," Luna suggested with a playful grin. "Let's have a session together."

Angelo was slightly annoyed by Luna's sudden invitation, but *who was he to decline such an offer?* With the bitterness between them now a distant memory, their newfound friendship was not just affirmed but strengthened by shared moments of laughter and care. Maybe he could now finish his dream with Akira.

Chapter 28

Snakes and Ladders

A convoy of sleek SUVs manoeuvred in unison along the road, their metallic bodies glinting in the sunlight. As the convoy approached, a welcoming signpost emerged on the horizon, proudly announcing, *'Welcome to Nevada.'* The saints had spent the past two nights ensuring they had food, supplies, and fuel to get them across from their base to another state.

Inside the lead vehicle, cool air from the air conditioning breezed quietly, offering relief from the heat outside. Angelo sat in the back seat; his eyes fixed on the passing landscape.

Nigel had brought two of his most trusted agents, Cherub Clyde and Faye, to accompany the Shawdowbreakers. Las Vegas was only a few miles away now. Humidity accompanied the dry terrain of land and desert. It had been scorching during the day, but dusk arrived as they got closer to Las Vegas. The purple sky hovered above, and the crescent moon arose in its glory, embracing regal tones of twilight.

Zayntopia was within reach. Angelo's memories of Las Vegas were coloured by family trips, yet the city had never claimed the title of his favourite.

"First time in Vegas, and so far, I'm liking it," Rex chimed in with excitement.

Nighttime had fallen. Las Vegas was decorated with glistening lights, and life bustled everywhere. The skyline sparkled with lights, creating a dazzling illumination on the lively streets. They drove past a flashing sign that welcomed them into the city.

"It's average. I've seen better, to be honest," said Angelo.

The saints reached the entrance of Zayntopia, a grandiose structure adorned with captivating shapes and a mermaid as its symbolic emblem. Angelo couldn't deny the charm of the entrance. This casino was a cash cow, judging by its size.

Two imposing guards stood sentry on either side of the door; their vigilant scrutiny focused on approaching visitors. As they approached the guards, Akira stepped forward. "ID, please," barked one of the guards, his stern gaze fixed on the approaching group.

Akira, an epitome of calm confidence, gracefully presented her fake ID.

The guard scrutinised it, then glanced beyond her, skimming over Nigel and his cherubs. His eyes landed on the four adolescents.

"Sorry, ma'am, but no kids allowed. Age limit is strictly 21," declared the guard.

Akira, undeterred, leaned forward, a friendly smile playing on her lips. "We're here to see the owner of Zayntopia, Zayn Hopkins. We made an appointment, and he should be expecting us. I'm sure you can make an exception."

A brief exchange in Spanish passed between the two guards. The decision seemed to hang in the balance as one of them disappeared inside the building, leaving the other to keep watch over the saints. A tense anticipation lingered during the minutes they stood waiting.

"Are we sure this is gonna work?" Shawn whispered.

"If this goes south, we're all screwed," Vanya added.

After a series of concerned whispers amongst the team, Akira chimed in. "Be patient. Just wait. We'll get in."

Finally,, the returning guard granted them entry. As Angelo stepped over the threshold, a luxurious red carpet graced with intricate patterns welcomed them. The opulence of Zayntopia unfurled before them—gambling machines humming with activity, fine dining areas exuding an air of sophistication, and extravagant chandeliers radiating a soft glow.

Zayntopia was a palace for the rich and must have been worth millions of dollars. Angelo observed people playing poker and other betting games. He thought that whoever invented gambling was a scammer. *What a dumb idea.*

"Ah, look who's arrived," a man greeted them with a welcoming smile, beckoning for the saints to follow him. "I'm Zayn, the owner of this casino. Nice to have some company. Right this way."

As the group trailed behind Zayn, Angelo couldn't help but notice the vibrant energy that radiated from the casino owner. Reports pegged him in his forties, yet Zayn Hopkins carried an unmistakable spirit of childhood youth. His features, fresh and handsome, bespoke a man at ease in his own skin.

Leading them through the labyrinthine corridors of Zayntopia, Zayn finally ushered them into an empty meeting room. "I hear you requested to see me about an ongoing investigation. Please, make yourselves comfortable. I won't keep you waiting long," he assured them, his hospitality evident in every gesture despite him being the potential murderer.

The man was suspiciously too jubilant for Angelo's liking. He was sure to catch Zayn out soon.

***

Angelo stared aimlessly into space to kill time as they waited. Shawn, Rex and Vanya groaned impatiently with their arms folded while Akira remained as calm as still waters.

"What could possibly be taking him this long?" Nigel questioned, growing irritable.

Suddenly, the room spun, its familiar walls morphing into a surreal landscape. A wave a dizziness pummelled Angelo. With effort he struggled to maintain his balance.

The rest of the team was equally disoriented, caught in the throes of an unexpected dislocation. The once-plain room transformed into a massive, checkered expanse, huge, coloured squares stretching out endlessly before them. Each square was the size of a room.

"What the hell just happened?" Angelo voiced the collective confusion.

A booming laugh echoed through the unseen corners of the space, disorienting them further.

"Welcome to my playground," Zayn's voice, now amplified through an unseen intercom, filled the air. "Before our meeting, I'd like us to play a fun board game. Who's up for some Snakes and Ladders?"

"Say what now?" asked Vanya, bewildered.

A die the size of a fist appeared. Gasps of astonishment escaped Angelo and his teammates.

How was Zayn doing this? Zayn's reputation as a magician and illusionist had been mentioned in the reports, but this level of mystical display surpassed their expectations.

"You'll find me at the very end of this board. The rules are simple. Each player rolls the die and moves according to the number they've rolled. There are one hundred blocks. Any attempt to move beyond the number you've rolled will be blocked by an unseen barrier, and you'll have to wait until it's your turn to roll again. There's eight of you but only one of you has to win for the game to end. You have 40 minutes to complete the game, or you die as the board self-destructs," Zayn's disembodied voice explained.

"We didn't ask to play your stupid game!" Nigel protested out of frustration. "Quit wasting our time."

"Nuh uh uh, you're my wonderful guests. My casino, my rules," Zayn declared with finality. "Now, let the game begin."

A colossal holographic timer materialised at the distant end of the gameboard. The atmosphere grew heavy with a sense of urgency as the saints found themselves reluctantly entangled in the whims of Zayn's dangerous game.

Vexation now resonated from Akira, mirroring the collective discontent that permeated the entire team. The absence of exit doors left them with no escape, and the ominous checkered terrain seemed to stretch endlessly before them.

Cherub Clyde glanced at Nigel with alarm. "It's not looking good for us, Seraph."

Shawn, standing amidst the tense assembly, broke the uneasy stillness. "I used to be good at this game. I have a special way of rolling dice. The game's pretty easy. If you land on a ladder block, you get boosted up the board, and if you land on a snake, you go down," he explained.

All eyes turned toward Shawn, and memories of past board game challenges with him flickered in Angelo's mind.

As the spectre of an ancient game unfolded before them, the saints shared glances, silently conveying the urgency of the situation as time was ticking away. The unspoken question lingered: Who among them would take the first roll in this perilous game?

"Don't worry, it's just a stupid game. We can beat this," said Rex and, with a confident grin, scooped up the die and gave it a vigorous shake.

The cube tumbled, revealing a favourable six. His initial steps on the gameboard were marked by triumph.

Angelo recalled that players could roll again when they rolled a six. Rex did so. Another lucky six came up.

Rex snickered with joy as he advanced effortlessly, revelling in the absurd ease of the challenge. "This is too easy," Rex boasted with exuding confidence. "That magician dude's got nothing on me."

However, the volatile nature of the game revealed itself when the next roll produced a four. Rex ran forward, but as he landed on a new block which revealed itself as a snake, his triumphant look shifted to one of disbelief. In an instant, he found himself inexplicably back at the starting block, frustration evident in his muttered curses.

"Shoot! I had a good streak going," Rex grumbled, his earlier confidence replaced with irritation.

The snake Rex had landed on stretched to the starting block.

Angelo had no desire to land on any snake blocks. It would only slow down the team's quest for answers and survival. He was annoyed at Zayn's time-consuming challenge. *All he hoped for was a simple meeting about their investigation, but if the saints were going to get to him, they had to beat the game.*

Angelo shook the die in his hands, anticipation building as the cube tumbled across the checkered floor. With each roll, the Shadowbreakers travelled an unpredictable path, each move dictated by the whims of chance. His first roll took him five blocks forward, but as he continued, an invisible barrier halted any further progress, reminding him that he couldn't leave the square beyond the number he had rolled. He'd have to bide his time and await the next opportunity to advance. When his turn came again, he rolled a six, moving swiftly along the checkered blocks.

However, the unpredictable nature of the game took a sudden turn. Zayn, the enigmatic mastermind behind this bizarre challenge, introduced an unexpected twist.

"Thought I'd add a little spice to the game and make you fight some bad guys," Zayn's voice boomed through the intercom, setting the stage for a sudden and treacherous encounter. "Let's see the Starlight Saints in action."

Three ninjas materialised within Angelo's block; their agile forms poised for battle. He was caught off guard, almost evaded a shuriken aimed at him as it scraped his shoulder and went past, leaving a bleeding cut. Instantly he was on alert and summoning two katanas with his starlight watch, engaging in a flurry of slashes against the imposing adversaries.

The ninjas effortlessly dodged his attacks, showcasing acrobatic feats with backflips and cartwheels.

Angelo stumbled and fell backwards.

The looming figures of the ninjas closed in, brandishing shuriken with lethal intent.

Angelo's predicament was dire as sweat trickled down his brow, an impending threat of being sliced to pieces. Adapting to the challenge, he swiftly drew a pistol from his arsenal, unleashing a volley of shots at the attackers.

However, instead of bloodshed, the ninjas dissipated into ethereal smoke.

Angelo began questioning the reality of the game. *Were these ninjas just mere illusions?* He examined his cut and started doubting, wondering how illusions were able to hurt him. *This was another one of Zanyn's magic tricks.*

As Angelo awaited his next round to roll, he observed the other participants. He caught a glimpse of Seraph Nigel engaging with a vicious fleet of cyborgs as he rolled, displaying fierce tenacity.

Cherub Faye shielded herself against more ninjas, and Clyde struggled against a bear a few blocks ahead while Shawn advanced with the help of a ladder.

A snake set Vanya back while Rex trailed several blocks behind, trying to catch up to the rest. With everyone's chaotic fight for survival, Zayn's game proved gruelling.

As Angelo's turn came again, he moved three blocks. Beneath his feet was a picture of a ladder painted on the block. *Ladders would be his best ally.* As Angelo teleported to a new block, standing next to Akira.

"Seraph? Looks like I took a shortcut," said Angelo with a grin. He turned his attention to the timer with fifteen minutes remaining. "We don't have much time."

Angelo's heart started pumping at a faster rate, and he had butterflies in his stomach. Being in Akira's presence was overwhelming as his feelings for her became more vigorous.

A sudden roar disrupted the moment, and before them materialised a formidable adversary — a sabertooth tiger, its massive physique exuding an untamed ferocity.

Summoning a spear, Angelo stepped forward, ready to face the beast alone. "You can stand back, Seraph. I'll deal with this thing," he declared with determination.

Akira, however, countered his bravado with a knowing smile. "What happened to teamwork? I thought we were in this together."

"You're right. We're meant to be together," Angelo went on without realising what he'd just said.

Akira stared at Angelo wide-eyed. Only a few seconds later did he realise his error.

"I mean, we're meant to work together," Angelo corrected himself, attempting to steer the conversation away from the unexpected confession. His body temperature rose to the roof out of panic and about to die from embarrassment. *Did he really just give himself away like that?*

The sabertooth tiger, indifferent to the emotional exchange, roared again, its aggression escalating, demanding their united attention.

"The tiger must have a weak spot. You distract it while I look for a spot to strike," said Akira. "Remember what you've learned in your training."

Angelo nodded and summoned a bladed staff. He rushed up to the eight-foot beast, ready for war. The tiger tried to pounce on Angelo, but he quickly moved out of harm's way. He spotted an opening and struck the tiger's side with the blade. Yet, nothing seemed to work, and the tiger was unmoved by any of his attacks.

Akira ran circles around the beast, looking for the weak spot, while Angelo kept it at bay.

The tiger became more vexed and began swinging its claws at Angelo. His energy was rapidly draining from dodging the tiger's ferocious attacks.

Angelo's staff finally disappeared, requiring a recharge. He was now at the sabertooth's mercy, and that's when an epiphany dropped. Trying to summon a snare, but it took much of his willpower and cognitive thinking.

The snare was forming, but Angelo's energy was straining. *Could he manage such a great feat?* Angelo contemplated trying to summon other more powerful weapons instead, like the fiery sword he'd seen Rex use in the previous mission, but the tiger proved immune to his strikes. *Catching the beast off guard seemed to be the only option.* If Angelo didn't project the snare he was as good as dead.

"Come on, work," Angelo prayed.

The tiger was inches away from its meal, and at the last moment, the snare finally took form on the ground. Angelo hurriedly dived out of the tiger's way. The tiger's feet landed in the trap, and its legs were bound together. The monstrous beast fell sideways and squirmed helplessly.

"I've found it!" said Akira, targeting the tiger's weak area.

"Now, Seraph!" Angelo yelled.

As Akira closed in, Angelo marvelled at her skill.

The tiger, now struggling within the snare, was vulnerable.

Akira projected her sword with a fluid motion, aiming for the creature's exposed neck. Every swing was deliberate, calculated, and executed with a precision that spoke of years of disciplined practice. The blade descended, meeting its target, and the sabertooth let out a final, thunderous roar before dissolving into nothingness.

As the illusion of the tiger faded away, Angelo couldn't shake the adrenaline coursing through his veins. He stole a glance at Akira, who wore a satisfied smile. The encounter with the tiger had tested their ability to adapt, and Angelo found himself grateful for the partnership, even if his feelings had been accidentally laid bare. He eventually collapsed to the floor.

"Good thinking back there, but that trap you summoned almost knocked you out. Be careful. You're not yet at that level to summon such complex devices. That's advanced," Akira explained, rushing to his aid.

Angelo couldn't comprehend the joy he was feeling. Being in Akira's arms was the paradise he had always dreamed of. His heart buzzed with more intense affection.

"Why're you smiling like that?" asked Akira, her eyebrows raised with confusion. A smile had snuck up on Angelo's face without him realising it.

"It's nothing. You and I make a great team," said Angelo, getting up and dusting himself off. Their collaboration only strengthened their bond.

***

The game progressed, and Angelo kept moving along the gameboard. Through hurdles and obstacles, Angelo was close to the end.

Unfortunately, Akira landed on a snake, which set her back.

Angelo was even more determined to win now. *If he could win this game for the whole team, Akira would be highly impressed.*

Angelo landed on block 90, and Shawn was surprisingly a few blocks ahead of him. *How did Shawn manage to get ahead of everyone else?*

Akira, Nigel or one of the cherubs should have dominated the board by now, never mind Rex. *Was Shawn destined to win Snakes and Ladders and save the team from certain death?* A twinge of jealousy nipped at Angelo, eager for his own moment in the spotlight. Yet, he couldn't forget that Shawn had always been the reigning champion of board games.

With a critical five minutes remaining, Shawn rolled the die, the anticipation heavy in the air. The die danced across the board, settling on a four. Shawn advanced, a mere three blocks away from victory, block 97.

"Oh no, this is bad," Shawn exclaimed.

"What is it?" asked Angelo.

"I've landed on a snake!"

Victory seemed so close, only to slip away once more. This game was impossible to beat. Snakes and Ladders would soon trap the Starlight Saints in its claws of death. With Shawn landing on a snake, a dreadful realisation came upon Angelo. He was their last hope, the closest one to winning and saving the team from certain death. The pressure intensified as Angelo braced himself.

CHAPTER 29

WELL PLAYED

Shawn met his doom. He would be hurled to a lower part of the gameboard. The saints had no way of winning, and this was it. It was up to Angelo to make the final stride. He waited for Shawn to go back, but nothing happened. Shawn just stood there. *Had Zayn put the game on pause or a complete stop?*

A door suddenly swung open, and a slim girl, probably around Angelo's age, emerged. The girl's glamourising spark lit in her eyes, alluring every witness. However, Angelo noticed the girl had a snake coiling around her arm and in her hand was a small crystal cube. A smile crept up on the girl's face as she glanced at Shawn, and Angelo couldn't help but harbour a bad feeling in his gut.

"I'm Tori, the referee of this game and Zayn's girl," she said.

Angelo's unease deepened; her seemingly innocent demeanour clashed with the peculiar situation they found themselves in.

Shawn, still captivated by Tori's presence, managed to stammer, "Since when does Snakes and Ladders have a referee?"

Angelo's heart skipped a beat.

Shawn was in awe of Tori, easily entranced by her lovely aura. She rubbed the cube with her fingers and put her ear close to it. "For you to win the game, you must answer a riddle. You have three attempts," Tori declared, her gaze fixed on Shawn.

Shawn, visibly caught off guard, struggled to find his composure. "What kind of riddle?" he asked, desperation seeping into his voice. The room held its breath, awaiting the cryptic challenge that would ultimately determine their fate in this game.

"This riddle is the key to helping you find the answers you seek," said Tori. "It's something that some of you lack."

In shadows deep where darkness weaves,
Unseen whispers, the secret retrieves.
Within the echoes that silence bares,
The intangible truth patiently flares.
What am I that binds everyone together,
Yet can never be seen, nor touched ever?"

Angelo's heart sank with the weight of the challenge before Shawn.

Once filled with anticipation, the room now froze as if afraid to disturb the delicate balance between the known and unknown. Angelo, trying to anchor himself in this unworldly reality, encouraged Shawn with a desperate plea. "Come on, Sparrow. You can solve it. You're good at puzzles."

The snake slithered away from Tori's arm, disappearing into the shadows of the illusory game. She, unmoved, placed her arms on Shawn's shoulders, the cube still cradled in her delicate grasp. The position they formed resembled that of a couple at a ball. Shawn's eyes met Angelo's, doubt etched across his face like a brushstroke on the canvas of uncertainty.

"You're the hidden truth," Shawn guessed, his confidence starting to waver.

"Wrong," Tori explained, her words like a gentle breeze that refused to reveal the secrets it carried. "Try again."

Shawn's eyes widened, realisation dawning on him. Two attempts left, and the pressure of the impending consequence pressed upon his shoulders.

"Think deeper," Angelo begged, a desperate plea lost in the game of Snakes and Ladders.

But Shawn, entranced by Tori's charm, seemed distant, his focus blurred by an invisible allure. Angelo began to have second thoughts as his jealousy resurfaced. Although he usually hated being the centre of attention, Angelo was desperate to have the spotlight this time and impress Akira. *It could only be done if he won the game and not Shawn.*

Angelo contemplated helping his friend further. If he let Shawn win the game, he would also be helping the rest of the team escape its deathly snare, but he would also miss his chance at impressing Akira. *Yet if Angelo didn't help Shawn, the burden would be placed on him to win, which wasn't so guaranteed, and he could end up costing the Starlight Saints their lives.*

In the grand scheme of things, the team's survival was far more important than a mere moment in the spotlight. Angelo swallowed his pride and decided to keep helping his friend.

Still, Angelo's attempts to break through to Shawn felt like desperate cries in a vacuum, swallowed by the illusion surrounding them.

Tori had Shawn ensnared in the grasp of her seduction, and Angelo, despite his efforts, had to face the painful truth.

Feeling the pressure of time slipping away, Angelo forced himself to contemplate the riddle's possible answers. The air suffocated with tension as the seconds ticked down, each tick emphasising how close they were to death.

"The answer is teamwork?" Shawn made his second guess.

"Getting warmer but not quite," Tori answered.

Shawn was wrong once again. One final attempt remained, and the imminent threat drew closer with each passing second. There was one minute left until all hell broke loose. Angelo, grappling with the pressure, mentally highlighted each keyword of the riddle: *intangible truth…binds everyone together…Unseen.*

The pieces clicked into place. *What is unseen and intangible is often what holds the most significance.* The third starlight motto rang in his head.

"The third motto!" Angelo exclaimed, urgency driving his words. "Think of that motto and what bound us together in the Journey of Faith."

Shawn clamped his hands onto his head in frustration, fingers tangling in his hair as he grappled with the answer. Then, in a sudden burst of realisation, his eyes widened, and the light of understanding settled in his gaze.

"It's trust!" Shawn declared, his voice cutting through the suspended tension. "Trust is the answer that binds us together. It can't be seen yet has huge significance."

Tori, taken aback, staggered backward, her shock evident in the widening of her eyes.

Taking his chances, Shawn reached for the die, his fingers closing around it with a newfound confidence. With a resolute roll, he sent the die clattering across the gameboard. As it settled, Shawn surged forward, navigating the last three blocks with determination. The finish line beckoned, and with a final, triumphant leap, he crossed it. It was game over.

The once chaotic illusionary landscape blurred and twisted, folding in on itself. The disorienting spin intensified, and soon, the saints found themselves back in the familiar surroundings of the main casino. The team, scattered around the room, was in a collective daze, each member attempting to reconnect with the reality surrounding them.

"Did...we win?" asked Vanya.

"Yeah, Shawn won the game for us," Angelo explained with a sense of relief.

"Shawn? That's the last person that could pull off a victory like that. More like a fluke," Rex scoffed. "Everyone knows Leclez would've dominated."

Suddenly, with an instant and unexpected movement, Akira materialised next to Rex.

In a blink, Akira's hand clamped down on Rex's arm, effortlessly putting him in a submissive arm lock.

Rex's groans of pain filled the room.

"Talking down on your fellow saints will not be tolerated," Akira declared. "We're a team, and what we're built on is trust and support."

"My apologies, Seraph," Rex conceded in desperate moans.

Akira released Rex from her vicious grip, and he rubbed his arm.

Rex wasn't so tough when he was at the seraph's mercy.

Angelo was tempted to laugh, but he dared not for fear of what Rex would do to him later if he did.

Akira locked her eyes on Shawn with a flicker of approval. "You did us proud, Sparrow. Your grit in the face of danger is to be commended."

"I got a little help. We're nothing without teamwork," said Shawn, looking in Angelo's direction.

"Yippie! Yay! Congratulations on beating my fun little game," said Zayn as he burst through a set of doors, clapping his hands like a child who'd just opened their present. "Our meeting can commence now. I'm sure you guys need something to drink."

An infuriated Nigel summoned a dagger and aimed it straight at the casino owner. "How about I just put an end to this? Enough of your dumb act!"

The tension in the room tightened, each heartbeat reflecting the possibility of a violent confrontation. Akira gracefully stepped forward, a calming force amid a rising scuffle, and gently gestured for Nigel to put his weapons down. With a slow, deliberate movement, Nigel lowered his dagger and followed Akira's advice.

Zayn smiled jubilantly despite Nigel's heated threat.

If the Starlight Saints wanted answers, they would have to keep playing along with this dubious magician until he gave them.

Chapter 30

Final Confrontation

Zayn extended a casual invitation, gesturing for the saints to follow him. Through a maze of endless corridors, they were ushered into an elegant lounge. Plush sofas surrounded a polished round table. Everything for the meeting was set.

"Get these guests our finest beverages," Zayn instructed a waitress. "Lemonade for these lovely kids."

Angelo sat with Shawn, Rex and Akira.

Tori, with an unsettling grace, joined the table and took a seat opposite Angelo. Despite the welcoming hospitality, Angelo couldn't shake his mistrust for Zayn and Tori as the saints had almost fallen victim to an intense board game.

Angelo shot Tori a detestable glance, to which she responded with a disarming smile.

Shawn, seemingly entranced once again by Tori's presence, was oblivious to the silent exchange between Angelo and the enigmatic referee.

Clyde and Faye, perhaps sensing the tension, swiftly excused themselves, claiming a bathroom break.

"That encounter with me was a test of trust, and you passed. You stay counting on your friends, and that's what us magicians love to see," Tori said to Shawn, her words carrying a force that only deepened Angelo's mistrust.

270

They were now in the presence of the final suspect. Angelo's objective was clear: he needed Zayn to confess to Don's murder or the murder of the dietitian.

"So, you guys wanted to see me about the investigation," Zayn said, breaking the tension as if making an innocent inquiry. "Where should we begin?"

The drinks arrived, placed on the table with a tempting array of flavours. Angelo hesitated as he stared at the icy lemonade, suspecting it may have been poisoned as part of Zayn's fake hospitality, but at the same time, thirst was beating down on his throat. His parchedness got the best of him and proved to be the bigger adversary. He took a big gulp of his lemonade, allowing it to quench his undying thirst.

"We're here because you're the last suspect on Don's enemy list. Don wrote that you were one of the people who might kill him," Akira explained, her words confrontational, like a challenge.

Zayn responded with a smile as if the accusation was nothing more than a punchline to a joke. "Ooo, very amusing. A fine woman like you shouldn't concern herself with such matters."

There was something irresistible about Zayn's attractiveness, and his charm oozed like honey. If Akira was dazzled by his looks, she didn't show it. She remained stoic and unmoved.

"That evidence led us to you. You were one of the best magicians, and you turned your back on my father," Angelo declared, his words cutting through the room like a knife.

Zayn's laughter echoed, "Oh, is that so? I find it funny how you think you know everything."

"You killed him! Admit it. You're an Illumiknight."

"Not exactly. Don and I were great friends. I'm no Illuminati member, trust me. I work alone, and I take no one's side. Not even Starlight Saints like yourselves," Zayn explained with an act of nonchalance, sipping his drink as if he were sharing casual gossip.

271

The revelation didn't sit well with Angelo, and he wasn't buying the claims.

Zayn spoke like a lone wolf, a figure unbound by allegiances. Yet, the air of mystery around him persisted, leaving the saints unconvinced. *There had to be more to the story, a hidden truth waiting to be uncovered.*

"I'll tell you the full story of what happened between me and Don," Zayn said, leaning back and gesturing for them to get comfortable. It seemed, for a moment, that he was finally willing to cooperate.

"Don and I were always close friends, or should I say besties? He was always amazed at my tricks as a magician and an illusionist. I showed him my greatest works of magic, and he became fond of it," Zayn narrated, setting the stage for an intriguing account. Holding a steel spoon, he slowly began to bend the metal using his bare hands, a demonstration of his mystifying abilities.

"One day, he brought me his enemy list and asked me to take revenge on people like Tom Chandler for him. He asked me to curse his enemies using my magic, but I couldn't bring myself to do that. I can't abuse such power," Zayn explained. "I know Don's innocent now, but at the time, I wondered what if he was guilty of the child trafficking allegations? I could bend spoons, but I had no intention of bending justice or democracy until I knew the truth. That would be wrong."

It was hard to believe what they were hearing. This didn't sound like his dad at all. Angelo wasn't buying the story.

"After I denied his request, he didn't take it very well. He added me to his enemy list, and our friendship went downhill from there."

"That's a lie. My father would never wanna curse people. He was a man of God," Angelo objected, amplifying doubt and anger.

"That's what I'd like to believe, too, but this was what he wanted," said Zayn. "My magic is unpredictable, and cursing individuals in high positions of power would only add fuel to the fire. I explained to him that we didn't need to resort to dark magic and being petty like he was, he held a grudge against me for the rest of his life."

Angelo was taken aback; *his dad was just trying to protect himself and the family. Or was there perhaps a darker side to him.*

"Well, the Illuminati was after him. You think he was a part of it?" asked Akira.

"I would think so because the way he acted was a cry for help," said Zayn, his words carrying the weight of a bitter truth. "He was probably trying to get out, but they wouldn't let him. Anyone with that kind of stardom and power is bound to have some connection with the Illuminati. They wouldn't let someone like him off the hook."

"But what if you'd just helped him? You could've saved his life, and he'd still be here today," Angelo retorted, frustration and rage punctuating his words and banged his fist on the table.

"I wanted to protect him, but he was too far gone. The Illuminati already had him. If I'd gotten involved, they would've taken me out too or even my daughter. No one would've been saved," Zayn explained, his tone carrying regret.

Angelo's trust started to falter as he grappled with the disturbing revelation. *This couldn't be. What Zayn was saying about his father simply wasn't true.*

He could not believe any of Zayn's words because, after all, weren't magicians known for being tricksters, manipulators and deceivers with the magic tricks they performed?

If he wanted the truth, Angelo would have to take a drastic measure, one that would involve death. "You're lying. You made that story up, and I don't believe a word you're saying about my dad." Angelo's hand emerged from beneath the table, clutching a gun aimed directly at Zayn.

The room fell into a shocked hush as the saints grappled with the sudden escalation. Even Nigel was taken aback by Angelo's display of assertiveness and gave a nod of approval.

273

"No more playing around. It's just us now, and you've got nowhere to go. Confess, or I pull the trigger," Angelo declared, savouring the power that the gun afforded him.

Zayn, unfazed, scoffed and continued to laugh. "You're right, I have nowhere to go, but I wouldn't be so foolish if I were you. I've still got plenty of tricks in the book," he said in a calm, soothing voice that defied his predicament. Was he not worried for his life? One pull on the trigger, and it should have been all over.

"Take a good look at your gun again."

Angelo, puzzled by the request, followed Zayn's instruction. To his horror, what had been a firearm seconds ago transformed into a hissing snake, coiling menacingly in his hand. Panic gripped Angelo, and he yelped, hurling the snake across the room.

"Shoot, that gun just turned into a snake," Angelo exclaimed in a frenzy. However, the others looked at him bewildered.

"What snake?" asked Nigel.

"Right across there." Angelo pointed to where he threw the gun, but there was no sign of the snake.

The weapon, now just a regular pistol, lay innocently on the floor. Angelo's forehead creased with confusion.

Had the snake slithered away? They had to have seen it. It had even hissed.

"Tell me you guys saw it too. I can't be the only one," Angelo implored, his eyes darting between the faces of his teammates, but the others remained unconvinced.

Was he the only one who saw it? Was his mind playing tricks on him? He looked back at Zayn, who was laughing uncontrollably.

Angelo's suspicion intensified, a flicker of realization surfacing. It was one of Zayn's illusionary tricks, some crafty manipulation. "How'd you do that?" Angelo questioned, too stunned by the trick.

"A magician never reveals his secrets," Zayn explained with a confident smirk. "I'm an illusionist, so I make people see things I want them to see."

"Are these the tricks you played on my father before you killed him?" asked Angelo, with bitterness now eclipsing the fear that had been there before.

"No. I didn't kill your dad," Zayn stated matter-of-factly, presenting a cell phone that showcased pictures of old emails as evidence. "Believe me, I tried to help him. My associates can testify."

Angelo felt a surge of pain at the realization that his dad had been fighting for his life but ended up losing it to the dark forces that held him captive. As he learned more and more about his father's death, his rage only grew. His hunger for vengeance cut deep.

The Illuminati would not get away with this. Angelo vowed to save the music industry and avenge all the fallen soldiers who lost the battle. *If Zayn wasn't the killer, then the saints had reached a dead end. All these leads had ultimately led to nothing. Was the killer still worth pursuing? Perhaps it was time to abandon the investigation and accept that they would never find the answer.*

As the tension in the room thickened, the doors suddenly burst open, and one of the guards came through with panic written in his eyes.

"Sir, there's a raid happening on the ground floor. There's people in masks shooting everybody they see," the guard urgently reported. "Our men are trying everything they can, but we can't hold them off."

A raid? Angelo's mind raced, grappling with the unthinkable scenario of one of the city's most prestigious casinos under siege.

"How'd they break through our security? The cops better be on their way," Zayn demanded.

"That's the worst part. The cops can't even get through. They blocked them off," the guard explained, his words landing like a heavy blow.

Zayn met the situation with a solid look of determination.

Angelo's gaze swept the team, realizing that Clyde and Faye were still absent. A sinking feeling settled in his stomach; they had been in the bathroom for an oddly long time.

"Nobody raids my casino and gets away with it," said Zayn, his fingers casually stroking his smooth, silky hair. "Tell everybody to vacate the area; I'll take things from here."

The building crackled with despair as they found themselves in the middle of a raid. Distant screams and gunshots resonated from outside the room, and chaos broke loose. Uncertainty clawed over the fate of the casino and all its occupants.

CHAPTER 31

LAST MAGICIAN STANDING

The raid unfolded like a storm, chaos rippling through the once untroubled surroundings of the casino.

"I assume you guys can get around since you're Starlight Saints. Everybody follow me," Zayn instructed, his voice cutting through the racket of gunshots and screams.

"Is this part of the game too?" asked Vanya.

"No, it's not part of the game! They're raiding my damn casino," said Zayn, frustration etching lines on his face.

Angelo still harbouring the remnants of mistrust towards Zayn but they would have to work together, or they would die in the raid.

The saints trailed behind Zayn as he led them out of the lounge, descending steps that seemed to cry with the distant turmoil. Gunshots reverberated, each one a thunderous bang.

On the ground floor, armed attackers, faces concealed by menacing masks and clad in leather jackets, moved with forceful authority. The air was thick with the scent of smoke, assaulting Angelo's nostrils and heightening the urgency of the crisis.

Angelo glanced up. "Fire!" Angelo exclaimed, his voice rising above the chaos. The rest of the group followed his gaze to the upper floor, their shock mirrored in shared panic. The situation had escalated into a desperate struggle for survival. *Yet, a nagging question lingered — why hadn't the fire alarm gone off?*

The saints crouched down to avoid detection from the intruders who held some of the customers.

"How'd this place catch fire? I need one of you to get a fire extinguisher and run up there before the fire gets worse. We'll need to get everybody out through the fire exits," said Zayn under his breath.

"I'll go," Nigel volunteered. He manoeuvred up the stairs with a growing urgency, each step a testament to the race against time.

Two women and a man, their hands and legs bound together, were tightly taped, helpless in the clutches of the assailants. Dozens of robbers, cold and cunning, stationed themselves around the hostages, forming a formidable barricade.

"These fools will pay," Zayn commented. "If they're foolish enough to raid Zayntopia, they got another thing coming. Nobody gets away with hurting my people."

A gunshot shattered the air, the deafening sound bouncing off the walls, sending shockwaves through the already panicked crowd.

"We have unfinished business, Mr. Zayn Hopkins. We had a deal, and we demand you to show yourself," announced one of the robbers in a gold mask, taking leadership authority. "We're aware you have connections with the Jacksons, too. We know Angelo's around here somewhere, and we want him alive."

A collective freeze took hold of the room.

The attackers were here for me, but the question was, why? Anxiety gripped Angelo's heart, a storm of questions raging within him. *What a group of terrorists wanted with an adolescent? Someone must've sent them. Was raiding Zayn's casino while the Starlight Saints were present just a coincidence?*

Nothing added up.

The unsettling realisation dawned.

Someone was watching their every move, but who?

"You have five minutes to make up your mind. If you want these people to live, you will do as we say," declared the gold-masked leader, presenting his ultimatum.

Confronting these terrorists, head-on would be suicide. Too many were armed, and the odds were insurmountable. There was no chance of taking them on with a group of eight. There was only one thing left to do.

Angelo had to turn himself in to save his team and the innocent hostages. He couldn't bear the guilt of others paying the price for his actions. The memory of nearly leading Rex and Shawn into an ambush haunted him, and he wouldn't let a similar incident happen again. Angelo refused to have any blood on his hands.

"Who are these guys, and what deal did you make?" asked Shawn in disbelief.

"It's the Illuminati. I should've known," Zayn admitted. "They wanted me to sell them my casino and offered me a big check. I agreed initially, but when I found out what they were planning to do with my business, I had to cheat my way out of the contract using magic."

A stunned silence settled over the group; all eyes fixed on Zayn.

So, the Illuminati had another enemy on their hands. They also knew about Zayn's affiliation with Angelo's dad, and that's when the dots connected. No wonder they were here.

"I'm gonna turn myself in. If they want me alive, they won't shoot," said Angelo resolutely. He took a step forward, but a hand grabbed hold of him.

"Are you crazy? You can't trust them," Vanya pleaded with Angelo, desperation in her eyes.

"I have to do it," Angelo responded. "It's the only way to save everybody. If I don't, then we all die."

Angelo wouldn't allow anyone else to go. It was him they wanted. No one else would have to step forward.

Akira wasn't putting up with Angelo's bravado, however. "You're not going anywhere. You'll stay here as I say."

"I hope you'll forgive me, Seraph," Angelo began. "I don't mean to defy you, but I know what's right."

Angelo rose from his crouched position. He bolted down the stairs, the urgency propelling him forward.

Rex and Vanya joined the mad dash, their footsteps following as they descended to the ground floor.

Angelo's hand gripped the door, and with a forceful push, it swung open, revealing the lobby swarming with masked intruders. "I'm right here! It's me you want," Angelo boldly announced, his heart pounding against his ribs.

The poor hostages were terrified and wide-eyed.

Angelo had his starlight watch ready to activate.

The man with a gold mask laughed and ridiculed Angelo's heroic antics.

Rex and Vanya stood on both sides, prepared to engage in combat despite their slim chances of defeating these armed enemies.

Angelo was about to activate his frequency box as a surprise attack until Rex halted his efforts and warned that it would harm the hostages in the process.

Behind them, doors burst open, and the rest of the team, apart from Nigel and the cherubs, streamed in, a united front against the intense threat. Zayn and his daughter added to the formidable presence.

***

"Mr. Hopkins, it's good to see you. Remember your old friend Ugo?" asked the man in the gold mask. "You agreed to give us your casino in exchange for 80 million dollars, but you somehow changed the contract and tricked us into terminating it. A typical magician, yes. I've read all about you and your amazing tricks."

"You were gonna use my casino to spy, gather data from people and control them as part of your new world system. I won't let you exploit my customers for your own agenda," Zayn declared.

Angelo was intrigued by the Illuminati's attempt to exploit people's tendency to gamble with their money to gather sensitive data. If the Illuminati had tabs on the people of Las Vegas, they would know how to control most of the city's population. The Illuminati would stop at nothing to grow and exert their influence.

"That's a shame," Ugo declared, pointing his gun menacingly at Angelo. "We're taking the boy with us too."

"Not without a fight," Akira asserted, stepping forward.

Ugo, dismissing the conventional, fired a shot into the air, the bang signalling the beginning of a deadly battle.

"Guns are pretty boring. We're gonna fight like real men and women," he declared with a wicked grin.

The metallic clang of weapons being unsheathed filled the room as Ugo pulled a black, rounded ball from his palm. With a swift motion, it transformed and extended into a sharp blade.

Other Illumiknights mirrored the action.

With the odds stacked against them, Angelo wished the rest of the team had stayed behind. How would they navigate this perilous encounter?

Akira lunged forward, katanas flashing, dispatching two Illumiknights with lightning speed. The clash erupted into a chaotic bloodbath as both secret societies collided.

Angelo, summoning a sword, engaged in a fierce blade-to-blade duel with an Illumiknight. Smoke billowed, obscuring his vision, and he couldn't help but wonder if Nigel had managed to extinguish the fire.

Angelo coughed relentlessly from the suffocating smoke, the Illumiknights surged in full force, and the onslaught became overwhelming.

The Starlight Saints found themselves in a desperate struggle to fight their way out of the building and save the hostages before the casino succumbed to the flames.

An Illumiknight knocked Angelo's sword out of his hand. Just as the attacker closed in for the final strike, a sudden grip on his throat sent him sprawling forward, defeated. A dagger protruded from the back of his neck. Angelo looked up, he spotted Vanya running across the walls with unparalleled grace. As she ran, she threw daggers at her targets with impressive precision. Great strategy using her star strides, thought Angelo. His sword disappeared, and he summoned a spear.

Across the room, Shawn and Tori, an unexpected duo, had teamed up.

"Just follow my lead," Tori directed Shawn.

Tori pulled out a card from seemingly thin air. A masked assailant leapt forward, but out of nowhere, their blade, once a deadly threat, began to bend like rubber.

Angelo's eyes widened in awe and disbelief, questioning if what he saw had just happened. The blade had curled up like a snake.

Tori took advantage of the Illumiknight's shock, and with a powerful blow of her fist, she sent the assailant crashing to the floor. It dawned on Angelo that this was one of the magic tricks Zayn had demonstrated earlier - the art of bending metal, now wielded in combat.

Another Illumiknight swung their blade at Tori and gave a fierce howl. It was a female behind the mask, as heard in their voice. As the attack unfolded, an uncanny phenomenon took hold - the Illumiknight began to slow down as if trapped in slow motion.

What foolishness was this? Shawn was evidently astonished by Tori's display of magic tricks and combat.

Angelo's gaze darted up the walls once more, searching for Vanya.

Vanya still ran across, but her agile run was short-lived with the crack of a gunshot. She lay crumpled on the floor.

"Tempest!" Angelo cried with desperation. In that heartbreaking moment, time seemed to freeze.

Vanya was hit, lying on the floor helpless, and there was nothing Angelo could do.

"I find saints and their walking strides annoying," Ugo's voice cut through, pistol in hand.

It was Ugo who had fired the deadly shot. *The only way to stop this madness was to give himself up, or more people would die.*

An enraged Angelo, fuelled by a surge of vengeance, tussled and fought his way to Ugo. he confronted Ugo, Angelo's spear disappeared, and in a gesture of surrender, he raised his hands.

"Just take me and leave the others alone," said Angelo with a desperate plea for mercy. "It's me you want."

"Wise decision, smart man," Ugo responded, his grip tightening on Angelo in an awkward embrace. The closeness was suffocating, an uncomfortable action in the midst of danger.

Angelo, unable to see beyond the mask, could almost feel the satisfaction radiating from Ugo.

Amongst the ongoing struggle, Ugo steered Angelo towards the exit, a dark passage awaiting them.

The Illuminati's intentions with him remained a mystery. If the Illuminati wanted him dead, they would've killed him by now, but they were clearly after something else. He recalled Tom Chandler's threat to sell him to the child trafficking agency, and a chill spread through his whole body at the thought.

Out of nowhere, Zayn emerged from a cloud of engulfing smoke, halting their progress. "You're not leaving my casino with that boy or in one piece," he declared.

A glimmer of hope arose in Angelo's mind. *Perhaps this was his chance to team up with the magician.*

Hope gave way to horror as Ugo produced a device. An electric shock buzzed through Angelo's body as the device pressed against his forehead, the electric shock coursing through every fibre of his being. The agony was so overwhelming that he was on the brink of unconsciousness. Ugo, maintaining calmness, caught him in the nick of time, holding the paralysed Angelo in his arms.

"Now don't try running away," Ugo's chilling words resonated as he gently placed the helpless Angelo on the floor.

Angelo lay there, a prisoner in his own body, unable to move his limbs. Panic and frustration erupted within him as he realised what Ugo had done.

Zayn and Ugo stood locked in a deadly confrontation, the casino's fate and Angelo's life on the line. "For the last time, no amount of millions will make me give away my business," Zayn's defiance could be felt as Angelo observed the standoff.

"Oh, Zayn, a great movement is happening worldwide, and you could've been a part of it. A part of something bigger than this. It's too bad you've sided with the Starlight Saints," said Ugo, his voice dripping with disappointment.

"I'm not on anyone's side," said Zayn. "I go solo, *Han Solo.*"

In a flash, Zayn pulled out a card, and a cascade of hidden knives arced towards Ugo.

Ugo dodged the incoming blades with light effort. He then retaliated, charging at the magician with lightning speed.

Zayn had another card up his sleeve—or rather, in his hand. With a flick of his wrist, time seemed to slow around Ugo.

Angelo chuckled at how Ugo was moving slowly, but his laughter vanished when Ugo surprisingly delivered a rapidly fast punch.

Zayn stumbled backwards and rubbed his jaw where Ugo's blow had landed.

"That trick won't work on me," Ugo declared with a self-assured grin. "You can't alter my perception of time when I have a sharp mind."

Undeterred, Zayn began crafting shapes with his hands, conjuring a legion of shadows that enveloped him. He seemingly sank into the ground, leaving only the shadows to swirl menacingly.

The shadows swarmed around Ugo like sharks, ready to devour their prey, and the onslaught of darkness left the Illumi-knight disoriented. "Stop hiding in the shadows and face me like a man," Ugo challenged.

Zayn materialised from the shadows, but Ugo's blade cut through him before he could retaliate. Blood oozed from Zayn's chest, and Angelo, witnessing the brutal scene, gasped in horror.

The shadows dissipated, leaving Zayn on his knees, struggling for breath. Despair set in; it seemed Zayn's fate was sealed, and there was nothing he could do to intervene.

As the two vulnerable figures remained on the ground, Ugo diverted his attention to a nearby vase. Picking it up, he positioned himself between Angelo and the wounded illusionist. He transformed his lethal blade back into an ordinary ball.

"Watch closely," Ugo instructed. "I've decided to show mercy to the two of you since you're lost causes. I'll put my orb in this vase and call a truce. Then I'll put my hand back and take out the orb."

A truce? Why spare Zayn in such a weakened state?

Ugo's sudden surrender took Angelo by surprise. He proceeded to follow through with his words. After a brief pause, he submerged his hand into the vase once more. To everyone's surprise, a gun emerged, not the expected orb.

"Ta-da! How do you like my magic trick? Thought I'd give you a taste of your own medicine before you die," Ugo sneered, taking aim at the defenceless Zayn. "You would've reigned with us in the new era that's to come, but you're just a useless magician."

As Ugo prepared to pull the trigger, he collapsed to the floor like a puppet that had lost its strings.

Zayn pulled out a small rag doll and made it stand straight.

Ugo stood up straight in response, accurately mirroring the doll's actions and became stiff.

As Zayn put the doll in an arch yoga position, Ugo started to bend backwards and fall into the same position. The savage cracking and crushing of bones made Angelo wince, and Ugo began shrieking.

Ugo, once a menacing force, was now at the mercy of a small rag doll manipulated by Zayn. He winced in pain and cried out, "Lord have mercy, how the hell are you doing this?"

"While we were fighting, I snuck a card into your pocket without you knowing," Zayn explained calmly, indifferent to the Illumiknight's suffering. "This card allows me to control people like puppets."

"Impossible," said Ugo, his voice strained with disbelief. "I thought I knew all the tricks in your book."

This was difficult for Angelo to watch, although Ugo deserved it. Seeing Ugo in such a position made Angelo's spine hurt. The pain was unbearable, for sure. Although the Illumiknight was a sworn enemy of his, he couldn't help but hold a tinge of sympathy as the feeling was coming back to his arms again, slowly gaining his mobility back.

Zayn continued his ruthless performance on the immobilised Ugo. "One thing about magicians is we always have one or two more tricks up our sleeves," he declared with a smirk. "Bending the rules and perceptions of the eye is kind of my speciality."

Zayn twisted one arm and one leg of the tortured Illumiknight. More bones cracked, and Ugo's howls of pain reverberated through the room. "I learned this trick from some magicians in Berlin,"

"Please, make it stop!" Ugo begged; his cries coated with agony.

Ugo lay on the floor, now limp and crippled.

A spark of sorrow for Ugo's gruesome torture touched upon Angelo. The fact that Ugo remained alive only intensified the pain of witnessing such brutality. He was grateful Zayn had never used this horrifying trick on him.

Footsteps plodded from behind, and as Angelo turned to familiar faces in the distance. Vanya miraculously materialised, and to Angelo's relief, she revealed her protective vest had shielded her and taken the blow of the bullet from earlier.

"I managed to free the hostages while we were fighting, but all the fire exits are blocked," said Vanya.

Everyone had reassembled at the centre foyer as the smoke and putrid odour of burning sulphur lingered. It was time to escape. They had to flee before the casino swallowed them in its fiery destruction, *yet something still feels out of place.*

CHAPTER 32

DEAD END ACCOMPLICE

A deafening gunshot shattered the air, and blood began to stain Zayn's chest. Seraph Nigel emerged behind the fallen casino owner, flanked by Cherub Clyde and Faye.

Tori's panicked scream pierced the chaos as she rushed to her wounded father's side.

"Nigel, what have you done?" Akira questioned, her voice trembling.

"I'm simply doing my job," said Nigel nonchalantly. The gun in Nigel's hand was now ominously directed at Angelo, prompting gasps from the onlookers.

Angelo, momentarily frozen by the sudden turn of events, felt a cold shiver run down his spine. Nigel's voice cut through the silence.

"So, here we are, still without answers to the investigation," Nigel began with an unsettling smile. "I can help with that. The answer is right in front of you. I killed Don's dietitian after he leaked the tape, and I planned this whole raid from the start, so you'd never be able to solve the case. I'm also the one who hired the assassin during the rituals."

The revelation hit the team like a thunderbolt. Wide-eyed disbelief painted their faces.

Angelo's heart sank, the weight of the confession impossible to ignore. "B-but why?" Angelo's voice quivered with a mix of confusion and desperation. "Why don't you want us to solve the case?"

"I did it to protect my daughter, Quinn Parkerson. She assisted with Don's murder as part of a deal," Nigel confessed, sending tremors through Angelo. The revelation that Casey's touring partner and girlfriend was involved in the murder fuelled the fire to the already unsettling case - A murder accomplice. Angelo needed to act. *Warn Casey and reveal the truth about Quinn.*

"So did you plan my dad's murder too?" asked Angelo.

Unfazed, Nigel claimed ignorance, asserting that the specifics didn't matter, for death awaited them all. "For many years, I served under the Starlight Saints and saw just how flawed it is. Grandmaster Rin failed from the day you were recruited. Today, I renounce my allegiance and assume my new position as Vice General Director in the Illuminati. They need someone like me."

"What about our positions you promised us?" Cherub Faye interjected. "You said if we helped you, we'd become high-ranking Illumiknights ourselves."

Nigel paused abruptly as if caught off guard. Then, with a cold smirk, he answered, "Oh, about that…there is no place for you guys. You've served your purpose, and I won't be needing you anymore."

Clyde and Faye's faces mirrored shock and bitterness as they realised Nigel had deceived them all along. "That's not what you promised! We had a deal," Clyde objected, stepping forward to confront Nigel.

In a split second, Nigel fired a bullet into Clyde's head.

Clyde's cranium shattered, and he collapsed to the floor.

Faye, now on high alert, projected a blade in an attempt to strike Nigel.

But Nigel was faster. He blocked the attack and instantaneously thrust the blade into Faye's throat, leaving the cherub to drown in her own blood.

Angelo and the others watched the brutal onslaught in disbelief. A Starlight Saint turning on his own made Angelo question if anyone could really ever be trusted.

Nigel pulled out a cylinder of green liquid and pulled the cap off, revealing a syringe.

"I'm an Illumiknight at heart. Ugo said this new variant of reptilian serum will do wonders beyond anything the Starlight Saints can ever think of," laughed Nigel.

Ugo groaned in response, still lying there like a rag doll.

"Nigel, no," Akira warned. "The sera are not meant for you. You must go through a ritual to develop immunity first, or you'll die."

"I already have. I've been in contact with the Illuminati for a while as they promised me my place in their society." Without hesitation, Nigel injected the substance into his neck.

Veins began to emerge prominently as the serum coursed through his body. A sinister smirk adorned Nigel's face as he revelled in the transformative power of the serum.

Clyde and Faye lay there dead on the floor, now out of the picture.

Angelo understood that once the serum's transformation was complete, they would face an unstoppable force.

Nigel, a loyal seraph dedicated to the Starlight Saints before, was now evolving into someone far more menacing with this new variant.

The Shadowbreakers, sensing the imminent battle, activated their watches in preparation.

Yet, just as a confrontation seemed inevitable, Nigel's triumphant moment took a sudden turn. He began coughing violently, blood gushing from his mouth.

Nigel dropped to his knees, trembling, his face contorted in agony. "What's happening to me?" he gasped, looking toward the incapacitated Ugo. "You said I was immune. You tricked me!"

Ugo simply let out a weak cackle, "Fool. There is no ritual for immunity. We made that up. A Starlight Saint will always be my enemy no matter what."

Angelo locked eyes with Akira, contemplating whether they should intervene. She shook her head sorrowfully as if conveying that there was no salvation for Nigel now.

"There's no way to reverse the effects. Once it's in your bloodstream, it's over," Akira explained.

Nigel lay on the floor, twitching uncontrollably until all signs of life gradually faded.

Angelo stared at the lifeless body of the once prominent seraph, which was now amongst those of the two cherubs, too stunned to comment.

Tori, standing beside her wounded father, began chanting an incantation while skilfully tending to Zayn's injury to stem the bleeding.

The group gathered around them, dreading the magician's fate.

"He'll make it, but we should leave before the flames take over," Tori informed the group with urgency. "Someone, help me get him up."

Without delay, Shawn rushed to Tori's side, and together, they manoeuvred Zayn toward the entrance, where a small escape route awaited. As the Starlight Saints and the hostages emerged into the night, they gazed back at the once prestigious casino now engulfed in flames. The top half of the building collapsed a fiery spectacle that signalled the destruction of whatever remained inside. They had left Ugo, Nigel, and the others to be consumed. They would be nothing but ashes the next day.

***

Akira's gaze fell on Angelo, and her frown was coated with anger. Despite trying to justify his actions, he faced the disapproval of his Seraph.

Akira's frown deepened, signalling her dissatisfaction with Angelo's choice. "You chose to disobey me after I told you not to give yourself in," she declared. "As a Starlight Saint, defying your seraph is a serious offence."

"But did I not save everybody? I did it for you especially," said Angelo, rationalising his choices.

Akira was not buying it, and she remained resolute.

Angelo should've known that Akira wasn't one to reason with. *Risking his life wasn't the best strategy to win the seraph's heart.*

"You still disobeyed me. When we get back to campus, I'll decide your punishment, and you will be dealt with accordingly," Akira stated firmly.

Accepting the inevitable his head sank to his chest. Angelo gave up as he clearly wasn't going to win this fight.

Akira hushed him into silence, but he dreaded returning to campus.

Whatever punishment awaited him, he knew it wouldn't be pleasant. Angelo vowed to himself that he would never again disobey Akira.

***

The police finally managed to get through and moved around the charred remnants of the casino, investigating the aftermath of the chaotic events that had unfolded. Zayn took the liberty to explain the situation to them. Who carefully omitted any mention of the Starlight Saints. Once the police were engrossed in their examination, Zayn gathered the team to share a crucial piece of information.

"I owe you all my life for saving me," Zayn expressed deep gratitude. "I know something that might be of help to you. Don used to keep a diary at his estate. Before our fallout, he trusted me as his close friend and told me he had it somewhere in an attic. Maybe you'll find something in there."

With the growing threat of the Illuminati's agenda, time was slipping away, and the team now had a new lead to explore.

Akira extended an invitation to Zayn, urging him to join forces against their common enemy.

Zayn, however, weighed the heavy toll on his casino, Zayntopia now reduced to smouldering ruins. "I'd love to, but someone needs to organise reparations for the casino," said Zayn, saddened by the destruction of his most prized business. "It's best for me and my daughter to stay in Vegas and see what else the Illuminati are doing around this city."

Akira accepted Zayn's choice with a solemn nod, recognising his strategic thinking. As the Starlight Saints prepared to depart, Shawn sought a moment with Tori.

"You sure you don't wanna stay with us?" Tori inquired, her hands clasping Shawn's. "You and I make a great team. I can teach you how to be a magician."

Apologising gently, Shawn affirmed his loyalty to the Starlight Saints. "Sorry, I'm a Starlight Saint, but we'll see each other again, I promise."

Touched by the sentiment, Tori planted a kiss on Shawn's cheek and handed him a book. "This book is a guide to all the basics of becoming a magician. I know you can master it," she said, a warm smile lighting up despite their turbulent night.

"Tori, you can't disclose our magical secrets like that," Zayn demanded, protective of their mystique knowledge.

"They helped save us, Dad. The least we can do for them is reveal the basics of our magic to help in their fight," Tori countered.

Accepting Tori's perspective, Zayn nodded with acknowledgement.

Shawn and Tori bid farewell, the Starlight Saints embarked on their journey back to the academy.

Angelo braced himself for the impending punishment awaiting him, a consequence of his disobedience to Seraph Akira.

CHAPTER 33

GOD SAVE THE INDUSTRY

Angelo grimaced as he scrubbed the toilets, repulsed by the sorry state of the bathrooms – it felt like a punishment fit for a disobedient apprentice. His only defence was a face mask, barely adequate to shield him from the unpleasant task. Armed with nothing more than a toothbrush, the chores for the evening seemed like torture. His body, weary from the day's activities, was on the verge of giving way. Wishing that he'd listened to Akira back at the casino.

With Seraph Nigel gone, there was a strange, unsettling void in the academy. The news of Nigel's betrayal hovered over the society like a plague, and trust between fellow saints began to waver.

"Look who's doing labour." Dwayne's voice came from behind, and it was the voice that irritated Angelo to the core.

"What do you want, Chandler?" asked Angelo, not even trying to mask his annoyance.

"I was just passing by," said Dwayne nonchalantly.

Angelo couldn't escape the aggravation provoked by Dwayne's presence. The constant pestering from his rival, who had no right to give orders, only fuelled Angelo's frustration. He had tried to make a truce with him twice and was unwilling to take another shot.

His focus returned to the draining task at hand, the rhythmic scrubbing providing a backdrop to his words. "What you said about my family before is pretty ironic," Angelo remarked. "We both know the truth now and if the other phoenixes were to find out who knows what they'd think of you?"

"I'm nothing like my father," Dwayne snapped.

Dwayne's mood had shifted dramatically. Denial was still written on his face from their encounter with the prosecutor.

Angelo couldn't blame him. However, with the leverage he had on Dwayne, Angelo could either give his rival payback by exposing the truth and turning the saints against Dwayne just like he'd done to him or simply spare him from the humiliation. He realized that shattering Dwayne's reputation wasn't worth the effort. There was a much graver matter at hand.

The safety of his family and solving the case.

"If your dad hurts my family in any way, just know that I'll show no mercy," Angelo declared.

"This is between me and him," Dwayne shot back. "You best stay out of my way."

Angelo had never seen Dwayne so pressed before but maintained a firm gaze. It brought a mixture of amusement and satisfaction to finally have his rival in the wrong. All those accusations against Angelo's dad had made a boomerang effect. Despite the punishment, pride surged through Angelo for being right all along.

Dwayne stormed out of the bathroom; his exit accompanied by a cloud of dramatic rage.

Angelo watched the spectacle with a knowing smile. He had clearly gotten under Dwayne's skin, peeling away more layers of secrets. As soon as he finished his current task, Angelo would send Casey a message. Two brothers armed with knowledge were better than one.

***

The Shadowbreakers journeyed to Don's prestigious estate, which had closed down after he died. Luna's arm had miraculously healed with the innovations of the sanatorium, and she was back in action. Shawn had attempted to learn the mysterious art of metal bending from the guidebook Tori had gifted him after the casino raid prior to the estate visit. But he had not come close to mastering it. Nevertheless, the Shadowbreakers were a full squad once again, ready to tackle whatever lay ahead.

Most of the family's belongings had long been cleared out of the estate, and the team anticipated that there wouldn't be much to find. However, they could try to puzzle out what happened on the day of Dad's death. The diary was the jackpot. Angelo was unsure of how he felt about returning to his old home— the place where it all started.

When the saints arrived at the estate, memories flooded Angelo's mind.

Years before, it boasted perfectly manicured gardens, but now it was scarce and desolate as if life itself was sucked out. The looming presence of Dad's legacy left Angelo downhearted, reflecting on what once was. They had decided to infiltrate the estate at night when they were sure no one was watching. The estate was said to be worth 100 million dollars and was up for auction sale.

Someone was still yet to buy this extravagant property. *Fortunately for the saints, there wasn't any security because why would anyone need to guard a vacant house?* This made things slightly less complicated for the team.

They walked across the grass with their headlights and surveyed the area. The moon also aided their vision, helping them to make out most of their surroundings.

In the distance, Angelo took a glimpse of the abandoned amusement park rides his dad had built as part of the estate. Nostalgia flooded him, and he recalled the days when other kids would come to visit and play with him on the rides. Reminiscing about the early childhood days added an extra feeling of sorrow to the already solemn environment. The joy had vanished entirely.

"This place had everything a kid could ever want," Angelo reflected. "This was my home till it was taken away from me."

"Life is a collection of seasons. Things change, and nothing remains the same forever," said Akira, offering her perspective.

Angelo noted her words, acknowledging the inevitability of change.

Akira was somehow always able to offer wise words of comfort when needed.

The saints had already heard the tape recording of Don's last phone call, so if they could recover the diary Zayn was talking about, they would find a crucial piece of the puzzle.

The estate, a silent witness to the highs and lows of Angelo's family journey, now held the promise of unlocking secrets. Secrets that maybe even the family didn't know. The mansion's entrance held an overgrown garden and exhibited a modern Tudor architectural design. At the pinnacle of the mansion, a massive clock adorned the structure. Ascending a set of stairs, the team marvelled at the spacious property.

Upon Akira's directive, Luna skilfully lockpicked the front door, granting them entry. Stepping inside, they were met with a desolate living room, a sight that triggered a sense of familiarity in Angelo. Progressing through the mansion's dusty remains of a kitchen, a dining room, and a toy room, unveiling the traces of an abandoned life.

Angelo replayed the days he had meals with his dad and Casey in his head. He recalled how his maid and butler would treat him with utmost care. However, he tried not to dive too deep into his memories and instead focused on the mission. Wondering if his old bedroom was still intact.

As they ascended a circular staircase, the mansion seemed to croak as if it had longed for guests. Angelo recalled the countless times he had raced up and down those stairs as a child. Now, with each step, he was on a journey to uncover the truth.

Reaching the attic, the Starlight Saints began searching the room. The place was stuffed, and the air was stiff. Some of the items in the attic had yet to be sold. Dusty rays of moonlight filtered through the small windows, giving a ghostly ambience to the environment. Angelo was surprised to see his old Mickey Mouse toy as it stared back at him.

As the Starlight Saints spread out in the cluttered attic, Shawn's excited voice echoed from across the room, signalling a significant discovery. "Guys, I've found it! The diary!" The red cover, worn and weathered, bore the name *"Don Leonard Jackson"* at the top. Angelo felt a mix of anticipation and anxiety. Finally, he would uncover the mystery that had eluded him for so long.

Shawn, armed with a flashlight, carefully turned the pages, each one revealing a piece of Don's life. Entries chronicled the struggles of a star icon navigating the complexities of daily existence. However, the team's interest heightened when they stumbled upon a page marked with special red ink and adorned with a mysterious symbol. These were highlighted diary entries:

2 October 20XX

I wish I knew,

I wish I'd known what these people were doing sooner. I've been in the entertainment business ever since I was 5. I had no idea what was happening back then. I was too innocent.

The Illuminati recruited me from a very young age, and I knew no better. I followed their customs and rituals, trying to figure out what I was getting myself into. I was helping an evil group move their goals forward, and I would give anything to leave. I blame my father for this. He's the one who sold us out. All he cared about was the money. Later in my 30s, once I discovered the Illuminati's sinister aims, I started to secretly resist them. In return, I suffered the consequences. This family is cursed, and I don't want my kids to go through the same thing I did. I am one of them.

Angelo was taken by surprise at the mention of his grandad, Ted. Grandad was blinded by money and might've made the biggest mistake by signing the family to a record company, as far as Angelo remembered from Aunt Erica's story about *Fusion*. *Who could blame him? Anyone with a poor family would've taken that chance.* Angelo wondered if his grandfather ever regretted the decision wherever he was.

The team skimmed and stopped at another page:

12 December 20XX

It may be too late,

The Illuminati have used entertainers like me to carry out their agenda for many years. They're gonna take over the world. They already ahead of schedule.

Infinite Magna is one of the projects they're working on. They'll implant this microchip into the brain, allowing people to listen to music by the will of their mind. No headphones or speakers are needed. It will also improve health and have other benefits.

The chips are being manufactured in 3 locations, and Illumiknights aim to finish production in the next 7 years:

Colin Storage Hub - Los Angeles

Lexton - Philadelphia

Nefa HQ - Detroit

The Illuminati plan to make humans immortal, but there's one thing they won't tell the public. The Frequency of Death. This music frequency will put death to a person's will and emotions, killing their soul and making them feel like they don't need God. The Illuminati themselves will become gods instead and make the rest of the population bow down to them. That's the New Age System. They know how powerful music is, and they exploit that power.

Real art is long dead. It's all about control and programming. I may be the world's last hope, but who knows if I'll wake up tomorrow? God save the industry.

So, this is why the Illuminati was after Dad. He had their secret plans in the palms of his hands.

"This sounds like some Mark of the Beast Revelations type plan," said Rex.

"Not quite, but it's pretty close. The Illuminati thinking they're gods is very antichrist," said Akira. " Their goal's always been to eliminate God, but *if there's no god or archangels guiding our purpose then let our existence be a lie.*"

Shawn kept turning the pages.

18 December 20XX
Blu J is the devil,
I'm trying to get out, and I will expose them. I started a movement called Sonic Scope Records Stink. Blu J can go to hell. The label owner wants everything he can get from me, and the Illuminati carry out his work. I just wanna protect Angelo and Casey from the secret society, but if I end up dead one day, Blu J is probably the one responsible.

This revelation was devastating for Angelo as tears streamed from his eyes. Not able to believe what he was reading. *The diary not only unveiled the true nature of Blu J but also exposed the depth of the conspiracy.* His father had been a victim of an Illuminati sacrifice orchestrated by someone they trusted. *Everything connected.* Blu J gave Casey a record deal months after Dad died, and Casey was in danger of facing the same fate as their father.

Akira, quick to respond, pledged to relay the information to the Seraph Council to halt the production of the microchips. *The truth was now clear, and the Saints were determined to bring justice.*

Angelo's feelings of betrayal and heartbreak fuelled his resolve.

300

The doctor, Tom Chandler, and Yato were mere pawns in a larger, more deceptive game.

The saints were now focused on dismantling the ultimate conspirator and avenging Angelo's dad.

Angelo, consumed by the need to protect his brother, burned with the desire to relay this critical information to Casey. The urgency of Casey's precarious situation hung over the saints like a dark cloud, urging them to act now.

"The case is solved," said Luna, breaking the intense silence that lingered for several minutes.

Angelo grabbed the diary and held it to his chest. Nobody spoke as the Saints left the attic, and they were met with another eerie silence. There was nothing but whistling wind and cracking of floorboards. He became increasingly unsettled as the team walked through the mansion. For a split second, he thought he caught a shadow of movement on the other side of the hall, and his heart raced. *No one had occupied this place for the last five years, and Angelo convinced himself his imagination was at work.*

"Before we leave, we should survey the amusement park too. There could be more things waiting to be discovered," said Akira as she stepped out of the mansion.

Angelo doubted they needed to keep searching for clues when they'd caught the big fish of the investigation. However, he dared not to oppose the seraph's orders like last time.

"Everybody spread out and come back to this fountain when you're done," Akira ordered.

The Saints would use their earpieces to communicate if they found any more pieces of information. As the saints split into different sections, he approached a carousel. He had a flashback of riding it with the kids who used to visit. Angelo then went into a mirror house with funny-looking shapes and reflections. He shined the headlight, distorted versions of himself appeared. Most mirror surfaces were dust-covered, but as Angelo explored further, he caught a glimpse of the former Angelo. The one he didn't want to see.

The clone from the dream he had the other night. Angelo jumped back at the reflection and activated his starlight watch.

"I don't know who you are, but I want you out of my head," Angelo yelled as he summoned a hammer.

He smashed the mirror with brute force, and the glass shattered into a million pieces. Angelo breathed a sigh of relief and headed towards the exit, knowing he'd find nothing else.

"Got nothing on my side, guys," Angelo spoke into his earpiece.

There was no response from anyone, and it was all static. Perhaps the signal in here was just weak. Angelo noticed another unfamiliar figure as he walked through the passage of mirrors. Instincts urged Angelo to summon a blade, but when he came into closer proximity with the figure, he dropped it immediately.

"Casey?" Angelo's voice trembled.

Casey, recognizing Angelo, approached cautiously, the worry etched on his face transforming into recognition. The brothers shared a tight embrace.

"Angelo, what are you doing out here?" asked Casey, his concern heightening. "I snuck away and came to investigate Dad's estate by myself. My record label's been acting weird, and I'm scared. What's that in your hand?" His eyes were on the diary.

Angelo, determined to share the burden of truth, revealed the diary's contents to Casey and the revelation about Quinn from Nigel.

Casey snatched it and flipped through the journal. This moment of revelation struck him like a lightning bolt. Casey's eyes widened as he absorbed the shocking contents of the diary.

"Oh god, I had a feeling something was wrong when I signed that record deal," said Casey under his breath.

"Blu J isn't who he says he is, and neither is Quinn. Blu J could be using you just like Dad. You may have joined the

Illuminati without even knowing and could suffer like Dad. Casey, you need to get out of that record deal," Angelo urged him.

"What? I can't. I'm trapped. There's no way out of the contract. You have to help me," Casey pleaded, his desperation palpable.

Angelo nodded resolutely, and the united siblings would team up against the mastermind behind this sick operation. Angelo motioned for Casey to follow him; a silent agreement forged in their shared determination.

"Come with me. I need to regroup with the other Starlight Saints and explain that you're with me. They can help us and possibly recruit you," Angelo proposed.

"Wait," Casey interjected.

Angelo turned to face him, only to find the cold, metallic gaze of a gun levelled at him. Before he could comprehend the danger, a brutal impact on the back of his head sent him into the clutches of unconsciousness, and it was lights out. Angelo drank from the cup of oblivion.

CHAPTER 34

THE WATCHER

The end had finally come. At least, that's what Angelo thought. He opened his eyes and recalled the moment right before he was knocked out. *Something wasn't right.* He scanned his surroundings and noticed nothing but eye-capturing landscapes of trees, ethereal icebergs, and bright celestial colours. His eyes even captured colours that he never knew existed. This wasn't the estate. Angelo might have finally died and made it to heaven. *If that was true, the first thing to do was try to find his dad. Were the rest of the team still alive?*

Angelo got up. This place gave him an overwhelming sense of joy and peace. What he felt on earth was nothing compared to what he was feeling now. It was as if all his sadness and pain had been wiped away forever by a wave of cleansing. He kept roaming, but oddly enough, no one else was present. *If this was heaven, then where was everyone else?* heaven had to be filled with all the saved people that God had gathered, but there was no one to be found.

"Hello, is anyone there?" Angelo yelled, but it was only silence that conversed with him.

Just as he was about to give up his search, there was a sparkling lake nearby and decided to investigate. Angelo walked closer, a figure shaped like a person. *Someone else was here!*

To his relief, the person came into view as he ran closer. When he arrived at the lakeside, he was struck with awe and magnificence by what he saw. It was a girl that looked almost his age.

She was one of the most beautiful girls he'd ever seen. Her skin was glowing with divine radiance, and her scent was as pure as the ocean.

Angelo's eyes widened, and he couldn't move as he was paralyzed with amazement. It warmed his heart when she smiled at him.

"You must be Angelo. Follow me," instructed the girl gently.

Angelo didn't even question her because his instincts told him he could trust her straight away. As they walked through the landscape, there was something familiar about this girl, even though he'd never met her in his life.

"Who are you and what is this place?" asked Angelo.

"This is heaven, a part of heaven. My name's Hayden, and I'm your guardian angel," the girl explained. "God assigned me to you when you were born, and I've been watching you your whole life. I know everything about you."

Angelo was mind blown. It amazed him how an invisible guardian angel had been watching him since he was a baby. That meant she also saw his embarrassing moments, which Angelo hoped she wouldn't bring up. *It felt honourable to finally interact with a spiritual guide.* Angelo had many questions *but could all of them be answered?.*

"So, does this mean I'm officially dead? What happened to my brother and my friends?" he asked. They stopped, and Hayden put her finger gently on his lips.

"All that will be answered soon enough, but I have something more important to tell you, said Hayden. "It's about Casey."

They found themselves in a cave full of screens that resembled diamonds. Different versions of himself flashed on the screen, from when he was one to when he was sixteen, etc.

these screens were displaying different points of his life. He spotted one memory of Casey saving him from drowning and another of him and Casey sleeping together. Seeing all these memories play out in front of him touched his heart. Hayden placed her hand on his shoulder.

"You and Casey have been through so much together, but your brother is not who you think he is," said Hayden. Angelo was perplexed. What did she mean by that?

"I know you've been looking for the one responsible for your father's death and you think it's Blu J," she continued.

Angelo became even more confused. He had no idea what she was going on about.

"It was Casey," Hayden revealed.

Angelo wasn't sure if he'd heard those words correctly. Casey did it? That was impossible. Casey cared about Dad and broke down at the funeral, so he couldn't have been the one to kill Angelo's dad. They were family, and no one turned their back on family. It was Blu J behind the murder, surely. Angelo was unwilling to buy into the angel's claims.

"It can't be," said Angelo in denial. "Casey would never do such. The killer is after both of us."

He would do what he could to defend his brother's innocence, but Hayden shook her head and gave him a look of sympathy.

"Angelo, I know how much you love your brother, but I have to reveal the truth to you," she said, pointing towards one of the screens.

The screen showed a moment when Casey met with record label executive Blu J.

Casey sat opposite Blu J, who had paper piles before him. Casey was eager to sign the contract and anxiously waited for Blue J to pass the pen over to him. The executive shook his head.

"Before we sign you, there's something you must do for us first," said Blu J. "You're aware that everything requires sacrifice, right?"

Casey responded with a gasp of confusion, not comprehending what Blu J was trying to say.

"You want to be successful right? We believe in you, and we can make you one of the greatest artists just like your father," Blu J continued. Casey frowned at the mention of his father.

"My dad doesn't support my endeavours. He don't want me pursuing a music career like him. He don't believe in me, but I'm thankful you do," said Casey.

At that point, it seemed like Casey loathed Dad and his success. To him, Dad seemed like a selfish prick who never acknowledged the potential and ambition of his own son.

"Your fathers just scared you'll surpass him. He doesn't want you to have the same level of success as him. That's why he'll do whatever it takes to stop you from chasing your dream, but I promise when you sign with us, you'll have triple the amount of success he had, sonny. You'll win Grammys, your albums will go platinum, sold out shows, and you'll always peak on the Billboard charts," said Blu J with a sly smile.

Casey paused for a bit and took Blu J's offer into consideration. Blu J must've seen something in him that his father didn't. After countless rejections from countless labels, Casey couldn't afford to let this opportunity slip away. He was one step away from superstardom.

"Alright what do I have to do for you to sign me?" asked Casey.

"Help us kill Don," said Blu J cold-heartedly.

Casey was immediately bewildered. This man was insane for planning to kill a family member despite Casey's detest for his dad. How would the rest of the family feel about this? Should he have reported this to the police? Casey objected and called Blu J a madman, wanting to leave the room, but Blu J simply raised his hand and asked Casey to calm down.

"Casey, don't you see? You can become a part of something greater. Forget about whether it's a family member. Think of the reward. The gains from this far outweigh the losses. There's a better family you can join," said Blu J, but Casey objected again and banged his fist on the table.

"This was just a ruse all along. I'm leaving," yelled Casey, taking out his cell phone. Before he could leave, two scary-looking men blocked his exit, and he was trapped.

"Casey, it would be rude for you to leave our meeting early. Your contract is waiting for you. You're a nobody, but we can make you one of the greatest rappers to ever live," Blu J explained. "Think of all the money and women you'll have. All you have to do is make one sacrifice. I promise it'll be worth it, and you'll thank me later. Your father doesn't want you to reach your full potential because he wants the spotlight all to himself. He's the only obstacle standing in your way to success, and you must remove that obstacle."

Casey took a moment to reconsider. As long as Dad was around, he would always be under his shadow, and nobody would ever acknowledge him.

"Okay, I'm in," said Casey, slowly nodding his head.

Blu J snapped his fingers. A contract and a pen were placed in front of Casey as he sat back down. One signature and his life was changed forever.

Hayden then showed Angelo the day Dad died.

The screen displayed his dad being rushed to the hospital. He remembered that day like yesterday. After the eleven-year-old version of himself had left the room, three doctors came in.

Angelo tried to dismiss what he was seeing. *This couldn't be real. This must've been a dream,* but no matter how hard he tried to convince himself, this was what he was witnessing.

One doctor revealed himself to be Blu J. He recognized the female doctor as Quinn. After giving Dad a lethal injection, another doctor revealed himself to be sixteen-year-old Casey. He delivered the second fatal injection.

"You see, Casey sacrificed your dad so he could get signed to Sonic Records," Hayden revealed.

Angelo contemplated the display of murder for a moment. He recalled meeting Blu J on Don's Memorial Day and how Blu J would take Casey under his wing.

Casey getting a record deal after Dad's passing should've been a mere coincidence, but it wasn't.

Angelo refused to let his views of Casey be shattered by this revelation. It had to be false. Before he could object to these accusations, Hayden pointed to another screen to play a different scene. Blu J and Casey were seated in a studio.

"You're doing great, but I wanna change the direction of your music," said Blu J.

The screen had fast-forwarded to a year since Casey had done the deed. If he was holding any guilt, he didn't show it. Blu J's words were like silk and sugar, always flattering and comforting no matter the situation. Blu J poured up a glass of tequila and continued the conversation.

"I think your music is too positive. You've had some great success so far, but you can go higher," said Blu J, sipping his drink. Casey appeared uncomfortable at first, but then he eased down and smiled.

"I want you to make gangster rap music about guns, drugs, and violence," said Blu J turning a knob on one of the mixers. "The frequency of this bass already appeals to the listener's ears, but now you should replace the lyrics."

"Isn't that corrupting the youth and promoting bad morals?" Casey questioned with scepticism. "I got so many fans that see me as their role model."

"We're not corrupting them. We're simply making ourselves more profitable by appealing to wider audiences. Especially those that come from the projects. They need someone to relate to, and you're that artist. The Illuminati's vision is far greater than your understanding. Trust me on this," Blu J explained.

Angelo battled to comprehend the scene before him. He refused to believe anything his guardian angel was showing him, but he could also see something was changing in Casey, and his expression appeared more sinister.

"You signed the contract, and I know what's best for business as label executive," said Blu J, *finishing his tequila.* Casey nodded and had no further objection.

The scene suddenly switched to Casey watching late-night news. He held a bottle of luxurious champagne and poured himself a glass. On his right side was a plaque of his latest record. Casey made a toast to it as if it were a friend.

"Gun violence and drug abuse have increased significantly over the last several months in Atlanta and other cities. More youths are ending up in prison, and crime rates are higher than they've been in the last decade. Some residents blame rap music and its influence on teenagers," A reporter announced.

"Oh, shut up, it's their parent's fault. The Illuminati know what's best, and I'm one of the biggest icons right now," said Casey to the television.

Casey sipped more champagne. Casey was deep into the secret society at that stage, and they might've brainwashed him entirely.

"Casey was hungry for more fame and status, so he made more sacrifices, including one of Erica's kids, whose death was staged as a car accident," said Hayden. That was Cousin Leo, whom the angel was referring to as Angelo recalled the accident years back. "The Illuminati got the best of him," Hayden explained.

The angel insisted that Angelo was deceived this whole time. She implied that Casey did a perfect job covering up and convincing Angelo that he was on his side, but the enemy was right in front of him the whole time. How could Angelo not have seen it? One of his closest family members outsmarted him, and he felt like an idiot. However, no matter how stacked the evidence was, Angelo would still not yield to the angel's convictions. His trust in Casey would not waver, and he knew his brother still had to be innocent.

"Casey was willing to sacrifice you next when you joined the Starlight Saints. He let you do it, so he'd have a good reason to kill you," said Hayden.

"I don't believe you. You're lying to me," said Angelo in Casey's defence. "My brother loved Dad. Take me back to earth and get me outta here."

"As you wish. It's hard to take this all in, but you must trust me," said Hayden. "Apply your starlight mottos and see how your perspective changes. It's up to you to accept the truth or continue allowing deception."

Angelo was simply not adhering to anything the angel was saying anymore. He wouldn't believe anything, but his doubtful heart ached at the shattering possibility that all he'd seen might just be true. What if Casey was part of the murder? Angelo would have to confront him and verify the truth for himself. He wouldn't be easily moved by the words of his guardian angel.

"God says it's not your time yet. You still have work to do. You have an important task on your hands. You should save your brother from himself and stop the record label and the Illuminati. You're equipped to handle anything," Hayden explained.

Angelo shook his head, and tears emerged from his eyes. "I can prove Casey's innocence. Just watch."

Hayden put a hand on Angelo's shoulder to calm him down. "This encounter was meant to strengthen you and develop your courage to face the impossible," she concluded.

After that, Hayden turned away and went in another direction, but Angelo had more questions he was burning to ask. He begged her to stay, but she kept walking. Angelo made a run for her, but as Angelo ran, Hayden began to fade away. All his surroundings started disappearing. Angelo found himself travelling towards a light hole through a tunnel. He couldn't move his body, no matter how hard he tried. All Angelo could do was float toward the end of the tunnel as the current dragged him. With all these abnormal occurrences, he hoped this was just one lucid nightmare. He wished he'd find himself in bed when he woke up and that none of this ever happened.

Most importantly, he knew this was just a dream and that none of what the angel said could be true. He had hope that Casey was on his side. Angelo clung to that hope like a teddy bear. Everything would be just fine when he got to the end of the tunnel.

Chapter 35

Case Closed

Angelo was confronted with dizziness and fatigue the moment he woke up. The disconcerting haze threatened to erase the boundaries of his consciousness, leaving him on the brink of forgetfulness, where even his own identity and the current year seemed elusive. The last thing Angelo remembered was blacking out and mysteriously meeting his guardian angel, but the rest of his memory was still clouded by fog.

As awareness slowly returned, Angelo's attempt to move was met with resistance – a persistent pull that seemed to restrain him. It was a tight rope. Struggling against the disorientation, he discovered his entire body secured to an immovable pole. When he examined himself, a horrible realization settled. All his gear was gone, and he was equipped with nothing but his black shirt and trousers.

Angelo's awakening was accompanied by a gentle throb at the back of his head—a reminder of the blow that had rendered him unconscious. *How long was Angelo out for, and who had knocked him out in the first place?*

His head was spinning, and he was close to losing his sanity. First, it was the estate, then heaven, and now this strange room. Waking up in different locations was driving him mad.

"Seraph? Rex? Shawn?" Angelo called out, only to be swallowed by the oppressive silence..

In this semi-dark chamber, he found himself alone, bound to captivity. For moments that felt like an eternity, he sat in contemplative silence, attempting to process everything that happened and what could have led to this. All he could think of was Casey.

Suddenly, footsteps resonated beyond the confines of the room, and they grew louder with every plod. Angelo was anxious to detect signs of life, but at least he wasn't completely isolated.

Angelo, tension coiling within him, prepared for the imminent arrival. The creaking protest of the door signalled the entrance of an unexpected yet familiar face—Aunt Erica. Relief cascaded through him like a welcomed wave.

"Erica? You're okay. I'm so happy to see you. I thought..." Angelo's words tumbled out, the rush of excitement momentarily overtaking his composure. "What's going on? How did I -"

"Stop talking. Keep your mouth shut and come with me," Erica commanded with an urgency that allowed no delay, her fingers working deftly to loosen the ropes that bound Angelo.

Erica's tone caught Angelo off guard. She was here to save him and possibly didn't want to alert nearby enemies. After untying the knots, Erica grabbed Angelo by the wrist and walked him out of the room. Despite the subdued nature of their reunion, a surge of joy accompanied Angelo's realization that his aunt had come to rescue him from the unknown binds that had confined him.

When they got out of this mysterious place, he would break the news to Erica about all of his experiences with the Starlight Saints and the investigation. It was time she knew about his recruitment into the agency.

Angelo's mind buzzed with a swarm of burning questions, but it was best to remain silent until they'd escaped.

Erica guided him through the corridor, the air taking on a disturbing chill that mirrored their mysterious surroundings.

Angelo spotted a door with an exit sign ahead and was instantly relieved. Once he got out those doors, he would be free from the grasp of his adversaries.

As Erica approached the door, she made a left turn, deviating and cutting Angelo's excitement short. A confused Angelo wanted to question why they didn't go through the exit. Though puzzled, Angelo suppressed the urge to question, choosing instead to trust his aunt's judgment. Erica pulled out a walkie-talkie, her voice shattering the silence.

"He's awake. I got him right here with me," said Erica to the device.

"What's happening? Who are you talking to?" asked Angelo.

"I said keep your mouth shut," Erica ordered, her tone allowing no argument.

Angelo maintained his silence; questioning Erica's actions seemed futile. The trust he placed in his aunt mingled with an ever-growing curiosity about their destination. *Where could Akira and the others be?* He thought.

As Erica ushered him into a large room crowned by a glass dome, Angelo's eyes were drawn to the astonishing display beyond. The descending sun painted the sky in shades of twilight, signalling the arrival of evening.

How many days had slipped away during his unconsciousness?

Without warning, Erica propelled Angelo to the floor, and the cold surface met his palms.

A sharp inhalation caught in his throat as he witnessed his aunt draw a gun.

"I got him! Angelo's here!" Erica's triumphant declaration echoed through the vast room.

"Erica, what are you doing?" asked Angelo, stunned by the sudden turn of events.

"Shut up and don't move," Erica commanded, her focus unwavering as she aimed the gun. Just as the words left her lips, her eyes softened for the briefest of moments. She raised her free hand to her lips, pressing a finger there – a small, almost unnoticeable motion – as if telling him to play along.

The gesture was there and gone in an instant but it left Angelo's heart racing for reasons beyond fear. *Was she trying to tell him something?* His world spiraled into disarray as he grappled with the incomprehensible sight of a gun pointed at him.

The air grew thick with disbelief, rendering him nearly speechless. His own aunt, his supposed rescuer, now stood as an unforeseen threat, weapon in hand. A sting of betrayal too great to understand.

Angelo's gaze swept across the room, and he discovered four other captives handcuffed and bruised.

The captives were Rex, Shawn, Luna, and Vanya. They'd been kidnapped, too. Desperation was written on their faces as they pleaded for help, but someone was missing. *Where was Akira? Was she being held somewhere else?*

Angelo couldn't help but question if Erica was behind this cruel set-up. Such a thought would shatter how he viewed his kind, loving aunt.

From the shadows emerged a weathered man with a subtle birthmark. Shock held Angelo in its merciless grip as his sworn enemy revealed himself—Tom Chandler, the astute prosecutor. The reunion was far from a joyous one.

A sadistic grin played on Tom's lips, an unsettling acknowledgement of his sinister delight. Angelo found himself once again at the mercy of the man who had once sought to destroy his family.

Tom's approving nod in Erica's direction sent a chill down Angelo's spine. "We've finally got the boy. You've done an excellent job, Erica."

Angelo trembled at the realization that Erica and Tom had some sort of alliance. They'd planned his kidnapping. Locking eyes with Erica, Angelo sought answers in the depths of her gaze, but all that stared back was a cold indifference.

It couldn't be true—Erica, his aunt, collaborating with the prosecutor who had tried to destroy his dad's career?

The reality unfolded before him like a grotesque nightmare, leaving Angelo to grapple with the unthinkable betrayal.

"Erica, how could you team up with this lunatic? You know he tried to ruin us," Angelo shifted his gaze to Tom, fury replacing his initial shock. "You put her up to this, didn't you?"

Tom crept closer to Angelo and gently held him by the chin while he was on his knees. The prosecutor smirked at Angelo's plight.

"I didn't put her up to anything," Tom retorted, his words accompanied by the acrid scent of tobacco cigarettes. "We've been in this together all along. Behind the curtain of conspiracy gaming."

Angelo, infuriated by Tom's taunting, spat in the prosecutor's face with vindictive grit, and the saliva landed in one of his eyes. He grew, incensed by the act, ruthlessly slammed Angelo to the floor in retaliation.

"You've got some nerve spitting in my face like that," Tom sneered, tightening his grip around Angelo's throat with one hand, depriving him of breath. "When the boss comes, I'll tell him to sacrifice you to the Gummy Bear Association!"

Tom was poised to crush Angelo's windpipe, the threat of unconsciousness looming once again.

"Let him go, Mr. Chandler," an authoritative voice bellowed from behind.

Instantly, Tom released his grip, allowing life-giving oxygen to circulate through Angelo again. As Angelo sat up, his blurred vision cleared to reveal two figures—Casey and Blu J—storming into the room, accompanied by others. Among them was Officer Gerald from the state prison where they had interrogated Dr. Marshall. The unexpected arrival of Quinn Parkerson and other Illuminknights only intensified Angelo's sense of helplessness.

Shock paralyzed him as his adversaries and loved ones seemed to merge into a disturbing conspiracy circle. What were Erica and Casey doing with these people?

"There's still one saint missing, Erica. Where is that woman? The seraph?" asked Blu J.

"She got away," Erica explained. "She escaped, sir."

Blu J, visibly frustrated but composed, nodded at the news. Angelo couldn't fathom that Akira had escaped, leaving them behind. Clenching his fists, he swallowed hard, grappling with the painful realization. How could she abandon her team like that? A prick of pain seared Angelo's heart, and the room seemed to grow colder. He tried to console himself. She wouldn't just leave us like that, he thought.

Angelo's gaze shifted towards Casey, who stood clad in glasses and a designer jacket. A surge of unanswered puzzles buzzed through his head at the sight of his older brother.

***

"Casey, what's going on?" asked Angelo. "Don't tell me you're part of the Illuminati. Step away from Blu J. He's not who you think he is."

Casey, however, remained immovable, displaying no signs of concern. Instead, he met Angelo's inquiry with an unsettling silence, allowing Blu J to take the lead.

"Your brother's one of us, but you decided to join the Starlight Saints, didn't you?" Blu J asked. "Do you realize what we do to saints? They're our worst enemy."

"What did you do to my friends? You killed my dad!" Angelo yelled. "I read his diary. It was you! Admit it."

Blu J simply scoffed at Angelo, revelling in the knowledge that his captive was powerless. He relished the helplessness.

Angelo's fury intensified, yet there was no energy left to manifest it.

318

"Don't make such accusations when I've been on your family's side throughout the years," said Blu J. "Why'd you join the saints? You're a Jackson and you were meant to take your place among us. To reign with us in this society. It's your calling Angelo but you ran away from it just like your father did. Now you'll suffer the consequences."

Angelo grappled with the disbelief that his older brother had been an Illumiknight all along—the same secret society that had oppressed their father.

Casey, stepping into the conversation, aimed to shape Angelo's perspective. "But he doesn't have to suffer the consequences if he joins us," Casey interjected. "Think about it, Angelo. You'll conquer the world with me. We can build our legacy as a family. It will be you, me and the rest. The Starlight Saints ain't your friends. They're roaches, and they're only using you as their puppet to get to our family's riches. Look, even your seraph abandoned you. Our goal is to enlighten the world and liberate the human race from their stupidity."

Angelo resented the possibility that some of what Casey said might be true. *A part of him still clung to hope in the woman he loved.* Recalling Akira's revelation of her secret identity and her promises to always be there, Angelo struggled against the doubt, clouding his judgment. Surely, Akira wouldn't just leave them like this.

"The seraph would never leave us. She's gonna come back, I know it," said Angelo, clinging onto a thread of hope that became increasingly fragile.

"It's been three days," Casey retorted, shaking his head dismissively. "She ain't coming back. Nobody is."

Angelo's heart sank at the mention of three days. So, what Casey said about the Starlight Saints was probably true.

"Maybe you're right. It's just that…I loved that woman with all my heart," Angelo confessed, vulnerability creeping into his voice. "Is anyone else in the family part of this?" he inquired.

As if on cue, Uncle Jace, Bobby, Loraine, and the other Jacksons entered the room, their presence affirming the unsettling truth Erica, and the family had hidden from Angelo.

"You're all in on this," Angelo exclaimed, the sting of truth hitting him like a wasp.

How could the Jacksons possibly be on the same side as people like Tom Chandler, who damaged the family's reputation?

Silence filled the place. *What if this was his calling? What if the Starlight Saints were the evil ones? What if they were the enemy?* Angelo's thoughts wavered and conflicted. *Perhaps it was time to give in and submit to his calling. There was little he could do either way.*

One question lingered on his mind, though.

"Casey, if Blu J didn't kill Dad like he says then how was Dad killed?" asked Angelo, his voice trembling.

"Overdose. The man was just going insane, and that's why he made that tape," Casey replied lightly.

Angelo's intuition rebelled against the simplistic explanation. The evidence from the autopsy report and the existence of the enemy list all contradicted the claim of a mere overdose.

However, restrained by his captive state, Angelo found himself in no position to argue further.

"Fortunately, there's always a way you can atone for your siding with the Starlight Saints," Blu J proposed. "You can join us like Casey said."

"If I join your society, will you let my friends go?" asked Angelo, filled with desperation.

Blu J's response was a dismissive laugh. He scoffed at Angelo's question as if mocking the very idea that such a deal could exist.

"Didn't your pops ever tell you nothing comes cheap or free? We have prescribed customs in this society. You must sacrifice your friends to be accepted. Sacrifice is a way of atoning for your sins, and you sinned against us by working for our enemy," Blu J explained. "Shedding blood will prove your allegiance to us."

Angelo felt an iciness crawl up his spine, a cold realization settling in. Blu J was dangerous - and twisted. This man had to be crazy if he thought Angelo would sacrifice his friends. How could he bear that kind of guilt? Family loyalty or not, he couldn't just hand over the lives of the Starlight Saints. No, he wouldn't do it.

"I won't do it," Angelo declared.

Casey, fuelled by anger and impatience, yanked out a gun, its cold metal reflecting the harsh reality of the moment.

"I'm the one who did it. Is that what you wanna hear?" Casey's voice dripped with a bitter admission; a hint of guilt detected. "I sacrificed Dad. When you secretly sent me messages about your mission, I did my best to sabotage your investigation by informing Officer Gerald about your prison visit. I didn't want you to solve the case, so I even worked with Nigel to make sure. I let you join the Saints so I could gather info about the enemy. Now I'm gonna sacrifice you too."

Those words cut deep and pierced Angelo's heart.

The truth, once concealed, now stood exposed, a blade cutting through Angelo's defences, and the soreness pounded in his chest. It couldn't be true. A desperate denial resounded in his mind. But deep down, he knew Hayden had been right all along.

Sacrifice meant more power and status.

Angelo trembled with fear, a dreadful realization gripping him as the cold steel of the gun stared him in the face.

321

Chapter 36

Atonement

"Why'd you do it? I thought we were family!" said Angelo. Tears streamed down his cheeks, each droplet carrying the weight of shattered trust and the ache of betrayal.

"The old man was losing his touch," Casey explained. "It was my turn to shine."

"Don had to be sacrificed, Angelo. We were always under your father's shadow," Uncle Jace added to the revelation. Other members of *Fusion* nodded in agreement.

"Plus, he was suffering anyway so I did him a favour and put him out of his misery. Remember that day at the hospital? While you waited for me, I was disguised as a doctor and I did what had to be done," Casey summarised.

Casey made yet another confirmation that the angel was right. Angelo's heart plummeted, and he felt like an idiot for clinging to the hope that his brother could still be innocent.

"Blu J, Chandler, Gerald. You're just like them," Angelo spat. "It's my fault for trusting you. If you shoot me, at least let my friends go." Angelo glanced toward Rex, Luna, Vanya, and Shawn.

He remembered Reverend Wilson's teachings about the apostles of the bible and how each had to give up their lives for the greater good. This was Angelo's apostle moment. He would die an

322

honourable death. At least he would finally be reunited with his father and glorified with the messiah. Although it frightened him, Angelo convinced himself that Jesus Christ would want him to do this. Being a privileged kid, he'd pretty much done everything most people didn't get to do in this life. Angelo had travelled, kickboxed, and lived the non-celebrity life he desired.

"This will hurt a lot," said Casey with a devilish grin, itching to pull the trigger.

The Casey that Angelo knew as his brother was long gone. This was someone else now, maybe a clone, if cloning was even real.

"Hold on," said Blu J. Everything came to a standstill. "Move the gun away from him, CJ."

Following Blu J's instructions, Casey obediently stepped back. Blu J advanced toward Angelo, whose confusion mirrored the uncertainty of the moment. Angelo couldn't fathom why Blu J had halted the impending violence. Blu J gently placed his hand on Angelo's head and began to stroke like the caress of a father soothing his son.

"It doesn't have to end like this, sonny. You still have a chance to answer your calling. I believe in second chances, and I'm willing to give you one last chance," Blu J's voice, though smooth, held authority. "Become an Illumiknight and learn the ways of self-enlightenment."

It took Angelo a moment to process Blu J's words. His initial instinct was to reject the offer again, but a flicker of realisation ignited within him—there seemed to be no other viable option. Blood was going to be shed one way or another. It was either him or his friends.

"Fine, I accept your offer. I'll join your cult by sacrificing my friends. I realise the Starlight Saints tricked me now, and I wanna atone for my faults," Angelo began. "If you can let me talk with them one last time before I make the sacrifice, I'll be grateful," Angelo requested with an idea to stall for time.

Casey wore a look of surprise and awe for the first time. Angelo's unexpected decision to turn his back on the Starlight Saints left Casey impressed, a subtle acknowledgement that Angelo was finally coming to his senses. The anger that once consumed Casey gradually faded, replaced by a sense of approval. Blu J ordered the other Illumiknights to bring the captives forward.

Soon, Rex, Luna, Shawn, and Vaya were presented in front of them, handcuffed and gagged. Angelo, steeling himself for the grim task ahead, prepared to do the deed that would forever alter the course of his life.

"You've finally seen the light. Your loyalty to us will be rewarded," said Casey with glee. "The most important lesson is to never turn your back on family."

There was a rule Dad always taught Angelo, and that was family comes first. The Illumiknights brought forth a sacrificial altar. *The time had come.*

"No guns, please. We do this the old-fashioned way," Blu J instructed as he presented a bloodthirsty knife to Angelo.

"Think of how our ancestors made animal sacrifices to atone for their sins. You'll be doing the same thing," Blu J explained further. With a slow, deliberate movement, he traced his thumb along his neck like a killing gesture to emphasise his point.

The realisation hit Angelo like a punch to the gut — he was about to cut their throats open. His heart froze, a shiver of hesitation coursing through him at the thought of delivering such a brutal death.

"I can't do this. I'm not a killer without reason," Angelo protested, staring at the knife. The blade held a distorted reflection, a hazy glimpse of the man he was about to become.

What would his dad or Reverend Wilson think of this?

"Someone has to make the atonement. It's either you or them," said Blu J. The barrel of a gun shifted, its gaze first on

Angelo, then on the captives, as if fate itself was pointing its judgmental finger.

"What if they join the Illuminati like me? Would that suffice?" Angelo pleaded.

"This is your inheritance, not theirs. Your grandfather made a covenant with our order. Your dad ran away but that doesn't have to be you."

Angelo couldn't bring himself to commit the act. If inheritance meant blood on his hands, he didn't want it. "Please, there has to be another way!"

"There is no other way. The Starlight Saints are corrupt and hinder our plans to enlighten the world. We must rid society of such a disease," Blu J explained. "I'll make this simple for you. You can sacrifice one and spare the other three. Do we have a deal?"

That proposal struck like lightning, tearing through the fabric of fate. Angelo muttered to himself quietly. This made things even harder, and the choices tightened around his conscience like a boa constrictor. He looked toward his friends, who remained distraught and despairful.

Rex's face etched with anger and desperation, Shawn and Vanya with terror, and Luna with a bitter resignation.

Tears welled up in Angelo's eyes. He was just like the Illumiknights. He had no right to call himself a Starlight Saint anymore. He stood there like he'd turned into stone, contemplating the unforgiving choice before him.

"I'm so sorry, guys," was all Angelo could whisper. There would be no coming back from his. He was one moment away from a permanent life change.

"This is taking too long. I'll choose for you," said Casey, shoving Angelo out of the way.

"Eeny, meeny, miny, Moe,
Cut the starlight by the throat,
Make a sacrificial oath,
This should be the one to go."

As the eerie mantra concluded, Casey's finger landed on Luna, who gasped in horror. Desperation written across her face, she attempted to speak beneath the tight gag, but only a futile scream escaped.

"Is that a mantra you guys use when sacrificing someone?" Angelo questioned.

"Nah, I just made that up," Casey chuckled, scoffing at the cruelty of Luna's fate.

Angelo refused to find amusement in the situation. While humour had its rightful place, this was not the time for laughter.

"Looks like we'll be killing the girl. I hope she's not your girlfriend 'cause it would be a real shame to see love die so young," Blu J mocked.

The time had slipped away, and Angelo couldn't stall any further. He held the knife with a firm grip and advanced toward Luna. He was looking down on her with sorrow and remorse.

There was rage and bitterness of betrayal in her eyes.

"Luna, I tried, but they won't listen. I'm the one who deserves to die, not you." As Angelo said this, he blocked everyone's view with his back turned toward them.

Luna's hands remained cuffed in front of her, and Angelo gently placed the knife in her hands. Her eyes widened.

"Kill me instead. I don't wish to die, but I can't live with the guilt of murdering you after you finally started trusting me. All the saints back at the academy think I'm the enemy. Why don't you prove them wrong and thrust the knife into my stomach?" Angelo whispered in gradual sobs. "Just get it over with. You're in this mess 'cause of me."

***

Luna's eyes started to water, and tears fell. Hesitation lingered in her gaze. In the tense silence that gripped the room, a sudden, deafening boom echoed, resonating through the walls. Startled, every gaze snapped toward the source of the disturbance.

"Did you guys hear that?"

The booming intensified again, accompanied by billowing smoke that engulfed the room. Coughs erupted amid the swirling haze, followed by the unmistakable clash of flesh against bone.

Angelo found himself disoriented, unable to see through the thick veil of confusion. *What was happening?*

When gunshots fired, he pinned Luna to the ground for cover.

Luna mumbled under the gag, and Angelo knew it was his signal to remove it. As the tape came off, Luna took a deep breath.

"Everybody lay down till the smoke clears," said Angelo as he glanced towards Rex and the others. Even though their handcuffs were still on, they could move.

"You idiot, what were you thinking?" said Luna, still bitter about the whole ordeal. "You were secretly communicating with Casey during the operation? Were you actually gonna make us join them? Traitor!"

Angelo's guilt slammed him heavily after Luna's rumbling. He didn't even get a thank you for saving her from the bullets flying across.

"It's the only way I could try persuade them not to kill you. I had to convince them I was on their side. I'm sorry I broke the code by communicating with outsiders, but I thought Casey could be trusted. I just saved your life from those gunshots. Hope that shows I'm still with you guys," said Angelo.

"We're probably still gonna die," Luna shot back.

As the smoke started to clear, Angelo removed Rex, Shawn, and Vanya's mouth tapes.

"Apple Jack isn't the traitor," said Rex in Angelo's defence. "Akira's the one who abandoned us and left us to die. She just took off without freeing the rest of us."

"Let's save the talking for later and find a way out of here!" Vanya urged.

JAYDEN GILMORE

The five adolescents raced to the other side as the smoke cleared but found the door locked. The group tried to force it open and lockpick but realised it needed fingerprint scanning. Angelo cussed under his breath. The only thing they could do was go back the other way. Bodies lay sprawled on the floor while strangers were engaged in combat. Angelo recognised a ring one of the people wore and immediately knew they were Starlight Saints.

Cherub Hugh and Skye were fending off menacing Illumiknights while Seraph Titus slashed the throat of another enemy.

To his surprise, Angelo observed a standoff between Dwayne and Officer Gerald. Gerald flashed a device in Dwayne's eyes, temporarily blinding and kicking him to the floor. The officer poised himself, a shadow blade glinting in his grasp, ready to drive it into Dwayne's chest.

Tom Chandler, noticing Dwayne's closeness to being stabbed, pushed through the sea of fighters, seized Gerald at the last second, and hurled him across the room, sending his own comrade tumbling through the air.

"Don't touch my son!" Tom declared.

As he helped Dwayne up, he was impaled by a trident that Dwayne had summoned from his watch.

"I'm not your son anymore. You're a disgrace to me," Dwayne declared as he drove Tom backwards with his trident. "I disown you from this day forward."

Angelo also caught glimpses of Zack, Kiko and Sanji holding off Illumiknights. A surge of relief washed over him as he realised the whole legion of Starlight Saints had come to their rescue. As he dashed for cover, a blade met him at his throat.

Quinn, with a fierce glare, locked eyes with Angelo, her eyes filled with murderous intent.

"You killed my father, Nigel, and I'll make you pay," Quinn declared.

328

"He killed himself. This clearly became about who can kill whose father first," Angelo shot back. "Well, two can play at that game."

Angelo felt the cold tip of the blade pushing into his throat as Quinn forced him to move back against the wall. Powerless and unarmed, Angelo was done for.

Quinn held up her shadow blade and went for the fatal slice until she was abruptly interrupted mid-way from making the kill.

Cherub Skye launched a well-timed kick into Quinn's side, causing her to lose her footing from the unexpected attack.

Angelo, gasping for breath, felt a rush of relief flooding through him once again. With heartfelt gratitude, he acknowledged Skye's timely intervention, a moment of salvation in the midst of peril.

"Put this on," Skye instructed as she handed Angelo a starlight watch. "You can't be exposed like this in a pit of scorpions."

Angelo gracefully accepted the accessory and wrapped it around his wrist. He fought his way through the room to catch up with Luna and the others. As he surveyed more of the chaotic scene, he found a surprise.

Akira was struggling with Blu J as their blades clashed with one another. She'd come back for them! Angelo's faith in his leader proved correct.

Blu J proved to be a resilient fighter, cutting his blade down on Akira with swift execution.

However, Akira displayed more precision and agility, making it challenging for Blu J to match her pace.

He finally started to grow weary. As soon as he dropped his guard down to give the slightest opening, Akira knocked Blu J to the floor.

"Surprised to see me Blu J?" Akira punctuated her words with an audible punch to Blu J's face. "Remember your protégé? Admit you set up my plane crash. Admit you tried to kill me," she demanded, each accusation fuelling the force behind her strikes.

Blu J, his nose now broken, gasped in horror as if a ghost from the past had come back to haunt him. "Akira? You're supposed to be dead. How the hell are you still alive?"

Akira offered a simple response. "I knew what you were planning and faked my death."

The revelation only fuelled her anger, and she continued to rain down blows upon the already defeated record label owner. "This is for taking all the money I made off my records and my rights to my music, you bastard. You used my posthumous albums and entire catalog for your own profitable gain and left my family with nothing!"

Blu J, his facade crumbling, attempted a feeble defence. "You were becoming a liability to my business. I had to clean out my closet," he admitted, a sinister undercurrent in his words. "You have no idea what we've planned."

"As a matter of fact, I do. We know your Infinite Magna plan to produce death frequency microchips. We're destroying your production warehouses as we speak," Akira let her last sentence drip into Blu J's ear.

A cold realisation dawned in his widened eyes, disbelief spreading across his face.

"Impossible. How did you find out about our plan? It just can't be," Blu J exclaimed.

"Don Leonard Jackson." Consumed by her unrelenting rage, Akira summoned a blade from her starlight watch with a swift, practised motion. She'd had enough of the wicked label owner. Without hesitation, she slashed the blade across Blu J's throat.

Blu J grunted as rivers of blood spilt out.

"Akira!" Angelo called out.

That was the first time Angelo had ever called his seraph by her real name. As the rest of the team materialised with their handcuffs off and starlight watches on, they rushed towards Akira, too.

"We thought you abandoned us, Seraph," said Vanya.

"I went to get some help. I'd never abandon my saints," said Akira.

Angelo was comforted. He should've known she'd come back. His affection for Akira grew stronger with the reunion. He swore never to doubt the seraph again and would finally confess his feelings for her.

"We have to get out of here. The other agents are taking care of business," said Akira.

"Did you see any of my family? I hate to tell you this, but they're part of the Illuminati, all of them," Angelo said. "My brother killed my dad."

If Akira was surprised, she didn't show it. They had to make their way out of here. "There's something else I need to tell you," said Angelo with butterflies in his stomach as his heart accelerated.

Now was the time – if there was ever a moment to tell Akira his feelings, this was it. Reunited with his sweet seraph, he could feel the words pressing at his throat, refusing to stay hidden any longer. That poem, those words he'd kept locked away, they were long overdue.

Angelo doubted if they were going to make it out of this place alive, and he figured it was best to unleash his truth now.

"You can tell me later when we get out of here. We must leave," said Akira. "And just so you know, I'm proud of you guys for hanging in there. You're all true saints. Now let's go."

A gunshot sounded before they could move further, and Akira fell forward from the impact. Her bulletproof armour absorbed the damage, thankfully. As Akira got up, Casey bolted behind the seraph and pulled out a device that paralysed her. The same device Ugo used on Angelo at the casino.

Casey held Akira by the neck as she screamed and slit her throat with a blade.

Akira collapsed to the ground with a thud.

331

A horrified Angelo froze at that moment and was too stunned to react. Blood covered Casey's blade. It all happened so fast that Angelo couldn't process it yet.

Chapter 37

Set Apart

Akira clutched onto her bleeding throat. Grunting, she felt the life draining from her.

"Akira! Hang in there!" Angelo's voice cracked with desperation as he yelled and rushed to Akira's side, struggling to find the right words. "You're gonna be okay."

Angelo knelt beside Akira, cradling her in his arms. His gaze locked with hers, witnessing the fading consciousness in her eyes. The exchange between them hung heavy, and Casey, sensing the need for space, took a step back, allowing the two to have their moment.

"Leave her and come with me. She killed the man who made my dreams possible," said Casey, looking over Blu J. His voice was shaking as if he was on the verge of sobbing himself.

"How could you?" Angelo's voice thundered with fury. In a moment of urgency, he reached into Akira's pocket and retrieved a gun.

"We're not letting her die. One of you, rip your shirt off and wrap it around the wound. That should slow down the bleeding till we get proper help," Angelo directed, his tone authoritative.

The weight of leadership settled on his shoulders, and Rex and Shawn responded, swiftly following his instructions. With the seraph down, someone else had to take charge.

Angelo, now armed, aimed the gun at Casey, the surge of rage threatening to engulf him.

"You already took away one person I cared about. I won't let you take another," said Angelo. "It ends here."

Casey produced his gun in retaliation and aimed it back at Angelo, the standoff intensifying.

Two pistols and the mere pull of a trigger could tip the scales into irreversible chaos.

"So, it's come to this? I thought you were with us. I told you the Starlight Saints are bad news," said Casey. "Come back to your real family."

"You're no family of mine after what you did," Angelo countered. "The Saints are more family to me than you've ever been. You sacrificed Dad, remember?"

"It had to be done. You still can't see that the Starlight Saints are using you. You'd rather be with them than receive your inheritance. You and I can run the industry and accomplish greater things than our father ever did."

Even though the family were under a deep covenant with the Illuminati, this wasn't his calling. It was the devil's work of making it seem like it was, but he was not like the other Jacksons. His heart belonged to the Saints. Angelo had studied his bible scriptures with Reverend Wilson and knew that the honourable thing to do was to suffer for the greater good, like Jesus and his apostles.

"I'm nothing like you guys. I've been set apart and chosen for a different purpose," Angelo declared.

The gun started to tremble in Angelo's hand. The hesitation to kill his own brother manifested itself.

Once again angered by his brother's refusal to become an Illumiknight, Casey held his gun firm and prepared to pull the trigger. "You can't even bring yourself to shoot me. The Starlight Saints have trained you to be weak-minded. I gave you a chance but now you're worthless to me," he sneered.

Angelo's fury boiled over, and in a fit of rage, he pulled the trigger. However, no bullets were discharged. The gun, it seemed, had run out of ammunition. Angelo's eyes widened in realization, a moment of vulnerability that Casey seized upon, snickering at his helplessness. The tables had turned, and Angelo, recognizing his defeat, raised his hands in surrender.

Now, it was Casey's turn to pull his trigger, and Angelo awaited his inevitable death. "Good riddance," Casey coldly remarked.

Out of nowhere, Erica emerged, gun raised, and aimed directly at Casey's head. Stunned and shocked, Casey's composure crumbled in the face of Erica's unexpected interference.

"Erica, what the hell are you doing?" Casey demanded, his voice indicating a tremor of fear. A surge of relief filled Angelo as he was seconds away from losing his life. However, he couldn't tell who Erica was siding with anymore. She had turned him in before, and now she had Casey at gunpoint.

"I've been in this dark society for too long. I knew my brother was gonna die the moment he tried to leave. I tried to stop him, but he wouldn't listen. He fought for his freedom till the very end while I was too scared to fight for my own," Erica confessed with the burden of regret. "Maybe it's time I do the same. I can start by ending you."

Angelo widened his eyes. Erica's words seemed to bring everything to a standstill, each syllable a testament to her years of silent suffering.

"You'd kill your own nephew? After everything, Grandad, your own father, built and sacrificed for this family. You wanna throw that all away?" Casey questioned.

"I'm sick and tired of being a puppet and always being told what to do," said Erica, reclaiming her autonomy. "I was told to keep this secret from Angelo until he was ready to be ordained, but now he knows. I won't be a part of this anymore."

As her finger tightened around the trigger, she was ready to break free from the chains that had bound her for so long.

Casey was one bullet away from death and could do nothing about it.

"You're too far gone to recognize your own greed now, so you're better off dead," said Erica. "My son, Leo? I figured it was you who sacrificed him."

Casey's eyes flickered with shock. Erica's words seemed to penetrate his consciousness. His clenched jaw trembled as he lowered his weapon. Angelo couldn't fathom this.

Was Casey really surrendering?

Casey's hands slowly rose, the gun slipping from his grasp and clattering to the floor. He turned around and faced Erica, and his eyes tinged with regret.

Had Casey realized his wrongdoing?

Shawn and Rex were still helping Akira, and she still looked conscious. She uttered a few grunts as she turned her head to observe the standoff unfolding.

"I realize the error of my ways now. I killed Dad, sacrificed many and now I've slashed the seraph. You're right, I was wrong and too blinded to see my own greed was hurting the people around me. Maybe I don't deserve to live because of the damage I've done to you, but I promise I can change if you give me a chance," Casey confessed.

Was this the turning point? There was always a possibility for change.

If Casey was genuinely remorseful about his actions, Angelo wasn't sure if he would forgive him.

Erica lowered her gun, and her eyes glistened with tears that held the promise of reconciliation.

The family would get back together.

Casey suddenly lunged forward, catching Erica off guard, and knocked her to the ground.

Erica's body hit the floor with a thud.

"Did you really think I'd let you end my career and get in the way of what I want?" Casey sneered. "You were always blinded by your naivety, Erica. The Illuminati gave our family power and everything we could ever want but you took that for granted. Shame on you. I'm CJ Maverick, and the whole world will remember my name!"

Casey's supposed remorse shattered like fragile glass, revealing the cunning manipulator lurking beneath the surface.

Angelo had a small hope that Casey could change, but that hope was snuffed out.

"You...you were always blinded by your ambition, and you fail to see the devastation you've caused. One day, you'll fall. Your fame will destroy you, and you'll end up just like any Hollywood star, gone and forgotten. You'll gain the whole world but lose your very soul," said Erica.

Casey's violent assault continued as he knelt beside Erica, tightening his grip around her throat. "Nobody's forgetting me. I'll make my legacy so big and have my name on every street corner! Every billboard and every magazine! I'll be more famous than my father ever was!" Casey exclaimed.

Reacting instinctively to save Erica, Angelo summoned a blade and hurled it at Casey. The blade found its mark, piercing Casey's shoulder.

The sudden pain forced him to release Erica, and he turned towards Angelo and the others. "You'll be sorry you did that. You had your chance, Angelo," moaned Casey as he clutched his bleeding shoulder, and the blade disappeared. "You could've had it all, but your stupidity also deprives you."

"You're wrong. We've stopped your plan to initiate the frequency of death. You've lost," Angelo shot back.

A faint smell of gas filled the room as Angelo and Casey were amid their confrontation.

"No plan of ours is ever truly stopped. Looks like the gas leaked. I'd get out of here if I were you, but mark my words, we will meet again," said Casey. "Bring Erica along! We'll deal with her later." Casey called one of the Illumiknights.

Angelo, driven by a final surge of determination, attempted to save Aunt Erica. However, two Illumiknights intercepted him, blocking his path and holding him at bay. Despite his efforts, Angelo could only watch helplessly as Erica was escorted away.

"I'm not finished with you yet, Casey! I'll never forgive you for what you've done. I'll make sure you pay," Angelo declared.

Casey limped away and made his escape. The smell of toxic fumes became stronger.

Angelo, while coughing, wasted no time going back to Akira. The others, having followed his instructions, awaited his assessment.

"She's still losing blood. We don't know how long she's got left," Shawn informed, the urgency in his voice mirroring the hopelessness of their situation.

Angelo, without hesitation, examined Akira's wound, pressing the makeshift bandage against it. Her breathing was alarmingly shallow.

"This is beyond us. She needs medical help at the hospital," said Rex.

Angelo cussed in frustration.

The nearest hospital was their only hope, but without phones to call an ambulance, they faced a daunting challenge. Their only option was to seek assistance from the other Starlight Saints, a bitter pill to swallow in the race against time to save Akira.

"Stay with us, Akira. I promise we're gonna get help. Oh Lord, don't forsake us now," Angelo pleaded, holding Akira's hand tightly.

Her mouth opened as if she wanted to say something. "Leave... now. Get out of here with the other saints," she uttered through a series of shallow breaths.

"Not without you, Seraph," Angelo asserted, refusing to abandon their leader.

A weak smile crossed Akira's face, and she whispered to Angelo, "When two stars collide, nothing can ever divide."

Angelo froze and questioned if he was hearing things. Those were the exact words from the poem he had written for Akira.

How could she know such lines unless he had presented the poem to her?

Before Angelo could question further, more saints arrived, coming to their aid in this critical moment.

"We have to go now," urged one of the saints, with Sanji standing beside him.

"We have to save Akira. We're not leaving her here," Angelo insisted desperately. "Get her help."

The agent among the saints checked Akira's pulse and shook his head sadly. "I'm afraid she's gone. You must leave now. Go with the rest of the crew before the gas kills you all," the saint ordered, the harsh reality sinking in.

Angelo, fuelled by grief and defiance, was prepared to fight further, but Luna intervened, placing a reassuring hand on his shoulder. He rebelled with denial.

"He's right, we have to report back to campus and let them know we've completed the mission. We've solved the case," Luna reasoned.

She pulled Angelo by the hand as they ran. Angelo, torn between grief and the urgency of escape, reluctantly cast one last glance at Akira's helpless body.

Casey had escaped, and there was nothing more they could do.

Angelo's heart ached as they left Akira behind. A haunting image burned into his memory.

They burst out of the building, the urgency still pushing them forward. Angelo ran with the team, Luna's firm grip on his hand providing a small anchor amidst the storm of turmoil's.

Akira's loss weighed on Angelo's shoulders as they rushed to one of the waiting vehicles, leaving the desolate area.

CHAPTER 38

THE GRAND ILLUMIKNIGHT

As the Saints returned to the academy, a heavy silence enveloped the vehicle. Angelo, grappling with the weight of grief, found no words to express the pain in his heart. Luna, Rex, Shawn and Vanya shared in his silent sorrow. Although Akira was dead, the saints had successfully stopped the Illuminati's death frequency operation, and the case was solved.

The academy lay decimated upon their arrival. Angelo's eyes caught sight of the Owl of Athena, a chilling symbol that only meant one thing. The unthinkable had happened—the Illuminati had discovered their secret location and launched a devastating raid. How was that possible? Lifeless bodies lay strewn across the ground, and remaining saints fought for their lives across the devastated landscape.

Angelo and the remaining Shadowbreakers, equipped with full artillery again, quickly armed themselves for another inevitable struggle against Illumiknights. As Angelo looked ahead in an ongoing battle, a figure in the distance steadily approached the team. As the figure came closer into view, Angelo's heart froze. Although unrecognisable at first glance, there was no mistaking that an old traitor had returned. Seraph Nigel, equipped with his starlight watch, eyed the entire team with fierce resentment. He was visibly injured and disfigured from the casino fire, his flesh burnt and scrapes of hair hanging loose, which made him a nightmarish sight. The seraph's unexpected survival left Angelo, and his friends stunned and bewildered.

"I thought he was dead," Vanya gasped in horror. "We saw the casino burn down."

"I'm more concerned about how he survived the reptilian serum," said Shawn. "That Ugo guy said he wasn't immune."

A twisted smile formed across Nigel's deformed face. He relished the team's perplexity at his miraculous resurrection. "It was divine intervention that saved me. A rare antidote given to me by one of Angelo's own. He saved me from turning into ashes before it was too late."

The Shadowbreakers gasped with collective shock. One of my own? thought Angelo. What exactly was Nigel implying? Angelo's friends stared at him as if he knew the answer, but he was just as clueless.

"Alright, Freddy Krueger, what game you playing at?" Rex questioned the seraph.

Behind Nigel, an elderly man with a briefcase in hand emerged. Sporting a vintage fedora hat, the man's ageing face displayed a look of great delight as his gaze landed on Angelo. Angelo's skin crawled immediately, his intuition telling him he'd met this stranger before. However, he still couldn't pin the man's identity to his memory.

"Angelo, my boy," the stranger began. "Recognise me? It's your grandpa. Last time I saw you, you was nothing but a shorty. Look at how you've grown."

The recognition finally clicked in Angelo's mind. Standing before him was his grandfather, Ted Jackson, who he hadn't seen for several years. Why did he suddenly choose to appear now? Angelo couldn't fathom the moment.

"I got word that you joined the wrong team. I happened to be in Vegas the same night that casino burned down, and I resurrected Nigel so he could help me find you," said Ted. "See this briefcase? It contains the last of the remaining Infinite Magna microchips that you Starlight Saints destroyed at our warehouses. I've got appointments with leaders to sponsor the production of these chips in other countries."

Ted dropped the revelation like an atomic bomb, revealing himself as an Illumiknight. If he got away with the briefcase, all the Starlight Saint's efforts to destroy production warehouses in the United States would be in vain. Suddenly, a Starlight Saint emerged, his katana ready to strike Ted. Within what seemed like a millisecond, Angelo's grandfather sliced a shadow blade. The Starlight Saint stood there frozen...until his head slid off. Angelo and Luna exchanged bewildered glances. Even Nigel backed away slightly. The decapitation occurred before they could even blink.

"Don't let my age fool you, kids," Ted laughed, taking note of the team's shock. "Gramps has got the speed of light."

Ted picked up the decollated Starlight Saint's head, stared at it with glee and chucked it away as if it were nothing more than garbage waiting to be disposed of. Angelo shuddered at his grandfather's display of cruelty. Ted was simply not human.

"You should know you belong with your family amongst the Illumiknights, Angelo. I shouldn't have to come fetch you," said Ted.

"No, I don't!" Angelo protested. "Where even were you when my dad got killed? When Casey sacrificed him."

"I was observing from behind the scenes. It was me who came up with the idea of giving Don the lethal injection. Blu J, Quinn and Casey simply took my advice." Ted revealed himself to be the ultimate conspirator. He had helped plan and coordinate his own son's death, making overdosing and the environment of a hospital the perfect coverup story. All Blu J, Quinn and Casey had done was seek guidance on how to execute the murder, but Grandpa Ted was the mastermind ultimately responsible for Angelo's father's death.

"You beat my dad, put him through hell…" Angelo's fists trembled with rage, ready to erupt as he recalled the abuse Ted had inflicted upon his father to make him a world-class musician. "Then you helped kill him, took his life away. What kind of parent does that?"

"Your father was gonna expose our secrets. He became a threat to the Illuminati and everything I'd built for this family," Ted explained. "Don turned against us, and I'm hoping you, my grandson, won't do the same."

Ted clearly had no remorse for his actions. Angelo's friends could only stare in wide-eyed surprise but made no attempt to comment or interfere in this family matter.

"You have one last chance. Leave with me now so we can fulfil our agenda," Ted commanded. "Or would you rather be massacred along with the Starlight Saints?"

A wave of Illumiknights stood behind Ted, some in masks, some barefaced, ready to slaughter saints to nothing. Numerous Starlight Saints lay dead on the floor, and some had fled into hiding. From the corner of his eye, Angelo caught another crowd of Starlight Saints approaching from the left, Seraph Titus among them. Although a fair number of saints were still standing, the Illumiknights outnumbered them, reducing their chances of winning or surviving, for that matter. As Illumiknights began to encircle the team, enclosing them, no one would make it out alive. Angelo locked eyes with each of his friends, dreading their inescapable fate. He carefully slipped out his frequency box.

"Don't even think of using that dumb toy," Ted laughed as he displayed a set of specialised earpieces already plugged in. "We took these from the saints we killed, so your weapon is useless. You better come with me."

Ted glared at Angelo as he put the frequency box away, awaiting his answer. Angelo had the chance to escape the massacre if he agreed to join his grandfather, but he couldn't bear the thought of leaving his friends and the rest of the saints to be annihilated. The code of the Starlight Saints had bound him to his secret society no matter what. Akira and they had come back to rescue Angelo back at the Illuminati's hideout, which put him in their debt. He could refuse Ted's request by fighting to the death and risk getting killed as a result. He'd done it before when he was ordered to sacrifice his friends, but there was no guarantee he'd make it out of this one. When Angelo weighed his options, his heart compelled him to stand with his true family - the Starlight Saints.

"I won't join you!" Angelo declared.

He projected two flaming swords, and his friends followed suit. They would fight till their last drop of blood. It was hopeless, and Angelo knew it. Before they could engage, the ground began to shake, sending a humming vibration that left everyone questioning if an earthquake had come. Without warning, mechanical vines sprouted from the ground, ensnaring the feet of Illumiknights. Angelo stared wide-eyed as his enemies were stuck with nowhere to go. They tried to free themselves by cutting through the vines with their weapons, but it was futile. How was this happening? Who was doing this? Angelo looked to the rest of the team, but they reflected the same perplexity.

Ted remained immobile, with the briefcase still in hand, confounded by how the tables had flipped. "What the hell is going on? You're only delaying the inevitable."

"You underestimate us," came a voice from afar.

As Angelo glanced ahead towards the right, Grandmaster Rin arrived in his authoritative glory. The grandmaster's attire glistened in the night despite the destruction all around him. His presence froze the atmosphere, and all eyes landed on him as if he were a messiah.

"I leave for two days to find my academy in ruins," Rin announced, infuriated. His eyes landed on Ted, who had no means of escape. "I despise your cause, all the suffering you've brought. How it disgusts me."

Rin then went on to explain how each Starlight academy or base had a unique secret defence system that only the grandmaster knew how to activate. This system was used as a last line of defence, which was something Illumiknights weren't prepared for, as shown by Ted's disbelief. To Angelo's amazement, this again reminded him that Starlight Saints were always ready and ahead of the game.

Rin's eyes shifted to Nigel, who remained the only enemy untrapped by the vines. "Nigel, shame on you. You were one of my most trusted seraphs, but you joined our enemy. You'll suffer the consequences."

"I was supposed to be grandmaster, and you know it," Nigel spat as he prepared his starlight watch. "Your society is flawed. Accept it."

In an instant, a shower of fiery blue arrows materialised out of thin air and flew towards Rin. With barely enough time to react, Rin shielded himself with his arms. Most of the arrows shrank before disappearing, but two of them managed to land their mark on the grandmaster's foot and leg. Angelo knew that since Nigel's arrows were made of energy projection, Rin must've had a special ability to dissipate that energy. As soon as the grandmaster was hit, the Starlight Saints launched a vicious attack. With Illumiknights pinned by the vines, the Starlight Saints had the upper hand. A blood bath transpired once again as saints sliced and diced their enemies. As Angelo surveyed the scene, he spotted Nigel and Titus engaged in a fierce battle.

"Watch out!" A sudden tackle drove Angelo to the ground as a blade flew over him. Luna pinned him and released him in a matter of seconds.

"We should lay low," she said.

"No, we gotta find that briefcase and destroy it," Angelo declared. "If my grandfather leaves the country with those microchips, it's over, and our investigation will be for nothing."

Rex, Shawn and Vanya gathered as the two rose to their feet. Angelo and his friends pushed through the chaos, scanning for any signs of the briefcase. In the far distance, Angelo spotted Ted, free and making his escape with the briefcase in hand. Ted had snatched a Johnny Skyblazer and a pair of star strides as he climbed up a building.

"We can't let him escape, after him!" Angelo urged.

The Shadowbreakers sprinted towards their target. When they got to the building, Ted had already reached the top.

Looking down, Ted called to Angelo. "You're too late. Didn't we teach once before that anyone who messes with a Jackson blows the wrong fuse? From tonight, you're no longer one."

"Fine by me," Angelo shot back.

Ted clipped the briefcase handle to his belt and began readying the jetpack. Angelo and his friends raced up the wall using their strides. Ted would not escape with those microchips. They couldn't allow it. Just as they reached the top, a chain yanked Angelo from behind, coiling around his waist, and his palms gripped the edge in desperation.

"Oh no you don't," said a familiar voice.

As Angelo looked down, it was none other than the disfigured Nigel scaling up the wall to catch up to them. As the rest noticed the struggle, they rushed to Angelo's aid. Luna chopped down on the chain with a projected axe, but it proved invincible. Nigel caught up and forced them out of his way to get to Ted. Angelo and his friends followed. The jetpack engine rumbled as Ted prepared for his ascent.

"You can't leave me here. I showed you where the base was, and I'm one of you." The former seraph approached Ted. "My daughter. I need to be with her. I know she's with Casey," said Nigel, referring to Quinn.

Angelo and his friends surrounded the two targets, drawing closer.

"Of course. You've proved yourself a great asset. Ugo was a fool to trick you," Ted began as he held out the Johnny Skyblazer controller. "You drive the controls while I hold you."

Angelo would do everything he could to prevent their escape. Behind his back, he summoned a harpoon spear that he knew Ted couldn't dodge in time. After everything his grandfather put his dad and his family through, Angelo would stop at nothing to eliminate Ted. With his boiling anger, he fired the spear, the tip aimed directly at Ted's chest. It was over, and there was nothing his grandad could do. In a matter of seconds, before the spear could hit its target, Ted forcefully grabbed Nigel and placed him in front, letting the spear pierce the seraph instead.

"No... what have you done?" Nigel drooled up blood, and the spear disappeared, revealing a large gaping wound in his chest.

Angelo hadn't hit his intended target. Ted's sacrifice of Nigel left him baffled. Nigel would be dead for good this time. Although Nigel declared himself an enemy, guilt still found its way to Angelo's heart. Killing the former seraph by accident frustrated him.

"That's blood on your hands," said Ted as the jetpack rumbled. "You rebelled like Don, and for that you'll die too when the time comes."

Without wasting any more time, Ted's feet began to lift off the surface as he launched himself into the night sky. Angelo and the team were too late to stop him.

"He got away. We failed," said Shawn with despair.

"There's nothing we can do now," Angelo admitted. "The Illuminati's plan hasn't been stopped. Those microchips are gone."

Angelo lowered his head in defeat. All his friends mirrored the same hopelessness while Nigel's corpse lay there. The Infinite Magna operation would continue in other countries, and death frequency would damn the whole world into disaster.

"Or are they?" a voice came from behind.

As they turned around, a masked Illumiknight appeared, holding a briefcase. The Shadowbreakers prepared to fight until the Illumiknight unmasked himself. Under the veil was a saint.

"Cherub Marc?" Shawn questioned with astonishment.

"That's right. When they launched their attack, I put on this disguise and swapped the microchips for a decoy," the cherub explained. "What the Illuminati don't realise is we've always got a plan."

Angelo breathed out a sigh of relief. Ted had ultimately been fooled, and the real victory was theirs. After a few moments, the saints gathered around a fire. Angelo was given the honour of casting the briefcase of microchips into the fire. The death frequency operation would be destroyed for real this time. The Starlight Saints decided that Nigel didn't deserve a proper burial for his treachery, and they also chucked his corpse into the fire. Seraph Titus limped, severely injured, while the grandmaster was patched up on a good recovery. The saints were given a chance to gather anything on the war-torn campus.

When Angelo returned to his room, he found his bible and the cassette still intact. He took the remainder of his belongings with him as the other seraphs organised for them to relocate.

CHAPTER 39

FRAMED

The Starlight Saints were prepared for disasters like this. It was a journey they hadn't anticipated making so soon, but fleeing was imperative. They had fought to the very end. Sizable trailer buses served as their means of escape, carrying the remaining Saints. The road stretched ahead as they drove. Amidst the rumbling engine, static crackled through the radio, and the frequency tuned into a news broadcast.

"We once again confirm that the owner of Sonic Scope Records, Jason Blue Radisson, was found dead in the headquarters of Sonic Records. We have reason to believe that this was a terrorist attack. Other unidentified bodies were found at the scene. A photo was captured by one of the witnesses. According to the evidence presented, one of the people involved in the terrorist attack was a 16-year-old boy by the name of Angelo Jackson."

Angelo's world seemed to freeze when he heard his own name. The report's inaccuracy struck him with disbelief, considering he had been fighting for his life against Blu J and his Illumiknights. He was disgusted by the label' terrorist.' How could they label him as such when he and the other saints were the ones kidnapped and forced into a deadly predicament? Everyone remained silent and listened carefully as the broadcast continued.

"Angelo Jackson, aged 16, is the son of the late star icon Don Leonard Jackson, but no other suspect has been identified yet. We have reason to believe that Angelo is part of a terrorist organization called the Starlight Saints. The rest of the family is still under investigation, but do not know Angelo's whereabouts. As we speak, Erica Jackson has been taken into custody, while famous rapper CJ Maverick has been called to testify about the incident. If you see any signs of this kid, please report it to your local authorities immediately, and you will be compensated for stopping this dangerous criminal. Be on the lookout."

"I've been framed," said Angelo shocked.

Trembling and feeling utterly helpless, Angelo cussed under his breath. The false accusations pressed on him, branding him a fugitive with a bounty on his head. Fortunately for Rex, Shawn, Vanya, and Luna, they'd dodged a big bullet of exposure from the media. They were off the hook, but how?

"This isn't right. Why me?" Angelo questioned. "They're gonna come looking for me. I've got no place to call home now. I'm stranded."

"Not with us. You're a member of the Starlight Saints now, which makes you family, which makes us your home," Cherub Hugh reassured.

Angelo grappled with the new reality that awaited him, forever changed by the events that unfolded. He had played a crucial role in discovering the Illuminati's secret plans from his dad's diary, and they had been stopped, not once but twice. It was a victory, but Angelo couldn't shake the emptiness that gnawed at him from within. The revelation about his family being Illumiknights had shattered him. He had been deceived this whole time. He wanted nothing to do with them or his inheritance. If these were the enemies he had to face, Angelo was prepared to confront them head-on, standing alongside his newfound family in the Starlight Saints.

"We're always gonna fight by your side," Skye commented. "You displayed the courage and resilience of a true Starlight Saint back there."

After several hours of travel from night to the following late afternoon, the saints finally arrived at their new academy. This location surpassed their previous one in beauty and space. The scenery embraced them with the warmth of a setting sun, the rustle of trees, and the melody of birds in the air. As they explored the area, other saints were seen settling in, creating a sense of community despite the tragedies that had occurred. Angelo walked by and spotted Dwayne and his friends. His guard immediately went up, wary of their presence. Surprisingly, Dwayne paid no attention to Angelo and continued walking, as if the past conflicts were forgotten or put on hold in this New Haven.

***

In the evening, after washing up and enjoying dinner, the Shadowbreakers—Rex, Shawn, Luna, Vanya, and Angelo—were scheduled to meet with Grandmaster Rin. As they entered the lodge, the room greeted them with an opulence befitting a grandmaster. Artefacts and jewellery adorned the space, reflecting a wealth that left Angelo in awe. The lavish setting and decorations hinted at Grandmaster Rin's substantial fortune, possibly even bordering on billionaire status if Angelo's estimation was correct.

The Shadowbreakers had been escorted by Skye and Hugh, and they were ordered to kneel, a gesture of high respect and reverence reserved for the grandmaster. Angelo, along with the others, complied, understanding the protocol in Grandmaster Rin's presence. Rin, all healed from battle, walked into the room and sat on his glamorous throne. Angelo looked up quickly and was reminded that the grandmaster's outfit was always prestigious. He averted his gaze back down, unwilling to make eye contact with the grandmaster.

"Young saints, I've requested to see the five of you for an important matter. Firstly, I want to say congratulations on completing your first mission. Your efforts have helped us with discovering our enemies' plan and stopping them from launching the frequency of death. Rex, Shawn and Angelo are no longer apprentices but have now become phoenix saints," said Rin. "Do not be complacent, though. The Illumiknights are bound to strike again. We must stay vigilant, and you will continue training because those who sleep open themselves to the enemy's attack. We must always be ready."

The grandmaster cleared his throat. "We also discovered an insider who broke one of our codes, leaking information about our operations and jeopardizing our secret location."

Angelo's heart almost jumped out of his throat at the mention of a broken code. He knew he had broken a code by communicating with Casey, someone he trusted, and now he would face the consequences. Fear gripped him, realizing there was nowhere to hide now. His actions were likely the reason why so many were put in danger and why Akira died. He wondered if he should confess his violation or let the grandmaster continue, but what difference would that make? Ready to face the consequences he believed he deserved; Angelo braced himself for what would come next.

"That's not why I've called you here, though. Seraph Nigel was the one who broke a code by betraying and giving us away."

Angelo was relieved but didn't want to show it in front of the grandmaster, so he kept his sigh to himself.

"We lost many valuable members recently, and you lost your beloved seraph. In the next few days, we'll be holding a memorial in the meeting hall in honour of her and the other saints who have fallen. Your team will be assigned a new leader and new members, but for now, you shall receive your reward money for completing the mission. 20,000 dollars added under your team's name, and you can split it amongst yourselves however you like. Our meeting is done," said Rin, bringing the discussion to a close.

The grandmaster dismissed everyone. The case tied to Angelo's father was solved, and the ugly truth was out.

Chapter 40

Secrets of the Universe

Angelo hadn't eaten much for the last few days, and a grievous weight pressed on his heart. The loss of Akira felt like he had lost a part of himself. Angelo would forever regret waiting for the right moment to ask Akira out. He'd waited for too long. He should've confessed his feelings to Akira when they stood at the fountain together, but it was too late. Love was to never be concealed.

In the solemn embrace of the main hall, the Starlight Saints gathered in a large crowd to honour the lives of their lost ones. Seraph Titus, whose injuries were healed, stood at the podium. As he faced the assembly, his eyes mirrored the collective grief of the saints.

"Dear saints," Titus began, his voice steady despite the weight of mourning. "Do not be discouraged. As we gather here to honour the fallen, let us also recognize the profound truth that holds us together. Even though we mourn today, let us not forget the victory that each of these brave souls sacrificed their lives for. Though they may be gone from our sight, they live on in the very essence of who we are as Starlight Saints."

Titus paused, allowing the substance of his words to settle upon the sea of agents.

"Though we were successful in stopping the Illumiknights from launching their frequency of death plan, we cannot let our guard down. Our enemy will return, and they will come back stronger. Do not fear though, for when our doors of perception are cleansed, we see beyond our limitations," Titus proclaimed.

Titus then turned his attention to Angelo. Angelo suddenly grew uneasy about the unwanted attention and awaited the seraph's continued speech.

"We would like to commend Angelo Jackson for his loyalty and bravery. He didn't turn his back on the Starlight Saints, and he stayed loyal to us despite his whole family being Illumiknights. Even with the darkness that intertwines with his own blood, his devotion to us is a beam of hope." Titus announced.

The hall erupted with applause, and Angelo felt a swell of mixed emotions as he stood there bathed in the praise of his fellow Starlight Saints. The unexpected praise for his heroic actions left him uncertain about how to react. As Angelo looked around, Dwayne was the only one who wasn't clapping. He caught Dwayne glaring at him with bitterness in his eyes. The applause continued, oblivious to the tension, but Angelo couldn't ignore the simmering resentment that emanated from Dwayne.

As the eulogies and speeches concluded and everyone left the hall, Angelo, having weathered a grievous storm, felt a sense of relief. In an expected turn of events, Dwayne approached him, and Angelo braced himself, anticipating another scuffle.

"Calm down," Dwayne began, showing no intention to brawl. "The day you joined this society was probably one of the worst, but after the tenacity you've shown, I have no choice but to give you credit. You've earned my respect."

In a gesture that caught Angelo off guard, Dwayne extended his hand. His rival was officially willing to make a truce. While traces of bitterness remained within Angelo towards his rival, the appeal of wiping the slate clean was too compelling to resist. Who was Angelo to refuse if his rival had acknowledged his efforts for the secret society? Angelo clasped Dwayne's hand in a firm handshake, solidifying their conciliation.

"I should give you credit, too, after the way you fought your dad and stayed loyal. The seraph should also give you recognition for that. Without you Tom would've taken and sacrificed me to his child trafficking agency," said Angelo.

"I did you a favour once, so consider yourself lucky. Next time, you might not be so lucky," Dwayne declared as he began to stroll away. "Don't let the praise get to your head. You're still an amateur in the ranks."

Although the fiery rivalry between Dwayne and Angelo had been extinguished, it didn't make Angelo's spirits any better. He still needed time to mourn and overcome the weight of Akira's death. The burden of guilt still clung to him, and he couldn't shake the feeling that all of this was his fault.

Angelo felt a comforting hand on his shoulder and turned around to find Titus standing there. With a silent understanding, Titus beckoned for Angelo to walk with him through the peaceful expanse of the campus gardens. The sunbathed everything in warm rays as summer reached its peak, shedding a soothing aura over the environment.

***

"Akira was dear to my heart. A close companion that made me feel unstoppable." Titus began, his tone pensive. "But one thing I know is that her spirit hovers over us."

"Nigel's betrayal also shattered my faith. I trusted that man with everything but that just shows the nature of man," Titus added.

Titus and Angelo halted by a small flower field. As the wind whispered through the blooms, tears welled up in Angelo's eyes, yet he also felt his mind easing up. He yearned for silence, wanting to embrace his surroundings in any way possible. A butterfly landed gently on his arm, and he made no effort to chase it away. The tranquil scenery of nature offered a temporary interlude from the heaviness of their shared grief.

"If you want to understand the secrets of the universe think in terms of energy, frequency and vibration. Everything holds a frequency, including you," Titus explained.

Angelo, sceptical, questioned, "How?"

"You're powered by a vibration that can never be destroyed, only transferred. Part of Akira's spirit vibrates in you meaning she hasn't truly left."

Angelo was mind-blown by Titus's profound perspective. It was a view he had never considered. "What is unseen, and intangible is what holds the most significance, that's it."

Titus and Angelo continued their journey, and Titus led him into a hall decorated with plaques and pictures.

"This is what we call the Hall of Remembrance. We have them in every academy. Luna told me how you were willing to sacrifice yourself for her. That's the act of a true Starlight Saint if you ask me," said Titus.

Luna said this? The praise warmed Angelo's heart, but it couldn't fill the emptiness he felt.

"The seraph still lost her life. I could've saved her if I was given more time, but we left her to die," said Angelo, choking on his words.

"You did what you could, Angelo," Titus responded. "Don't beat yourself up about it. If you stayed there any longer, you also would've died."

Angelo contemplated on the seraph's words. Throughout the nights, the haunting memories of Akira's helpless form had tormented him. He couldn't stop faulting his actions, and it devoured him from the inside. Angelo faced a choice – to either continue blaming himself or to move on and accept things as they were. There was no use looking back, and tormenting himself wouldn't solve anything. It was better to continue Akira's legacy and honour her by serving the agency. Titus insisted that this was only the beginning of Angelo's journey.

Angelo observed the pictures hanging on the wall and became curious. Titus pointed up the wall.

"These are all the Starlight Saints who served the agency and refused to be consumed by the darkness of this world. You are part of a lineage that has fought to preserve the goodness of mankind for generations," Titus explained.

The images on the wall depicted the faces of individuals who had dedicated themselves to the cause, leaving an indelible mark on the legacy of the Starlight Saints. Angelo felt a sense of connection to these unseen heroes. He gazed at the plaques, astounded by how high they went. His heart tightened, each word resonating with his very soul.

Angelo observed a plaque with *Starlight Johnny* written on it. This was the former student Cherub Hugh had mentioned and praised after Angelo completed the Circle of Transformation.

"Starlight Johnny was once consumed by darkness, but then he saw the light and became a saint. He was just like you in some ways. Our paths are interconnected, and the lessons we learn today will shape the future," Titus elaborated. "If you want to make Akira proud, then you must continue to honour her sacrifice and advance in the order."

As the seraph's words sank in, Angelo's gaze became distant. His jaw tightened, and he clenched his fists. The memory of Akira's smile, voice, and the moments they shared together tugged at Angelo's heartstrings. A tear trickled down his face.

"My brother's still out there," Angelo declared. "I'll make him pay for what he did."

"Remember, you're a fugitive now. The safest place for you is here, and now you must be discreet on your missions. You'll no doubt see Casey again," said Titus.

Angelo was forever separated from his family. He questioned when he would confront Casey again. If he ever did, he would deliver justice. He promised himself he would never forgive Casey for what he did. Angelo had to avenge the two closest to him, but the day he'd fulfil that vengeance remained uncertain.

"Hey Angelo, when you're done, come over here so we decide how we split the money," Vanya called from outside.

Titus dismissed Angelo with a nod and gestured for him to go join his team.

Chapter 41

The Poem

The team gathered around a table with a briefcase, as Angelo entered the room, and all eyes were fixed on Shawn, who held a steel spoon in his grasp. A hush of anticipation enveloped the room.

As Shawn's brows furrowed in deep concentration, a subtle energy seemed to stem from him. To the team's surprise, the steel spoon in his grip began to bend. The team's collective gasp and wide-eyed amazement revealed their astonishment at Shawn's extraordinary skill.

"Yes! I did it. I'm finally getting the hang of metal bending," Shawn praised his own display of magic.

Angelo stared at the bent spoon in awe.

Shawn had grasped the basics of Zayn's mystical tricks but still had more to learn.

As the praise died down, Rex did the honour of opening the briefcase and in it lay the stacks of money they'd been promised.

"We get 20% each, that's the deal," said Luna.

"But shouldn't Angelo get less since he's already rich…oh wait, he can't go back home, never mind," said Shawn, brushing off that suggestion as quickly as he brought it up.

They carefully counted and divided the stacks of money, each bond comprising 100-dollar notes. The process took some time, but they successfully split it evenly. Each member received $4000. The agency provided a trust account for each saint, offering a secure place to deposit their money.

"Now I have enough money to cover the remainder of my uncle's lung transplant. The other $2000 can be for me," Rex declared, his face beaming with triumph. "What about you guys?"

"I could give some to my parents and show them that I'm actually getting paid for this so-called internship program," said Shawn.

"I could do some shopping or maybe plan a cruise," Luna added.

"I could use a vacation somewhere in the Bahamas," Vanya chirped in.

The team glanced at Angelo last, awaiting his two cents. "I don't know what to do with my money. I'll probably donate some to charity, or some of you could have it. I don't really care much about cash anyway. My brother needs to pay for killing our seraph, and I got a feeling the Illumiknights ain't finished like the grandmaster said," Angelo confessed.

The rest of the team paused for a moment. It was a grave truth they couldn't deny. Each member's spirits had been low after the void Akira left. Things just weren't the same anymore.

"You're a wanted criminal now, and it won't be easy going out there," Luna warned.

"I know, and that's why I'm counting on you guys to fight by my side. You saw what we did back at Sonic Records and the academy. Luna, you told me the one who's persistent should be more feared than the one who's gifted. The Illumiknights should fear us now if they dare to strike again," said Angelo with determination.

The fight wasn't truly over, and training would only intensify from here. Angelo thought about how proud his dad would be of him. He knew Dad had to be looking down on him with approval of how much his son had accomplished. The thought threatened to unleash a wave of grief, but he pushed it back, locking the sorrow away.

***

"Wait, Apple Jack. There's something I should give you," said Rex, reaching into the depths of his pocket.

Rex retrieved a crumpled piece of paper and carefully unfolded it, a small smile playing on his lips. "I almost forgot."

Was this a note? Rex handed Angelo the paper, and the unexpected exchange took him by surprise.

"The seraph had something to say about your poem," Rex added.

Angelo glanced at the note with anticipation. Unfolding the crumpled paper, he was met with the sight of a big heart doodled onto it. He realized it was the poem he had written for Akira, the same poem he had poured his feelings into. He thought he'd misplaced it before, but it was Rex who had taken it without his knowledge. Upon closer inspection, Angelo recognized Akira's handwriting at the bottom of the page. Confusion mingled in his mind, and the room seemed to hush with a burst of intrigue.

"Rex, how did you…?" Angelo began. His voice trailed off. "You went behind my back and gave Akira my poem when I didn't ask you to. Why would you do something like this?" Angelo fumed with an overwhelming gush of self-consciousness. "I thought you were my -"

"Now, before you get mad at me, just read the damn note," Rex insisted.

Angelo's heart skipped a beat as he silently read Akira's message.

This is a beautiful poem you've written for me, Angelo, but I honestly see you more as a sweet friend. I cherish our friendship even though…

362

"Come on. Read it out loud so we can all hear," Rex encouraged with a sly grin.

Angelo, still shaken by a mix of shock and embarrassment, found himself in an unexpected predicament. The note, initially intended for the private exchange between him and Akira, now faced an audience of curious friends. He had never gotten the chance to confess his feelings, but Rex had unnoticeably done it for him. Feeling exposed and vulnerable, he didn't know whether to thank Rex or hate him. He was ready to storm out and end their friendship, yet again, he couldn't deny that Rex had done him a favour.

Angelo had to realize it was his fault for hesitating and waiting too long, which had led to this moment.

Akira had even quoted the two lines from the poem as her final words before her life slipped away, and that's when sense finally clicked.

Taking a deep breath, Angelo swallowed his bitterness and composed himself as he read the note out loud, bringing Akira's response to light.

"This is a beautiful poem you've written for me, Angelo, but I honestly see you more as a sweet friend. I cherish our friendship even though I'm hard on you sometimes, and I think we're better that way. I'm an adult, and you're just a teenager. Maybe, if you were older, I would consider going out with you. Perhaps in another lifetime or universe. You're kinda cute and brave for asking me, though. I won't deny that <3 :) xoxo

I knew you had feelings for me from the very beginning, but I know someone else who might like you ;)."

Angelo felt a flush of embarrassment as he read out Akira's playful message. He remembered the fear that held him back from giving the poem to her, but after reading the message, this meant he had a chance with the seraph. *But only in another lifetime or universe.*

363

A powerful lesson dawned on Angelo at this moment. He realized that being with his celebrity crush, someone he'd admired his whole life and someone way older than him, was ultimately a distant fantasy. The weight of the age difference created a barrier that simply shouldn't be crossed. As Angelo went into deeper reflection, he understood that circumstances would never allow him to fulfil his desire to be with the seraph, even if Akira was still here. As his heart ached from this painful realization, there was something else he could still cherish. Their friendship.

"You needed a little push 'cause I knew you'd never have the balls to show it to her yourself," Rex explained, snapping Angelo out of his thoughts.

"I was going to show her eventually, but I waited too long," said Angelo with regret. He skimmed the last few sentences of the note again. "She thought I was cute and brave, huh?"

"Well, it seems like Akira definitely saw something in you." Rex chuckled softly. "*Akira 'Til Infinity.*"

"She knows of someone else who might like me too," Angelo tried to comprehend what Akira had written.

Out of the corner of his eye, Angelo caught Luna blushing, her face gradually transforming into various shades of red. However, lost in his thinking, he brushed it aside and thought nothing of it.

Angelo's smile grew, gratitude and sorrow tugging at his lips. Akira may have gotten the poem, but now she was gone. Angelo's gaze became distant. As Angelo placed his hand on the table, Luna reached out and gently held it. Her compassionate gaze met his, a silent understanding passing between them. In a shared minute of grief, Angelo found comfort in the presence of his friends.

"Not to spoil the moment, but maybe next time, stick to someone your age," she added playfully.

Angelo couldn't help but chuckle. Luna was right, and Angelo had been too blinded by his feelings to discern the rational reality of things. Acknowledging Luna's advice, he folded the poem with Akira's message inked onto it and tucked it safely into his pocket, a piece of her spirit he could carry.

***

An unexpected guest breached the room, and as Angelo looked up, his surprise reflected with widened eyes. He found the last person he expected—Tori Hopkins, Zayn's daughter. The rest of the team were also taken aback by her sudden appearance.

"What are you doing here?" Angelo questioned.

"I thought long and hard and decided I should join the Starlight Saints to help you guys fight for justice," Tori explained. "My dad agreed, and he sent another trusted magician to teach his arts to Starlight Saints."

Shawn's face lit up with excitement at the prospect of Tori joining the secret society, a spark of enthusiasm glinting in his eyes.

Angelo, too, welcomed the idea, finding gladness in the addition of a new member.

"I've already unlocked the basics," Shawn smirked, presenting his bent spoon.

"Impressive. Told you you'd make a good magician," Tori responded. "Titus said I need to go through some rituals first before I join the team so wish me luck," she added with an enthusiastic grin.

As the anticipation of Tori's initiation into the Shadow-breakers hung in the air, a subtle acknowledgement passed through the team. It added newfound hope, but the aching truth remained - no one could ever fill the void Akira had left.

***

Under the starlit sky, Angelo found himself at the fountain where he and Akira once stood while his friends enjoyed themselves in the gaming lounge. The gentle sound of water filled the air, a soothing backdrop to the memories that flooded his mind. He gazed at the stars above. He whispered his thoughts into the night breeze. As the water sparkled in the moonlight, Angelo knew he'd never be able to return to Rockingston.

From living the non-celebrity life of a teen to living the danger-filled life of a Starlight Saint was something he couldn't wrap his head around. This was his home and family now. This was where his heart belonged. As he pulled out his poem, and stared at it with tears, fighting to come out.

Suddenly, his sixth sense detected an unexpected presence. As soft footsteps drew closer, Angelo turned around.

"I've had enough rounds of gaming. I thought I'd just come hang out here like you," said Luna, her facial features glowing in the night. "What's on your mind?"

"Just thinkin' about how proud my dad would be right now," Angelo shrugged.

Luna moved closer, and together they stared up at the stars. "I'm sure he would. Both my parents drowned in a boat accident, and I was orphaned until the Starlight Saints found me."

Angelo, touched by Luna's vulnerability, offered his condolences and took comfort in their shared sorrow. "I never knew. Guess you and I are more alike than I thought."

Luna cracked a smile, and the stars seemed to radiate brighter as they locked eyes. Angelo was staring into a pair of eyes that bore untold stories of pain. Luna, leaning in as if she had a secret to share, moved closer, but Angelo's attention returned to the vast night sky.

"Wanna have a session in the sound room?" Luna asked, breaking the silence.

"Don't mind if I do," said Angelo with gladness. The sound room was now their treasured location.

As Angelo stepped away from the fountain, he clutched the poem in his hand, the words etched in ink a piece of Akira's memory - *Akira 'Til Infinity*. With a bittersweet smile, he tucked the poem back into his pocket, knowing that part of Akira would be with him everywhere he went.

The battles against the shadows of the Illuminati proved deadly, but the ever-burning light of the Starlight Saints proved unshakeable.

About the Author

Jayden Gilmore (whose real name is Michael) is an author dedicated to his artistic vision and bringing his stories to life. He is also a famous musician who goes by the stage name Kdaxx. His albums have gained recognition from over 100,000 listeners worldwide and he continues to shine his light.

ACKNOWLEDGEMENTS

Writing *Starlight Saint* has been treacherous journey for me to say the least and I am grateful for all the support I had along the way. There were times when I lost hope, and I thought I'd never finish this book. Firstly, I'd like to thank Joe Bunting and the Write Practice community for teaching and guiding me in the art of writing. To my amazing book coach, Taylor Kimble who helped me develop the story. To my incredible editor Kyle Cisco who helped me perfect the story with his excellent editing skills. To my mother, father and the rest of my family who kept encouraging me along the way even when I was ready to give up. I give praise to God who gave me my creativity and story ideas. I'm extremely grateful for this journey and I look forward to many more in my writing career.

Printed in Great Britain
by Amazon

56852569R00207